Division One: Break, Break, Houston

by Stephanie Osborn

Chromosphere Press

Huntsville, AL

Break, Break Houston
© 2019 Stephanie Osborn
ISBN 978-1-950633-18-0 (print)
ISBN 978-1-950633-19-7 (ebook)
Cover art © 2019 Darrell Osborn
Fiction

First electronic edition 2019

This is a work of fiction. All concepts, characters and events portrayed in this book are used fictitiously and any resemblance to real people or events is purely coincidental.

Chromosphere Press
P.O. Box 252
56 Hughes Road
Madison, AL 35758

www.chromospherepress.com

Table of Contents

Chapter 1

"...What the damn hell do you mean, I'm not the mission commander any more?" an indignant NASA astronaut Scott 'Scotty' Chadwick demanded to know. "Shit! I've been training on this advanced bird since the beginning, dammit!"

"I understand, Scotty," Morgen Kirby, NASA Chief Astronaut, noted, green eyes flashing in sympathy as he stood before her in her office. "It was originally supposed to be you as commander, George as pilot, then Megan as MS-2—and that, only because she didn't have the military experience you and George had; in my opinion, she was better qualified to take the pilot's seat than George. Then she vanished out in west Texas some place, and George developed that little inner-ear quirk that washed him out of the astronaut office. Don't get me wrong: Dan is good, and his training is coming along nicely, but it's too late in the training—he's just not going to be up to being the pilot under you as commander, not in time for this mission—I gave him every chance I could, but we all knew it was a long shot. So you know as well as I do, when we lost Megan, it left us short a major member of the crew manifest. She would have been the backup pilot. And we could have upgraded her to pilot when George's medical disqualification came up, and Dan would be fine in the MS-2 slot. But now, with George transferred out to a desk job and Meg...dead..." she ignored Chadwick's wince, "we needed another member of the flight crew. It just wasn't an option any more."

"Yeah, but when you bring 'em in, you put 'em UNDER me, not OVER me!" Chadwick declared. "That's just broken, Morgen! I'm the one still on the manifest with the most experience with the new drive! How the HELL did he manage to replace me as the commander?!"

"He has extensive on-orbit flight experience," Kirby pointed out, "and, well, 'connections,' if you know what I mean."

"Yeah," Chadwick said, bitter. "You mean he got his father

to pull strings to get the slot."

"I didn't say that."

"You didn't have to! Everybody in the corps knows this guy! His dad's head of the House Committee on Science, Space and Technology, and he makes damn sure everybody knows it!"

"I'm sorry, Scotty, but that's the way it's gotta be," Kirby said, firm. "Peter Dianus is now the SP-1 mission commander. You're *Kitty Hawk*'s pilot. And don't worry; Peter promised me he'd work hard to come up to speed between now and launch."

"There's no way in hell he can ever manage to come up to my level with *Kitty Hawk* and the new prop system," Chadwick averred. "I've had YEARS to learn this, work with the bird! He'll have scant MONTHS!"

"And I expect you to help him learn," Kirby ordered. "The matter is settled, Scotty."

"Yeah, I get it," Chadwick said, still intensely annoyed. "I bust my ass to see this mission gets done right, and he waltzes in at the last minute and takes over. That is SO Dianus!"

"This conversation is ended, Chadwick."

"Yeah, yeah, I know. Mark my words, though, Morgen. The whole situation's busted to hell and back. Trouble will come of this. I only hope we all live through it."

"That's where I'm counting on you, Scotty."

"I'm not Superman, Morgen."

"You shouldn't have to be. Peter is a professional."

"Sort of," Chadwick muttered, well under his breath.

"What?"

"Nothing."

"You don't think he's qualified."

"Not for this," Chadwick protested. "He's cocky, arrogant, and an obnoxious know-it-all. This baby is gonna need a delicate hand. And one that knows the systems, that helped develop 'em. He's got none of that!"

"Which is why you're the pilot. If I need to, I can always order him to pass the stick to you."

"You need to."

"I'll see what I can do," Kirby said with a shrug. "Meanwhile, you need to deal with it, Scotty."

"Yeah, yeah, whatever," Chadwick said, sullen, annoyed... and secretly deeply worried. "Permission to return to duty?"

"Granted."

He spun on his heel and headed for the door.

* * *

"...So they are on the way?" Pan-Galactic Coalition President Lord Pulgey Entiyti remarked to his oldest human friend, former chief bodyguard, and brother in all but blood.

"They are, Pul," Division One Director Fox, formerly known as Franz Levy—and still known that way in certain galactic circles—noted as they spoke on the vidcall. A relaxed, cheerful Fox sat comfortably in his office, at his desk, looking at the face of the big Draconan on one of the wall screens. "When your physician notified us that you were finally up to a few excursions and planning some 'special events,' I sent them on, like we'd planned. I was notified that they took off about half an hour ago in a small saucer from Penn Station. Listen, I wanted to thank you for this; I can't help but think your generous offer will help win back Alpha One's reputation after that huge pile of excrement landed on 'em that came out of the Ennead's fact-finding attempts getting so twisted by Adita's Coup. Never mind the fact that it helps out you and Suud on some scheduling conundrums."

"As you would say, 'no shit,' my friend," the white-scaled lizard-like face said, his flexible black horns crossing in mild irritation. "And believe me, it is greatly appreciated! Assassination attempts galore, usurpations, getting your top Agents in trouble for doing the right thing...how are the injured doing, after they finally ousted the fake Adita, anyway?"

"Most are doing better, Pul," Fox said. "The least-injured are already back on duty; the most seriously injured are coming along pretty well by this point. It's taken a bit of doing, and several of 'em had to get 'dunked,' as the medlab staff is terming the regeneration process these days. Even the agent with the broken back is now on the mend and walking again, albeit still in physical therapy, and with crutches. But the agent with the brain injury isn't progressing quite as fast as the others."

"But he is progressing?"

"Yes, he is," Fox said with a nod. "Kappa is getting better!

We had some serious consultation with the Edeptan physician Doron about him, and that brilliant little fellow even came to Earth for a few days to examine Kappa and design a new process for the regeneration, expressly for that agent. It helped Kappa a lot, and now they're just...retraining him, I guess you could say. When the damaged brain areas regrew, they perforce lost some of the information base, I suppose is a good way of explaining it. It's a form of physical therapy, but more intense than the other patients are getting." Fox shrugged. "I understand there was also a little bit of memory loss subsequent to the tissue regrowth, but they're looking at how they might recover at least some of that with brain bleacher technology."

"Ah. Well, that all sounds quite promising, then."

"Very much so. But speaking of such things, Pul, you need to know...Omega is still suffering from PTSD, and Echo has been a bit down over the whole damaged-reputation thing. Actually, if I had to guess, I'd think he's downright depressed over it, only he's doing his damnedest to hide it." Fox sighed. "They need and want to work with you, certainly, but it's my considered opinion—and I verified that opinion with Zebra—that they are going to need a bit of time to themselves, as well. So please take that into consideration when you schedule their shifts. And while I know you want to spend personal time with them—and they, with you—please be sure to allow them a smidgen of free time, too. They need it badly."

"Aha. But Omega is getting counseling, yes? How is that going to work around her being here?"

"That's not a problem," Fox said with a grin. "Ambassador Zz'r'p is her counselor."

"The telepathic Deltiri from Arcturus VII?"

"The same."

"Oh, well then, that will not be a problem at all," Entiyti chuckled. "He can counsel from there to here as well as in his office! But perhaps, rather than putting them in the main house, I should quarter them in the guest house?"

"You don't mean the dignitary house in the back of the garden, do you?" Fox wondered.

"I do."

"I think that is an excellent idea, Pul," Fox averred. "That's a VERY nice, rather luxurious little house! They can spend their off hours wandering the garden, maybe sitting at the reflecting pool, and generally 'zen-ing out' a bit." *And maybe,* he thought, *they'll go ahead and take advantage of certain amenities, instead of waiting for the Ennead to come through with the farkakt amendment... 'some day soon.' If they wait until that happens, they could still be waiting when they're MY age.*

"That was what I thought," Entiyti said with a nod. "And as a recently betrothed couple, they likely crave a bit of time alone together, especially after that whole 'Omega is about to become the Persan premier's new concubine' mess. Never mind the 'let's brain-bleach Echo and send him away' giis-shttt."

"Exactly."

"I'll contact my house steward Ssutav and have him take care of matters, then," Entiyti decided. "Do not fear, Franz, I will see that they are as properly seen-to as they shall do for me. They are, after all, 'family,' in this big inter-species clan that we seem to have formed. That YOU seem to have formed."

"It wasn't my idea, at least not originally! I rather think that was Omega's doing, and I'm not sure how much of it was planned, versus it sort of growing," Fox noted. "I'm rather inclined to think it just developed on its own, to a large extent, as she got to know us and grew fond of us. But...yes. And I am part of it, and—as between us—glad to be." He shrugged, hoping his face didn't flush. "Because, well, frankly, Omega isn't the only one enjoying how nice it is to have a family again."

* * *

The pair were silent for a long moment; Entiyti was well aware that Fox had lost his entire extended birth family in the Nazi concentration camps. Aware, too, that such an admission from the reticent Director was significant. After all, the Draconan considered, that same concentration camp experience taught him to withhold signs of emotion, so no one could take advantage of those feelings. *Yet I was just privileged to bear witness to such a deeply-felt, telling admission,* Entiyti realized. *Which admission includes me in that family, without doubt. At least where Franz is concerned.*

"All right," he said then, after a suitable time had passed

for Fox to regain any lost control of those emotions. "I will see to it you are notified when they arrive, my old friend."

"That's good, Pul. Meantime, I guess I need to get back to it. Talk again soon?"

"Indeed, my brother. Entiyti out."

"Fox out."

* * *

When Alpha One arrived at Emdali, their ship was directed past the transfer station, straight to the Entiyti estate outside the capital city. By this time, a large, triple-reinforced force field dome had been permanently established, and it now enclosed the core of the estate, including the gardens and several guest houses, though not the fields surrounding, where crops were being worked. A special 'gate' was built into the dome to allow for trusted craft coming and going, and it was through this that the *D1 Calypso* entered, landing lightly on a section of the side lawn now reserved for such.

After several minutes, the hatch opened and extended a ramp. Alpha One emerged, composed of Alpha Line chief Echo—a handsome, well-built human male with a strong hint of Native American in his features—and assistant chief Omega—a tall, beautiful, platinum blonde. Both bore themselves with confidence, though perhaps not quite as much as their friends were used to seeing in them. They walked close together but not touching; small travel kits were slung over their shoulders. Ssutav Kegen, Entiyti's estate steward, a large Reptoid of imposing and reserved manner, met them at the foot of the ramp.

"Agents Echo and Omega?" he queried.

"The same," the male said. "I'm Echo, and this is my partner Omega."

"Come with me," Ssutav said, then turned and led the way straight through the big manor house, out the back, and deep into a lush garden, some of which was very formal, though some of it was delightfully random and almost wild. Here and there streams flowed into limpid pools of various sizes; from time to time they encountered finely-carved animal sculptures in the local stone. A couple of fountains wafted soft, susurrating music through the air. Bird-equivalents sang from their

6

hidden perches in the trees.

After several minutes of walking, the pair saw a small, white stone structure ahead. Moments later, they stood before the door of a goodly-sized limestone cottage, 'little' by comparison with the manor house, but in no wise cramped. A small stream emerged from the trees on the edge of the lush lawn, before meandering around the side and back of the house, whence it disappeared. A large patio and veranda could be seen peeping around the opposite side of the structure.

"This is the dignitary guest house," Ssutav noted, handing them each an electronic key card. "Lord Entiyti felt that you would be most comfortable here. It is a great honor we bestow, to be placed in this house. We—the household and staff—welcome you here as friends and family of Lord Entiyti, and thank you for your intent to protect him from further harm, even as he is recovering from the last...giissht...attempt upon him—forgive my language."

Echo and Omega exchanged a surprised, somewhat dismayed glance.

"Please thank Lord Entiyti for us," Echo said, "but we don't need such fancy quarters. We'll be just fine in the bodyguards' barracks with the others."

"Right," Omega agreed. "We don't want, or need, special treatment or favoritism."

"No, no," Ssutav averred. "You do not understand. We WANT to do this. Milord has already discussed the matter with myself as chief steward, as well as Lord Guurn, his son Duuniiss, and Chief Dalgaard—together those three now comprise the chief bodyguard, assistant chief bodyguard, and head of household security. And we have, in turn, ensured that the staff—including all the bodyguards under them, and the inside and outside servants under me—understand you are honored guests nigh unto family, and that milady here," he nodded at Omega, "has had...a difficult time of it recently. No, no, fear not; no more detail was presented than was necessary, milady. But they do know that you have been stalked, mind-raped, and that an attempt at physical rape was made—no more than that; no details were given or requested. And Agent Echo, the situation with your reputation was already known, and we understand and want you to know that you are welcome. Nor do we believe the besmirchment of your reputation was in any wise warranted."

Alpha One exchanged glances once more; this time, the expressions on their faces were those of mollification and relief.

"Well, thank you, then," Omega murmured. "We...appreciate that."

"All of that," Echo added.

"Very good," Ssutav averred. "So. Given 'all of that,' it was generally felt that a nice, quiet, private lodging would be... beneficial. For both of you. And this place is far and away the best suited for such." Ssutav swept a clawed hand over the subtly-manicured surroundings; no other dwelling or artificial structure was visible from their vantage save a few small landscaping sculptures, and the environment was peaceful and quiet—a well-appointed dwelling in a forest clearing. "When you are not attending Lord Entiyti, you are quite free to enjoy the gardens. In case you did not think to bring your own, there should be suitable swimming garments within," he indicated the guest house, "to allow you to enjoy the pools and streams, as well. Some are formal swim pools, and some are more what you would term ponds or small lakes, I think. So you have your choice."

"Well...thank you," Omega said again, offering a grateful smile. "VERY much. I appreciate that more than you know."

"So do I," Echo agreed. "And I think if the truth be told, we really could both use some peace and quiet in our down time, after the last few months."

"Very good," Ssutav said, breaking his reserve by smiling. "We had all hoped you would feel so. Lord Entiyti says you are to take your time settling in, and come to his suite whenever you are ready. Though Lord Suud recommends you come by the guard headquarters first, so he may introduce you properly to those with whom you will be working."

* * *

The visiting-dignitary guest house was indeed spacious and luxurious, and Omega and Echo were delighted by the opportunity to stay there.

"But, um, it's only got one bedroom," Omega noted, flush-

8

ing slightly. "The bathroom's really big, and there's doors partitioning things like the toilet, so that wouldn't be an issue. But the bedroom, I mean, um. It's just, uh, it's plenty large, and we can make it work, I only...I wonder what Pulgey thinks. I mean, he knows we're engaged, and Fox said he handled our life partnership application, so now we're permanent in THAT way, so..."

"It's a definite temptation," Echo admitted with a sigh. "I know you're still a little scared, after what Slug did when you were little, but...I dunno if you know how hard this is for me, baby."

"I...I get it, Echo," Omega murmured, tucking her head. "Just because I'm kinda scared about, about certain things, doesn't mean I don't, I mean..." She flushed even deeper.

"Well, that's good to know," he said with a slight smile. "Do you think we can manage to share the bedroom, if we don't share the bed?"

"We've done it before, more'n once," Omega said with a shrug, her face cooling. "So I guess so."

"Good. Because I had a hunch something like this might come up at some point—if not here, then on some of Pul's political excursions—so I packed the air mattress in my kit, along with some extra bed linens."

"The hovering thing?"

"The same. You take the bed, I got the air mattress. It's not like the bedroom's exactly cramped. We got plenty of room to set the thing up."

"Brilliant," Omega declared with a grin. "Problem solved! Ace, I gotta tell ya, I'm looking forward to this. Especially with this house situated in the gardens like it is. It's just beautiful."

"I know. I'm thinking after our work shifts are over, we do some long walks, a few moonlight strolls, swimming, some stargazing, maybe even a picnic," Echo said, plopping his kit down on the bed and digging inside to find the air mattress. "And did you see the hot tub in that big huge bathroom? With a one-way picture window overlooking the pond in the back?"

"Oh hell yes! Big enough for both of us, so we put on swimsuits an' hop in and relax! An' a big ol' shower, an' two sinks an' a whoppin' big vanity..." She shook her head with a wry grin. "Maybe we should come back here for our honeymoon!"

Echo stifled a snort.

"I don't think so."

"Why not? It's lovely."

"It is, but do you really think that, with certain persons in the manor house, we'd have all the privacy we want for a honeymoon?"

"Oh..." Omega flushed, then scrunched her face. "Good point. Pulgey is a wonderful friend, but he might be a little, um, TOO solicitous."

"Exactly my point. And with Suud to add to the mix..."

"Oh boy. Yeah, no. Pretty as it is, we go someplace else for a honeymoon. Hell, I'd be happy just spending some time at your beach house in Ipswich."

"Well, I expect we can do more than THAT," Echo noted. "We can talk about it some while we're here, maybe. Brainstorm some ideas."

"Okay."

"Hey. While I get this air mattress inflated and made up, why don't you go find the kitchen and see what we need to get in the way of food, then we can ask that Ssutav fella where we can go into town and get groceries suited to humans?"

"It's a plan," Omega said, dumping her kit beside Echo's. "Then I'll come back and we can finish unpacking, before we go see Suud and Pulgey."

* * *

It didn't take long before they were all settled in, ready to work alongside Entiyti's standard bodyguards to ensure the galactic president remained safe during the remainder of his recovery period. The estate's steward had already ordered the kitchen of their guest house duly stocked with human-style foodstuffs, and once they unpacked and decided everything was where they wanted it, they set out to meet with Suud and Entiyti.

"Hey," Echo asked, as they walked toward the manor house, "I forgot to ask. Is it ready yet? Are you gonna give it to him now?"

"No, not yet," Omega told him, "so keep it under your hat for now. I checked just before we left Headquarters. Madrid will bring it when it's ready. And we discussed it, and he'll ensure he's escorted by Fox and all the pertinent personnel."

"Okay," Echo said with a grin. "Lips zipped."

"Good deal."

* * *

Suud Guurn and his son Duuniiss were waiting for them near the back door of the manor house, and together, they promptly introduced the pair to the rest of the bodyguards, whose quarters and office were down the corridor nearby. The enthusiastic, welcoming response was heartening to the human pair.

"This does not surprise me, and I believe it is a very good plan," Goobop Ogoobah, an Alaygoon from Lambda Andromedae III and one of the bodyguards who had been with Entiyti during the attempted assassination, averred. "The two of you are very well known in the galactic community, highly qualified and quite capable, and I have felt it was most unfair, the way you have been treated in the media and such."

"Thank you," Echo murmured, touched despite himself, and trying with only mild success not to show it. "I—we—appreciate the support, and I promise you all, this is in no wise an attempt to show up any of you. Quite the opposite, in fact—the reputation of the bodyguard corps for Lord Entiyti is so high, it was felt that it could only reflect favorably on Meg and myself if we assisted."

"Yes, the Entiyti Bodyguard Corps has developed a certain reputation of its own, in the years that Pulgey has been Coalition President," Suud acknowledged. "I rather think that Franz had somewhat to do with that upswing. And those of us, his successors in the role, have worked hard to maintain the unit's stature. At least in as much as Pulgey would allow us." He shot a meaningful glance at Sigrund Dalgaard, who nodded.

"Indeed. I think if the bodyguard corps had had a little more leeway, we might have at least seen the attack coming, perhaps. At any rate, we are very glad to have you here, now," Dalgaard declared—he was formerly Entiyti's chief bodyguard during the recent attack, now the head of security for the estate and responsible for the 'tabernacle force field' as they called the triple field about the estate—which was based on a stratagem Fox had devised for starships, and which he'd dubbed a 'tabernacle maneuver,' resulting in the field name. "I think it is a great help. Milord will be going off-world soon, for short jaunts such as will not exhaust him, and as I am now limited to estate security by my own choice for my family's sake, and Suud cannot always go with him due to familial obligations, the two of you—used to running Alpha Line—can serve as the head of his security detail."

"Just so," Suud agreed. "It helps immensely. As the head of the Guurn family now, I have certain obligations that conflict with some of Pulgey's plans in upcoming weeks, so this is excellent. Granted, Duuniiss is my assistant, but he is not experienced enough quite yet to run the entire corps."

"And I know it," Duuniiss admitted. "And I am needed at some of those same family obligations, as well."

"True. It also helps the two of you," Suud continued, addressing Alpha One, "by displaying the trust that Pulgey and the rest of us have in you. I think this is all very well thought out."

"Well, good," Omega murmured. "And none of you have any problems working with us? Even reporting to us, on occasion?"

Heads shook in the negative throughout the small but efficient corps of guards.

"No, madam," one of the new guards, Bisun Pujai, Entiyti's first Ganotian bodyguard, affirmed. "We have all had your unclassified personnel records from Lord Guurn, as well as the story of how your reputations were inadvertently damaged, and I think I speak for all of us when I say we are honored to have you working with us."

"And we trust you without question," Pyxffurn Vuxia, a Xemlon damale on Entiyti's bodyguard staff, noted. "We are in agreement, the entire bodyguard corps. This can be nothing but good for all of us."

"Given Omega's status as the head of training for the Alpha Line department," Suud added, "I think we are all rather hoping she might look over our corps training regimen and offer recommendations, as well."

"Y'all know that's as much Echo as me, right?" Omega

pointed out. "He and I tend to work out training routines in our own efforts to stay in shape and ready, and then I analyze 'em and look at whether or not they'd fit into the department training—if not overall, then for certain teams that might could use the added practice, experience, or whatnot."

"I suspected as much, though the others, perhaps not," Suud noted. "I know both of you reasonably well by now, all things considered, and I know how well you work together—and LIKE to work together." He shrugged. "Still, you have the analytical experience to look over our program and see what might want changing. If Echo wishes to help, it will only be better for the both of you working on it."

"Consider it done, then," Echo averred, and Omega nodded her agreement.

"Is it true you are betrothed?" Vuxia wondered.

"Yes, we are," Echo confirmed. "We expect to be properly married—er, go through the formal, religious espousal ceremony—once the Council amends the Division One Agency charter to include such ceremonies."

"Which we hope will be soon," Omega added.

"How long will you be here?" another guard asked. "Is it a permanent reassignment?"

"No, it's not permanent," Echo said. "Meg has an event she wants to be back on Earth to watch, in a few weeks. And it's not something that the galactic news media is apt to pick up, so we HAVE to be back on Earth to watch. But we'll be here long enough to help out on those offworld jaunts for Lord Entiyti, for sure."

"What is it?" Duuniiss wondered. "Agent Omega, what is the event you want to watch?"

"Oh, it's not any big deal," Omega said, dismissive. "Remember how I was a civilian NASA astronaut before Echo recruited me? Well, I try to keep up with the major milestones they make—I've kinda gathered Fox and Pulgey, er, Lord Entiyti, are looking to me for a notion on when Earth might be ready to have, um, certain technologies released, if you get my drift—and there's a milestone launch coming up. I just wanted to get home in time to watch and see how it went, that's all."

"Now, I think that is enough questions for the moment,"

Suud noted. "And they have yet to even greet Lord Entiyti, so I believe Dalgaard and I shall escort Alpha One to see him. The rest of you, see to your duties."

* * *

"Oh my younglings, there you are! Welcome, welcome," Pulgey Entiyti exclaimed from behind his big desk, giving them a broad smile. Alpha One stood in his office before the desk, flanked by Suud and Dalgaard, even as the big Draconan rose from his chair and came around the desk to greet them. In moments even Echo found himself enveloped in a familial hug. "It is so very good to see you both! How are you doing? Forgive an old Draconan's familiarity, but by now I think of you as family, you know."

"Um, we understand," Omega said with a slight smile, flushing. "Because, uh, well, we know about Fox and, uh..."

"Sigrund knows about the bonded-brothers ceremony," Entiyti noted. "And Suud is one of the brothers—it is we three, you see—Suud, Franz, and myself. So while it is not public knowledge nor is it desired to be, here you can speak freely, Omega."

"Oh!" she said, smile deepening. "Okay, then. Well, we get it, 'Uncle' Pulgey," she added, smile morphing into a grin. "Fox is kind of the 'family patriarch' for our little adoptive family back on Earth, and you and Lord Guurn are his ceremonial brothers, so that makes you uncles, sorta..."

"And so why am I not 'Uncle Suud' then?" Suud wanted to know.

"Because you hadn't invited Meg to call you that yet, Suud," Echo pointed out with a grin. "And she's not the sort to go presuming on stuff like that."

"By all means, then, let us not stand on such formalities. I am Suud, 'Uncle' Suud if you like, Omega. And Duuniiss is your 'cousin,' and we shall have to introduce you to my wife and three other children at some point, I suppose."

"I'd like that," Omega said with a broad smile.

"Don't forget Lyddhu," Entiyti pointed out. "We 'adopted' her as a niece, too."

"Oh, that is right," Suud remembered.

"Oh wow," Omega murmured, overwhelmed. "Echo,

thanks, hon."

"For what?" Echo asked, startled.

"I lost my birth family to Slug over a decade ago, and lots of aunts, uncles, and cousins in that tornado I told you about one time, even longer ago," Omega reminded him. "On Earth, I really don't have much in the way of a genetic family left. But I think I've got more 'family' now than I ever had, before... well, before everything. The tornado, and Slug, and joining the Agency." She laughed. "And what's even cooler is, they're definitely more, ummm, 'assorted' than my genetic family ever was!"

They all laughed.

"So, Pulgey, how is your...well, how are you getting on after, um..." Echo tried.

"I miss the wing, Echo," Entiyti sighed, sobering. "From time to time I forget, and still try to flex it, and it feels...odd. Skin, muscles, nerves, all gone; even the bone is truncated. There is simply nothing left there to flex."

"And they can't clone it?" Echo asked.

"Draconan tissues do not clone well," Suud offered, quiet. "And the wings are, per my understanding, one of the most complex features of Draconan physiology."

"Cybernetics?" Echo pressed, but gently.

"None of our people have yet developed a suitable cybernetic replacement for a Draconan wing, and to my knowledge, no one off-planet has even considered it," Entiyti sighed. "We are not small beings, and...well...the matter has proven more complicated than might otherwise be expected. Ah, well. It is what it is, I suppose. I am not quite strong enough that I could have attempted flight yet, in any event, but the notion that I cannot ever attempt it again is...depressing."

"Aw," Omega whispered, biting her lip.

"Now, now, none of that," Entiyti remarked, overhearing. "You have had more than enough on your plate, my dear girl, without taking on my troubles. And I am alive and well and growing stronger each day, thanks to your friends and colleagues—your 'family,' or perhaps I should say OUR family, and their friends." He turned. "Now, let us go over my upcoming schedule, so you can familiarize yourselves with it, and work with Suud and Sigrund for the personnel staffing, and start to plan."

* * *

The Agent pair eased into their new bodyguard duties, and Omega designated herself Entiyti's nursing assistant in addition, watching over his medications and ensuring he did not wear himself out by trying to do too much.

"You did good today, baby," Echo observed as they strolled through the garden that evening, hand in hand. "He almost forgot his nutritional supplements to speed his recovery, never mind losing track of his pain medications—twice. And you kept him on schedule, through all of it. And that's good for several reasons, because it also ensures someone is watching over his pills, and nobody can slip him something."

"Well, I've done it for you a time or two," she said, a twinkle in her eye.

"You have," he agreed without rancor, "and I hope I've always been appreciative. I know I can be a grumpy-as-hell patient, but I always valued having you around to help me remember all that shit."

"I know. And you were. Appreciative, I mean."

"Good. I never want you to feel taken for granted, or rejected. Or just ignored."

"I know. And even when it might look on the surface like you do—usually 'cause you're busy as hades—I remember that, and try not to take it that way," Omega told him. "I mean, I know I've been kinda...messed up, lately. So I've reacted like you have taken me for granted, at least a few times, I guess. But deep down, I know you DON'T." She sighed, then squeezed his hand, and felt his own fingers tighten on hers in response. "You've been bearing with me an awful lot, and I want YOU to know that I appreciate that, too."

"I know. And it's the same for me, in that I have a pretty good idea what's going through your head, anymore," he admitted. "I understand what you're dealing with, baby. And I'm proud that you're dealing with it as well as you are despite all the shit you've been through, and that you have enough sense to recognize that the counseling is a good thing."

"Yeah, I can tell it's helping," Omega confessed. "Zz'r'p

is a really good counselor, too. He gets it all, every bit of everything I tell him, and he's taking the time to THINK about what sort of things I need to hear...and then he TELLS 'em to me. You know what I mean? The things that make me consider it all, the stuff that makes me readjust my perspective. Sometimes it even gives me a whole 'nother angle that I never knew existed! So...yeah, it's a good thing." She paused, eyeing him, then added, "Meantime, how are YOU doing?"

"What do you mean?" he wondered, evasive—she knew, because he didn't meet her eyes.

"Don't give me that! You might be able to fool the rest of Alpha Line, but you don't fool me for one second—I KNOW you're depressed about your wrecked reputation."

* * *

Echo sighed.

"Most days, you read me like a damn book," he noted, and the statement was half grumble, half appreciation. "No matter how hard I try to hide things. Yeah, I'm pretty down about it. It just hasn't quite bounced back the way I'd hoped it might. And I threw my whole life into this job, because I love it, so... it hurts. But I'm a guy, kinda old-school at that, and a pretty damn reticent hombre when you get down to it, so I tend to hide it, just out of instinct. I dunno; maybe, with you, I need to open up about stuff a little bit more. I'm just still getting used to the notion that I have somebody beside me that I CAN do that with, you know? Somebody I can talk it all out with, the feelings, and the what-ifs, an' might have beens, the oughta-dones, an' all that shit."

"Yeah, I get ya. But..."

"'But' what?"

"What about X-ray? Couldn't you do that with him? Y'all were best buds before I came along..."

"Aw, well, yeah, to an extent," Echo said with a shrug. "When I was younger, he usually had to worm it outta me, though. You know what I mean: 'Son, I can tell something's bothering you. Now, are you gonna own up to it and talk to me, so I can maybe help, or am I gonna have to get creative?' kinda thing. And if it was serious enough, we'd sit down and have a talk. But as I got older, and more confident in general life stuff, that got a lot rarer. He respected my personal space, whether physical or mental. He knew that if I decided I NEEDED his advice, I'd come to him for it. But he had kind of a warped sense of humor, which got the better of him sometimes. So there were things that I sorta didn't WANT to discuss with him, because I didn't feel like getting picked at about it, ya know?"

"Oh, okay. I haven't ever done that, have I?"

"Nah, not like what I'm talking about. You...you're sensitive, and, and gentle, and when you tease me about something, you're doing it to make me smile, and I know it. And it generally works, unless I'm just too wrapped around the axle about the subject...which, with you, is rare."

"Good, then. I've always tried to be careful about that. I'll remember this, and be even MORE careful."

"You're fine, baby; don't sweat it. You do good. So anyhow, I'm dealing with it, the whole reputation mess. I have hopes that this little jaunt with Pulgey will end up setting things to rights...maybe not immediately, but reasonably thoroughly, by the time everything's done. And you're standing staunch beside me. Well, beside, behind, in front of, around; you've been right there for me, no matter what. Like a damn big, strong bulwark, or maybe a three-sixty force field perimeter or somethin'. And this adoptive family that seems to have coalesced around you, they're standing right in there with you."

"Coalesced around US," she corrected, and he smiled slightly.

"Okay, around US," he capitulated, understanding her point of view. "And having you and all the others supporting me...it helps, a whole damn lot." He squeezed her hand gently, then raised it to his lips and deposited a light, affectionate kiss on her knuckles. "So I'm starting to get my hopes up, my perspective back, and my general outlook lifted, I guess."

"Good. And yeah," Omega considered, "I'm thinkin' maybe we both need to start opening up to each other more. 'Cause I'm bad about that, too. I mean, that's what bein' married is about, isn't it? Getting each other's backs on EVERYthing, not just assignments an' missions an' junk. It isn't just, just stuff in the bedroom, it's a whole lot more—it's sharing everything, the good an' the bad, and fulfilling each other's needs when you can, sticking by each other through it all. And so we gotta know what each other's needs are, in order to do that."

"Yeah, you got a point, baby. Okay, I'll try my damnedest to do that, if you'll try, too. Deal?"

"Deal!"

Just then, Echo's wrist chronometer let out a soft beep. He glanced at it, then at her with a surprised expression.

"Wup, it's getting late—time to head back to the house," he said. "But I really enjoyed our stroll."

"Yeah, it was awful nice," Omega agreed, as they turned toward the guest house. "A nice way to work off dinner, too."

"Yup. Do it again tomorrow night?"

"Sure, why not?"

"Okay. Now for tonight, I got the air mattress completely inflated and made up earlier, so all we gotta do is get ready for bed our own selves. We can even chat for a while after we climb into our respective beds."

"Yeah, I like that idea. I dunno if I ever told you how much I liked it when you did that up in Ipswich at your beach house. Never mind how safe it made me feel, what with everything going down."

"And it's gonna be even better once we're married and can share the bed," Echo noted. "Never mind the whole sex thing, we can cuddle together and talk. Make plans for the future, rehash the day, or just discuss the latest movie. The best friend I've ever had in my life is also gonna be my wife and lover. Maybe eventually the mother of my kids, if we can figure out the genetic problem. And I can't imagine anything better than that."

"I've...never really heard you say anything like that before," a shy Omega said. "It...makes me feel really, really... good."

"Aw. Well, you know me, Meg. I don't say what I'm feeling that much," he admitted. "But with you, I can, and I will. Especially now you know I love you, an' I know that YOU love ME. 'Cause now *I* know you won't laugh, or reject it out of hand, or be offended, or...whatever. I can pretty much tell you anything I'm feeling, if I can come up with the words to express it, and choke 'em outta my mouth. An' for you, I'll try my damnedest."

"Aw," Omega echoed, and smiled. "I never would have laughed, or rejected it, you know."

"Yeah, but..." Echo shrugged. "You know what I mean. I wasn't sure how you felt about, about us, and I didn't wanna mess up the partnership, never mind the friendship, if you didn't love me the way I loved you."

"Uh-huh. An' I had the same considerations, which was one reason why we talked past each other for so long, I guess. Neither of us wanted to mess up the wonderful relationship we already had, just in case the other one didn't feel the way we felt. And it coulda totally hosed up the top partnership in the department."

"Yup."

They were silent for several moments, as they meandered back to the guest house in the moonlight, still hand in hand.

"Hey, you wanna bedtime snack?" Echo wondered. "I noticed they had imported shortbread in the cabinet, and Earth milk..."

"Ooo!"

"I'll take that as a yes."

They laughed.

Chapter 2

So the first couple of weeks passed relatively smoothly. Alpha One accompanied Lord Entiyti on his daily rounds—which also allowed the regular bodyguards to have a bit more time off; most of them had been keeping rather long shifts since the assassination attempt on the galactic leader, and the cadre was just now getting up to numbers that satisfied Fox and Suud. This attendance included Alpha One walking with the Entiyti clan chief about the estate, as he determined how caretaking was proceeding.

"Because I view myself as the caretaker, not the owner, of the clan estate," Entiyti explained, as the two humans walked with him, and he showed them details of the grounds...which extended well past the force field perimeter into the areas being actively farmed, thus requiring his two diligent guards. "Yes, I am the clan leader, and yes, this estate is in my name. But it is not truly mine. It belongs to my family as a whole, my clan. Unless a miracle happens and I find a wonderful Draconan female, I am unlikely to produce an heir of my body, and so when I die—which has almost happened already—the estate proper will go to a cousin of mine, here on Emdali. The monies, investments, and such which I have made over the years will be split between Suud, Fox, and Lyddhu, but the lands truly belong to the clan at large."

Thus they accompanied him on his day to day activities, helping to attend to his needs and ensure he neither overdid, nor missed his medications, as well as watching out for anything untoward—it had escaped no one that there was still organized crime on Emdali, and while the particular crime syndicate involved in the transfer-station assassination attempt had been taken down, there were at least two moore. "And we don't know what their attitude is toward Pulgey," Echo pointed out.

In the evenings, they sometimes dined with Entiyti at his invitation and insistence, and sometimes retired to the guest house to dine alone together. Afterward, they found ways to quietly amuse themselves, ranging from stargazing sessions where Omega attempted to put together Earth constellations as seen from Emdali, or create 'constellations' based on her decidedly exhaustible knowledge of Emdalian mythology; to strolls through the gardens, often by the light of Emdali's moons; to swimming in one of several pools and streams that ran through the gardens. Occasionally they simply stayed inside and kissed and cuddled on the sofa as betrothed couples so often do. Lastly, they retired for the evening, with Omega nestled in the big bed and Echo cozily settled in the inflated hover-bed...though chit-chat, ranging from wedding plans to honeymoon destinations to new concepts for Alpha Line, tended to continue between them for at least another hour after retiring.

This went on for three weeks before a private message arrived for Omega.

* * *

Old girl,
It's ready. I'm en route to your location as of five minutes ago. Escort detail duty: Fox, Zarnix. Took a bit of doing in both instances; had to let Zarnix in on the thing. Fox annoyed. Be prepared.
-Madrid

* * *

"Ooo," Echo hummed as he read the email on Omega's tablet, over her shoulder. "Looks like it's time?"

"Yep," Omega said, excited. "Oh, I hope this works right!"

"I guess we'll find out soon," Echo decided.

* * *

The *D1 Exodus* touched down next to the *Calypso* on the estate's lawn. A puzzled Entiyti, Suud, Duuniiss, and Dalgaard waited with Alpha One, just outside the front door of the manor house. After several minutes the hatch opened, and three beings climbed out—Director Fox, Medical Chief of Staff Zarnix Chifejuz, and Weapons Department chief Madrid, who carried an oblong package under one arm. Captain Prrt, the *Exodus* pilot, slipped out behind them, headed for the servants' quarters, where she would billet until the *Exodus* was needed again.

"Well, we're here," Fox grumbled, walking up to Entiyti and Suud and offering them male hugs. "Madrid was damn insistent we three come here at once. I have no idea WHY, or why I had to come along—I had a shit-ton of work to do—but here we are."

"I think that would be for Omega to tell, old chap," Madrid remarked, handing her the package he carried. "After all, it was HER idea and design."

"Yeah, but you made it, Madrid," Omega commented, trying to hand the package back to him. "You should be the one."

"Why the hell is Zarnix here too?" Fox wanted to know. "Obviously you two—you three," he glanced at Echo, "are up to something, but I'm not seeing it, based on who-all is here."

"Gimme that," Echo said in exasperation, taking the package from Madrid and Omega, who were passing it back and forth like the proverbial buck. "There. Now, Meg, why don't you explain, and then Madrid, you can demonstrate."

Madrid and Omega exchanged thoughtful glances, while an annoyed Fox, an amused Zarnix, and a bemused Entiyti, Suud, Duuniiss, and Dalgaard looked on. Finally the pair nodded.

"That'll work, I think," Omega averred.

"Indeed," Madrid agreed.

"ON with it!" an out-of-patience Fox all but roared.

"Okay, okay! So guys, y'all know me an' flyin'," Omega began. "And when Echo told me about, um, 'Uncle' Pulgey losing his wing, it 'bout ripped my heart out..."

"Oh, dear child," Entiyti murmured, "I keep telling you to stop that."

"I know, but you might as well tell me to quit breathin', Pulgey," she told him. "So I sat down and kinda delicately picked Fox's brain about your flying ability. I didn't really mean to, at first; I was just curious, and thought it might do him some good to reminisce, 'cause I could tell it hurt him, too..."

Fox flushed slightly, but said nothing, neither confirming nor denying the matter. He did, however, settle down a bit.

"So anyway, it was when he showed me some video of you flying, Pulgey, that I had an idea," Omega admitted. "And so I went off to work when we were done, only it stuck in my head, and then I started to sketch, and..." She shrugged. "So then I scheduled an appointment to talk to Madrid. And I showed him what I had, and he liked it. And more important, he thought it would work." She turned and swept him a fluid bow. "Take it away, Madrid."

"Well, my mate here had a grand idea," Madrid said, reaching for the tape holding the package sealed. "And we set to on it in our spare time."

"But at a certain point, it got a bit beyond my 'hands-on' abilities," Omega interjected, "'cause I don't make this kinda stuff every day, like he does. Never mind missions an' stuff. So I stepped back and let him finish it."

"And here it is," Madrid said, producing an intricately folded metallic item in a dark matte silver alloy. He shook it gently, and it unfurled slightly. A stunned Entiyti gasped as he recognized the pattern of the device.

"Oh great Maker, you didn't," he breathed in astonishment, as Fox, Suud, Duuniiss, and Dalgaard turned to stare at him. "Omega, child, you do not mean to say that you and Agent Madrid..."

"We did," she declared, beaming from ear to ear, even as Madrid activated the device, and it abruptly expanded, unfurling to its full length. "We built you a cybernetic wing to replace the one you lost!"

Echo beamed with pride in his partner and fiancée; Madrid and Omega just grinned. The others erupted into excited chatter.

* * *

"And now I know why we had to bring Zarnix along," Fox observed, as the physician prepped Entiyti for the minor outpatient surgical procedure in the little but well-appointed hospital wing of the manor house, and the others sat in the waiting room. "And why Madrid was so insistent I come along for the ride."

"Yup," Omega said, still beaming. "Oh, I so hope the whole neural interface works like we thought it would!"

"I'm better than ninety-nine percent certain it will, my dear," a sanguine Madrid noted with a smile. "I tested it very thoroughly in the lab, even to the point of connecting it into some cloned Draconan tissue, happily donated by one of my offworld consultants, expressly for the purpose. The hardest

24

part was cloning the tissue!" He shrugged. "I destroyed the tissue when I was done, of course, to ensure everything was ethically done. But it worked nicely."

"So we just wait?" Fox wondered, antsy and verging on the fidgets; of the lot of them, he was the only one not yet in a chair.

"We just wait," Madrid confirmed. "I had already given Zarnix a heads-up as to what we were doing, just to ensure he brought the right equipment with him. He's all prepped and ready to go, and knows exactly how it ties into Entiyti's nervous system, because I showed him."

"At least nobody's in danger this time, Fox," Echo pointed out. "Just relax. Even if it doesn't work, Pulgey will be fine. And if it does work, he'll probably be over both moons."

Fox chuckled, then parked his behind in the nearest empty chair, pulled out a tablet, and began to work while he waited.

* * *

A few hours later, a dazed Entiyti awakened on his stomach in a hospital bed, as the anesthetic slowly wore off. Gradually he became aware that his lower body was encased in a kind of trouser—somewhere between lightweight pajama bottoms and scrub pants—for the sake of privacy, and a light sheet draped his body up to the bottom of his ribcage. The soft buzz of whispered conversation sounded around him, and he recognized voices, realizing that his 'family members'—Fox, Suud, Duuniiss, Echo, and Omega—awaited his awakening. He grunted, and tried to roll over.

"No, no," Zarnix's voice said from somewhere above him, and the Draconan felt strong yet gentle hands on his shoulders, holding him in place. "Just hold still here, until you wake up a bit more. Otherwise you'll roll off the bed. And that won't feel good at all."

"Sick and giissht tired of lying on my belly alla time," a groggy—but irritated—Entiyti grumbled to himself. "Ready to sit the hiigeessht up."

"All right, all right, settle down there," Zarnix said, his amusement audible to the slightly addled Draconan. "Let me see what I can do, here. I do wish we had Ooossi Duurg here to give me a hand; that medtech was one big strong Reptoid!"

25

"Let me help, sir," Duuniiss' voice said. "I am not so big as Duurg is, but I am strong, and I had to help in the military mobile hospitals a few times during my service, so I know what I am doing."

"There we go," Zarnix said, and Entiyti felt four hands contact his body, sliding over his scales, easing into position to help him move. "All right, Pulgey, follow our lead and just shift your body weight as we nudge you around, okay?"

"'Kay," the still-woozy galactic leader agreed.

The Chesharilzi and the Reptoid functioned smoothly together, as they shifted the big Draconan's weight around. Moments later, Entiyti was sitting upright, leaning forward slightly, propping himself up with his hands on the sides of the bed as his lower legs dangled off the end.

"Ohhh, that is much better," he decided, looking around with bleary eyes. "Hello, everyone."

A small chorus of cheerful greetings was his reply. Entiyti drew a deep, contented breath as he stretched, and let it out in a sigh.

* * *

"Ohmigosh, OMIGOSH!" Omega cried in delight as Entiyti stretched. She jabbed an index finger in the direction of the galactic president. "Echo! Madrid! Fox! LOOK!"

"That's terrific, baby!" Echo exclaimed, equally pleased, as Madrid grinned in pride and Fox leaped to his feet.

"PUL!" Fox burst out.

"What?!" Entiyti said, mildly grumpy and apparently still not fully awake yet.

"Pul, when you stretched, you instinctively flexed your wings!" Fox explained. "BOTH of them!"

"I wha-?" Entiyti tried, then he shook his head. "BOTH wings? But..."

Suddenly he seemed to remember why he was in the estate's tiny hospital, and he shoved himself off the bed, rising to his full height, even as Zarnix and Duuniiss grabbed for him to steady him. Then he very deliberately flexed both wings, the leathery and the metallic...

...Which suddenly unfurled and spread to their full wingspan, brushing the walls.

"IT WORKED!" he roared in glee.

* * *

"Slow down, my friend," Zarnix said some time later, when everyone—except Entiyti—had settled down a bit. "Yes, the cybernetics are hooked into your nervous system now, and your new wing will work more or less as your original flesh wing did...we think. But it might be good to do a little physical therapy and actually FIND OUT if there are any differences before you go jumping off a cliff someplace."

"It is amazing, children!" Entiyti declared, continuing to move his wings about, savoring the sensations. "The neural inputs are perfection! It feels so natural, so much like my original wing did, that I forgot, when I was awaking from the anesthesia and thus still a bit befuddled, that it was NOT my original wing!"

"Capital, old fellow!" Madrid said with a smile. "I am very glad it seems to be working so well! But Dr. Zarnix is right; we can't be sure it will do everything your original did, so we'd best go slow and make sure it'll do all you want, the way you want it, before committing yourself to making it hold you aloft!"

"I'm so happy for you, though!" Omega said, giving the big Draconan an enthusiastic hug. The alien male responded by wrapping her in a gentle embrace.

"I know, my dear girl, I know," he murmured. "You and Madrid have done wonderfully."

"It was her idea," Madrid said, modest. "And her basic design; I simply followed through on the engineering and construction. I mean, cybernetic limbs exist, but nothing so sophisticated that it can serve as a Draconan WING! I thought it was gobsmacking."

"I know, and I am appreciative to you both. But Omega! To even come up with the notion! You are utterly amazing, child, in so many ways. I think I have never known a being with so large, so great a heart."

"She is," Madrid agreed. "And she has."

"Amein," Fox said.

"Alla that," Echo averred. "I'm one damn lucky man."

"You are, indeed," Entiyti confirmed. "And if I did not

know you as well as I do, I would admonish you to take good care of her. But as I DO know you well, and I know you already do, I shall refrain from making the statement."

They all grinned.

* * *

But Entiyti proved to be quite determined, even more so than usual. While Fox and Madrid headed home to Earth the next day, Zarnix stayed a little while longer and worked with Entiyti alongside his personal physician Werfer Eretigen to ensure his new wing worked well and he had good control of it. It was a kind of physical therapy, but he cared little for the difficulty or the tedium. He was nearly obsessed, and spent every spare moment he could, working with the cybernetic wing, mastering its use and ensuring it would do everything he wanted...or figuring out how to MAKE it do what he wanted.

But no one expected, after only a little more than a week, to find him perched on the highest turret of the former castle turned manor house, and clambering over the railing onto the ancient 'launch pad.'

"NO!" Omega wailed in dismay, from her vantage on the ground, as Alpha One ran onto the lawn, the bodyguard corps having been alerted by the alarmed household staff. "Echo, what is he DOING?! I NEVER meant for him to do a thing like THIS!"

"Hellfire an' damnation!" Echo exclaimed, alarmed. "How the hell do we get up there from inside the house? I'll run in and try to stop him before he does something stupid!"

"No, hold," Suud said, laying a hand on Echo's arm. "I know what he is doing. He is not mad, but he is...experimenting. And from what I saw of his therapy this morning, I believe he is ready."

Just then, Entiyti leaped from the railing into the wind, flinging his arms outward. His wings unfurled, caught the breeze, and suddenly instead of plummeting, he was soaring... graceful and free. A roar of delight reached their ears, as he caught a thermal and rose higher...careful, nevertheless, to stay below the tabernacle force field.

Zarnix came running outside, along with a significant portion of the remainder of the household staff, servants and bodyguards alike.

"Oh damnation," Zarnix grumbled. "I was afraid he'd do something like that. All on account of a successful, long-duration hover in therapy today. Anybody have a coronary?"

"Nearly," Echo averred, gesturing to Omega, "both of us. Shit!"

"Well, look, guys," Omega pointed upward, "we have got one helluva happy dragon, flying around up there!"

"We do, indeed," Suud agreed. "But I still intend to 'give him a damn good reaming-out,' as Fox used to say, when he lands."

"Let me help," Zarnix added, raising an eyebrow.

* * *

Zarnix and Suud did indeed administer a decided attitude adjustment to the big Draconan, who became extremely perturbed and contrite when he realized how he had upset Alpha One—especially Omega—and he promised to be more considerate of his friends and family.

Together, Zarnix and Eretigen gave Entiyti one more thorough going-over in the hospital wing, ensuring that all was well. Then Zarnix assigned several more intensive physical-therapy exercises, pronounced Entiyti hale and hearty, if not quite ready to resume regular work as yet, and contacted Fox, who immediately sent the *Exodus* to return the Chesharilzi to Earth.

* * *

As soon as Zarnix reached Grand Central Station in Headquarters, he found a summons from Fox waiting, in the form of dark-red lighting between the tiles of the floor. So he headed straight for the Director's Office off the Core.

"I'm here," Zarnix said, poking his head through the open door as he rapped his knuckles on the doorframe, and Fox looked up from his interminable paperwork.

"Good. This shouldn't take but a moment," Fox said, waving first at a chair, then at the door. Zarnix closed the door and sat, as Fox added, "How was everyone doing?"

"Before or after Pulgey jumped from the observation tower?"

"WHAAT?!" Fox all but bellowed. "Aw, damnation. Tell

me you're shitting me, meyn khaver."

"No, not in the least," Zarnix said, grinning. "Fortunately, that wing Omega and Madrid ginned up worked to perfection. He flew over half the estate, I swear he did! But not before nearly giving Omega and Echo...and quite a few others, such as Suud and Ssutav...coronaries. Echo was prepared to sprint the whole way up the tower stairs in an effort to stop him, if someone could have shown him the way in time."

"Oh, farkakte," Fox said, smearing a palm down his face. "That was meshuginah, Pul! Well, at least the wing worked."

"Yes, which was his intent, I expect," Zarnix noted. "And we had already pretty much determined it was apt to hold his weight in flight, because at Omega's and Madrid's instruction, I anchored it firmly in the bones of his back, which were well-healed by that time. I had just wanted to run a few more tests first!"

The two males stared at each other for long moments, then broke into prolonged laughter.

"Ah well, that always was Pul," Fox finally managed to gasp. "Where business is concerned, he is the very definition of professionalism. But in personal matters? Impulsive, he can definitely be."

"It would surely seem so!" Zarnix agreed, still laughing. Finally they sobered.

"Oy! Oh me. Okay, next subject—what about Alpha One?" Fox asked.

"I suspected that was coming," Zarnix said, nodding. "Insofar as I can tell, they are doing rather well. I made a few specific queries of Omega, and she IS keeping up with her counseling with Zz'r'p, using a telepathic 'remote' connection, let us call it. They talk, and he determines what her current worries and anxieties are, then discusses them with her, often giving her something new to think about. Then he assigns her various little exercises to do with the matter, nothing that takes up more than a few minutes at any given time, but all of which has significance to HER. And she does them—'religiously,' as she put it—and declares they help." Zarnix gave a thoughtful nod. "Our Deltiri ambassador seems to be a very skilled, and very wise, counselor; I am glad to have him working with us."

"That's outstanding. And Echo?"

"Is considerably more cheerful than he was," Zarnix averred. "The pair are well-respected by the guard corps, and that is proving a boon to his wounded spirit, as well. There are a few other matters coming up that, Pulgey insists, he will turn to Echo's advantage, as well—somehow, as he says. And I have little doubt but that he can, and will. This might actually work, my friend."

"Excellent," Fox said, satisfied. "What about the relationship between Echo and Omega?"

"It seems to be progressing nicely. Of course they are the soul of professionalism when on duty, but I watched them take several long walks through the grounds, hand in hand, after hours. There were a couple of heated kisses, too, though I did not mean to observe THOSE, and always left my observing post whenever they started. And Pulgey has them staying in some lovely little guest house in the back, in the gardens."

"Very good, then," Fox said, even more satisfied. "I think maybe things are developing just the way they need to, for a lovely happy-ever-after for those two."

"I'd have to agree," Zarnix declared.

"All right, meyn khaver, that's all I had, and thank you," Fox said then. "Head on down to the medlab; I know you're dying to find out what's happened while you were gone. Though, according to Zebra, it's been fairly quiet."

"Which is just what a hospital chief of staff wants to hear, after a prolonged absence," Zarnix averred, as he rose and departed.

* * *

Four days later, Alpha One accompanied Lord Pulgey Entiyti offworld, the pair heading up his bodyguard contingent. They were headed for Aleancë, there to attend a big press conference scheduled for Entiyti by the Ennead. This was largely intended to allow the galaxy to see that he was well and healing.

The big Draconan arrived at the conference with a large, charcoal-gray cloak carefully draped around his body; Alpha One worried about him as they arranged his security.

"Are you all right, Pulgey?" Omega wondered, as they

prepared to enter the big room off the Ennead council chambers, where the press conference would take place. "You're all wrapped in a cloak. Are you cold?"

"No, no, dear girl, I am fine," he noted with a slight, almost wolfish, grin. "No, this is to hide the new wing."

"But..." Omega broke off, face falling; it had only just occurred to her that the artificial look of the cybernetic wing might be a source of embarrassment in public events.

"Oh! No, no, no, my dear Omega!" Entiyti exclaimed, spotting her expression and correctly interpreting it. "No, I am most proud of it, and of you and your friend Madrid! No, this is a little surprise. I am feeling rather mischievous, you see, and as it has become known that my natural wing had to be amputated, but we have largely kept it quiet that I have a new artificial wing—save for my household, I suppose—I thought to have a little revealing ceremony!"

"Well, um, but...I mean, if you...I'm sure we can change the surface of it, so it looks a little more natural..." Omega bit her lip.

"And certainly, when they begin to be made for other Draconans who have been injured thus—did I tell you, there have been discreet inquiries regarding licensing and commercialization, coming through Werf, my physician? I have directed them to Fox to have his people work out the business details for you, but provided you agree, you and Madrid should be receiving some nice royalties if a deal can be made—I am sure once that occurs, it will be a consideration for other Draconans, youngling," Entiyti said, as Echo moved to her side, reassuring. "But for me? Not at all. In fact, I should resist any such attempt! No, you did this for love of me, child, and I would have the entire galaxy know it!"

"Aw," Omega sighed then, and flushed, even as she offered a shy smile. "O-okay."

"Better, baby?" Echo breathed, as he leaned over her.

"Yeah, I'm good."

"The bodyguards just headed out into the room and are securing it. We three head out in about two minutes." He glanced at his wrist chronometer. "Mark."

"Very good, then," Entiyti noted. "Omega in the lead, you

in the rear, and me sandwiched between?"

"Exactly," Echo averred, watching his chronometer. "Ready, Meg?"

"All over it, Ace."

"Goggle-glasses on."

"Why?"

"It's more intimidating that way," he pointed out.

"Oh. Good point. No wonder why Mu always wanted to wear his sunglasses, when he was guarding the U.S. President," Omega realized, and Echo chuckled. They slid on the eye gear. "Okay. Ready."

"Then..." He held up his hand, while still watching his chronometer. He dropped his hand and looked up. "Go."

Omega headed for the door, followed by Entiyti, as Echo guarded their six.

* * *

When Omega led Entiyti into the hall, a perturbed whispering sprang up, but when Echo followed him, the room fell dead silent. The trio, well aware of this response and its cause—given the smear to Alpha One's reputation—nevertheless ignored it; Echo kept his head held high and his shoulders even, while Omega lifted her chin and squared her own shoulders. A calm Entiyti strode over to the podium, and Alpha One flanked him, as intimidating as they knew how to be—which was considerable—even as the bodyguards spread through the room took up apparently-relaxed ready stances, as Alpha One had instructed.

"Greetings, my friends!" Entiyti boomed, and various and sundry imaging devices—still and video —went off, even as microphones picked up his statements. "Welcome, welcome! I am, as you may well imagine, very happy to be here!"

Polite, enthusiastic applause greeted this statement.

"Now, normally," Entiyti continued, "I would have some sort of prepared statement at this point, but this is not really an announcement. I simply desired to let the peoples of the galaxy know that I am healing nicely, and while my friend Teela Krimnet has been doing a fine job of heading the Ennead, I am now strong enough that she has begun adding me to the distribution for discussions and such. Much to her relief, I think! Which is to say, while I am not back in harness as yet, I am now back in the loop on important matters. So this is, to my way of thinking, very good news. And with that said, I think I would like to simply open matters up to questions. Mind, you can ask until you are ultraviolet in the face about the day to day details of the Council, but I cannot answer; I simply do not KNOW just yet! Teela forwards the important items to me at my home on Emdali, but the more commonplace items that do not require great cogitation have been taking place without me." He shrugged, then grinned. "Which is not a bad way to do the thing! I might even keep that up after I come back to work!"

Laughter went around the room, and several hands went up. Entiyti pointed at one being, a blue-point Bastian, who stepped forward and initiated a tiny mic.

"At what point do you anticipate coming back to work, milord Entiyti?"

"Ah! I should have brought my personal physician," Entiyti exclaimed. "He has not told me, so far. I think he also wants to obtain the feedback of some of the other physicians who assisted in saving me; Dr. Zarnix Chifejuz, Medical chief of staff at Division One Headquarters, visited me quite recently, and only went back to Earth last week. But while he was here, he and Dr. Werfer Eretigen, my personal physician, collaborated on a general physical, and they were pleased with my progress. However, the best I have been able to get out of them has been, 'In a few more weeks!'" Another chuckle was shared by the room's occupants, and Entiyti added, "I expect I shall be back in the office in roughly another standard lunation, give or take, provided all continues to go well with my healing."

Another appendage went up. This being was a Tethanoid, a giant, decapodal crablike being with a leg span of over six feet.

"President Entiyti, how are you handling the attack? Does it disturb you mentally or emotionally?"

"This is not the first time, nor, I expect, will it be the last time I have been in danger," Entiyti noted, calm. "If you do not believe me, ask Division One Director Fox, sometimes known in galactic circles as Lord Franz Levy, how we met! No, I am doing fine. The matter does not unduly concern me. I do have some considerable regret about the loss of my bodyguard, Uussa Cuusseer, who died in the attack due to my own carelessness in excitedly running ahead of my guard unit. I learned my lesson; I shall never do that again! And I have apologized as profoundly as I know how, to my old friend Suud Guurn and his son Duuniiss, as well as the Cuusseer clan; Uussa was betrothed to Duuniiss, and they were only a few lunations from their espousal ceremony when she was killed. I do feel great and very deep regret for that." The celebrated being paused and drew a deep breath, letting it out in a sigh as his gaze grew distant and sad for a moment; the room was silent in respect of his sorrow. "But has it left me with a fear of open spaces? Of space stations? Of...anything else? No. It has not. I am solid and as strong mentally as ever."

A diminutive Edeptan raised her hand.

"Lord Entiyti, may you remain always healthy! Is it true that even our most famed healer Doron was unable to save your wing?"

A buzz went through the listeners, even as Entiyti held up a clawed hand to pause the murmuring.

"It is true...to a point," he admitted, when the room was silent once more. "It is possible that, had he been available and able to consult with my team of physicians sooner, it might have been saved, though from everything they have told me, I am in doubt of that. But at my own recommendation made well prior to the attack, he was off helping to successfully quell a multi-planet pandemic in the Valestia system, and thus was unable to be reached. He is a very dedicated healer and often positions himself in the more remote regions, to ensure that all in need of medical attention have that attention available. Unfortunately, this sometimes renders him out of range of communications, even our most sophisticated means. Do not misunderstand; he was doing what he should have done, and I do not blame him in the least for what happened to me."

"Does that cause you anguish? The loss of the wing?" a Kinti in its natural tiger-like form asked without raising a paw, following on from the Edeptan's question.

"It did at first," Entiyti remarked, "but no longer. The matter has been...dealt with."

* * *

At that, Echo and Omega both perked up, expecting their

friend Pulgey to whip off his cloak, revealing the artificial wing.

But he did not, merely selected another media being and kept going.

Echo glanced at his partner and saw her shoulders seem to wilt, ever so slightly. It was not a motion that any other being in the room was apt to even see, but to him, it was obvious. He bit his lip, wondering how to offer loving solace that no one else would notice.

* * *

A Skulian, an intelligent seaworm from the Kusheer system, waved its pseudopod-like antennae, gaining the galactic leader's attention.

"President Entiyti, are you truly well?" it asked. "We have all noted that you are heavily wrapped in a thick cloak. Do you find the room unduly chill? Are you, perhaps, feverish? Or does the remnant of your lost wing cause pain that the warmth of the cloak soothes?"

"Heh," Entiyti chuckled. "None of the above, my friend, none of the above. No, call it a touch of the dramatic. For I wished to unveil a little surprise at this event!"

He whipped off the cloak in a smooth, graceful move, tossing it to Echo, who caught it nimbly and laid it aside. As soon as the cloak was clear, Entiyti flexed his back and expanded the wings to their full spread. Despite the matte surface of the alloy on the artificial wing, the smooth polished joints glistened in the light.

A gasp went up, then cries of delight, and finally applause, met Entiyti's surprise display. Called congratulations filled the room.

"Indeed, indeed, and I thank you kindly," Entiyti said with a delighted grin. "Yes, this is a gift from some brilliant friends, and I can already tell you that it works excellently well! I have already flown with it a couple of times." He relaxed the wings, and they folded neatly against his back, as was their natural wont.

A Dorian, age indeterminate as was typical of that species until near death, said in a somewhat snide tone, "I am sure we are all very happy for your good fortune in obtaining what we presume is a very sophisticated cybernetic replacement for your natural wing, Lord Entiyti. And I do hope that your personal coffers were up to the cost, and that no galactic funds were inappropriately utilized to pay for it! But do you not think, in the circumstances, that you could have found rather more reliable escorts for your travel? After all, it is a matter of galactic discourse how Agent Echo, there, disobeyed direct orders in a most delicate first-contact negotiation. And how Agent Omega urged him to do so."

Omega and Echo squared their shoulders and scowled. Entiyti seemed to swell visibly in response, his flexible black horns crossing over his head in his wrath even as his folded wings arched, creating the impression that his body had grown in size. Together, the trio presented an impressive, and highly intimidating, picture of displeasure. The room fell silent, as an uncomfortable electric current seemed to flow through it. The Dorian took an instinctive step backward.

When he spoke, however, the galactic leader's voice was deceptively quiet.

"How dare you speak to what you do not know," he declared. "Not only is this pair fully trustworthy, they are leading my security at this event. In point of fact, Agents Omega and Echo were set up to take the blame by the Persan usurper, Humn Aggum, who murdered and impersonated Ennead member Ordik Adita. He used Adita's position to ensure that the Alpha One team, here, was placed in a no-win scenario by grossly twisting a fact-finding assignment, which had been combined with the diplomatic mission...which was NOT a first contact; the first contact had already occurred. I know that for a fact, because I was part of it! Omega never urged Echo to disobey orders; Echo's orders, as twisted and issued by Aggum, stated that he was to give the Persan Premier anything he wanted. What the Premier wanted...was Omega as his concubine. And even that was twisted, perverted by the usurper, because the Premier thought he was doing as he had been requested, in taking Omega into his harem."

A soft murmur went around the room.

"Not only does this render it effectively slave trade, which is illegal in the Coalition, it would have ensured Omega's death, as humans and most species of the Persis Federation are not sexually compatible," Entiyti continued. "AND...Echo and Omega were, at that time, newly betrothed, never mind Alpha Line partners of long standing and patent merit. Worse, the coup attempt intended to assure Omega was killed, along with the Premier, framing her for the Premier's death in order to ensure Aggum's succession to power—it was a no-win scenario, several times over. So I ask you: if your chosen mate were about to be taken from you and killed in what amounted to illegal sex-slave trade to further a successful hostile take-over of the entire galaxy, what would you have done? Rescue it, or leave it to die? The moral thing, or the letter of the law? More, which was the RIGHT thing to do?"

The room was silent for long moments, then various heads and head-equivalents began to nod.

"And do you see this?" He flexed the cybernetic wing, partially unfurling it once more. "Do you know who is responsible for this? Agent Omega, Echo's partner, who has been included in the slander of his hard-won reputation. It was SHE who had the idea, who created the design, and who enlisted a talented friend, Agent Madrid of Division One, to help her construct it! OMEGA...when as yet no Draconan engineer had been able to find a way to build so robust a system! And she did it... as a GIFT. There was no exchange of funds. At all. More, it is my understanding that the time which Omega and Madrid took to design and construct the thing was donated from their off-duty hours, and the materials used in the construction were either surplus or expressly purchased by their own finances." He paused, then laid a hand lightly on Omega's shoulder for a moment. "It was a handsome gift, indeed."

Omega blushed, as another murmur, more approving, went around the room. A proud Echo thrust out his jaw, his chest appearing to expand until the buttons of his shirt seemed threatened. He pressed his lips together to control the grin that threatened to break his professional-tough-guy image. Entiyti saw it, however; he smiled, and laid a gentle hand on the human male's shoulder. Then he turned and replaced his other hand on Omega's shoulder.

"These two are trusted friends and colleagues," he declared. "Not only of myself, but of my entire bodyguard corps. You see them around the room? My bodyguards? They are reporting to ALPHA ONE. By their own choice. They were not ordered to do so; each and every one of them CHOSE to work under these two. Because they TRUST THEM. One of the most highly-regarded guard corps in the galaxy."

At that, every bodyguard in the room nodded, then stepped forward, one at a time, in clockwise order, and saluted the trio who stood behind the podium.

"It will not do. This ongoing maligning of Alpha One, and particularly Agent Echo, simply must stop," Entiyti declared. "Do you want to know what he really did? He most likely saved TWO galaxies from a despotic rule! Because in rescuing Omega from certain death, he enabled her to bring out information that she had discovered while imprisoned in the harem, which led to the exposure of the plot, and the capture of the assassins and accomplices, as well as the attempted usurper himself. You would, every one of you, be under the oppressive rule of a tyrant if not for them. Aggum PROVED this in his usurpation of authority in Division One. They have seriously injured agents on Earth who are still recovering, and some who may never fully recover...because they were so severely 'punished' by Aggum's vicious and bloodthirsty soldiers, in the guise of 'enforcers'—enforcers who beat these agents nearly to death—that it may have left them permanently disabled. It is my understanding from Lord Levy that one agent DID die, in the effort to oust the usurper." He paused, then looked around the room. "And if ALL of this is not properly and fairly reported in the galactic media, I intend to see that there are investigations into obstruction of justice...for it is only justice to see Agent Echo vindicated from the unreasonable charges which were levied against him, at the influence of Aggum. And that, in the galactic consciousness, not merely in the courts of law, which latter has already been done long since, and in no less a court than the Ennead itself."

The room was deathly silent. Many faces had paled—those capable of doing so, at any rate—and everyone stared at the suddenly-fierce galactic president.

After long moments, the little Edeptan raised her hand, and

Entiyti waved a clawed finger at her.

"Might a very grateful Coalition citizen say thank you?" she wondered.

* * *

The press conference was immediately followed by an informal reception. Most of the members of the Ennead showed up for it, mingling with the media, and greeting Entiyti and Alpha One with enthusiasm. Lady Teela Krimnet was especially excited about Pulgey's artificial wing, and she was vociferous in her praise of Omega, much to Echo's delight. The male Agent stood near his partner, his shoulders automatically and instinctively squaring each time someone praised her design work.

"And Agent Madrid helped you with it? With the building of it, I mean," Teela verified.

"Yes ma'am," Omega said with a smile. "In fact, he did most of the construction; he's more experienced with that aspect of it than I am. But we started it off together." She shrugged. "Alpha Line had an unexpected little incident over in China, when Echo and I had to help corral that gurfdin that shouldn't have been there in the first place. Then things got kinda busy with organizing the new departmental branches at the various Offices, and that put paid to my being able to work with Madrid on it much, anyway."

"Great Maker," Teela said blankly. "A gurfdin? Seriously? And you are both still in one piece? Nor even injured?"

"Oh, well, we got a few of what I call boo-boos," Omega admitted. "You know what I mean—small cuts, scrapes, and bruises; things like that. But then, we nearly always do, when there's something loose like that. Wild animals an' all, you know. We keep bottles of Rejuvic handy for those, Echo an' me. No big deal."

"They are good at what they do, Teela," Entiyti noted... while also privately observing—with considerable amusement—the way the various members of the media were eavesdropping on the conversation...and taking voluminous notes on various small hand or wrist devices. He gently elbowed Echo to indicate the fact; the Agent's eyebrows rose. "Is it any wonder they head the toughest, most resourceful group in their, and

40

possibly any other, Division? Have you seen the training video they made recently, with Fox's help? You should have a look some time. I think it is in the open-source literature, at least for the rest of the galaxy; something about a 'Nazi zombie apocalypse,' I think Franz called it?"

Then he subtly elbowed Echo again, watching the reporters jerk out various implements to locate the video being referenced, and both males stifled snorts of amusement.

* * *

After that, galactic demographics showed Alpha One's overall reputation and approval rating had increased more than an order of magnitude, and Echo's solo rating improved nearly two orders.

"I should say that takes care of that," Entiyti decided.

"Looks like it," Echo agreed, even as Omega fairly beamed her pride.

* * *

When they returned to Emdali from the highly-successful press conference, Entiyti did as he had once promised, taking Alpha One to his favorite glide park and seeing to it they were each suitably outfitted with a set of the most sophisticated glide wings available for offworlders. Though the wings were largely fixed in position and served essentially like a hang-glider on Earth, the torso harness was more of a body suit, and the wings had slight movement, sufficient to make some rather radical midcourse adjustments by simply flexing a few muscles. Then Entiyti joined both Omega and Echo in a flight through the park.

"Come with me!" he called, as they launched into the air from a high pinnacle, and the wind quickly caught beneath their wings, holding them aloft. "I will show you some of the fun, more exciting things to do in the park!"

"WAHOO!" Omega screamed in glee, as Echo, paralleling her, grinned from ear to ear. "You mean it gets BETTER?!"

"Indeed it does, my dear girl! We shall find thermals and fly high! I will show you how to shoot through an obstacle course, and swoop down on drone prey! You will learn today what it is to be a true dragon!"

"You up for this, Ace?"

"Are you kidding?! Just because I'm not as obvious about it as SOME people are, doesn't mean I don't like me some speed and some altitude, baby! Remember, there's a reason you nicknamed me 'Ace'! Let's GO!"

And they were off.

* * *

Suud remained on the ground, watching; Reptoids, unlike Draconans, did not naturally possess wings, and never had. As a consequence, they tended to eschew heights; even their houses were typically sprawling, one-story dwellings, as opposed to Draconan houses, which were multi-story and either built on hilltops and mountain peaks, or possessed tall turrets, or both. And while Suud himself was an excellent pilot, he still preferred to keep his feet on the ground...or deck, as the case might be. In Suud's world, it was one thing to fly inside a well-maintained craft, another altogether to be dangling in the wind.

But he could still appreciate the enthusiasm of his adoptive brother, let alone his 'niece and nephew,' as he was coming to think of the Alpha One pair. And when he heard all three voices raised in shouts of excitement as they soared, swooped, and dived, he grinned to himself.

"Based on Franz's experience with those things, as well as Pulgey's enforced inactivity of late, I expect the lot of them are going to be very sore on the morrow," he decided. "But they are having fun now, as well as obtaining a substantial bit of emotional release, and Maker knows, all three of them need THAT."

So he found a comfortable seat that commanded a good view of the peaks and the obstacle course, then parked himself for what promised to be a long, enjoyable afternoon, watching his friends swoop and soar and play.

* * *

They WERE sore the next day. But as Omega had certified as a massage therapist by then, Echo had had his certification for years, and Dr. Eretigen had a massage therapist in his practice—never mind hot tubs available for all and sundry, to help loosen stiff muscles—the three managed to get most of the aches and pains eased before it became necessary to do anything of significance.

And Suud had had the good sense to schedule Alpha One for an extra off day.

Chapter 3

"Come ON, Pete!" an intensely annoyed Dan Hollifield, the flight engineer/MS-2 for the *Kitty Hawk* complained in his soft Southern drawl. The entire crew of five sat in a tiny flight cabin, the full-up simulator for the new space plane system, complete with controls for the new propulsion system which would be under test for their mission. "With me AND Scotty BOTH telling you not to do that, and you did it anyway?! And crashed the damn simulator while you were at it? It's not designed to DO that!"

"And if you do that on orbit, you're apt to get us all killed," Scotty said, tight.

"So...what now?" Pat Pate, the payload specialist and expert on the new propulsion system under prototype testing, wanted to know, cutting Peter Dianus off before he could respond. "With the simulator down, does that scrub training for the rest of the day?"

"It depends," Scotty noted, seeing as how a sullen Dianus was now refusing to answer. "If they can reboot it and bring it back up pretty quick, we'll just have a delay for as long as it takes 'em to do that. If it's a hard crash, we're prob'ly done for the day. They'll have to bring in the techies and go off and fix it. Maybe tomorrow."

"Which slides everything else in the training by a day, when we're behind schedule already," Robert Vancel, the MS-3 payload commander, observed with carefully controlled irritation; given that Vancel tended to be easygoing and always in an upbeat mood, this was a good sign of the crew's general level of displeasure with their new commander.

"Sim Sup to *Kitty Hawk*," came the audio on the speaker just then. Dianus ignored it, so Scotty hit his mic button.

"*Kitty Hawk*. Go, Sim Sup."

"*Kitty Hawk*, the simulator techs say they'll have to do some work on the simulator before they can get it up and running again. We're standing down the simulations for the day.

We will resume simulations across all control centers tomorrow at 13:00 GMT."

"Sim Sup, *Kitty Hawk*; copy that. Resume sim at 13:00 tomorrow," Scotty said. He glanced at the others meaningfully. Several sets of eyes rolled in disgust.

"And another entire day wasted, thanks to ego," Dan grumbled, sotto voce.

"I heard that," Dianus snapped. "Hollifield, let me remind you—let me remind ALL of you, especially you, Chadwick—that this crew complement is NOT a democracy. You do NOT get a vote."

"Funny, I thought that was the reason for an odd number of crew members on any given mission," Vancel observed. "So the crew could VOTE, and not have a tie. This isn't the military, Dianus."

Dianus ignored the comment and continued.

"...I am the most experienced astronaut on this manifest, and I am the commander of this mission," he went on with his rant. "I will tell you what you will do. You will treat me with respect, and you WILL do what I tell you. Do I make myself clear?"

"Then I recommend you try acting in a manner that's apt to GET you respect," Scotty snapped, and stalked off.

* * *

"Morgen, it's just not working," Scotty declared in her office behind closed doors. "HE's not working! I dunno what the hell happened on his last mission to give him such an outrageous opinion of himself, but it's gone to his head and then some. He acts like a tyrant, tells us we all have to do what HE says, even when he's WRONG, even when we KNOW he's wrong and HE knows we know he's wrong...and then pulls a stunt like today, with Dan AND me both telling him NOT to do what he did! The sequence he tried to use was so bad, it crashed the simulator, and I don't mean the usual slow deterioration to failure, I mean he locked up the whole damn system!"

"Ooo," Kirby murmured, green eyes widening. "That's really bad. That...if that were real life, that means—"

"Exactly," Scotty confirmed. "One lost space plane, and five dead astronauts! Never mind losing the new propulsion

44

prototype."

"Is the rest of the crew in agreement? I mean, about the, uh, personnel problems?"

"I couldn't tell ya for sure," Scotty said, "because we haven't been able to have a crew meeting without Dianus! Pat is starting to wonder if he's got us all bugged, the way he shows up every time we try to get together without him—even just for beers; he's a real party-pooper, 'cause he's the only teetotaler in the entire astronaut office. And then he thinks he can order us NOT to drink in our off hours! Never mind what we eat, how we exercise..."

"You're kidding," Kirby said, jaw going slack in shock. "In your OFF hours?"

"Lord have mercy, I wish I was."

"It's never affected anybody's performance, has it? Like, a hangover or something?"

"Nah, Morgen. 'Cause we're not stupid. None of us have more than one or two, and we always got a designated driver, an' all that shit. We're responsible, hon. Besides, Pat is our clock."

"Huh?"

Chadwick grinned.

"Okay, do NOT tell her I told you this," he said, grin growing wider. "But Pat, being on the petite side of the corps requirements, has a smaller bladder than the rest of us. Which means that after about one an' a half beers, she's gotta go—it's like clockwork. Bob and I have even timed it, without her knowing. So as soon as she has to go 'give back to the porcelain throne,' we know it's time to stop with the alcohol. We finish what we got, and switch to sodas or something. Or go home."

Kirby slapped her hand to her face, lips twitching. Chadwick, watching, let out a lone bark of laughter, then slapped his own hand across his mouth, murmuring a muffled, "Sorry."

"...Okay," Kirby finally managed to choke out in a slightly strangled tone, deciding to get back to the original topic. "What about the crew's response to him?"

"Well, like I said, I can't say for certain, 'cause we never get a chance to talk in private. But to judge by the reactions, I think so. I mean, even Bob was pissed off."

"Damnation," Kirby exclaimed, surprised. "He got under the Teflon Astronaut's skin?"

"If that scowl on Bob's face was anything to go by, oh HELL yeah."

"All right," Kirby sighed. "Let me see what I can do. You clear out while I get Pete in here."

"Gone," Scotty said, making a beeline for the office door. Kirby leaned over and thumbed a switch on her intercom.

"Carol, could you get hold of Peter Dianus and have him come to my office in about ten minutes?"

* * *

"Peter, you remember what I already told you," Kirby told the space plane commander, after a thorough raking over the coals. "If you don't know, if you even THINK you MIGHT NOT know, then let Scotty handle it."

"That self-righteous son of a bitch? No way in hell," Dianus snarled.

"Did you just refuse a direct order by the chief astronaut?"

"Respectfully, when the chief astronaut doesn't know the attitudes of the crew involved? Yes ma'am," he declared.

"So you're telling me that this is Scotty's fault?" Kirby eyed the man. "And that you are not responsible for the crash of the simulator and the delay of training across multiple field centers?"

"Yeah! Well, indirectly," Dianus tried. "His attitude just gets under my skin, Morgen! You have to be there to see!"

"For all intents and purposes, I was, Peter," Kirby noted, calm and cool. "I just finished a quick review of the simulator video. I didn't see Scotty do ANYthing, or SAY anything, that should have raised ANY sort of ire in you. I did see him... AND Dan, AND Pat AND Bob, repeatedly telling you NOT to do what you then went ahead and did anyway. Which resulted in an immediate hard crash of the simulator—extra work and unnecessary overtime, across the board, when you know we're behind schedule, never mind short on funds this late in the year, PLUS possible damage to the simulator!—and which action, according to a quick poll of the other four crew members, all of whom are more experienced with the advanced system than you are, would have resulted in catastrophic loss of the bird and all crew."

"Buncha damn suck-ups," Dianus muttered under his breath.

"What was that?"

"Nothing."

"I asked you a question. Answer it. What did you say?"

"They think that Chadwick is gonna be the commander over me," Dianus burst out, "and they're sucking up to him!"

"If you keep this up, they may be right," Kirby snapped. "I reserve the right to rearrange the crew, putting Chadwick back in the command seat, Dan in the pilot's seat, and you in the MS-2 seat. One more incident out of you, one more negative report to this office, and that's what will happen, if I have to go all the way to the Administrator to do it. Do. You. Understand?"

"Sure, Morgen. Whatever."

"What?"

"Uh...yes, ma'am."

"That's better. Dismissed."

An irate Dianus rose and marched out of the office.

* * *

Two weeks later, Coalition President Pulgey Entiyti attended the opening of the brand-new Division Five Slliith City Office, in his official capacity. Suud Guurn was unable to attend; there was a Guurn clan event over which he had to preside. Upon the arrival and successful debut of Alpha One as bodyguards, Duuniiss also decided to go to the clan event, with Entiyti's full permission; there was to be a private, family-only memorial to Uussa Cuusseer, his deceased fiancée, and he greatly desired to be present to participate and honor her memory. Doctor Eretigen attended the Office opening, just in case he was needed; he did not consider Entiyti quite up to full strength as yet, but he was pleased at this particular event.

"Because it is high time this facility was built and operational," Doctor Eretigen noted privately to Alpha One, as Entiyti and Division Five Director Taassass Siisshiiss cut the ribbon to much applause. "To have no PGLEIA Office in the home city of the long-standing coalition president has been neglectful at the least. Now he has personnel that can be called

47

upon in an emergency and actually RESPOND in a reasonable time."

Director Siisshiiss moved to the nearby podium, with Entiyti flanking him, and Alpha One shifted their positions slightly, to provide due guard, even as Eretigen moved back, out of the way. Behind them, near the Office entrance, stood Goobop Ogoobah. On either side of the plaza stood Bisun Pujai and Pyxffurn Vuxia with some dozen other colleagues, all clad in the burgundy-and-black uniform of the Entiyti Bodyguard Corps. Accompanying them were several Division Five agents, including Piradu Madru of Tath, the Division's top agent, and Eessaan Niirsseen, the top Emdalian agent, considered second only to Piradu in the Division as a whole. All of the security team, Agents and bodyguards alike, scanned the area intently, looking for any sign of a potential threat.

Siisshiiss said a few words of welcome and gratitude for the new Office, then introduced Entiyti to address the crowd of citizens, politicians, and more. Entiyti stepped to the podium with a broad smile.

"Greetings, my friends and fellow Emdalians, Reptoid and Draconan alike! Welcome to this new Pan-Galactic Law Enforcement facility! I am pleased—"

"Oh shit!" Echo exclaimed, gaze fixed at an angle upward. "Meg! You see—?!"

"I got it!" Omega cried, following his gaze. "Get Pul!"

Echo dived for Entiyti, efficiently tackling the much larger being and taking him down to the pavement, even as Omega pulled both blasters. Instantly the other guards and the Division Five agents were in ready mode, weapons brought to bear...as a shot rang out from somewhere above and slightly to the right, followed by a tiny explosion and spray of rock chips behind them, as the projectile impacted the heretofore-pristine stone of the building's façade. Several more shots followed, peppering the front of the new building with tiny pockmarks. Siisshiiss, Goobop, and several Division Five agents dove for cover, drawing their own weapons.

Given Draconans stood some two to three feet taller than he, and Entiyti was a particularly tall Draconan, Echo spread out to cover Entiyti as best he could, crying, "Stay down, Pul!

Stay down! Keep your head down!"

Omega, in turn, stepped forward and took aim with her primary blaster at a point on the balcony of the building across the street and down the block, and fired twice. A scream rang out, and a being fell from the second-story balcony onto the sidewalk below; simultaneously the projectile gunfire barrage ceased. Police and security of various persuasions rapidly converged on the fallen being, even as the rest of the Entiyti Bodyguard Corps surrounded Pulgey. Eretigen eased into the group, crouched, and began to check his patient for injury, swift and sure. Echo shifted, moving to crouch beside the Draconan, and the others helped the pair to their feet.

"Are you two okay?" Omega asked, urgent.

"Thanks to your partner, I am, indeed," Entiyti confirmed.

"Doctor?" she addressed Eretigen.

"Yes, he is fine," Eretigen verified.

"Ace?" Omega pressed.

"I'm fine, Meg," Echo murmured. "Is anybody else hurt?"

"No," Director Siisshiiss declared. "For a wonder."

"Good," Echo said. "Let's haul ass and get Pulgey out of here to someplace safe. There could be others."

* * *

As soon as Entiyti was safely back in the manor house with Eretigen, Echo, Omega, Piradu Madru, and Siisshiiss returned to the Slliith City Office, where the perp was being held...and given medical care into the bargain, as he had two small, deep holes in the musculature of his shoulder; Omega had been deadly accurate, but had chosen to wound rather than kill, in order that they might have a chance of getting information out of the would-be assassin.

It turned out that wasn't as hard as they had expected.

The perpetrator was one Sebvuv Yiitssahn, a Draconan university professor of astrophysics, just entering early middle age, and already developing the somewhat portly figure characteristic of a sedentary lifestyle. He was normally a law-abiding, peaceful, somewhat pacifistic citizen of some reasonably respected standing in the university faculty. More, he had no permit for a projectile weapon of any sort, nor was there any record of how he had obtained it.

49

"No, no, you don't understand!" the deep-olive-scaled Draconan confessed, desperate and babbling. "The weapon is not mine! They made me take it! I didn't want to! I didn't want to do ANY of this! I LIKE Lord Entiyti! I think he is an excellent galactic leader! I didn't have any choice! They are angry about increased PGLEIA presence on Emdali, and blame him for the additional PGLEIA Office being built. But I aimed at the wall, not him!"

"Explain," Echo snapped. The Draconan seemed to wilt.

"My family. They have my wife and children," he sighed. "They said they would kill them...slowly...if I did not...try to kill milord."

"WHO?!" Echo demanded.

"Asssshh Hiiisss Geessht," Yiitssahn explained.

"'The Sixteenth Level of Hell,'" Piradu Madru translated. "It's an Emdalian crime syndicate. One of three...well, there's really only two left, after we were done with the whole 'Adita's Coup' grag," the Tathian agent noted.

"Well, they overstepped their bounds this time," an angry Director Siisshiiss declared. "Whatever their problem is, they made their little vendetta interstellar by attacking Pul. That means PGLEIA is involved now. And unlike the local police, who are understaffed, WE will flatten their asses. Emdali will only have one crime syndicate for the locals to deal with, when we are through. If that."

"The first thing we need to do is rescue this male's family," Piradu said.

"Agreed," Siisshiiss said.

Echo and Omega exchanged a glance.

"Count us in, if you don't mind," Omega noted.

"Done," Siisshiiss agreed. "In fact, I was hoping you would assist. I shall pair you with my two top people, and you four can take the lead on the case."

* * *

Given the galactic level of equipment, technology and ability that the PGLEIA agents could bring to bear, the number of PGLEIA agents pulled into the task, and the pristine new, state-of-the-art Office facilities they had in which to work, coupled with the somewhat overweening pride of the crime syndicate, it did not take long before the location of the kidnapped family was pinned down by the elite team. This was largely based on some quick detective work by Alpha One, who swiftly derived a list of possible sites, then reconnoitered them with the help of Madru and his partner.

That same elite team, consisting of Alpha One, Tathian agent Piradu Madru, and his partner, Reptoid agent Eessaan Niirsseen, entered the dilapidated old shipping warehouse where intelligence information said the wife and two small children were being held by three members of the syndicate, and which Alpha One had confirmed that afternoon. Another quick reconnoiter verified the intel was still correct and the perps had not moved the targets, and the four agents withdrew to plan specifics.

"There's three of them and four of us," Echo noted. "Meg, you just go get the mom and kids. We'll take out the guards. Watch yourself, though."

"Perhaps Eessaan should do that," Piradu considered. "The mother may relate to her more."

"No," Echo countered, "because the mother could think Eessaan is part of their kidnappers' organization. She'll take one look at Meg and know she's not part of the mob."

"Eh. Good point," Eessaan agreed.

"All right, you good with that, baby?"

"All over it, Ace," Omega noted, as they re-entered the 'abandoned' warehouse, waving certain small gold rods at the overall volume of the building as they progressed, thereby ensuring that no one in the syndicate would know exactly what was happening via any monitoring devices. But it also meant they needed to move fast, so no one in the syndicate could FIGURE OUT what was happening, once those monitoring devices went down.

In seconds the four agents had spread out. Echo, Piradu and Eessaan located each of the three criminal guards and prepared to render them unconscious in various ways, as Omega homed in on the small family group.

* * *

Omega eased her way toward the little family, which consisted of a female Draconan and two tiny 'baby dragons,' as she immediately thought of them; she had never seen Draconan children before, and even Suud's youngest child was an adolescent. *Though,* she thought, *that doesn't necessarily mean that Reptoid kids look like Draconan kids, I expect. Same genus, different species.*

The biggest of the two imprisoned children was no more than two feet tall, if that; they had stout, roly-poly bodies, oversized heads, short wings, and stubby little tails that Draconan adults did not possess, as they tended to be absorbed into the body as maturity neared. Judging by the way the children were using their tails, they were intended for stability and balance as the little ones developed coordination in running and flying. *Oh, they're adorable!* Omega thought briefly, immediately stifling the reaction in order to remain alert.

As soon as the mother saw Omega, crouched and creeping toward the little family, she tensed, then relaxed slightly and cocked her head in confusion.

"Shhh," Omega shushed with a friendly smile, even while she approached the small group. "I'm here to rescue you. Be quiet, and come with me."

"But will they not stop you?" the anxious and frightened mother whispered. "They are all much bigger than you are..."

"I've got equalizers, and I'm not alone," Omega breathed with an infectious grin. "Hush, and listen."

From the right, a soft male voice fairly snarled, "Bastard," seconds before the smack of flesh hitting flesh sounded. Silence reigned from that direction thereafter. Omega held up a finger.

Within seconds, from the left came a muted electronic *zap!* followed by a series of low spatting sounds. Then the area fell quiet. Omega raised a second finger.

Fractions of a second later, from the far left came a soft Reptoid growl, followed by a truncated grunt and a soft thud. No further sound issued from that direction, either. Omega held up a third finger, still grinning.

"That's all three guards. By now they'll be restrained, as well as unconscious. C'mon, let's go before they send somebody else over," she murmured.

"Children, come with me," the mother said, holding out her

arms for the younglings. She scooped up the larger of the pair, Omega the smaller, and Omega led the way back toward the doorway, moving fast.

* * *

The other agents fell in beside them; first Eessaan, then Piradu, then Echo. The three other agents formed a small, horseshoe-shaped phalanx around the little family and the Agent who assisted them. When Mrs. Yiitssahn stumbled badly over a broken brick on the floor, obscured in the dim lighting, Echo quickly grabbed the little toddler before she could drop it, even as Eessaan caught and steadied Mrs. Yiitssahn. The group halted.

"Are you okay? You didn't hurt your foot or sprain your ankle, did you?" Omega asked, and Mrs. Yiitssahn shook her head.

"I will be fine. Just get us out of here," she hissed. "Is Sebvuv all right?"

Omega restarted the group, as Piradu drew his blaster, given that the other three agents were either carrying children, or steadying Mrs. Yiitssahn.

"He is well, madam," Piradu noted. "He has a few mild injuries, but they have been treated and will heal quickly."

"What about Lord Entiyti?"

"He is unhurt."

"And...is Sebvuv under arrest?"

"Mm, call it house arrest. Your husband will have to answer for his actions, but given the blackmail, and the fact that he admits to pulling his shots so as NOT to hit Entiyti, any punishment meted is apt to be small to none. He is waiting for you."

"Oh, thank Maker," she breathed, as they exited the building. "Thank Maker."

* * *

Chief Siisshiiss was waiting outside with a large contingent of field agents. He personally led the small group over to an armored vehicle, waiting nearby. "Get in, all of you," he murmured, opening the back, and the group of five adults and two small children piled into the rear.

He closed the door firmly but quietly, assuring it latched

and locked properly, then knocked on the side panel and waved toward the cab of the big truck—which only marginally resembled an analogous vehicle on Earth, being, among other things, possessed of antigrav instead of wheels. It hummed, then pulled away from the warehouse, headed toward the Sl-liith City Office. He turned back to the waiting agents and keyed a comm device, ensuring several remote teams could hear his orders.

"Take 'em out," he growled. "Every last gsshtt ssllit-thhssshhtt of the lot. Wherever they are, across the whole gsshtt planet. By the time tonight is over, I want the Asssshh Hiiisss Geessht stamped into the soil. Preferably all the way down to Geessht. If we have to personally introduce them to Aarg'sshiibeek itself, so be it."

The agents spread out swiftly, disappearing in the darkness.

* * *

Professor Sebvuv Yiitssahn was indeed waiting for his family when they arrived at the Office, the armored vehicle driving right through a special force-field door in the building's side, and into a secure kind of courtyard within. Omega and Echo had carried his children the entire way, much to Omega's not-so-secret delight; the child she carried—finally feeling safe, and deciding the human female was nice and smelled good— had fallen asleep against her shoulder, but she had watched in captivated fascination as Echo sat the other 'baby dragon' in his lap and played with it while they rode back to the Sl-liith City Office. The youngling laughed and cooed, and Echo grinned.

Wow, she thought, happy. *If I can ever figure out how to get around my genetic issue, we might actually have some kids together, one of these days, him and me. And if that right there is any indication, he'll be a terrific dad. I guess the interaction with kids he's had in the last couple years has been a GOOD thing.*

But as soon as the rear doors of the vehicle opened and the two Yiitssahn children saw their sire waiting in the courtyard, three shrieks rose—the third being Mrs. Yiitssahn—and they fairly thundered for the door, running and flapping. The four agents followed, easing to the ground. One of the local

54

PGLEIA physicians accompanied the Professor, and she led the entire group toward Medical.

"Are any of you agents injured?" she wondered, glancing back.

Omega, Piradu, and Eessaan shook their heads, but Echo held out his hand. The knuckles were raw and bloody.

"Ouch," the physician winced.

"OW!" Omega exclaimed, surprised. "Ace, what'd you DO?!"

"I forgot what Reptoid scales can do to human skin," he said with a sheepish grin.

* * *

A medtech had carefully cleaned Echo's knuckles and was finishing off the first aid by anointing them with Rejuvic, while a team of physicians checked the Yiitssahn family for injury or abuse. Just then, Piradu came in with a tablet.

"Echo," he said, "after, um, events last month, I thought you and Omega might want to see this."

Echo took the tablet with his good hand, as Omega leaned over his shoulder to look at the screen.

The tablet displayed a galactic news website—it looked to be GNN's site—and it depicted the top story of the day in a huge headline.

MALIGNED DIVISION ONE AGENTS RISK LIVES TO SAVE GALACTIC COALITION PRESIDENT

Beneath was a large photo. It depicted Entiyti sprawled on the sidewalk in front of the Slliith City Office, Echo on top of him and shielding him with his own body, while a scowling Omega stood astride them both, blasters drawn and aimed, firing at something in the distance.

"Whoa," Omega murmured.

"That," Echo agreed.

"Exactly," Piradu said with a grin. "Somehow I don't think either one of you is going to have any sort of problem with ruined reputations for long, after this."

* * *

By the next morning, the Yiitssahn family had been

whisked into hiding for their own protection; Echo's knuckles were nearly healed, and Chief Siisshiiss had returned with news.

"That is pretty much the end of that," he declared, grim. "The idiots actually tried to fight back, and had NO IDEA how many agents I had ready for THAT battle. Frankly, I have been expecting the like ever since the attack on the transfer station, and I have NOT been idle in preparing. Asssshh Hiiisss Geessht is no more. Virtually all of their people are dead or in custody...and most of THOSE are being treated by various and sundry medics." He glanced at the four agents. "How are you four, and what has happened with the Yiitssahn family?"

"We are fine, sir," Eessaan noted. "The Yiitssahn family is in hiding with a bodyguard contingent out of Security, and the poor professor could not stop apologizing."

"Well, the fact that he deliberately shot to miss says a lot about the being," Siisshiiss pointed out. "He was doing his best to keep his family alive, and everyone else, too." He shrugged his big shoulders. "Somehow, I doubt the charges are going to be particularly severe, in the circumstances. I plan to have a long talk with the prosecutor on the matter, anyway." Then he eyed the four. "As to the lot of you being 'fine,' what was the report I heard of someone being treated, then?"

"Oh, that," Echo said, waving a dismissive hand. "I pulled a mild stupid, and barked my knuckles on a Reptoid stooge's scales." He pointed to the last of the scabs on his knuckles, most of which had already peeled off, revealing new, pink skin. "It was a brain fart on my part, and the injury wasn't really very bad, but it was bleeding all over everything, and I had been trying to hold one of the kids, and..."

"Ah," Siisshiiss said with a slight grin. "Mustn't bloody the Suit, eh?"

"Something like," Echo said, returning the grin. "Anyway, that's all there was to it."

"Why did you even hit him, though, Ace?" Omega wondered. "And I heard you call him 'bastard' right before I heard the punch..."

"I got a look at the kids, just before I took the guy out," Echo admitted, "and it made me mad that this jerk would even consider hurting two little bitty kids like that."

"This from the hardcore Agent," Siisshiiss chuckled.

"Why do you think I'm an Agent?" Echo asked, mildly puzzled. "The badass reputation is for the sake of the perps! Makes things simpler that way. I prefer keeping innocents from getting hurt by trash like those guys. And little kids are generally innocents. Especially that small."

"Good male," Siisshiiss decided, patting his shoulder.

* * *

The very next morning, back at the Entiyti estate, Pulgey called the pair into his office.

"There are a couple of things you need to see," he told them. "First, I assume you saw the first reports of the attempted assassination? 'Division One Team Risks Lives for Coalition President'? That sort of thing?"

"Yeah, Pulgey, Piradu showed that to us before Siisshiiss ever got back from the raid on the main mob HQ," Echo noted.

"I'd lay odds you have not yet seen this, then," he said, and handed them his 'outboard brain' to read the article. Once again, the headline was in bold block letters.

DIVISION ONE'S AMAZING ALPHA ONE TEAM
TAKES LEAD IN FIGHT AGAINST
ASSSSHH HIIISSS GEESSHT

The sub-headline read,

Alpha One Rescues Family Held Hostage
Before PGLEIA Wrath Descends On Crime Syndicate

Underneath was a photo, taken by a Division Five recorder, of Echo and Omega, each carrying a child, leading the Yiitssahn woman out of the warehouse and flanked closely by Agents Eessaan Niirsseen and Piradu Madru.

"Wow," Omega remarked. "I know that Siisshiiss asked us if they could photograph us, but I didn't even think about THAT. I hope Piradu and Eessaan don't take offense at being back-seated."

"Yeah," Echo agreed. "Nice publicity, all things considered.

57

But I agree with Meg; I hope those two don't get hacked at us. They're really good agents, and I'd like us to all be friends."

"Indeed," Entiyti averred. "Very nice, indeed. Do not worry about Piradu and Eessaan; they have already sent their congratulations at the recovery of your honor, along with their pleasure at being able to help in the matter. And here is the other thing."

He handed them a document.

* * *

The Rrgllbrrgll do hereby notify Lord Pulgey Entiyti, of Slliith Saaarn Entiiytii, that they have invoked the Hiiissh Aarg'sshiibeek Ssluthiissht, that neither we, nor ours, shall go against the Lord Entiyti, his extended family, his any descendants, nor the Pan-Galactic Coalition or galactic law. This we do swear.

⊙cꓷ8

* * *

"What the hell...?" Omega murmured, puzzled. "I'm sorry, Uncle Pulgey, but I don't quite understand all that. I mean, the whole bit about not going against you, or the law, or the galactic government, that all sounds good, but..."

"I get a bit more," Echo admitted, "but what the hell is 'The Curse of the Death Demon'? And what is that series of symbols at the end?"

Entiyti chuckled grimly.

"You have a spiritual being known as Satan, or the Adversary, do you not? In your personal religion?" he asked. "Franz and I have talked...Christo-Judean, or something like that..."

"Oh! Um, yeah," Omega said, nodding. "Most ministers I've heard think he's a fallen angel who used to be named Lucifer."

"Well, we call it Aarg'sshiibeek, which as Echo notes, simply means 'Demon of Death,' though it has more of a connotation of spiritual death than physical...though there is that, too," Entiyti explained. "Think oblivion, I suppose. At any rate, the Rrgllbrrgll, or 'Brotherhood' in Reptoid, is the last of the three principal crime syndicates left on Emdali. It seems, according to this, that they have invoked Aarg'sshiibeek in a specific ancient, and rather nasty, curse. You see, the Hiiissh

58

Aarg'sshiibeek Ssluthiissht, when invoked, means that the swearer—or in this case, swearers, plural, as apparently this document is now effectively mob 'law' over the entire syndicate—subject themselves to the curse if they fail in fulfilling their oath...which in this case, is basically to follow galactic law and not harm me or mine. Which, I intend to ensure they know, includes my entire adoptive family. The Guurn clan, Franz and his family, you and Alpha Two, Lyddhu...all of you."

"And the symbols?" Omega wondered.

"Are simply the mark of the oath as sworn."

"Mm," Echo hummed. "And what does the curse involve, if they fail?"

"Oh, nothing much," Entiyti said with a wolfish grin. "The invoker is simply disemboweled, alive, over hot coals, by the demon. Slowly. While being forced to watch."

"Damn," Echo said, shocked, as Omega gaped. "Ouch."

"Exactly," Entiyti declared, then roared with triumphant laughter.

* * *

"Well, it's time to go," Echo noted, as they stood in Entiyti's office with their kits, three days later.

"Aw," a sorrowful Entiyti sighed, as the bodyguard corps ranked themselves in the entry and corridor, and what members of the household staff who could get away from their duties clustered behind the guard group. "The time has gone far too quickly! Well, I know you have business to attend to on Earth, and a department to oversee. But I shall miss you, children."

"We all will," Suud noted. "You have done several great services for us, younglings. We will not forget."

"Hey, Suud, you know that works both ways," Echo pointed out. "Y'all helped Meg and me—mostly me—regain our badass reputations."

"And we have been very glad to do it," Suud noted. "Not only for your own sakes; you never deserved what was done to you. But you have done an amazing amount for Pulgey. And you know we all appreciate that...and myself especially. Even as I am sure Franz does." He met their gazes with a meaningful glance, and they knew he referenced the fact that he was Entiyti's 'brother in all but blood'...as was Fox.

"And I cannot tell you, for my sake, what you have done," Entiyti added, voice soft and low. "Saving my life is only part of it. Likely the biggest part, but still." He barely flexed his wings in a very deliberate, but subtle, gesture. "Never mind giving me back my life. In many senses of the word."

Omega hugged him. "It was my pleasure, Uncle Pulgey," she told him. "I don't think I could have NOT done it."

"I know," he murmured. "It is only one of many reasons why I love you, youngling." He wrapped one arm around her in a gentle embrace, while reaching for Echo with the other arm. Echo eased into the hug in a subtle male fashion, wrapping an arm around Entiyti's back below his wings. "Ah, children," the Draconan sighed, "go with my blessings. And be sure to send an invitation to your wedding, when the time arrives. I will drop everything and come. And bring Suud and Duuniiss. And as many of the rest as I can cram aboard the *Hsshthh*!"

"We will," Omega declared with a smile, as she moved to hug Suud and Duuniiss, and Echo began shaking hands with the guards.

* * *

Moments later, Alpha One exited the manor house between two phalanxes—one, the full bodyguard corps, all at attention and saluting; the other, the entire household staff, applauding.

They entered the *D1 Calypso* and prepped it for launch.

* * *

"...And the prodigals return, rather the better for wear, if the reports I've been getting from around the galaxy are anything to go by," Fox said, when Alpha One stopped by his office to report after arriving back in Headquarters.

"It went great, Fox!" Omega enthused. "Just like we hoped it would! Alpha One's reputation is back! ECHO's reputation is back!"

"Echo?"

"Hey, Fox, I got no complaints," Echo declared. "Meg's right. After that press conference, never mind after the attempted hit on Pulgey, every time I went someplace in public, you'd have almost thought *I* was the galactic president! Or at least a high mucky-muck," he added.

"I was so proud of him!" Omega announced, as Echo

flushed, and Fox grinned.

"Excellent," the Director noted. "And the two of you?"

"Meg's the inventor of the hour, for that cybernetic wing design," Echo said, "so Alpha One's reputation is flying high."

"That's good, and there is some paperwork for you to sign about taking that design into commercial production, Omega," Fox informed her. "But I meant the two of you as a COUPLE."

"We're good," Omega averred.

"What she said," Echo agreed. "Pulgey, Suud, and Dalgaard made sure we had plenty of time off, which was nice, and we took advantage of it. That garden in the back is damn pretty!"

"And the guest house?"

"It was really comfy," Omega said. "The chief steward, Ssutav, kept the kitchen pantry well stocked, which was good because MAYBE about half the time we ate with Pulgey, and the other half we cooked for ourselves...and it was at least as good as the ritziest hotel I've ever stayed in."

"The accommodations suited, then?" Fox pressed, but gently.

"Well," Echo said, eyeing the Director, "it was a good thing I brought along the air mattress, 'cause there was only one bedroom. But I'm betting you knew that already."

Fox sat back in his chair with a sigh.

"You DO both realize that you're officially life partners now, right?"

"Fox, I..." Omega ducked her head. "I only wanted..."

"Hush, baby," Echo said, easing an arm around her shoulders. "I understand, and I'm totally on board with waiting for the formal marriage amendment to come down...provided they don't back-burner it again. FOX should understand, too. But it's our business anyway, baby, yours and mine. Nobody else's. We'll handle things when we're both ready."

"All right," Fox capitulated. "You're right, and yes, I do understand. I think going ahead and taking your relationship to the next level would do good things for your self-esteem, BOTH of you, but that's your call. And I won't push any more. But other than that, you liked the guest house?"

"We loved it, Fox," Omega said.

"In fact, Meg was liking it so much, she said maybe we should come back for our honeymoon," Echo said with a grin. "But I sorta nixed that idea. I'd rather not have 'Uncle Pulgey' right there every time we came outta the house."

Fox fairly guffawed. Alpha One grinned, watching him double over with mirth.

"And he would, you can believe it," he finally gasped around his laughter. "I know that Draconan like my own face! Not that he would mean to be in the way; he just cares about the two of you. And it's 'Uncle Pulgey' now, is it?"

"It is," Omega declared, impish. "And Uncle Suud, too. After all, they ARE your Emdalian blood brothers, 'Dad.'"

"Or maybe that should be 'Abba,'" Echo added with a smirk. Somewhat to their surprise, Fox grinned.

"Oh, I think I rather like the sound of that," he decided. "'Abba Fox.' It has a good ring to it."

"I am NOT calling you that in public," Echo proclaimed. "I reserve the right to decide whether I wanna call you that in private, either."

"I'll call him that...in private," Omega avowed. "I like the sound of it, too."

"You do that, tekhter, you do that," Fox said with a smile. "Now, you've had a very busy time of it away from home, and I've already had a full briefing of all events from Suud and Pul, so what I want you both to do is to take the next Division day off and get settled back in. Then you can report back to your offices in the Alpha Line Room day after tomorrow. That sound good?"

"Sure does, Fox," Echo noted. "Meg?"

"Sounds great, 'Abba Fox,'" she said with a smile, and Fox's shoulders suddenly squared proudly. "I needed to unpack and see about some laundry anyway."

"And stock up the pantry, and a few other things like that," Echo agreed. "Maybe a nice dinner for two tonight?"

"I think that can be arranged, if we can get the pantries restocked in time," Omega said with a grin. "Or maybe tomorrow night, if not tonight."

"That'll work," Echo decided. "Might be better that way, anyhow; we can rest up and plan it and not feel rushed. Okay.

Tomorrow night it is."

"Off with you both, then," a tolerant Fox said, waving them out the door.

* * *

It turned out that Fox and Alpha Two had, between them, already arranged to notify Supplies that Alpha One was on the way home and their larders needed restocking, as well as ensuring that Laundry knew to bring fresh Suits and the pair's recently-cleaned-from-before-they-left casual wear, so all Echo and Omega really had to do was unpack, throw soiled garments into the laundry chutes, and get themselves organized. The automated vacuum robots—recently added after modifications to the household computer system in the wake of the Mark Wright incident—had kept their quarters clean and dust-free while they were gone, so there wasn't a great deal to do past that.

They changed into casual clothes, fixed snacks, and settled in front of the television, cuddling together under a certain Orion Nebula throw blanket, for a binge-watching session of their favorite missed shows, streamed from the Agency's servers. For dinner that night, they ordered Trifle's Pizza, delivered, and planned a lovely candlelight dinner for two—and prepared by both—for the next night.

Chapter 4

The pair had barely returned to duty after what Fox had declared was a well-earned day off, when a notice came in for Omega.

"Oh shit," she decreed, reading the automated email that had popped up on her computer screen. "It's that time already. Past it, rather."

"Time for what?" Echo wondered, turning in his desk chair to look across the Alpha Line Room at his partner.

"My semi-annual physical," she sighed, morose. "I hate those things."

"Aw," Echo murmured. "Anything I can do to help, baby? I mean, I get it now..."

"Yeah, you do," she said, sitting up straight and thinking for long moments. "Hey, listen, there might be something you can do; it's just...well, maybe you can't." She bit her lip.

"I'll do whatever I can to ensure you get whatever you need, Meg," Echo said, serious. "You should know that by now."

"I know," she said, offering him a smile. "But I mean, what I was gonna ask would interfere with your shift duties."

"What, you want me to go with you?"

"Umm, yeah," she admitted. "I mean, you DO know everything now, and you'll get what Zebra is driving at with all the testing, and..." She shrugged. "You can cheer me up when nobody else can, Ace. And believe me when I say that, given all the memories the testing dredges up, I could really use that."

"When is she wanting you to come in?" Echo wondered.

"Day after tomorrow, if I'm available around missions. Gives her a chance to get everything set up, and me a chance to get anything outta my gut that might interfere with...'observations.'"

"Right," Echo said, pulling up his master schedule on his desk computer and studying it. "Mmm...no, actually, you're clear, and I might be able to do this. Given my new status as your life partner, we'd probably have needed to do something like this anyway. And you'll need to come by with me for my next physical, too, just to get on board with my medical status. I mean, we're already the legal voices for each other, but you don't actually know my detailed medical history an' shit. And you should." He pulled up another tab and began typing swiftly, then hit <enter>.

"Oh, I get it," Omega said, turning to her computer and replying with a confirmation of the appointment. "But what about the Alpha Line meeting an' stuff?"

"Well, Alpha Two handled it while we were away, with Alpha Four backin' 'em up," Echo pointed out. "I'll ping 'em and explain, ask if they can handle the meeting that day, while I'm in the medlab with you."

"Will Fox be okay with it?"

"I just pinged him," Echo said. "I'll know in—" An alert sounded, and Echo pulled up the email. "Yeah, he's okay with it."

"Do you mind?"

"Not at all, baby. If it helps you get through it, I'm so there."

"Okay, let's do it."

"Consider it handled."

* * *

"There you are, girlfriend!" Zebra remarked as Omega and Echo entered the medlab. "You are way overdue for your six-months' tune-up!"

"I know," Omega answered with a wry grin. "But we were kinda busy at that point, if you'll recall."

"Ain't it the truth!" Zebra agreed. "Echo, I'm on this now. Thanks for seeing she got here."

"You're welcome, but I'm here for the duration, no offense," Omega's partner told the physician.

"Oh? How's that?" Zebra wondered.

"Well, I pretty much know everything about what Slug did to Meg, now," Echo noted. "She's even told me about the, um, the various origins of the genetics that got spliced into her. And she showed me the abduction and, and, 'modifications,' back when her telepathy was ramped up during Wright's little visit. So when you reminded us that she needed her checkup, she asked me if I'd come on down with her and give her a little

65

moral support."

"Oh," Zebra said, seeming to deflate slightly.

"No, no, Zebra," Omega said, voice soft. "It has nothing to do with you, hon. I couldn't ask for a better, more understanding physician...and friend. Family. 'Stepmom.' It's just..." Omega sighed.

"It's the procedures themselves," Echo filled in for her, his own voice just as quiet. "It wouldn't matter WHO did it. I could do it, assuming I had the medical qualifications, and it would still bother her. Because it all reminds her of the abduction."

"An' I guess it always will," Omega sighed.

"Oh," Zebra reiterated, more hopeful. "All right; I can see that. And you two are a couple now."

"Right," Omega said, flushing. Echo gave them both a slight grin.

"So she thought it might be a little easier if her boyfriend came along," Echo added, teasing Omega gently, then he sobered. "I can usually manage to make her laugh when nobody else can, and get her mind off shit, so we figured..." He broke off, then shrugged. "I thought it might help, in general."

"Okay. I see now, and I can understand that. Then let's get this show on the road," Zebra decided.

* * *

"How's it going, Zebra?" Echo asked several hours later. "Everything showing green with Meg so far?"

"You sound like that's a loaded question, Echo," Zebra noted, as she prepped the MRI for a full-body scan on Omega. Omega sat beside him in a chair, clad in a medlab jumpsuit, resting quietly.

"It's just that, what with...everything...that's happened in the last couple of months, Meg has been...really, really tired," Echo remarked with a concerned sigh. "I...worry about her."

"Well, what do you expect?" Zebra said with a huge grin, bordering on an outright smirk. "Pregnancy does that to a body."

"WHAAT?!" Omega shrieked, and Echo gaped. Abruptly, his face closed in a dark, angry scowl. He turned to his partner.

"Meg? You want to explain this?"

"I, I," Omega tried, face pale and horrified. "Ace, I swear

66

to you! This is...I DIDN'T...the only, only possibility is...Mark Wright! That...that night he got into my quarters...Zebra, how-how far along...?" Abruptly and unexpectedly—and uncharacteristically, save for recent weeks when artificially-enhanced hormones had induced truly outrageous stress levels—she burst into tears. Shocked and suddenly worried, Echo knelt in front of her and pulled her into his arms, as a dumbfounded Zebra watched, astounded and uncertain.

"Hush, baby," he murmured, as she sobbed into his shoulder. "It's okay. We'll...fix it, some kinda way. If we have to put the baby into the regen pod as soon as he...or she...is born, we'll make this work. I swear."

"Oh, Echo! I don't WANT...I never...if I'm gonna have one, I want it to be YOURS!"

"Ssh. I know. It's okay."

"Wait, wait, wait," a stunned Zebra said, holding up both hands. "Do you mean to tell me that you two are a couple, an ENGAGED couple, life partners in the Agency, for a couple MONTHS now...but you're not...?"

"Sleeping together? Of course not," Echo finished for the physician, glancing over his shoulder at her. "I thought you knew us better than that, Zebra. That was the whole point of getting the charter amendment, at least for us. Meg's an old-fashioned Southern lady."

"An' Ace is a, a S-southern gentleman," Omega sniffled, briefly raising her head. "He'd never...Oh, dear God, help..." She buried her face back in his shoulder.

"Hush, baby. It's okay. It's okay."

"You mean you're still WAITING for the Ennead to come through on the Agency charter amendment?!" Zebra exclaimed.

"Yep," Echo verified, terse. "They said it should be only a matter of weeks, now."

"Oh man, did I just screw up," a perturbed Zebra muttered, raking a distracted hand through her hair. "That was supposed to be a joke, guys. Omega isn't pregnant. I...wasn't thinking."

Both members of Alpha One froze, falling silent immediately, and Zebra bit her lip in apprehension, fully expecting to get a deserved and very efficient double-teamed reaming-out. Omega raised a tear-stained face to stare at the physician in confusion.

"A...JOKE?" Echo said, rising to his full height and glowering, as he stood protectively over his partner. "After all that shit back in the summer with Wright? And you think it's a JOKE?!"

"I know, I know. I'm...sorry. Really, really sorry," Zebra said, unhappy. "Like I said, I wasn't thinking. I mostly just wanted to get a rise out of you, Echo."

"So to speak," Omega fussed, and Zebra flushed.

"'Get a rise out of' me? What the hell does that mean?" the angry male Agent wanted to know.

"I figured, if you thought Meg was carrying your baby, and note I WAS thinking it would have to be YOUR baby, there'd only be a couple possible reactions to becoming a father," Zebra explained. "Either you'd freak the hell out like I've never seen you ever do, or you'd turn into a big bowl of mushy oatmeal, all cuddly an' junk. Which I've also never seen you ever do." She offered a weak, wry grin; Omega, who seemed to be getting Zebra's point, returned it in kind, but Echo was still scowling. "I...didn't think about the possibility you weren't, um, sleeping together yet. Let alone that you might get mad at Meg for presumably cheating on you...or worse. I didn't lie," she added, face falling as she hung her head. "I never actually SAID Omega was pregnant. I just..."

"Implied the hell out of it, to make us think it," Echo grumbled.

"Ace, settle down," Omega murmured, taking his hand from behind and lacing her fingers through his. "I think I get this now. You an' me, we're not the average agents around here, and I can see where she's coming from. After all, you and I have already discussed how we're gonna proceed if the Ennead back-burners the amendment again."

"Which they still might, given all the shit that came down after Adita's Coup that they're STILL digging out of," Echo sighed, turning to his fiancée and partner. "I know. I just..." he broke off and smeared his free hand over his face, raking his fingers through his hair. "That was one hell of an eye-opener."

"Tell me about it," Omega whispered, still pale. "But I get it. That was her affection speaking, wanting to tease us, and it never occurred to Zebra that we might be...that old-fashioned. That *I* might be that old-fashioned. 'Cause it's me," she added to Zebra. "Echo is a little more relaxed about it. But he's such a gentleman, he doesn't pressure me."

"But he also doesn't have all the shit in his history that you have, Omega," Zebra told the younger woman. "I...really shouldn't have done that. Especially given your personal history. I really, truly just...didn't think." She sighed, dejected. "And the sorta-kinda stepmom fails miserably, while the physician compromises her objectivity. Don't worry, Echo. I'll notify Zarnix and Fox, and put myself on report."

"Don't do that, Zebra," Omega pleaded. "Please. I understand, hon, and I'm not mad. Granted, I'm still tryin' to recover from the bad scare, but I'm not mad."

"And if Meg isn't mad, I can't stay mad, either," Echo decided. "I get it, too. You were trying to tease me, get me to react..."

"And it went down in flames," Zebra said with a wry grin— that didn't begin to reach her eyes. "I'm still gonna tell Fox what I did, though. And probably Zarnix, too. But if you don't want me to put myself on report—I mean, I think I should, but if you really just don't want me to..."

"I don't," Omega interjected, firm.

"Me neither," Echo noted.

"All right. Then I won't," Zebra agreed. "But Zarnix still might."

"I'll talk to him," Echo offered. "I'll tell him it was intended to be a family joke that went south."

"That'll work," Omega confirmed. "Because that's exactly what happened."

"Open mouth, insert foot," Zebra said with a sigh. "Well, one good thing came out of it. At least for Meg."

"What's that?" Echo wondered.

"After the magnitude of that scare, we need to call a halt to further medical testing for today," Zebra said. "Otherwise we won't get accurate readings as new baselines. Meg, you can get dressed and either go home, or back on duty, whichever you two need to do, honey. We'll reconvene in the morning, whenever's convenient for you, and finish up. We weren't far off done, anyway, so it won't take long." She turned. "And so in that case, um...Echo, why don't you come with me, and we'll let Meg have some privacy to get dressed? I'll go find Zarnix, we'll link Fox in on a vidcall, and I'll 'fess up."

* * *

By the time Omega could change from the medlab jumpsuit to her regular Suit— all the hook-and-loop fastenings on the jumpsuit tended to make things complicated without a medtech to serve as 'valet'—Zarnix and Fox both knew about Zebra's gaffe. Given the physician was already upset, and Echo explained the 'family' aspect of the attempted joke, neither the Director nor the Chief of Staff of Medical chose to reprimand her.

"Though we'll probably have a nice long talk when you get home, bubeleh," Fox told his own spouse. "I get where you were going with it, but that was meshuginah, Tei-yerinkeh."

"I know, I know," Zebra moaned, as Omega entered the open door of her office. "There's nothing any of you can possibly say that's as bad as what I've been telling myself for the last ten minutes! It's been a long day of doing all the usual tests on Meg, we were all tired, I wanted to try to raise everybody's spirits a little, and..."

"A tired brain went the wrong way with it," Omega said.

"Yeah," Zebra sighed. "I mean, to be honest, I thought that your stint on Emdali was about as much by way of honeymoon as guarding Pul to help out and prove your reputations were still deserved! It just...I never realized..."

"Well, she wasn't there back during that whole mess with the trumped-up charges, anyway," Echo observed. "She was taking care of Pulgey."

"True," Fox agreed. "So she didn't see your interactions, kinder."

"In all honesty," Zarnix noted, "if I had the kind of almost-familial relationship with the two of you that Zebra does, I might have tried a similar joke, just to lighten the mood after a long day, as she says." He shrugged. "So I'm not in any position to criticize."

"All right, fair enough," Fox decided. "If your department

chief chooses to let it go, your Director isn't going to fuss, even if he is your mate." He fixed Zebra with a stern gaze. "But watch it, bubeleh," he warned. "I can't—and won't—show favoritism just because we're life partners." His video image looked around the room. "And that goes for all of you, you know. I can only do so much."

"I know, honey," Zebra groaned. "I put both feet in this one. And then jumped up and down on it. So if you want to reprimand me, do it—I deserve it, and I know it."

"Over my protest," Zarnix noted.

"And Alpha One's," Echo averred.

"No, Zebra, not this time," Fox declared. "But oy, gelibte—THINK next time!"

"I will," Zebra moaned. "Lesson learned, in spades."

* * *

Alpha One went back to finish up the last couple of tests the next day, after their departmental meeting, and while Zebra was a bit tense at first, Omega soon set her at ease, with Echo's help. And for a wonder, nothing new came up in Omega's physical; she was well, and healthy, and she and Zebra began to consider that they might finally have found the limits of the 'tweaks' that Omega had experienced.

And in the end, the matter blew over. Everyone knew Zebra's intent had been to cheer them up toward the end of the long day, so no one stayed upset. In fact, it caused Alpha One to draw closer to the physician, as they grasped her behavior had been simple, affectionate teasing.

It became something of an in-joke within the 'family' as a result; after the next group dinner, when Alpha Two got too rambunctious, Omega informed them, "Behave, y'all, or Zebra will misdiagnose you pregnant!" The entire dinner table burst into laughter...except for Romeo and India, who were at once confused, mildly horrified, and chastised. A slightly sheepish Zebra explained to Alpha Two, and everyone had another good laugh.

* * *

Two days later, Echo came out of the Alpha Line Room to find his partner pleading with the Director and his assistants, as they all stood in the Core.

"...Please, Fox. Just the launch," Omega pleaded.

"Oy! Omega," the black-Suited Director replied sternly, "just watch it on your computer! If I put every NASA space mission on the Core's wall screens, we couldn't use it for anything else. Between them and the various commercial space companies vying for business, they've really ramped up activity in the last couple of years."

"Fox, when have I ever asked you to put a space plane mission onscreen before?" the blonde agent with the long, platinum French braid argued reasonably. "Just this once. I swear."

"What's up, Meg? I mean, I get you're trying to keep up with NASA's milestones, by way of advising Fox and Pulgey on technology developments in the field, but why is this particular one so important to you?" her tall, rugged, experienced partner enquired curiously, as two colleagues, a certain beautiful Afro-Asian woman and her partner, a handsome black man, walked up to the little group standing in the Core. Fox's two young assistants, Bravo and Lima, nodded in agreement with Echo.

"Well, okay, it's like this. The pilot's an old friend," she admitted sheepishly, and the black Agent grinned.

"Sounds more like an old flame o' Meg's, if ya ask me," Romeo, the handsome black man, commented.

"Which nobody did," Fox pointed out.

"Um...well..." Omega stammered, blushing, as Echo's eyes narrowed, "yeah, he is. Was. Sorta. I mean—"

"All right, Omega. Just this once," Fox acquiesced, gesturing to Lima and Bravo, who immediately set to work on the controls for one wall. "How long 'til launch?"

"Uh, lessee," Omega glanced at her Agency-issue wrist chronometer, "they'll be coming out of the planned T-minus-nine-minute hold in...five, four, three, two, one—two minutes. So launch is in eleven minutes."

"For how long?"

"Through MECO."

"MECO?" India, the Afro-Asian woman and Romeo's life partner, echoed.

"Yeah. Main Engine Cut-Off," Omega explained. "'Bout twenty minutes, total."

"All right, Boys. Got it?" Fox asked his assistants at the hidden console in the corner.

"We got it, Fox," Lima noted. Abruptly, the entire wall displayed the space plane on the launch pad, creating a nigh-seamless mosaic out of several panel screens. The Core's various transient denizens, both alien and agent, glanced up temporarily, then continued on their way.

"Ohhh..." Omega sighed quietly with a slightly dreamy smile, and her companions eyed her momentarily. Echo moved close.

"Everything all right, Meg?" he murmured. "You sound... regretful."

"Did I?" She glanced up at him. "I didn't mean to."

"You didn't answer my question."

"It's...a long story, Ace."

"What's his name?"

"Scotty. Scott Chadwick."

Echo opened his mouth to speak again, but just then, Romeo leaned over to nudge her. "Jus' think, Meg, if you hadn't run inta Echo, you coulda been aboard 'er," he teased.

"Actually, Romeo, I would've been."

"Whaat?!?" The Director, the other half of the Alpha One team, and all of the Alpha Two team straightened up, startled. Bravo and Lima even paused in their work to look up at the Alpha Line assistant chief, as she explained to her bemused colleagues.

"Scotty and I were in the same astronaut class. We had the same assignment," Omega clarified. "This is the new, advanced space plane, with the prototype interplanetary engines—phase one of the program they wanted me for. If I hadn't joined the Agency, I'd be the lead Mission Specialist and backup pilot— the flight engineer, or MS-2—onboard right now." She paused. "Actually, I heard the pilot got a medical disqualification for a problem that cropped up, so I might have ended up the pilot. Anyway, that's...the main reason I wanted to watch."

Echo's dark eyes scanned her face, then dropped to the floor.

"Meg...I—"

A slim fingertip covered his lips.

"Hush that," she said softly, with an understanding smile. "You've taken me a helluva lot farther 'out there' than those guys are going, even with the new prop system test." She jerked a thumb at the screen, then smiled at her companion again. "I'm happy, right here. Thanks, Ace. For everything." She took his hand and held it, lacing her fingers through his.

Echo's brown eyes warmed, the hint of an answering smile in them, and he opened his mouth to speak.

"Hey, guys," India interrupted, "the count's resumed..."

* * *

The Director and the top two teams of Alpha Line, the Division One Agency's special forces department, watched the final countdown with interest. From time to time, Omega explained a detail, or answered one of their questions, but her answers grew terser as the launch neared. So they also watched their colleague Omega in some amusement as she tensed with adrenalin at the imminent launch. In the last seconds, she began echoing the countdown, under her breath.

"...APU start..." she murmured. "Seven, six...switching over to internal...and...four, three...main engines!...rock, and... BOOM! YESS!" Omega punched a fist into the air. "Go, Scotty! Godspeed!"

"Houston, roll complete," the screen said.

"Was that your Scotty talking?" India asked.

"Yeah," Omega answered briefly, eyes glued to the large screen, where a small white craft ascended on a pillar of fire.

"Was he—"

"Oh, India, please shush for a minute," Omega interrupted urgently.

"Why?" India blinked, confused.

"The *Challenger* point is coming up!"

"Huh?" India and Romeo both looked puzzled.

"The time after launch when the *Challenger* space shuttle blew up," Echo explained quietly, drawing them away from the tense agent. "I gather it's a thing that pretty much all NASA people kinda grit their teeth to get through, any more, even on the new space planes. It was the first actual in-flight disaster NASA ever experienced, and it was traumatic for just about everybody who worked the program—or in Meg's case, remembers it from the time she was very little. Apparently she'd already decided she wanted to work in the space program, and I think she told me once that she had started a correspondence with the teacher who was on board. Anyway, '*Challenger* point' isn't an official term, it's just what Meg calls it. There's a point during the ascent where the atmosphere puts the most stress on the shuttle—or in this case, space plane—as it accelerates, and so it throttles back, to ease the stress. Then, when the air thins a little, they throttle back up. That's about when *Challenger* blew, because of the whole aerodynamics involved in the SRB—uh, solid rocket booster—blow-by and associated stresses, and it's coming up." Echo watched his partner closely, concerned.

"Whoa. How do you know all that, Echo?" India asked, curious.

"Who's my partner, India?" Echo shot back, slightly amused at the question. "Never mind fiancée. Yeah, Meg was a little kid when that accident happened, but it really affected her, and she learned all she could, especially after joining NASA, including reading all of the accident reports cover to cover. She's told me all about it. Here it comes."

"Sshh," Omega said.

"*Kitty Hawk*, you are go for throttle-up," said the screen.

"Roger, go for throttle-up..." came the response.

A supportive Echo moved beside his partner, only to discover she was holding her breath. He poked her gently in the ribs. "Meg, breathe." He watched her, poked again. "Meg—BREATHE."

She waved a dismissing hand at him, pointing silently at the screen.

"Meg, if I have to punch you in the belly and knock the air out of you to make you breathe, I will. Now breathe."

"SRB Sep," commented the screen in one voice, then continued in another. "SRB Sep confirmed. Engines at one-oh-four."

"UuuUUHHH!" Omega sucked in a deep breath, then exhaled slowly. "Ahhh. Okay. They're home-free, now."

"Omega, why are you so anxious?" Fox wondered. "I understand you have a history with the pilot, but..."

"I saw *Challenger*, Fox. I knew the teacher, though I'd never met her face to face, because I'd started a letter correspondence with her when she was named to the mission. And while I'll admit I was still pretty much a wet-behind-the-ears newbie at the time, I was there for *Columbia*, on console, and I knew the crew. NO flight controller who was there for either day...reacts any differently than I do." The others studied Omega's bleak face and distant, haunted eyes of memory; then they nodded silently.

"*Kitty Hawk*, single engine ATO. All engines nominal," sounded in the background. Omega smiled then.

"Okay, Fox," she said, "they can make it to orbit on one engine, and they still have all three good ones. I'm happy now. Thanks."

"You're welcome, Omega," Fox answered, gesturing at Bravo and Lima, who resumed 'normal programming.' Then he turned to the four Agents. "Now...don't you think it's about time Alpha One and -Two got back to work?"

"On it, Fox," Echo answered, and the two teams headed out on routine patrol.

* * *

"...Nah, it's just a CYA move on the part of the crew procedures people," Dianus averred.

"No, Pete, it's not," Pat Pate, the crew's specialist on the new propulsion system being tested during the mission, declared. "It's an essential part of the checklist. We could have a mess if we don't follow this, step by step."

"You're just a payload specialist," Dianus noted. "You're not even a real part of the crew, and you're sure no astronaut. So just siddown and shut up, and do what I tell you."

"No," Robert Vancel, the MS-3, declared. "She is every bit as much a part of this crew as any other person on board the *Kitty Hawk*, Peter. Officially, most payload specialists are not astronauts, true. But she IS part of the astronaut corps; she simply took this position because, once we lost Meg, Pat's the most knowledgeable about the science and the guts of the new prop. And you can go up against me if you want to. I AM the payload commander, and I'll say how the payload gets handled, not you. And I'm telling you, we are going by the checklist, to the tiniest detail. The Atom system is a relatively high-thrust ion drive, and if we don't do things right, we could have a mess."

"You're countervening my orders?" Dianus said, pushing up from the command chair and getting in Vancel's face. Vancel didn't budge.

"Where the Atom is concerned? Yes," Vancel confirmed, calm; he was called the Teflon Astronaut throughout the astronaut office because, in a corps of generally unflappable people, he was the least flappable. *'Forget water off a duck's back,'* some said of him, *'that duck's made of Teflon.'* And the nickname had stuck.

So Dianus' intimidation tactics got nowhere, as far as Vancel was concerned. Given Vancel's status as the payload commander, he could indeed countermand Dianus's orders on anything to do with the Atom testing.

"Got it," Dan Hollifield—the MS-2 and flight engineer—agreed immediately; he hadn't been thrilled about being bumped down from the pilot's position by Dianus' grandstanding, any more than Chadwick had been. "We follow the checklist to the letter."

"Copy that," Chadwick added. "Wilco. Follow detailed checklist."

An irked Dianus turned and pushed off, floating into the middeck, away from the others.

* * *

In the end, Dianus had things his way, since he refused to follow the payload checklist in detail, skipping over those steps that he felt were unnecessary or too cumbersome. The others followed the procedures, but whenever Dianus was scheduled to work part of the setup and prep, he went his own way without asking anyone else.

"Pete, you can't keep doing this," Chadwick said, having gotten him away from the others and sequestered him in the sleeping berths for a private discussion. "The rest of us have been working this mission for years, dude. We've been over and over these procedures, over the checklists, over everything, with a super-fine-toothed comb. We've long since worked out what needed inclusion and what didn't, and had all of the extraneous stuff removed from the procedures and the timeline.

77

The payload flight data file has been pared down as tightly as it CAN be. Trust me on this."

"Then you didn't do your jobs," Dianus snapped. "Because there's a shit-ton of stuff in there that doesn't have to be in there."

"NO, Pete, there's NOT," Chadwick insisted. "The Atom system is NOT like the standard propulsion! If it's there, it's because it NEEDS to be there. Because something BAD will happen if we skip over it."

"You ever think maybe what you guys needed was somebody to come in and look at this project objectively, for a change?" Dianus said.

"Oh, and you think that's what you're doing?" Chadwick shot back. "Get a grip, Pete. Admit that some of us might actually know more than you do about this thing."

"The hell you say," Dianus said, insolent. "Get outta my way, Chadwick, and do your job the way it's SUPPOSED to be done."

"I am," Chadwick retorted. "Can you say the same?"

Dianus ignored the remark, pushed the pilot aside, and moved into the middeck. Chadwick sighed and stared after him.

"Dear God, don't let him get us all killed," he murmured, fervent.

* * *

Two Division days later, the worst happened.

The Alpha One team had been following up on the Spleekanus family's latest arrival, and were now headed back to Headquarters after a requested visit with the alien Dendroid family.

"Oh, weren't they so cute, Echo?" Omega gushed with fond affection. "And now Preeg has a little sister!"

"Mmm," responded Echo noncommittally as he drove. "Least I wasn't involved in the emergency situation this time. Berta and Como got the job of getting the midwife there for the birth."

"Yeah, but just think—Preeg and his older siblings think you hung the Moon, hon," Omega pointed out. "And they're adorable."

"You're the expert on that," Echo replied. "I'll take your

word for it."

"You don't like kids after all, huh?" Omega said quietly. "I thought you did great with that little Draconan toddler, but..."

"Meh. Depends on the kids, I guess." Echo shot her a quick glance.

"Meaning?"

"I dunno, Meg. Human kids only have two arms, for one thing—and they're not that flexible. When Dendroid children hang all over you, they really hang all over you."

Omega burst out laughing as Echo's cell phone rang. Calmly steering with one hand through Manhattan traffic, he thumbed a switch on the dashboard; a panel opened up, revealing a special earpiece. He grabbed it, stuck it in one ear, tapped it, and answered the phone.

"Echo." A pause. "No." Another pause, as Omega's attention focused on him. "Oh, damn."

"What is it?"

"Yeah, Fox, we're on our way." Echo tapped the earpiece to deactivate the call, leaving the device in his ear, in case of follow-up calls.

"Echo? What's up?"

"Meg? Lemme turn into this back alley, here, to get us outta sight. It's time to morph, baby..."

* * *

Moments later, they stood beside Fox in front of one of the giant Core wall viewscreens, which once again displayed the NASA live feed. Omega scanned the imaged mission control room onscreen, listening intently to the audio for a moment, and studying the telemetry being displayed on Mission Control's big screen. Echo and Fox watched her, concerned, saying nothing. Abruptly the female Agent paled and grabbed for a chair, sitting heavily.

"Oh, dear God," she whispered. "*Kitty Hawk* is coming down. And there's nothing they can do to stop it."

* * *

"What exactly happened, Meg?" Echo asked his partner, as she buried her face in her hands.

In a muffled voice, without raising her head, Omega replied. "They've had a major rupture in one of the fuel tanks for the primaries, likely in a chain reaction from a weird malfunction in the Atom test drive. In the attitude and trajectory they were in—they were on the return leg of a trans-lunar injection—the venting fuel acted like a main retro firing, and they didn't achieve proper orbital insertion, back at Earth. So... they're coming out of orbit. And because of the rupture, they don't have fuel left to boost themselves into a nominal orbit, stabilize themselves, or control the time of re-entry. And with that hole in the belly, they won't survive re-entry. The bird will come apart. Just like *Columbia* did."

"I'm sorry, Omega," Fox said gently. "I thought you'd want to know as soon as possible."

The blonde head suddenly came up. Blue eyes blazed with intensity.

"Fox, we—"

"No, Omega." Fox interrupted and shook his head, firm.

"But, Fox, we can save hi— them."

"No."

"Why?!"

"Because it does not fall in our jurisdiction, tekhter," Fox explained, trying to be gentle. "It is dreadful, certainly, and I am very sorry for your relationship with one or more of the crew, but it sounds as if the part in question was simply poorly designed."

"I don't think so, Fox," Omega noted. "I think you really need to have Sciences and Forensics look into—"

"Omega, tekhter...no." He drew a deep breath.

"But Fox, it really—"

"Omega...we are a secret galactic-government agency, remember?" The Director sighed. "If an alien had caused it, it would be different, and we could take action on the matter. But it was an accident. An equipment failure. We can't interfere. I really am sorry."

Omega stood, shooting him a hard glance, while completely ignoring her partner. As she spun on her heel and walked away, Echo thought he faintly heard, "Yeah. The hell you are."

Fox sighed even deeper, and turned away, headed for his office.

* * *

Echo found her in her usual refuge, the Headquarters roof. It was twilight in New York, and Omega sat silently on a blanket outside the observatory dome, watching the sky darken and what few stars that could be seen from the heart of the city —without the light-fence perimeter—appear. Wordlessly, he joined his partner on the blanket. They sat together for a long time, saying nothing.

"You told me you didn't leave anyone behind when you joined the Agency," Echo finally commented.

"How the blazes—and I use the word deliberately—am I supposed to deal with this?!" Omega burst out suddenly. "I know those people—knew those people—and I'm supposed to just sit back and watch them come screaming into the atmosphere like that meteor??" she asked, pointing as a shooting star fell down the sky.

"Meg...I know it's hard..." Echo began.

"Really? Have you ever had to sit back, utterly helpless, and watch someone you once...cared about...just...die...knowing you had the power to save her?" Omega asked point-blank. Echo sighed.

"Well, I've watched people die, yes. Sometimes even people...close to me. But to sit back and do nothing, when I could have stopped their dying? No." He paused, then added, "Though Ma comes close, in some respects, I guess. At least I THOUGHT I was going to have to sit back and watch, with my hands tied. And probably would have had to, if not for you."

"Echo...I don't know if I can take this. They were my FRIENDS, Ace! Colleagues. Trusted ones. Every bit as much as the people I work with now. Because we all knew our lives depended on each other, same as now."

"I know." They sat quietly for several minutes. Then Echo asked, "What do you want me to do?"

"...There's nothing you can do, Echo." Omega bowed her head. "Stand...stand by me, I guess. Um...hon, I...I need to be alone for a few minutes. Would you mind...?"

Echo stood immediately, headed for the rooftop door and thence to their connecting quarters downstairs. "I'll go start some supper."

"Don't bother fixin' me anything. I...I'm not too hungry."

Echo shot a concerned glance at his despondent partner and soon-to-be mate as the door closed behind him.

* * *

Late that night, Echo woke, to hear the faint sounds of restless pacing drifting through the 'back door' connecting his quarters to his partner's. He flung back the sheets and sat up, threw on his robe over the knit boxers and tee he now wore as pajamas, leaving the robe unbelted. Then he meandered out of his bedroom, through his apartment, and over to the connecting back door.

A flickering light shone in Omega's study, and her dancing shadow paced against the wall. Occasionally, it bent over the shade of a computer terminal and keyed a few strokes, then resumed pacing. The soft sounds of the NASA broadcast could be heard in the background. A groan of frustration rose over the television's volume as the shadow Omega ran a hand through her loose hair.

Echo's shoulders sagged slightly, and he turned and went back to bed.

* * *

All night long—Alpha One had yet to fully transition from Emdalian days, which were similar to Earth's—Omega studied the launch video in detail, comparing it to video captured by the Agency's PGLEIA orbital technology. Hour after hour she worked, looking for a discrepancy, an inconsistency—anything that would provide proof for what she had seen without realizing it at the time—but had recognized for what it was, as soon as she had seen the nature of the malfunction.

This was no ordinary malfunction, she thought. *It had 'help'…that wasn't from around here. There's no way that tank could have ruptured that spectacularly otherwise. And yet the fuel itself didn't ignite, and the oxidizer tank didn't rupture, either. So that argues for 'help.' Something was put there that blew. And it coulda been sabotage, granted…but if it was human sabotage, I don't see the fuel tank rupturing without the oxidizer tank going, too, because Earth doesn't have anything that could do THAT much damage without busting both tanks. Which, actually, doesn't argue for sabotage at ALL, whether human or alien; you'd think a saboteur would have gone for max damage, which means 'let's blow the oxidizer at the same time, so the hypergolic fuel ignites and blazes holy hell outta the whole mess.' Hm. Gotta be here. GOTTA be here.*

Abruptly she sat up straight, staring at her laptop screen.

And there it is, she noted, grabbing an interactive stylus and circling two places on the split-screen, lighting up the circles in bright red. *That's the smoking gun, the change in color that marks the location where the 'help' was placed. And... Oh shit. LOOK at that carnage! It's even worse than I thought. I don't think I have TIME to convince Fox first. I don't even have time to grab Echo...never mind risking getting him in trouble again so soon after that whole Persan attempted coup he got tangled up in. I gotta move, try to stop this, THEN ask forgiveness...and hope, based on this, that I get it. Otherwise, it's MY hide that'll get busted for insubordination. And that'll mean imprisonment, since they can't brain-bleach me. But I have to do this. It's the right thing.*

She rose and scurried for her bedroom, pulling out her travel kit and stuffing items into it as fast as she could go.

* * *

"Meg?" Echo called early the next morning—only a couple of hours after Omega reached her conclusions—exiting his bedroom in shirt and trousers, hair still damp from his shower. "It's your turn to make breakfast."

No answer.

"Hm," he murmured to himself, heading through the back door.

There was no appearance of life in his partner's quarters, although there was a sign...on her bedroom door:

BREAKFAST IN OVEN —>

"Well, at least she fed me well," he remarked, pleased, pulling the ham and egg biscuits out of the warming oven moments later. Biting into one, he raised a pleased eyebrow, nodding with satisfaction; then he headed purposefully back into Omega's living area, where he stood munching as he scanned the room. After only a few seconds, he murmured, "Uh-oh..." and went into her study, where he woke her laptop and studied what was on the screen. "Oh man," he murmured, as the import of the computer display and the stylus markings on it struck him, then he hit several key commands before making his way into her empty bedroom. One quick glance told him all he needed to know.

"Oh, shit!" Echo exclaimed then, and sprinted through the back door, flinging what little remained of breakfast at his dining table on the way to his bedroom.

Moments later, a lone Alpha Line Agent emerged from the front door of his quarters at top speed.

* * *

Omega was already at the Chicago Station spaceport—the required launch site to hit the correct orbital inclination for rendezvous quickly and easily—powering up a small saucer and running through check-out. She had used her authority as assistant department chief of Alpha Line to obtain the spacecraft, though it had taken a bit of doing, and longer than she had hoped; she didn't intend to get any more 'official' authorization than that, from either the Director or the department chief. For one, she knew Fox wouldn't give it; for another, she didn't want Echo involved. For his own sake. She would be in enough trouble as it was, when this was over.

So when the deep voice behind her asked, "Just what the hell do you think you're doing?" Omega froze, a look of pain on her face.

"Ace...don't ask. Just go." She closed her eyes and willed Echo to leave.

"No."

"Are you here to stop me?" Omega turned her head to look at him over her shoulder. Echo stood calmly, arms folded, in the doorway of the saucer's flight deck.

"No."

"Why are you here, then?"

"Why didn't you ask me?"

"What do you mean?" Omega asked, puzzled.

"We're partners, Meg. We're engaged to be married. I thought we had an understanding, you and me. Last night, you asked me to stand by you. I agreed. With no restrictions on the standing by, let me add. I'll always stand by you if you ask, baby—and over ninety-nine percent of the time even when you DON'T ask. You KNOW that. So why are you going off on your own today?"

"I don't think I have to tell you, Echo. You know why."

"Well, I can think of two reasons. One, you're about to get into enough deep shit for any thirty-six people, and you're trying to protect me," Echo responded, walking across the deck toward his partner. "Two, you don't want another man along when you reunite with your old boyfriend." Omega turned the pilot's chair to watch him as he continued, "Which is it?"

Omega smiled, shook her head whimsically, and rested her chin on her hand.

"You know me way too well, Ace. What do you think? Do you really want to muck out the stalls with me when I'm done with this?"

"We've mucked out a few stalls together before." Echo shrugged with a grin. "Literal AND metaphorical. Why stop now?"

"What about gear?" Omega inquired. "You don't have a kit."

"You didn't see me walk on board," Echo replied. "Come on. Let's get exo before anyone catches on."

"Strap in and let's go, then," Omega answered. "Checkout's complete, and we don't have a lotta time. THEY don't have a lotta time."

"Roger that," Echo said, sitting down and fastening the seat restraints. "Let's go catch us a bird."

"And fix its broken wing," Omega added.

* * *

"All right, Meg, how do you wanna do this?" Echo asked his partner as their craft achieved orbit. "Calculating the bird's decaying orbit is gonna be tricky."

"Yeah."

"Sounds right up your alley, 'Doctor Astrophysicist.'"

"Yeah," Omega answered, "just like bringing the saucer in to dock is yours, 'Mr. Ace Pilot.'"

"Well, I guess that's how we'll do it, then," Echo remarked, checking the saucer's readouts.

"I don't have a problem doing it the other way," Omega

85

added, pulling up the data on the *Kitty Hawk* from the ship's sensors. "We swap up pretty well."

"No, let's stick with what we've each got the most experience in," Echo considered. "This is gonna be complicated enough as it is." He assumed the controls as Omega bent over the navigational computer. Five minutes of intense work later, she raised her head.

"All right, Echo, transferring projected trajectory to your console."

"Got it," Echo confirmed. "So...what? They're coming in from a trans-lunar return trajectory, right?"

"Yeah. They went out past the Moon to test the Atom propulsion system—partly AS a test of the system—and on their way back, kablooie. Which means that, while they've managed to achieve a geo orbit, they came in a little too steep. They wound up with an eccentric orbit whose perigee is at too low an altitude, so that means the drag is increased, and the orbit's decaying fast as a result, so..."

"Right. We'll catch up to them in about ten minutes. At two minutes to intercept, punch up the comm scrambler. I've got the cloak and sensor scrambler already on, but I'll make the sensor scrambler directional and drop the cloak as we get close to rendezvous. We want the bird to know we're here, just not the ground control."

"Wilco. No sense letting all of NASA know what's going on up here. We're in enough hot water as it is."

"And it just got hotter," Echo sighed. "Incoming message."

"Let me do it, Echo," Omega offered. "This is my baby, anyway. And we only just got your reputation recovered from the whole Persan mess."

"Suit yourself." Echo shrugged. She punched the comm button.

"*Phoenix* here."

"Omega, you and Echo get your insubordinate asses the hell back down here, NOW!" Fox's angry voice cut through the cabin atmosphere, razor-sharp. "Farkakte, verdammt, merde, glagaram, and argdun!"

"I'm sorry, Fox. I can't do that."

"Echo? Echo, talk some sense into your partner."

Echo opened his lips, but Omega spun and clamped a hand tightly over his mouth, signaling him to be silent.

"I'm sorry, but Echo's...indisposed, Fox," she lied. Echo's eyes narrowed in shock.

"Meg?!" his muffled voice could barely be heard under her hand. Desperately, she motioned for him to be quiet.

"What the hell?!" Fox's voice bellowed. "Omega, is Echo on that saucer with you, or not?"

"Yes and no," Omega answered, meeting Echo's eyes, pleading, as she spoke. "Yes, he's on the saucer. No, he's not...'with' me."

"Explain."

"Echo caught me trying to leave. He couldn't talk me out of it, and I couldn't let him walk away to report me, so he...'came along for the ride,' you might say." She dropped her hand from Echo's face.

"Aw, Meg," Echo whispered, pained, as he understood what she was trying to do.

"Omega," Fox asked, "are you trying to tell me you kidnapped your partner?"

"...Yes."

"Uh-huh," Fox remarked skeptically.

"No, Meg," Echo said clearly. Omega shot him a horrified look.

"Echo? Echo, is that you?" Fox's voice asked over the speaker.

"Yes, Fox, it's me."

"Echo, I told you to SHUT UP!" Omega shouted desperately, slapping her hand hard against her thigh to provide convincing sound effects. Echo merely stared at her, and she dropped her gaze, stifling a sigh.

"Nice try, Omega," Fox remarked, "but I never knew Echo to let another fight his battles. You're both on report. Now, Echo, turn around and bring that saucer back."

"What's that, Fox?" Echo asked, flipping the comm switch off and on. "Your signal's breaking up."

Omega, head still bowed, smiled slightly.

"Well, at least you didn't try 'reversing the polarity,'" she murmured, and Echo's lips twitched upward.

"—Cho, you qui— lipping that —damn —itch," Fox ordered. "Echo, I'm —arning —ou, I —ean it."

Omega's smile widened, and she glanced up at her partner. Echo was watching her with dark eyes as he flipped the comm off.

"Thank you," she whispered, sobering. "I-I tried...I just wanted..."

"I know. And thanks, but we're good, you an' me. No matter what happens after. What time is it?" Echo interrupted, turning back to the pilot's console and surveying the sensor readouts before flipping several switches.

"Oh!" Omega dove for the comm scrambler switch. "Scrambler on."

"Check the NASA transmission."

"Roger that. Bringing up NASA air-to-ground."

Amid the background squeaks, squeals, and chittering of the comm scrambler, a lone voice could just be made out.

"...Houston. Do you copy? Houston, this is *Kitty Hawk*. Do you read? We have massive interference. Do you copy?"

"Anything from the ground?" Echo asked.

"Flipping virtual directional antenna...there," Omega remarked.

"...*Kitty Hawk*, Houston. Do you read? We have lost your signal. Radar shows you in position, but we have unexplained L-O-S. Repeat, we have unexplained loss of signal. *Kitty Hawk*, this is Houston. Do you copy...?"

"Well, that worked," Omega remarked. "Oh, this is interesting. The bird has seen us."

"...Break, break, Houston! This is *Kitty Hawk*! If you copy, we have unidentified spacecraft approaching! Repeat, we have unidentified flying object on approach! The bogey is an estimated two thousand feet and closing! Houston, do you copy?!"

The two Alpha Line Agents looked at each other.

"Was that him?" Echo asked.

"Yeah."

"Will he recognize your voice?"

"Dunno. Maybe. Been a while, though. Want me to try?"

"Do it."

Omega keyed the comm. "*Kitty Hawk*, this is *Phoenix*. Do

you copy?"

"*Phoenix*?! We don't have..."

"*Kitty Hawk*, this is *Phoenix*. Our comm indicates you have seen us out your port windows."

"You're the bogey?"

"Affirm. Hi, Scotty. Request permission to come aboard."

"You know my...the...the voice...oh, no...But-but you're..."

"No. I'm not. It's all right, Scotty. I'm—we're—going to help."

"PROVE IT!"

"*Kitty Hawk, Phoenix*. Repeat transmission, please."

"Prove you're really her!"

Echo watched silently as Omega sighed.

"All right. Tabasco, this is Sharpshooter. Target acquired and approaching coffeepot. Do you have visual?"

There was a long silence. Echo glanced curiously at Omega.

"I told you once about that practical joke war in the astronaut office," she reminded him.

"Aha. He was the one who put the Tabasco in the coffeepot, then?" Echo verified.

"Yup. But nobody knew that but me, 'cause I caught him at it. Later on, I told him I was the water rifle sniper. Before I got caught, I mean."

"Mmm."

They waited quietly. Finally, a response came...but the voice was different, and far more grudging.

"*Phoenix*, this is *Kitty Hawk*. Permission to dock and come aboard granted."

"Roger, *Kitty Hawk*," Omega replied, as Echo began the docking maneuver. "Docking in progress."

* * *

"Okay, lessee. We need to match speed AND cabin conditions," Echo noted.

"Oh, that's right," Omega said. "Otherwise, there'll be a nasty little gravity gradient at the hatch. Never mind the air pressure. And I guess I need to extend the sensor scrambler field, too. Not to mention initiate that holographic 'replacement' we brainstormed while we were on ascent, and ginned up while we were catching up to 'em." She hesitated, then added, "After we blocked Fox's transmission."

Echo cut her a quick, concerned glance, and she shrugged.

"I just feel bad that he..." She broke off, then tried, "I can PROVE we gotta do this, he just won't listen. And it hurts."

"So that explains why you were a little distracted while we set up the hologram."

"Yeah. Sorry about that."

"Not a problem, baby. Are you up to this now?"

"Uh-huh. I'm just not looking forward to trying to get Fox to listen to my explanations when we get back."

"...Right. Try to relax about it, though; I think it'll be easier than you think, honey. Okay, we're coming up on the space plane; can you handle adjusting the environment settings and initiating the 'decoy,' while I line us up to dock?"

"Oh yeah. I'm all over it, hon."

"That's my girl. You ARE my girl, right?"

"No sweat, Ace," Omega reassured, reaching for the cabin-environment controls. "That was over a looong time ago, almost before it got started."

"You sure? If, uh, if I need to...to step aside..."

"I'm SURE. I'm right where I want to be, sweetheart. But see, when we decided we weren't cut out for romance, we stayed friends..."

"Oh. Okay. I get it now," Echo decided, settling a bit. "He was your closest friend...until I came along."

"Right, in so far as I HAD a closest friend. I could be kinda...reserved. Still am, it's just that my current 'family' took the time to get to know me, is all. But even so, he and I were never as close as you and I have been. You and I...we clicked, almost from the get-go, I think."

"Okay. But you gotta do this for him, same as you'd do it for me."

"More or less, yeah. But it's in our jurisdiction, Ace, I promise you. This wasn't due to a defective part or design, I swear it wasn't. I pored over all the video an' shit all NIGHT last night, to try to prove it."

"I know. I saw the data on your computer screen; you forgot to shut down before you left this morning. It's why I'm here, now."

"Oh. All right. And, um, thanks."

"Not a problem, baby. You know how I feel, how I think. As soon as I saw that? Hey. I saw what you were getting at, pretty much immediately. So I'm here. We'll get it worked, you an' me. On-orbit, an' on the ground at Headquarters." He made a minute adjustment in their trajectory. "Ready docking clamps."

"Sensor scrambler field extended; holographic imagery initiated. Bumping off the last of the artificial gravity, so make sure you're strapped down good. Docking clamps ready..."

* * *

"Fox?" Bravo said, as he and Lima bent over a tablet in the Core, where a deeply perturbed Fox was watching the scenario unfold on one of an entire constellation of the Agency's advanced—and heavily cloaked—observing satellites, displayed on several of the contiguous wall panels; given that the *Phoenix* was only using passive cloaking at this point, and the sensor scrambler field was directed at the NASA ground stations and the Tracking and Data Relay Satellite System that NASA used, the sophisticated Division One ObSats could depict the entire milieu, including the *Phoenix*.

"Yes, zun?" he replied, upset and worried. "I'm rather preoccupied at the moment..."

"I know. But this is important, and you really, I mean REALLY, need to see this," Bravo said.

"Besides, it's ABOUT that," Lima added.

"About THIS?!" Fox echoed, jabbing a thumb at the wallscreen image as he glanced at them. When he glanced back at the wallscreen, however, the image flickered, and both the *Phoenix* and the *Kitty Hawk* faded from the field of view. But the *Kitty Hawk* almost immediately returned...with a much smaller hole in its belly. "Mm," he murmured, "looks like they're using a one-two combo—sensor scrambler, and solid hologram projector. That's some nice work. But I don't guess I'm going to be watching any more of the actual rescue." He turned back to the Boys. "So. You have something about this?"

"Yeah, Boss," Lima averred. "As in, this explains everything."

Fox moved to their side.

"Let me see," he demanded. Lima handed him the tablet, and he studied the display intently. Abruptly his eyebrows shot up. "Where did you get this?"

"Echo sent it...from Omega's personal laptop in her quarters," Bravo explained. "About an hour and a half ago, so probably a little while before Alpha One launched, but we're just now seeing it. He strongly recommends analysis by Forensics. You already know what it means, Fox."

"Yes," Fox declared. "It means forget putting Alpha One on report, and get me at least two more Alpha teams and half a dozen standard field agents down to the Cape as fast as we can get 'em there."

"On it, Fox," Lima said, pulling another tablet and issuing the orders. "Aha! Good news—Alpha Two and -Four are available. Which one you want?"

"Both. Send 'em. NOW."

"Both teams?!"

"Both teams. With a full complement of standard field reinforcements. Headquarters or Atlanta Office field agents, I don't care which, but send 'em."

"Okay. Done." Lima tapped the tablet screen several times. "Anything else?"

"Yes. See if you can raise Alpha One aboard the *Phoenix*. I suspect they've switched off the air-to-ground comm, but keep trying, just in case. If you get through, tell Echo I got his message, that Headquarters is on board with their plan, and see if they need any help. If you can't get through on the standard comm, try an Alpha Line message relay to their phones. I want to make sure they have backup if they need it. And get that video, along with the freeze-screen graphic, to Forensics for analysis, five minutes ago."

"Wilco, sir," Bravo agreed.

"Who do you think did it?" Lima wondered.

"This," Fox waved the tablet, "indicates two possibilities, at least to my mind. Either we have another lot of imperialists from Va'du'sha'ā, intent on causing us trouble by way of 'retribution' for capturing and stashing the F'al—"

"Again," Lima sighed.

"I wish they'd get a life," Bravo grumbled.

"All of that. —Or it could be a group of joyriding Teludals, probably kids on holiday break. Hard to say who, and just based on this, hard to say if it was deliberate sabotage or a stupid accident...which is why we need Forensics looking at it with twenty-three fine-toothed combs. Though, based on this video, I'm leaning toward accident; I'd have thought saboteurs would have gone after both the fuel AND oxidizer tanks. But Omega and Echo were right to go after the *Kitty Hawk*; the cause of damage WAS one or more offworlders interfering, and that puts it squarely in our jurisdiction. And it's up to us—to them—to set it right."

And it's up to me to learn...again...to trust my Agents' hunches, he sighed to himself, as he turned toward his office. *After all, if Omega was originally assigned to this mission, she should know enough about it to be able to tell if the failure mode doesn't make sense. And damnation, but she was right— this doesn't make sense any other way than something was planted against the tank and exploded. Meanwhile, I'm trying hard not to show favoritism, especially after the shtik drek that went down with Adita's Coup, but maybe I'm going overboard the wrong way.*

* * *

The airlock hissed, and Omega floated through, followed by Echo. Immediately a tall, brown-haired man in a blue NASA jumpsuit enveloped Omega in a bear hug before she could get two feet from the hatch. She returned the greeting enthusiastically.

"MEG! Megan! Oh, dear God! It really is you! Oh, honey, we gave you up for dead nearly two years ago! Where the hell have you been?!"

The other crewmembers drifted around in confusion, staring at the former astronaut apparently returned from the dead. Suddenly they all noticed Echo, a tall, dark, imposing figure hovering silently behind Omega, watching. The discomfort in the cabin became palpable.

"Um, Scotty, this is my partner, Echo. Echo, Scotty Chadwick, best damn pilot in NASA." Omega smiled, attempting to lighten the mood. "Scotty, this is Agent Echo, best damn pilot in all of the Division One Agency.”

“Nice to meet you, Scotty.” Echo moved forward and shook the pilot’s hand. “I understand you and Meg...go back a ways together.”

“Oh, we have a history, you could say,” Scotty grinned. “But I don’t understand. Who exactly are you, what is ‘the Division One Agency,’ why does Meg need a partner, where has she been, and how the hell do you have a bird as...sophisticated...as that baby parked outside the airlock??”

“How long have we got, Echo?” Omega asked. Echo glanced at his wrist chronometer.

“Long enough for you to catch him up—if you’re quick.” He turned back to the airlock. “While you’re doing that, I’ll go get the suits ready.”

“Thanks, Ace,” Omega said softly, and the astronauts all clustered around.

* * *

“...And that’s the story, Scotty,” Omega concluded, as Echo emerged onto the *Phoenix*’s flight deck with two spacesuits.

“But...I don’t get...Meg, are you trying to say you’re an alien?” Chadwick asked, brow furrowed.

Omega opened her mouth to reply, but Echo interjected.

“No. She’s as human as any of us. But she had...a genetic atrocity, among other forms of atrocity...perpetrated on her by an interstellar criminal.” He floated over to the group.

“I’ve been modified, Scotty,” Omega said quietly, glancing at her partner, who returned her gaze inscrutably. “I’m not... what I was. What I should’ve been. And never will be.” She turned away, eased through the connecting hatch, and busied herself in readying one of the spacesuits.

Scotty’s eyes met Echo’s behind Omega’s back. Chadwick nodded slightly in the direction of his old flame; Echo’s lips tightened a bit, and he sighed and nodded. Chadwick’s hazel eyes grew sad, his expression one of deep sympathy and caring. Echo watched the other man’s response.

“The whole story’s too damn cockamamie,” Peter Dianus, the commander, suddenly grumbled. “Trying to feed us some bullshit line about aliens and a secret government conspiracy—”

"Look out the window," Echo responded, blunt. "Explain away a real flying saucer." He turned, ignoring the man, to help his partner. Omega carefully concealed her grin of amusement...from everyone except Echo, who bit his lip to prevent an obvious grin in return.

"What are you going to do?" the payload specialist, Pat Pate, asked nervously. Omega looked up then; she saw the anxious crew staring at the two Alpha Line Agents, and understood. She smiled, soothing.

"It's okay, Pat. We're here to help. We're gonna go EVA and repair the orbiter so you can make a safe re-entry and a controlled landing."

"Why?" Dianus demanded. "If you're so secret, why don't you just let us burn up? Saves you the trouble of a cover-up."

"You don't know Meg," was Echo's only answer. Chadwick nodded agreement.

"Meg's never been one to let something just...happen...if there was anything she could do to help," he told his superior. Then a thought struck. "But...Pete's right; it saves explaining." He caught the look that passed between Echo and Omega. "You two are in trouble for this, aren't you?"

Neither answered for a moment. Echo began to hum quietly, under his breath, as he initiated the life support units on the EVA suits preparatory to donning them. Omega glanced at him, recognizing the tune of *Stand By Me*, and smiled; it was a tired expression.

"Let it go, Scotty," she sighed. "Echo and I'll take care of it."

"Speaking of taking care of things...ready to suit up, Meg?" the man at her side asked.

"Yeah, Echo. Let's go do it."

"Lower deck egress?"

"Exactly. The two hatches are why I picked this particular craft. One to connect with the *Kitty Hawk*, the other to go EVA."

"Roger that."

* * *

"Okay, Meg, you're the one that studied this bird for years. You're the surgeon," the white figure with the black 'E' inscribed on the left breast said, tethering himself to the interior of *Kitty Hawk*'s payload bay with a second retractable tether. "Orders?"

"That's a switch," remarked the smaller figure, 'Ω' on the chest, wide black stripes distinguishing arms and legs, with a grin. She, too, attached a second tether to the space plane; both Agents had tethers that led to the interior of the *Phoenix*'s airlock, as well. "Okay. For starters, let's go take a firsthand look at the damage. Then we can plan what needs doing, and in what order."

"Roger that," came his reply, and the two Agents floated carefully over the side of the spacecraft, unreeling tethers. "Damn," Echo said immediately.

"What you said," Omega agreed, quiet.

"I take it, it's bad?" Scotty's voice remarked over their headsets.

"Not good," Omega acknowledged, staring at the carnage of bent, torn metal and broken heat shielding.

"It could be worse," Echo considered. "We can handle it."

"Can we see?" Pat's voice sounded.

"Yeah," Echo answered. "Punch up the small monitor I set up in the middeck of your craft. I've got a camera on my helmet."

There was a pause, then soft gasps came over the comm.

"Easy does it, guys," Omega soothed. "We came prepared. I got a decent look at it on the Agency satellite feed before we left, Echo. I brought some patch equipment suitable to the repair."

"Yeah, I snuck a peek, too, and I added to what you brought. Want me to unstow the stuff from the cargo hatch?" Echo asked, turning back toward the *Phoenix*.

"No, not yet. Let's see how much hydrazine contamination we've got, first, then we'll set about smoothing the edges of the rupture."

"Wilco. You're the boss."

"Riiiight." Omega's voice was full of dry amusement.

"In this instance, you are, baby. You know way more about this bird than I do."

"All right. But you've got more experience with this sorta

thing."

"No argument. So you analyze and explain to me what needs doing, and I'll take the lead in doing it."

The pair set to work as the NASA crew watched via video, pulling equipment from stowage areas of the sophisticated Agency spacesuits, and testing the area of the rupture for toxic contamination by the highly-reactive hydrazine fuel. Upon discovering there was relatively little, Omega was surprised.

"...'Cause with that much of the shit vented overboard, I'd have expected the whole belly of the bird to be coated," she noted.

"Did you see any of the venting?" Chadwick wondered. "I mean, I figure, with that craft you've got, you probably have some really good orbital observing platforms an' shit like that?"

"We do, and I saw a little," Omega confirmed. "But not a lot; the platforms weren't looking in the right direction to see you initially."

"Oh," Hollifield said then. "Then you didn't see how it went, ma'am. I'm still not sure exactly how it happened, but we could see the jet of fuel from the cabin, and it was below us."

"Ah," Echo noted. "So it was fairly spewing. Which means that most of it shot away from the bird before it could re-deposit ON the bird."

"That'd be our take," Chadwick agreed. "We had a significant thrust for a couple seconds, there. I'm sure the tank rupture itself has some contamination, and the secondary tank is still full; we managed to close the valve before the whole lot vented overboard."

"Well, I guess that's good," Omega decided. "The special decon cycle in the *Phoenix*'s airlock ought to take care of any contamination we pick up on the suits."

"True," Echo averred. "In that case, let's get started, I guess."

So the pair initiated the process of repair. From time to time, Scotty offered commentary, or confirmed Omega's recollections, assisting the two Agents in their analysis. Then they started laboriously cutting away damaged heat-resistant plates first, using a laser cutter, and carefully saving the plate fragments; the process was a slow one. Once they had an outer surface free of ragged edges, the pair commenced bending ruptured metal back into position, in order to weld it seamlessly. Little was said, the two Agents working in coordinated concert, hour after hour.

"Damn, you two are good," Scotty remarked in admiration from within the space plane.

"Thanks," Omega replied absently, as she and Echo concentrated on bending a metal plate.

"You don't even have to talk to each other?"

"No," Echo answered shortly, applying pressure with a special tool, as Omega positioned the superalloy plate.

"She's probably reading his mind," Dianus's voice dripped sarcasm.

"Shut up, damn you—" Scotty's voice cut off as the comm went dead. Omega and Echo paused, glancing at each other in concern.

"Scotty, drop it, hon', before you get in trouble," Omega said softly. "It's not worth deckin' your C.O. over me. Besides...sometimes I have."

No answer.

"Chadwick?" Echo queried.

"...It's all right, Echo," Chadwick answered, grudging. "But if Dianus makes another crack about Pook again, I'll—"

"Shoot 'im out the airlock in his skivvies?" Omega grinned.

"Yeah," came the amused response.

The two Agents bent back over their work, but Echo murmured into the mic, "Pook?"

"Uh, yeah," Omega replied, as her face flushed with embarrassment beneath the helmet visor. "It's an old nickname."

"Pook."

"Yeah."

"Sorry, Meg," Chadwick's voice said with chagrin. "It slipped out."

"'S okay."

"Pook." Echo never stopped work. Omega stared at her partner through her visor. Echo stared back, unperturbed, and thoughtfully reiterated, "Pook."

"Yeah, Pook!" Omega burst out, amid the faint sound

of laughter in the background on the audio. "In the—what? whoppin' five months we dated, Scotty gave me a cute little teddy bear for Christmas that year, and it came with the name Pook 'cause it was a character out of some fantasy story, and somehow he started applying it to me. That's the whole flippin' tale. Can we just get on with it??"

"I never stopped," Echo pointed out, as an exasperated Omega bent back over the metal shard, and more faint laughter could be heard on the comm. "You don't look like a Pook," Echo observed. Omega shot him a dirty look.

"Yeah, well, appearances can be deceiving."

"In other words, nothing is as it appears."

"Right."

"Okay, Pook."

"AArrghhhh...!"

Chapter 5

"All right, one last chunk here to bend back into place, and I think we can start welding and patching," Omega said sometime later, as she and Echo commenced work on one particularly ragged shard of metal. "Whadda you think, Ace?"

"Looks good to me, Pook," Echo answered with a straight face. "I can't get a good angle on this with the torque field inducer, though."

"Here, give it to me," Omega said, and Echo untethered the device from his gauntlet and handed it to her. "I think I can get to it from over here."

"All right, I'll hold it in position," Echo offered, fitting actions to words. They worked for several minutes, as Omega struggled to find the best angle to apply pressure.

"Dang," she muttered, "this one's the worst of the lot. Lemme try this." Omega wedged herself into position against the base of the wing and tried again, exerting all the force she could muster to bend the twisted metal back into a semblance of its original shape.

"WATCH IT!" Echo exclaimed, as the plate abruptly shifted. Omega, off balance and exerting considerable pressure, lunged forward as the tool slipped off the edge of the shard. A sharp, loud hissing made itself heard over the comm, and Omega stared down in horror at the jagged tear in the body of her exo suit.

"Suit breach!" she gasped, the air in the suit already growing thin as she struggled to stabilize her position against the venting gas jet.

"Meg! POOK! No!" Chadwick shouted over the comm.

Echo took one look at the rip, reached into one of his spacesuit pockets, then slapped his palm down over the puncture. When he raised his hand, an Ergisol Insta-Seal covered the breach. But the damage had been done: Omega was not moving, and appeared unconscious. Echo grabbed his limp partner around the waist, unclipped the secondary tethers from the *Kitty Hawk*, and leaped for the *Phoenix*'s middeck airlock, as the suit tethers automatically retracted in a frantic effort to keep up with the swiftly-moving Agent.

Inside the airlock, he slammed his hand down hard on the 'emergency decon cycle' switch. In seconds, the suits had been decontaminated, the inner hatch opened, and he dragged his limp companion into the ship's cabin and straight through the adjacent opening to the flight deck, where there was room to work.

The *Kitty Hawk* crew floated into the open hatchway between the vessels, Scotty forcing his way through to help Echo. Together, the two men practically tore off Omega's helmet, and Echo flung it aside. The woman inside the suit was very pale, eyes closed, breath undetectable.

"Meg? Meg?" Echo swiftly doffed a gauntlet, reaching for her throat, finding the pulse point. "Meg, say something. C'mon, baby; don't do this to me."

Abruptly, she sucked in a deep breath, and Chadwick turned away to hide his relief. Omega opened her eyes and looked up into a brown gaze containing the merest hint of anxiety...which was more than anyone else could see.

"You okay, baby?" Echo asked softly.

"Will be," she croaked. Then, gratitude in the blue eyes, she silently mouthed, "I could hug you, Ace."

Echo's expression never changed, but the smoky eyes warmed.

"'...Not in front of the Kronons, Jim,'" he quoted in a murmur, eliciting a weak grin.

"Okay. Your loss," Omega rasped, and an odd expression flickered in her partner's brown eyes. "I'm still kinda limp, here. Help me outta this thing."

* * *

"How long were we out?" Omega asked, and the *Kitty Hawk*'s commander replied, curt.

"Max EVA plus eighty-six minutes. Your suit supply is better than ours."

"Roger that," Omega responded thoughtfully. "Almost seven and a half hours, then. Echo?"

"Pulling it up now, Me-Pook," Echo answered expression-

101

lessly, bending over the navigation console in the Agency saucer, and Omega bit her lip to hide the grin as snickers sounded behind her. "Here. Have a look."

"Mm," was all Omega said as she studied the readout.

"Yeah," Chadwick murmured in agreement, giving the console display his expert eye as well. Echo raised an eyebrow at his rapid grasp of the readout. "We don't have much time, do we?"

"No," Echo agreed. "And now Meg's suit is out of commission. Well, time to get back to work." He reached for his helmet and gauntlets.

"Echo..." Omega said softly, and he glanced at her. After a moment, he shrugged, then nodded, and turned back to the deck hatch.

"Where's he going?!" Dianus demanded, as Echo headed down to the middeck through the deck hatch.

"To finish the job," Omega answered quietly.

"Alone??" Pat wondered, shocked.

"Yes."

"No," Scotty said firmly.

The others stared at him.

* * *

The couple gazed at each other, alone in the saucer's middeck.

"Are you sure about this, Scotty?"

"Positive, Pook."

"You don't have to."

"You know me better than that."

"Yeah, I do," Omega sighed. "Listen, um...I'm...I'm counting on you to..."

"I know," Chadwick answered with a lopsided grin. "I get that he's somebody special to you. I'll do the best I can to back him up for you. I don't have one of those slick instant-suit-patches up my sleeve like he does, but you know the training. It'll work."

"Okay," Omega said, hugging him tightly. "Be careful."

"I always am. Hey, you didn't tell HIM that!"

"No need."

"You think he's better than I am, just because he's got fan-

102

cier gadgets?" Chadwick jerked back, out of the embrace, offended.

"I didn't say that. I said I didn't need to tell him."

"What's that supposed to mean?"

"Scotty," Omega said softly, laying a hand lightly on the white-clad shoulder, "remember when we were training together?"

"Yeah. We were good. A real team."

"And the longer we worked together—"

"The better we got. Sometimes we didn't even have to talk..." Chadwick's voice tapered off in realization. "...Like you two did on the EVA earlier. And you've been together a couple years, now...prob'ly working pretty damn close..."

"And we're a really damn good match, partner-wise, Scotty. Echo's...well, he's the closest friend I've got. That I've ever had."

"Are you two—" Chadwick began meaningfully. Omega nodded her head.

"Yeah, we are now. We...just got engaged a few weeks back. I'm not sure how it's all gonna work out, all things considered, but I love him, and he loves me. He doesn't care about...about the genetics an' stuff." She shrugged. "We...connect, Echo and me. Almost from the first, we understood each other. It didn't take long before we could...communicate without communicating, if you get me."

"So that look you gave him...when he was coming down here...and then he nodded...THAT was you two communicating..."

"Right. And I didn't need to tell him, I mean to actually SAY it." Omega nodded affirmation. "He already knew."

* * *

"No," Echo said firmly.

"Echo, I can help," insisted the white-suited figure with the American flag on the left arm, floating beside the space-suited Division One Agent whose left arm displayed the ancient zodiacal sun-cross symbol for Earth in black, overlaid with a red 1.

"How? You're not trained on this equipment."

"So teach me."

"No. Meg was extensively trained, and she still nearly bit

it," Echo rejoined, curt.

"So maybe her trainer goofed," Chadwick shot back, and Echo scowled beneath the solar visor.

"Scotty...Echo trained me," Omega said quietly over the comm, distressed by the trend of the conversation. "He's... well, let's just say Echo's THE Agent, so to speak."

"Oh," Chadwick said, then, "Well, shit happens. Train me."

"No time," Echo insisted, as the anxious crew watched through the various ports.

"Surgeon!" Omega suddenly interjected over the mic.

"What??" both men responded, turning to look back at the saucer window, where a silver-blonde head was visible, peering out.

"Echo, remember when you told me I was the surgeon, working on this injured bird?"

"Yeah?"

"Now you're the surgeon—and Scotty's the nurse."

"Head nurse," Chadwick corrected. "I know this baby's guts inside and out."

"All right," Echo grudgingly acquiesced. "It might be good, at that. You ARE more familiar with the bird than I am. But I'm way the hell more familiar with the equipment we'll be using for repair, so you do only what I tell you, how I tell you, when I tell you. Got it?"

"I have good copy," Scotty replied. "You tell me what, how, when: Wilco."

"Roger that. Hand me that ceramic solder."

* * *

As the two men worked, Omega busied herself bringing the patch materials out of the cargo containers and placing them in the saucer's airlock, as the crew of the *Kitty Hawk* peered down from the flight deck, watching. Then she closed the inner hatch, and cycled the airlock.

"All right, Scotty," she said into the mic at the pilot's console on the flight deck, a few minutes later. "The repair stuff is sittin' in the airlock, all ready for you and Echo."

"Copy that," Chadwick responded, watching Echo fine-tune the edges of the hole in *Kitty Hawk*'s belly. "Ready for it, Echo?"

"By the time y'all get it here, yeah," Echo verified without looking up from his task. "There'll be a small pressure vessel. Black, with a white nozzle. Bring that, first. Hold off on the rest."

"Small pressure vessel, black with white nozzle. Wilco."

"Scotty, it's in front," Omega informed him.

"Good girl," both men said in unison, then glanced at each other. After a moment, they nodded an unspoken acknowledgement and continued their respective tasks. Inside the *Phoenix*, Omega merely rolled her eyes, grinning.

Well, at least they're bonding a little, she decided. *And that makes me happy. My current partner and my old 'partner,' not that NASA ever worked QUITE like that, seem to be getting along okay, even if it was kinda rocky there for a bit.*

* * *

The work was long and tedious; Chadwick made many trips back and forth between airlock and repair site, but the hole in the bird's gut was slowly and steadily closing. Omega kept an anxious eye on the navigation display.

"How much time we got, Meg?" Echo asked, studying what was left of the damage; about half an hour earlier, he had stopped using the Division One patch materials, and begun using the NASA materials aboard the *Kitty Hawk*. It wasn't as sophisticated, and unlike the Division One patch, the NASA patch material was patently obvious, but after considerable discussion during ascent, he and Omega had decided that was how it needed to be. "Because otherwise," he had noted at the time, "it'll look like the thing was miraculously repaired, whereas we just want it to look like it wasn't as bad as they first thought."

"About four hours out from serious atmospheric density issues, Ace," she replied.

"Okay, I think I got about fifteen, maybe twenty, more minutes here, then it'll be sealed," Echo noted. "Then I'll wanna do a tanking test like we talked about, and Chadwick here and I can observe it."

"Copy that," Omega replied. "Prepping for tanking, while you finish sealing."

"Roger." Echo pointed; Chadwick handed him what he

wanted, and the two men kept working.

* * *

"Hey, Fox," Romeo's voice said over the Director's cell phone. "Alpha Two an' Four reportin' in."

"What's the news, zun?" Fox asked.

"Turns out it was your second idea," Romeo replied. "Teludal kid got loose from th' tour group and used her abilities t' sneak inta th' VAB, then into th' guts o' th' space plane. I'm still not entirely sure what she did, but near's we can figure, she's a science geek—think middle school student—an' wanted t' get some measurements of...I dunno what, eezackly; she wadn' that clear on it...but she put some sorta measuring device in the plane, b'tween th' fuel tank an' th' hull, but awful damn close to th' oxidizer tank, too. Only she didn't realize that th' space plane ain't as fancy as our saucers an' shit, an' that area wouldn't be protected from radiation, 'specially once th' thing went t' th' Moon an' back..."

"Aha," Fox murmured. "I see that coming. The sensor took a cosmic radiation hit, overheated, and blew."

"Right, but 'cause of its design, it acted sorta like a shaped charge, an' blew open jus' th' fuel tank. If it'd cracked th' oxidizer tank too, way I understand it, th' whole shebang woulda gone instantly, an' th' ship 'd probably come apart immediately, with loss o' all hands. We got lucky. DAMN lucky."

"Oy vey," Fox sighed. "No shit. All right. Drop her off at the Atlanta Office; that's where our juvenile department is, and they can handle things like getting in touch with her parents and such. Tell 'em to give her a VERY stern talking-to, so she understands exactly what she did. And why she should never do it again."

"Wilco, Fox."

* * *

"Hey, I'm curious," Chadwick piped up after a few more minutes of intense work alongside Echo.

"Meg, can you take questions?" Echo murmured absently as he worked. "I'm kinda focused, here..."

"Yeah, I got it, Echo," Omega answered from inside the cabin. "Whatcha need, Scotty?"

"Well, we got the NASA patch stuff out, but we're only

106

using your stuff—or we were, until just a bit ago. Now we're only using the NASA stuff. What's up with that?"

"Oh," Omega said, monitoring statuses on both ships. "It's actually pretty simple. Remember, nobody is supposed to know about us..."

"Except you know NASA an' NORAD an' every DoD installation with the ability to spot us is watching us right now," Dianus interjected in a more-than-slightly snide tone.

"No, they're not," Omega came close to snapping. "Because we extended our sensor scrambler field to include the *Kitty Hawk* as soon as we got close. Nobody can even see us—either ship—right now. HOWEVER, since Echo and I have some skills with solid hologram tech, what they THINK they see is the *Kitty Hawk* ALONE, with a hole in the belly—smaller than what you've really got—and a couple of your crew on EVA, working on it."

The hot mic picked up an indecipherable muttering from the *Kitty Hawk*; judging by the tone, the Alpha One team adjudged Dianus was cursing under his breath. Just then, Vancel interjected, confirming their judgement.

"Stuff it, Dianus. You jumped the gun on the Atom test, before Pat and I even finished the checkout, so you should just be glad the bird is in one piece, with all of us still alive in it, and that they're here and willing to help."

"That strange chick already—"

"'That strange chick' was part of our crew, a couple years back," Chadwick interjected, tight.

"Yeah, yeah, but she ain't now, is she? She ain't even human. Besides, she already said this wasn't anything to do with us, or the bird. It was some alien dumbass that did it."

"No, what she said was that it was alien interference that CAUSED it," Vancel did snap. "Which off-nominal condition we might have SEEN, if you hadn't decided to override our procedures and protocols, and do things your way."

"Let me remind you who's commander of this flight, Vancel."

"Not any more," Echo interjected, voice firm. "I hate to tell you, but an Alpha Line team overrides everybody—including NASA hierarchies."

"The hell you say."

"Yeah, I say," Echo noted calmly. "Per agreements with the UN Secretary-General, the U.S. President, the NASA Administrator, most of the world's leaders..."

"Some secret," Dianus noted, caustic.

"You'd be surprised what people do and don't remember," Omega said, smirking despite herself; she had already decided she was looking forward to brain-bleaching this jerk.

"Then how the hell do you prove they even agreed to it?"

"For one, the signatures, which are demonstrable," Omega responded. "For another, just because THEY don't remember it, doesn't mean we didn't download and archive their memories of doing it. Those memories can be returned, under certain conditions." She paused, then added, "Like it or not, Dianus, Echo is in control at this moment."

A sullen silence emanated from the *Kitty Hawk*.

* * *

Given the fact that Dianus had shut up for the moment, Chadwick decided not to bring up the notion that Alpha One had disobeyed orders to come and help...which might negate that newly-established chain of command. *Still,* he decided, *Pook and her partner seemed fairly certain she could convince the top dogs in her chain that she was right.* Just then, Omega commented.

"Anyway, Scotty, to finish answering you, we have some pretty sophisticated stuff, and you can probably tell, the patch stuff we used blends in—"

"Awful damn well," Scotty finished for her.

"Right," she confirmed. "But the NASA stuff was designed to be more obvious, so they'd know what to look at on the ground..."

"Oh. So it'll look like the damage wasn't as bad as we first thought, and we got it patched up ourselves."

"Exactly."

"What happens when the rest of us talk?" Dianus wanted to know.

No one answered him.

"I SAID, what happens when—"

"We heard you," Echo noted. "We just chose not to answer."

"Let me remind you that I'm—"

"Let me remind you that we don't care," Omega barked. "Now get off the loop so we can coordinate this."

* * *

In the cabin of *Kitty Hawk*, the other crew members were ignoring Dianus, going about the business of prepping for re-entry and return, occasionally responding to one or the other member of Alpha One by doing as requested, then reporting the results.

'EARN our respect,' he heard the memory of Chadwick's voice in his head.

Damn straight, he thought. *First thing, I gotta get ridda the bitch and her shack job. And I think I know just how to do it.*

* * *

"Okay, Meg, I think that's got it," Echo said on the comm. "Chadwick, you stay out here with me to help check for leaks, and move over there." He pointed at the port wing. "You're gonna watch wing to wing, and I'm gonna watch nose to tail."

"Copy that," Chadwick noted.

"All right, Meg, go ahead and mate up to the fuel inlet, and tank about a third of the amount we discussed on ascent. Lowest pressure our systems will handle. I don't wanna risk blowing something back open by using too high a pressure."

"Wilco, Ace."

* * *

Omega commenced connecting the *Phoenix* special tank to the *Kitty Hawk*—the *D1 Phoenix* had been designed and intended for just this sort of repair mission, which was why Omega had selected it, and she had ensured the correct fuel had been put in the 'refill' tank. Now she watched closely as the remote delicately mated with *Kitty Hawk*'s fuel valves, adjusting to the NASA hardware as readily as it adapted to Pan-Galactic craft, regardless of planet of origin. Occasionally she typed a command into *Phoenix*'s computer, or toggled a joystick, to adjust the angle of the remote. Then she bumped the fuel pressure down as low as it would go, to avoid potentially blowing out the patch job. She entered the quantity of fuel to be transferred, then keyed the mic.

"Omega to Echo. Initiating fuel transfer...now."

She hit the button to begin fueling the standard hypergolic fuel into the tanks for the primaries, via the *Phoenix*'s remote manipulator system.

* * *

Echo watched the belly of the *Kitty Hawk* with an eagle eye. A quick glance out of the corner of his eye told him that Chadwick was doing the same. The two men stared at the belly, looking for leaks or distortions of the heat shielding that might note an undue pressure increase from the inside.

"First tanking complete," Omega's voice reported in his headset.

"I show clear here," he observed. "Chadwick?"

"Clear from this angle," Chadwick reported. "Dan? Do the instruments show anything?"

"We have nominal," Hollifield's voice answered. "I show a bit under one thousand kilos of fuel, say 853 kilos; oxidizer remained—and remains—unaffected by the malfunction."

"Perfect," Echo said in satisfaction. "Chadwick, will you ingress, please, and prepare for a short hotfire test? I'm going to maneuver myself into an out-of-the-way position to watch, just to make sure all goes as planned, then I'll ingress, myself."

"Maybe you should ingress and watch from inside your craft?" Chadwick suggested.

"Well, I thought about it, but if I need to do any fixes, it'll probably have to be fast, so it'd be better if I'm already out here. You go ahead and ingress, and I'll be back inside as soon as it's done."

"Copy. Chadwick ingressing through *Phoenix*."

* * *

Dianus unceremoniously nudged Hollifield out of the way on the flight deck, and sat down at the controls.

"Notify me when Chadwick is inside," he ordered. Hollifield stared at him for a moment in disgust, then shrugged and headed for the middeck and the hatch.

* * *

All of the crew except Dianus met Chadwick inside the mated hatch as he utilized *Phoenix*'s two-hatch system to ingress *Kitty Hawk*. Omega had waved as he passed through the flight deck, concentrating on following Echo's progress as he maneuvered his way to a location where he expected to be able to safely watch the *Kitty Hawk*'s heretofore-un-timelined hot-fire test.

"Damn," Chadwick said, as soon as Vancel and Pate helped him remove his helmet, "those two are GOOD. I think we might actually pull this off."

"Pete's already in the seat," Hollifield noted. "He wanted to know as soon as you were aboard, Scotty."

"Roger that," Chadwick grumbled. "Echo and Meg wanted ME doing this."

"And he knows that," Vancel pointed out. "That's why HE took the seat."

Together the crew headed forward.

* * *

"Okay, I'm almost in place," Echo noted, grabbing his tether and flipping it carefully. "I need to get this damn tether unkinked from the empennage first..." He tried again. "Guess I shoulda gone the other way 'round."

"Come back this way, Ace," Omega instructed. "I've got a good view of it from here, and I think if you come back about five meters, then go 'round the vertical stabilizer like you said, you'll have it."

* * *

"There you are," Dianus said, watching Chadwick lead the rest of the crew into the flight deck. He turned back to the controls. "All right, let's get this show on the road."

"Don't you think you should let Scotty handle it?" Hollifield wondered, pointed.

"No, I don't," Dianus noted, setting up the hotfire parameters. He reached for the switch.

"STOP! WAIT!" Hollifield cried. "We haven't got the go-ahead yet!"

"NO! NOT YET!" Chadwick shouted at the same time. "ECHO is still out there! He hasn't given the all-clear!"

Dianus hit the switch.

* * *

"OH SHIT!" Omega cried, as she saw the glow of the engines coming online. Her hands danced over her console, grabbing the *Kitty Hawk* in a solid tractor beam and trying to compensate for the thrust with the *Phoenix*'s own drive. "ECHO! Grab something and hang on!"

"What?!" Echo responded, startled.

"HANG ON, ACE!"

And the *Kitty Hawk*'s engines ignited.

* * *

Echo's tether was still hung, taut, in the *Kitty Hawk*'s empennage, and he had just started coming back toward it to free it when the engines fully ignited on the *Kitty Hawk*. Echo, his boots on the horizontal stabilizer, flew aft as the *Kitty Hawk* slammed forward. His tether, taut across the vertical stabilizer and the opposite horizontal stabilizer, snapped in two places, cut like a giant knife. The piece still attached to the airlock hatch of the *Phoenix* recoiled, slamming into the hull of that craft.

The other two pieces whipped back toward Echo; one slapped him across the chest, the other wrapped around his legs. The double impact sent him flying away from the Kitty Hawk, back toward Earth.

A soft, faint hiss came to the tangled Agent's ears, even as he strove to free himself of the bonds that had once been his lifeline.

"Aw shit," he murmured, watching as the *Kitty Hawk*—and the *Phoenix*, beyond—drifted farther and farther away with every moment.

* * *

Omega had her hands full, controlling the *Kitty Hawk* with the tractor beam, and keeping both spacecraft in their proper orbit by countering the *Kitty Hawk*'s thrust with the *Phoenix*'s own propulsion system. Once she got things stabilized, she hit the ship-to-ship mic to connect to the flight deck.

"DAMMIT, Scotty, what the HELL did you think you were doing?!" she snapped. "Did either Echo or me give you the all-clear for that?? NO! Shit dammit to hell an' back!"

"You're cussin' at the wrong man, Pook," Chadwick's voice came back, calm. "Let me put Commander Dianus on and you can cuss at him. HE was the one that took over the seat. And chose to do it his own way, in his own time. As usual."

"Oh really?" Omega said, voice dropping into her lowest register, and fairly glazing with ice.

"Um," Pate murmured into the comm, "Meg? I think you might wanna check on your partner..."

"Oh shit," Omega whispered, glancing aft, toward *Kitty Hawk*'s empennage. A small piece of tether still draped loosely across the vertical stabilizer, gradually drifting free...but no white-clad figure floated there. She began scanning the vicinity quickly, then finally spotted Echo against the circle of Earth, almost camouflaged by its clouds, and already at least a hundred meters away. "Oh shit, oh shit, oh shit," she breathed, scanning her control panel and bringing up a virtual heads-up display. "He's on the wrong side, I can't get a good angle, and I'm still compensating for that unduly-hot hotfire test..."

The hatch filled with four bodies, peering into the *Phoenix* flight deck; the only member of the *Kitty Hawk* crew who was NOT there was Dianus.

"...No. Oh, dear God, no," Omega whispered, watching the space-suited figure drift farther and farther away. She keyed the external comm. "Echo?!"

"I read you, Meg." Echo's voice was very quiet over the comm.

"Echo! Honey? Are you in one piece??" Omega asked urgently, as the *Kitty Hawk* crew watched, intent.

"Yeah, I'm in one piece. For the moment."

"Thank God. Listen, Echo, I'm coming to get you...!"

"Do you have the kick from that—damn hot—hotfire test damped out?"

"More or less, yes. I could grab you with a tractor beam, but from this location, I can't get a good angle—the *Kitty Hawk* is in the way. I could turn us around so *Phoenix* is on your side, but after all she's been through, I don't want to manhandle *Kitty Hawk* quite that much; even with the tractor beam, that'll torque her frame a fair bit, using *Phoenix* to make the maneuver. So I'll have to seal the airlock, detach the docking hatch, and come get you. Then we can come back here and finish—"

"No, Meg. There's no time."

"But, Ace, we're too close to atmospheric interface. You'll re-enter..."

Chadwick watched while Omega's pale face contorted with pain as she spoke.

"It doesn't matter. My suit's breached anyway. I've got a slow leak."

"How slow?"

"Put it this way: not slow enough."

"Then I'm—"

"Meg, we came up here to save a NASA space plane. Because it's our JOB." Echo's voice paused. "You can't save both of us. There isn't enough time. You know it, and I know it. Finish the job you started out to do. Don't add another, and end up fritzing on both."

"But, Echo—"

"Meg. Do it. That's a direct order." He paused, then added, "I'm sorry, baby. I guess it just wasn't meant to be."

There was a click, and the comm went dead.

Omega went white to the lips.

* * *

A pale, mute Omega woodenly went about the task of prepping the space plane for its re-entry. First—and now that she knew for certain that the bird could handle the milder stress—she used the tractor beam and the *Phoenix* to VERY gently tug *Kitty Hawk* laterally into a marginally more stable orbit, working to correct the kick that Dianus's hotfire test had given it. Then, extremely carefully, she loaded a small amount—a scant 1,758 kilos, and she threw in a few tenths of a kilo, to make it look like that was all that was left in the tank after the leak—of standard hypergolic fuel into the tanks for the primaries, via the *Phoenix*'s remote manipulator system. The crew of the *Kitty Hawk* watched in silence; even Dianus floated in to see how matters were progressing. Once the fuel transfer line was in place and properly mated, she initiated the transfer with a single command. Seconds later, the fuel was aboard the *Kitty Hawk.*

"There," Omega said, very subdued. "That'll be just enough to get you home safely, without looking like you got a refill. Use it sparingly."

"Why the hell don't you give us a little margin for error?" Dianus protested.

A furious Omega suddenly kicked off the cabin wall, moving at speed and aimed directly at Dianus, slamming the commander into the opposite bulkhead hard enough to knock the wind out of him; it was a zero-g fighting maneuver that Echo had taught her, and she had learned to execute it well and amazingly swiftly. She tucked her feet into the nearest holds to provide leverage—without even looking—then grabbed him by the collar of his flight jumpsuit, tightening it until he grew red-faced. Between the double impact and the choke hold, Dianus began to pant for air.

"Be thankful you're getting home at all, you damn bastard," she growled through gritted teeth, scowling fiercely. "Let Scotty fly the *Kitty Hawk* home, if you're so worried for your own damn hide. That fuel I tanked for you earlier was NOT all meant for the burn test! If YOU hadn't jumped the gun on the hotfire test, AND kicked it into the damn afterburner mode to make it as hellaciously hot as possible so you could show off what a hotshot pilot you think you are, you'd have HAD more margin for error, instead of making matters worse! I wasn't supposed to have to use the *Phoenix* to adjust YOUR shitty orbit! And Echo would be here helping me right now, instead of preparing for his own re-entry without a ship!" The other crewmembers gathered around, watching silently, refusing to defend their erstwhile commander. "Instead, you'll be safe at home in a few hours, and I'll go home alone, without my partner. Without the man I'd promised to marry. The man I'd have gladly died for."

A hand fell lightly, gently, on her shoulder. Omega glanced back into Chadwick's thoughtful face.

"Maybe not, Pook," he told her. "I've been thinking..."

* * *

Omega's fingers flew over the pilot's console as she detached the *Phoenix* from *Kitty Hawk*. A few more quick key entries dropped the solid hologram and tightened the sensor scrambler hard around the *Phoenix*, revealing the real *Kitty Hawk* to the universe once more.

She glanced out the window at the concerned faces peering out of the other ship's port—three faces, out of the four left on the ship—and gave them a brief salute. Then she turned her attention to the display on her console: It showed two ships and a small blue blip, all headed—at different rates—toward atmospheric boundary, which appeared as a fuzzy red arc on the display. Not that the atmosphere was at all hard-edged, but there was an altitude at which the density became great enough to create drag sufficient to ensure re-entry. And the lower the altitude, the faster it happened.

Echo was low. And getting lower.

"Not much time," she muttered.

"No, but just enough," the man at her side answered, encouraging, as he helped her set a course for the blue blip. "We'll reach him in time."

Omega laid her hand lightly on Chadwick's forearm.

"Thanks, Scotty. You always were right there when I needed you."

"The feeling's mutual, Pook," he said in a soft voice, and smiled gently, patting the hand on his arm. "Let's go get your man."

"Huh? MY man?"

"Yeah, you're engaged, aren't you?"

"Well, yeah, but hon...I don't OWN him! Echo is his own man."

"Uh-huh." Chadwick's tone was tolerantly disbelieving. "I saw the looks he gave you, when he thought nobody was watching. And that you gave him. He's all yours, or I'll eat my gauntlets. So don't give me that."

"Scotty..."

"What?"

"Look, I, um, okay, so yes, we're engaged, but, but...after everything that's happened, I...I'm still trying to get a grip on the notion that he loves me. Stop and think about what was done to me, about what I am, and you'll get what I'm talkin' about. I mean, half the time, I feel like I'm waiting for the other shoe to drop, you know?"

"Aw. C'mon, Pook, don't do this to me."

"Do what?"

"You KNOW what!" Chadwick flung his hands in the air, then grabbed for the nearest handhold to keep from floating off at the motion.

"Eep!" Omega exclaimed, "lemme get the artificial gravity re-established before we bash around the cabin!"

"Okay," Chadwick agreed in some surprise. "I didn't even know you HAD that. But I guess I shouldn't be surprised. Lemme get my feet on the deck, or I'm gonna take a tumble..."

"All right," Omega agreed, already beginning to adjust the settings that allowed for the gravity field to resume, Alpha One having shut it off before docking with the *Kitty Hawk*. "There we go."

"You guys have some serious souped-up shit," Chadwick decided. "I'm kinda jealous of it. But you're not getting off that easy, Pook. I know your diversions. Don't play games with me, now."

"Uh..." Omega began, confused. "Well, Scotty, I really don't know what you're talking about..."

Chadwick sighed.

"Are you and Echo an item or not?" he asked. "If you're not, then I want the chance to try again. If you are, then I'll back off and stay out of the way."

"I...I think...well, I know we're an item, him and me—assuming we get to him in time," she said pointedly, and Chadwick immediately moved to her side and began assisting her in plotting a course that would intercept Echo's trajectory before atmospheric interface. "But, I mean, sometimes there's this little voice that wonders, you know?"

"Why?"

"Because A—Echo loved someone else, once. B—what man would really want me? I'm not human. Not any more, anyhow."

"Well," Chadwick remarked, pulling her close, "I dunno 'bout A. But I can answer B, for sure." He hugged her, then let go. "Don't worry, Pook, I won't take advantage. Just...if that doesn't work out with him, remember me, okay?"

"Um, okay," Omega responded, uncertain.

* * *

"There he is," Omega whispered, pointing out the cabin window at a distant white form.

"Damn," Chadwick said softly. "He's not moving. He said he had a slow leak, but I thought that was his excuse to... You

117

think...?"

"I don't know," Omega said, deeply worried, the hint of a groan in her low voice. "Let's find out." She keyed the comm. "Echo, this is the *Phoenix*. Do you copy?"

Silence.

"Echo, this is Omega, aboard the *D1 Phoenix*. We have completed repairs on the *Kitty Hawk* per your orders, and now we're here to rescue you. Do you read?"

Still no answer.

"Echo, it's Meg. Please answer, Ace..."

When she still got no response, Omega lowered her head into her hands.

"Oh, Ace," she whispered, in deep pain, "I'm so sorry...I'm so sorry. I couldn't go any faster. I just couldn't go any faster."

A hand gently touched her shoulder.

"Come on, Pook, and let's get him," a sympathetic Chadwick told her. "At least you can take him home."

* * *

"EVA One, *Phoenix*, for a status," Omega spoke into the microphone.

"*Phoenix*, EVA One," Chadwick's space-suited figure replied, using the *Phoenix*'s standard maneuvering unit to make his way toward the limp, white-suited figure. "All systems green. Three meters and closing. Looks like he's all tangled up in the remains of his tether. Even if he had another one of those instant-patches, I'm not sure he could have gotten to it, not the way they have him all tied up."

"Hurry, Scotty," Omega urged, glancing at the re-entry display. "We're running out of time fast. And we're getting damn close to atmospheric interface, and that means real soon, the air will be dense enough to maybe damage your suit, or even break the tether, especially moving at these speeds. I don't want to lose both of you."

"Got 'im, Pook," Chadwick replied, grappling the lifeless form and tethering it to his own suit with snap rings. "Initiating automatic tether retraction..." and the line connecting him to the *Phoenix* began reeling him in with his burden.

"All right; I'll adjust the Higgs field to make it easier to get him into the ship."

"The who-wha?"

"Umh, the artificial gravity. You've heard of the Higgs boson, right? Well, the scientists in the Pan-Galactic Coalition learned how to manipulate a Higgs bosonic field to generate artificial gravity, tractor beams, force fields, all sorts 'a cool an' useful shit."

"Oh. Copy that. Okay, I'm at the hatch. Ingressing now."

In moments, Chadwick was carrying the limp form of Omega's partner into the saucer's flight deck.

Without a word, Omega led Chadwick, bearing Echo's body, back into the *Phoenix*'s cabin. She pointed to a bunk, and Chadwick gently laid Echo down on it. He strapped the body down as Omega carefully removed the spacesuit helmet.

"Echo?" she ventured softly. "Ace, please...say something. Honey, it's Meg; PLEASE say something, sweetheart!"

No answer. Omega swallowed hard and paled.

"Pook?" Chadwick's voice was almost tender as he hesitantly got the Agent's attention. "I'll go set course back to the *Kitty Hawk*."

"Hm? Oh, right. Gotta get you back aboard, or it'll blow the Agency's cover wide open."

"...Yeah."

"Go ahead, then," Omega agreed. "Strictly speaking, you're not certified, but you're one of the two best pilots I know—knew—and you caught on fast enough to co-pilot us here. Besides, medical protocol says I have to administer a specific regimen of medications, mostly of pent-ox compound doses, for what it's worth at this point. And I won't skimp on this guy, no matter what—not now, not ever. You go on; I'll be forward in just a minute."

"Copy that."

* * *

"Fox, it's Lima," the assistant's voice came over the Director's intercom.

"What's up, Lima?" Fox wondered, looking up from his paperwork.

"We've got what appears to be a live, REAL image of the *Kitty Hawk* again. It looks intact now, and they're maneuvering for a retro fire and deorbit burn."

119

"Ah! Alpha One must have been successful," Fox said, pleased. "Hook me into the Agency air-to-ground, please."

"All over it, Fox."

* * *

Omega administered the pent-ox sequence—complete with peripheral galactic pharmaceuticals—per established Agency medical protocols, then waited; Echo showed no response. She choked back a sob, bit her lip nearly bloody in a desperate effort to maintain control, and headed for the flight deck.

Chadwick looked up as she entered, a wordless question on his face. She shook her head, and he sighed.

"I'm...really, really sorry, Pook," he murmured. "If that son of a bitch Dianus hadn't jumped the gun, your fiancé would still..."

"No," Omega replied, shaking her head again. "That exacerbated the situation, yeah, but..."

"What do you mean?"

"I dunno. I look at this whole thing and I think I musta screwed up from the get-go. I didn't mean for him to even find out, let alone come along. Then I got careless and punctured my own suit. I just..."

"Hush that. You did what you had to do, what you should've done, and he did, too. Don't shoulder the blame for an egotistical, too-well-connected space plane commander." He paused, then added, "Oh, and uh, there was an incoming comm for either you or...or him...earlier. I...didn't answer or acknowledge, because...well, because I didn't want to get you in WORSE trouble..."

Omega nodded, then reached for the momentary toggle beside the blinking green light.

"Might as well get this over with," she decided. "It really can't get any worse, anyway. Not as far as I'm concerned."

"Can't Houston hear it?"

"No," Omega explained. "It's a tight-beam, encrypted signal; only the receiver at which it's directed is gonna pick it up."

"Oh." Chadwick nodded, and she flipped the switch to continuous comm.

"Ground control, this is Omega, aboard *Phoenix*."

"There you are! Omega, this is Fox. I thought you'd want to know, we have the Teludal responsible for the damage to the *Kitty Hawk* in custody. How are repairs coming?"

"Wh-what?" Omega stammered, then corrected herself. "Uh, Ground Control, please repeat...?"

"It's all right, Omega," Fox said in a soft voice. "Echo sent me your files before you launched. Forensics verified your conclusions, and I sent Alpha Two to the Cape, to lead a retrieval team that included Alpha Four, and about a dozen standard field agents out of the Atlanta Office. We're waiting for your and Echo's final evidence, but we do think, at this point, that it was accidental; the adolescent admits to, ah, 'tinkering' when she got away from the tour group, but she didn't mean any harm. She's in the hands of the Juvie department in Atlanta now."

"So that explains it," Chadwick murmured. "You HAD to help, because..."

"Right," Omega confirmed. "It was definitely our jurisdiction. I just was expecting to have to explain when I got back, and hope I had enough evidence to prove it. Evidently Echo took care of that before coming to meet me at the *Phoenix*... which I didn't know he was gonna do, either."

"Right. And he did," Fox averred. "Was that your old friend Chadwick?"

"Affirm, Fox," Omega confirmed. "He's been, uh, helping out. This...it hasn't gone well, Fox. Not at all."

"Uh-oh. What do you mean?"

"We...we lost...we lost Echo."

"WHAT?!"

Omega opened her mouth to reply, but nothing would come out. Her face crumpled, and she had to fight to keep the tears in check. Chadwick leaned over to the mic.

"Ground Control, this is NASA astronaut Chadwick. Omega is...indisposed...at the moment. The damage was very bad and very...ragged, I guess is a good word. We nearly lost her to a suit breach, but Echo slapped a patch on it and hustled her into the cabin, and he and I got her helmet off, and she's doing okay...from that. So then I went out with him, and, well, same song, second verse, sorta, only he went flying off with the force—the commander of my craft jumping the gun on the engine test didn't help that at ALL, and you do NOT want to know my opinion on THAT—and a slow leak in his suit into the bargain, and evidently no more insta-patches. Plus, he was tangled in the remnants of his own tether, so he mighta had trouble reaching it, or applying it in time, even if he HAD another patch. His last words ordered Omega to finish the repair. Which we did, then we went after him, to...to bring him home..."

"Ai, HaShem. Oy vey. So the *Kitty Hawk* is repaired?"

"Yes sir, and safely en route home."

"Did you get him? Is Echo there in the cabin with you?"

"Yes, sir. Well, he's in the sleeping berths, aft."

"Omega, did you administer the pent-ox protocol?"

Omega opened her mouth in another effort to speak, but her voice refused to work, so she simply nodded again.

"She indicates she did, sir," Chadwick relayed. "She's...not really able to talk right now. She's trying, it's just not coming out."

"Right. I understand. Omega, tekhter, can you hear me?"

She nodded, then gestured at Chadwick, and pointed at the mic.

"She says yes, sir."

"Good. Get your friend Chadwick back to his ship—"

"No sir," Chadwick interrupted. "With all due respect, sir, Omega's already indicated I might be able to join your organization, and that's what I intend to do. I wanna work with this outfit; you have some serious spaceflight capability, and I wanna be part of it."

"All right, Chadwick. Are repairs complete? Is the space plane able to return safely? Wait, you said yes a bit ago..."

"Yes sir. We took care of all that before leaving to retrieve Echo. Per his orders."

"Then listen closely: you sacrificed yourself to perform the repair work. I'll have a team waiting at the landing site for the *Kitty Hawk*, as part of the ground crew, with new memories to that effect for the rest of your fellow crew members..."

"Um, okay, sir," Chadwick agreed, mildly confused at the orders. "I...don't get it, but if you say so."

"Don't worry, zun, I'll explain later. Just remember what I'm telling you, and everything will be okay. Omega, tekhter, I need you to return to your launch site as fast as you can. I'll have a medical team standing by; if Echo is only 'mostly dead,' we can still fix this."

Omega's head shot up, her eyes wide.

"You...you mean...uh, um, wilco, sir."

"You left from Chicago?"

"Yes sir."

"All right." The sound of rapid-fire typing could be heard in the background. "There. Emergency teams are on the way; Chicago flight control has just been notified of an emergency inbound, and to put you on top priority."

"C-copy that, Fox. Um." Omega struggled to dig up the proper protocol statements, but she was badly rattled and upset and they refused to come to the fore, so she simply asked, "Do you want me to bring Scotty with me?"

"Yes. And 'Scotty'?"

"Yes sir?"

"Am I correct in that you helped her rescue Echo by going EVA, and even sitting in the copilot's seat?"

"It's where I am right now, sir."

"Good. KEEP helping her. See that she gets back here safely; I know she's...distracted, right now, and may need assistance in staying focused. She's one of my top Agents, but even top Agents can become...distraught."

"Understood. Wilco, sir."

"Good. Don't worry about the *Kitty Hawk* now, Omega. You did your job and you done good, tekhter; we'll take it from here. Consider this an emergency deorbit. Head straight for the Chicago Station Spaceport as fast as you can safely go. I'll see the way is cleared. Don't worry about anything else."

"Yes sir," she managed to murmur.

"Now GO. Fox out."

"*Phoenix* out," Chadwick said.

Chapter 6

Omega's hopes revived with the notion that Echo might be revived, but she was still upset and spoke only when she needed to do so, to instruct Chadwick in the deorbit.

Chadwick, in turn, watched her carefully, accepting and obeying her commands, but also following Fox's orders—there was no doubt in his mind that Fox was right, and she was distracted. *Still,* he decided, *she's handling it okay, and I haven't seen her even close to making a mistake on this. Damn, she's good. She was always good, but now...wow. Whatever Echo taught her, he did a damn fine job. And she obviously took to it like the proverbial duck to water.* He shook his head, making sure she was glancing at the console on her other side before doing so. *I wish she'd been at the controls instead of Pete. I bet things would have gone a lot different. I only hope the* Kitty Hawk *gets on the ground safe, with him at the controls. Damn egotistical idiot. Shit. I hope he gets permanently grounded. The corps would be a helluva lot safer for it.*

So they powered down through the atmosphere toward the Chicago Station Spaceport—which, while affiliated with and run by the Chicago Office, was separate from it, outside the city proper to provide for more room—trying to get Echo to medical help before it was too late.

"I know we gotta haul ass, but we still have to watch out not to create a shock wave," Omega noted, adjusting the trajectory to bleed off velocity as they went deeper into the atmosphere. "The last thing we need is to wipe out half of Chicago, like that asteroid nearly did to Chelyabinsk in Russia a few years back."

"No shit," Chadwick agreed. "Just tell me what to do, Pook, and I'll see it gets done. I might not be Echo in terms of experience with this bird, but I still know what I'm doing. And I'm a quick learner."

"I know," she said, offering him a wan smile, "or you wouldn't be sitting where you're sitting. Okay, pay attention; we're coming up on the navigation beam..."

* * *

Zebra and Zarnix together headed up the full medical team waiting at the Chicago spaceport hangar. Chadwick stood aside, and Omega led the team back to the sleeping berth where Echo's body lay.

But to her shock, that body was...breathing.

"Only mostly dead, then," Zarnix observed, as Omega gave a strangled cry. "Let's go!"

* * *

Within moments, the medical team had their patient— plus two—aboard an emergency medical maglev transport to Headquarters. A warp passage opened directly from the medical transport gate to the emergency section of Medical. In the waiting room there, Fox awaited Omega and her new recruit.

"Omega, welcome home, tekhter," the Director murmured, placing a light, sympathetic hand on her shoulder. "Don't worry, meyn kind; Echo will be fine. You, and the medical team, got to him in time. So. Is this your old friend from NASA days? Our newest agent?"

"Yes," Omega responded, monosyllabic. He turned to Chadwick, offering that same hand in greeting.

"Good. Welcome to Division One Headquarters, Chi," Fox added. "I'm Director Fox; I run the place. Sort of."

"I-wha?" Chadwick began, blinking, as he accepted Fox's hand and shook. "Chi?"

"Your new code name," Fox said with a slight smile. "Did Omega explain about Earth not being ready to know...?"

"About the galactic civilization? Yeah," the newly-minted Chi confirmed. "Oh, okay. Now I get it. I'm not Scotty any more, I'm Chi. Short for...Chadwick?"

"Exactly, zun. Tell me how you want to pronounce it— 'kai' or 'chai,' or hell, even 'key,' if you prefer an Oriental take on things, though it's spelled differently, I think—and I'll see it gets into the system that way."

"Um, what do I call YOU, sir?"

"Just Fox will do. Director Fox in formal situations, but this isn't one of those. So...just Fox."

"Okay, Fox. I think I'll go with the more Greek pronunciation of 'kai,' then," the new agent decided.

"Consider it done, Chi. Omega, meyn kind, I know you want to wait on word from Echo," Fox said, laying that same light hand on the female Agent's shoulder once more, and offering a gentle, fatherly pat. "I'll take Chi under my wing and brief him, then have Lima and Bravo put him through induction. Don't worry about another thing; sit here and try to relax, and consider that the rest of us are tag-teaming you, all right?"

"Okay, Fox; thanks," Omega murmured, staring at the door through which the medical team had vanished with her beloved partner. "Um...is Dihl here?"

"Not yet. But she's on her way from the Ranch, as fast as she can," Fox noted. "I sent a special maglev to fetch her from Dallas, and it's running at emergency speeds—and I had Joe get her to the Dallas Office, to that maglev, in a designated airskimmer that's been modded to my personal specs, and moves like a bat out of hell...if not QUITE as fast as the *Schmaltzblitz*. She'll be here inside half an hour, maybe only a quarter-hour; I'm not entirely sure when the train departed. Tell her to go straight through and report to Zebra when she arrives. Omega, please, for Echo's sake, try to sit down in the waiting room and be patient, tekhter. Or as patient as you can be, in the circumstances, I guess. I know you're eighteen dozen varieties of upset, and I don't blame you, but trust me, it isn't going to do him any good if you wear yourself out, pacing or what-not. Try to relax, as much as you can. Chi, come with me, zun. Let's get you processed in."

Omega slid into the nearest chair, never taking her eyes off the door into the emergency medlab, as Fox slipped out with Chi.

* * *

Some five minutes after Fox left with the former Scott Chadwick, Omega felt a gentle touch on her shoulder.

"My dear girl," Dihl's voice murmured in her ear. "I have finally arrived. Is he here?"

"He's in there." Omega gestured at the door into the emergency suite. "Fox said for you to go straight on through. Zebra will be waiting for you. Or, well, she'll be working on Echo, but she knows you're coming."

"Do you want me to come back out and tell you how matters are going, once I check on things? Before I join in on working on him, I mean."

"No," Omega decided, glancing at the elegant Apache woman with the black braid, who looked much younger than her years, thanks to the very same medical capabilities that they hoped would bring Echo back to them. "Just set to on him, and get him all patched up, as fast as you can. I-I thought I'd lost him, Dihl," she added, biting her lip. "I thought...I..."

"Hush now," Dihl said, hugging the younger woman, the woman who was about to become her daughter-in-law; she was Echo's birth mother, a highly skilled nurse recently recruited to the Agency to help flesh out the medlab staff, and had become very fond of her son's partner in the months since her recruitment. "All will be well, shich'ee'ké; try to relax."

"Shi-shich...what?" Omega tried, glancing at Echo's mother. "I've never heard that word before. Apache, right?"

"Yes," Dihl said with a smile. "Echo told me a while back that you had rather adopted me as a mother-figure—much to his AND my delight, let me add—and as you will be my daughter-in-law, hopefully soon, I thought perhaps I would call you 'daughter' as a mark of my affection. If you prefer, I can call you 'shich'ee'ké-ŏ,' my daughter-in-law, which you are, or will be; but personally, I prefer 'daughter.'"

"I think I do, too," Omega replied, offering a wobbly smile, then flung her arms around the other woman. "Oh, Dihl!"

"Hush, hush," Dihl murmured, hugging Omega again. "You truly thought he was dead, then?"

"Yes!" she sobbed, burying her face in the other woman's shoulder. "And I didn't know, I mean, I couldn't...didn't...how could I ever...? What was I gonna...? Without him, I..."

"Shh, hush, child, hush, it is all right now," Dihl whispered, cradling the distraught younger woman. "You retrieved him, you followed the emergency medical protocols, and it revived him. All will be well now."

"Well, it won't be, if I keep you any longer, 'cause Zebra will go ballistic," Omega said, pushing back and trying to laugh as she wiped the tears from her cheeks. "Get on in there and help 'em get him back to me."

"'All over it,' as you and my son like to say," Dihl said with another smile. She patted Omega's shoulder, tilted her head and surveyed Omega to ascertain that the Agent would be all right, then disappeared through the door.

Omega scrubbed the remaining tearstains from her cheeks with her hands, then settled back in her seat, folded her arms, and tried to be patient...as 'Abba Fox' had told her.

* * *

As soon as the *Kitty Hawk* touched down on a runway on the Rogers Dry Lake bed inside Edwards Air Force Base—with Hollifield in the pilot's seat, Vancel beside him; the remaining crew had ganged up on Dianus and informed him that he WOULD be sitting in the back seat, or ride home forcibly strapped into a sleeping berth—the ground crew came out in full MOPP gear and swept the spacecraft. Its orbital maneuvering system used the standard NASA fuel for such, monomethyl hydrazine, a chemical that was hypergolic, meaning it required no igniter, merely mixing with its oxidizer, usually dinitrogen tetroxide...which had been why it was so fortunate that the young Teludal's device had NOT ruptured both tanks. Unfortunately, all hydrazines were extremely toxic, and the crew was not allowed outside their craft until the 'all clear' was given.

This sweep took some twenty minutes, during which time Dianus fumed in his rear seat; the first thing he intended to do was to report the crew for mutiny. The second thing he intended to do was to report the strange spacecraft and its crew that had shown up to rescue them. *And 'report it' far and wide, if I can glom some media,* he decided, resentful. *So as soon as I get outta this damn tin can with wings, I'm lookin' for a press credential.*

But when the crew exited the hatch and came down the stairs, they were surprised to be immediately whisked off to a waiting van.

"We want to make sure you're all right after your ordeal," one of the ground crew members said, "so we're taking you for physical examinations and psych evaluations. Stress and all, you know."

As soon as all four remaining crew members got into the van, the door closed. The driver—who was wearing wraparound, goggle-style sunglasses; they were in the desert in

California, after all—released the brake and headed toward the nearest building...which was still some distance away. This was a dry lake bed, chosen for an emergency landing site because it had plenty of room. Abruptly the man in the passenger seat, who was also wearing sunglasses, turned around and held up a cell phone.

"Smile," he said...

...And a multicolored, strobing, holographic flash went off.

All four crew members froze, eyes wide and glazed.

"You got the scenario that Fox wanted programmed in, right?" the driver asked his partner.

"Yup," the other man said, tucking his brain bleacher back in his inner pocket. "The rupture wasn't quite as bad as they were afraid of, and Chadwick was able to patch the hole and salvage enough of the fuel in the tank to get 'em safely home, but he bit it in the process—suit breach, and they couldn't reach him to retrieve him. And now that's what's in their heads, instead of anything to do with Alpha One...who never existed, as far as they're concerned."

"But wouldn't there have been another crew member on EVA with him?"

"Evidently not. I mean, yeah, there shoulda been, but given that, in reality, none of their crew backed up Alpha One EXCEPT Chadwick, hey." He shrugged. "And that was with Chadwick overriding his commander every step of the way, it sounds like. So it wasn't like anybody else was really given a chance, ya know? Strictly speaking, with Alpha One on EVA and Chadwick essentially functioning as the IVA crew member, they had the matter taken care of per regs, though. And when Omega ingressed and Chadwick egressed, they just swapped roles. Still, you'd think, wouldn't ya? But you'd be dead wrong."

"You're kidding. The commander actually ordered 'em NOT to help save their craft?"

"According to what Fox fed me from Chadwick's debrief, yeah. How the hell he thought they were gettin' home otherwise, I got no clue."

"Damn. Speaking of which: what about the commander's attitude?" Agent Driver asked. "And the reaction of the rest of the crew to him?"

"THAT...we didn't touch," Agent Brain Bleacher noted with a smirk. "Fox said it was up to the NASA guys to work THAT shit out."

* * *

Nearly two hours later, Zebra came out with Dihl. Omega jumped to her feet.

"There you are," the assistant chief of Medical addressed Omega. "Sit, sit. I knew you'd still be out here, waiting patiently."

"I dunno about being patient, but I'm here," Omega replied, offering a wan smile at Dihl, who winked at her rather mischievously. The Alpha Line Agent sank back into her chair. "Not sure where else I'd be, really. What's the word?"

"He's alive but not yet awake; still, apparently everything's in good working order," Zebra noted. "There's some concern about a few things to do with oxygen deprivation, so Zarnix and I decided to 'dunk him,' as Whiskey has been terming it of late—we threw him in a regen bath, and we're gonna leave him there for about a Division day, day and a half, mostly just to get his tissue oxygenation up to levels we're happier with, 'cause it's really good for stuff like that—but we don't see any problems, offhand."

"Oh, thank You, God," Omega breathed, closing her eyes and slumping in the chair in relief.

"Yes, and we fully expected that you were still sitting out here, all by yourself, no food, no water, no rest, tense as a drum skin," Dihl noted.

"And it looks like we nailed it on the drum head," Zebra added.

"Um, well, I, uh," Omega began, looking sheepish.

"Uh-huh," Zebra replied, fixing Omega with a glare—benign, but stern for all that. "On that note, Dihl, could you please escort Omega either home, or back to the Alpha Line Room, whichever one she needs to be at, depending on her shift schedule...? Then come back here." The physician and the medtech folded their arms and waited for Omega's answer, entirely prepared to issue a medical countermand if it were needed.

Omega glanced at her wrist chronometer, then did a double-take.

"That looks like it should be home," Dihl observed.

"Yup," Zebra agreed.

"Well, yeah, but if you'll let me swing by the Alpha Line Room long enough to do a bare-bones report for Fox, and see about Scotty-uh, Chi, he is now, I swear I'll go home in about ten, maybe fifteen, minutes," Omega tried. "I didn't realize it was so late. But I need to at least start a debrief kinda thing."

"You were zoned out, sitting here waiting, weren't you?" Zebra wondered. "Mentally reliving the whole big pile o' shit. Moment by moment."

"Uh...yeah."

"You know I'll notify Zz'r'p to discuss this one with you at your next counseling session, right?"

"That's fine," Omega agreed. "I kinda figured it would come out with him anyhow. Right now, I mostly just want to give Fox a little more info, and see how far along Chi's induction is coming. And then I'll go home and try to rest a little." She eyed the two older women. "You'll notify me if anything happens, right?"

"You're his designated 'voice' if something happens, honey," Zebra reminded her.

"Yeah, but Dihl is his MOM," Omega pointed out. "She'd do just as well for that as I would, and she'll be right here."

"No, she won't...well, sorta," Zebra noted. "I plan on seeing her off to one of the little rooms with cots we keep for on-shift staff downtime, as soon as she gets back from escorting you to see Fox...who I'm going to call and tell you're coming, so he can see you get home from that debrief with him." Dihl nodded affirmation of Zebra's statement. "But Dihl was just coming off duty at the Ranch when Fox notified her to haul ass up here on accounta Echo," Zebra added.

"Oh." Omega bit her lip.

"Anyway," Zebra continued, "his mom Dihl may be, but his legal representative when he's out of commission, she's not. That's you, and only you, Meg, unless and until Echo says otherwise."

"Well, but it's only 'cause he hasn't thought about it yet,"

Omega pointed out.

"That's as may be. The legalities still say YOU are his designated representative, kiddo."

"And that is fine by me," Dihl added. "Omega has had the benefit of knowing him as an adult for far longer, and she also has much greater knowledge of the Agency system. Never mind becoming his wife. All is as it should be, and it does not offend me."

"I swear I'll call you, honey, trust me," Zebra added. "Now git."

With a sigh, Omega rose and turned for the exit. Dihl dropped in beside Omega and they headed in the general direction of the Core.

* * *

"There you are," Fox said, waiting in the Alpha Line Room as Dihl escorted Omega through the door. "No, don't you even sit down at the desk, tekhter. Zebra called and gave me a heads-up you were en route and why, but I think there's no need for a debrief, now. I already had all the pertinent details from Chi, including how his last-minute-assignment, string-pulling, rich-politician-father commander was part of the problem—and our landing team is handling some of that right now, by the way—and we got Chi halfway through processing into the organization before he himself started showing signs of wear and tear, likely from all the spacewalks the three of you did, and I sent him off to temporary quarters for some rest while we get his own things brought in from Houston. So there's your update on Chi—I dropped him off at the TDY billets half an hour ago, and I expect he's already crashed hard, by now—and any formal after-action reports can wait until in the morning." Fox extracted his cell phone and hit a button. "There we go. Alpha Two got back from the Cape a bit ago—they dropped the delinquent Teludal kid off at the Atlanta Office to be, ah, handled, and hopefully disciplined and straightened out; among other things, I instructed Office chief Frank to make sure it was emphasized to her NOT TO TOUCH. Anyway, Romeo and India are now en route here to escort you home; they ought to arrive in just a few minutes. And I will be going to fetch Zebra right after that, in order to take her home and see that SHE is properly fed and rested; Zarnix was just coming on duty when the shit hit the fan, so he should be good for some hours yet, but she was about to go off duty, and needs some sleep, herself. Dihl, thank you, *meyn khaverte*, and you may return to the medlab to get some rest as well."

"Thank you, Fox," Dihl murmured, then slipped out, even as India and Romeo entered.

"We're here, boss-man," Romeo declared. "Y' want us t' see th' pretty lady home, right? Look after 'er, see she gets there okay, gets fed an' junk?"

"Yes, zun, if you please."

"Consider it done, Fox," India averred. "C'mon, Meg, let's go, girlfriend."

With a tired, discouraged sigh, Omega followed them toward the elevator banks.

* * *

"...I won't be able to sleep, guys," Omega murmured, once they had her back in her quarters. Romeo and India had commandeered her kitchen; Romeo was heating up a can of stew— beefing up the flavor with Echo's trick of adding some red wine and a few herbs—while India made a small, fresh salad, the Alpha Line medic having insisted Omega eat properly after such a strenuous mission, before going straight to bed. To that end, and with India's insistence, Omega was already ready for bed and attired in pajamas, with her favorite black silk robe over all. "What with knowing Echo isn't next door, and the back door being all dark? After everything that happened, and the 'video' of events playing over and over in my head? Sleep? No. I just won't."

"Then I'll dig out my medikit and give you something to help that sitch, Meg," India declared. "But you ARE going to eat, and then you ARE going to bed and getting some sleep. One way or another. I promise you that."

"Yeah, you were bad 'nuff last Christmas, when Echo got shot," Romeo reminded. "Leastways 'e made it almost a whole 'nother year b'fore nearly doin' himself in again."

"Not counting crashing the *Trojan Horse* on the protoplanet this past spring," Omega recalled.

"Ooo, yeah, I forgot 'bout that," Romeo remembered. "An'

'at nearly got BOTH o' ya! You two need ta ease up jus' a smidge, pretty lady, don't you WILL get y'rselves killed. An' I kin think o' several folks b'sides me, who wouldn't be too happy 'bout that. Never mind you two gettin' a chance t' grow old t'gether."

"What he said," India agreed. "Okay, the salad's ready—saturated with balsamic vinaigrette the way you like it, Meg. How far off is the stew, Romeo?"

"Jus' dishin' it up in a bowl now," he reported. "I'mma slice a big hunk o' cheddar, add a piece o' buttered Texas toast, an' bring it t' th' table. Go siddown at th' table, pretty lady. Me 'n India'll grab a couple brews outta your fridge an' join ya, so's you're not eatin' alone, at least."

A grateful Omega sighed, immeasurably tired and anxious, and did as she was told.

* * *

India did indeed give her something rather potent to help her sleep, and Omega woke the next morning feeling somewhat better than she had when she went to bed. Rather than bothering to prepare breakfast just for herself, however, she simply grabbed one of the Agency's special meal replacement bars on her way out the door. Given that it was intended for full nutrition on the go, came in several flavors, and several of those flavors resembled a commercial breakfast bar, she decided it made a reasonably palatable breakfast, all things considered. And it was decently filling.

A quick call to the medlab first thing upon awakening ascertained that there was no need for her to go down there just yet; Echo was still in the regeneration pod and would remain so most of that day...though he was coming along well enough that there was no longer a consideration of keeping him in the pod until the following morning. More, his mother—after a short sleep herself; she was on normal 24-hour days at the Ranch, and Zarnix had spent most of his remaining shift in the regen room—had been sitting with him after she awoke, so Echo would not feel isolated in the pod, in the unlikely chance he should awaken.

Therefore Omega headed for the Alpha Line Room—as assistant department chief, with Echo in the medlab, she was run-

134

ning the department. *So, even though I really wanna be there with him,* she thought, *I have certain obligations. And he'd want me to take care of 'em. An' I'm not gonna let him down.*

* * *

In the Alpha Line Room, Omega found Fox waiting for her with Chi; the latter was now fully attired in the Suit of a Division One agent.

"Hey there!" Chi exclaimed as soon as she came through the door. "You look like you feel better!"

"A little, yeah," Omega admitted with a slight smile. "I got a good, solid night's sleep thanks to India's meds, and now it's a waiting game for Echo to get out of the medlab."

"Excellent, tekhter," Fox declared. "Very, VERY good! And I had the rest of the story from Chi this morning, after HE got a good night's sleep. I gather that NASA's EVA suits are even harder to work inside than ours are."

"Oh yeah," Omega averred. "Speaking as somebody who's dealt with both, no doubt—NASA's are definitely harder to work in. The Agency suits have more structure, and are partly compression suits, so they aren't so much like trying to operate inside a giant, human-shaped balloon."

"Lotsa that," Chi agreed. "It'll plain wear you out. It's why there are regs limiting EVA duration for NASA, unless it's just a flat-out emergency...which this was, I guess."

"Right," Omega said. "In spades. Damn. Um, Fox, I should have downloaded all of the video and data an' junk from the *Phoenix*, but what with the emergency response on Echo..."

"Don't worry, meyn khaverte," Fox held up a forestalling hand, "I thought about that, and had Hangar Maintenance take care of it for you. I've already seen all of it, AND I sent it off to Forensics to analyze and add to the material you and Echo provided before departure." He paused. "May I ask a question?"

"Sure," Omega said, shrugging.

"Why did you not send it to me directly? Why did Echo do it?"

Omega sighed, then sat in her desk chair, slumping; she was physically rested, but the topic of discussion revived a certain mental tiredness that she was finding it hard to overcome, all things considered.

"Because I got one good look at the belly of the bird, combined with the orbital decay curve, and I didn't think I had time," Omega confessed. "I wasn't sure what it would take to convince you that I wasn't just...I dunno, making it up or something, to help out Scotty and the crew. I know you don't play favorites; I just wasn't sure I had enough evidence to prove it to you yet. But I figured I needed to get on orbit as fast as I could and hope I could get the repairs made before they got too low..."

"And Echo convinced you differently?"

"No. Echo wasn't even awake yet when I left my quarters. I guess he figured out something was up, checked my laptop, and saw the same things I did...especially since I'd used my stylus to circle the pertinent sections of the imagery."

"Ah. So then he fired it to me, grabbed his own gear, and hightailed it after you."

"Apparently so. I...hate that," Omega admitted. "I was trying so hard not to get him into trouble. I figured I could probably convince you of the jurisdiction after I got back, with all the evidence I already had, let alone what we saw during the repair work, but I didn't want to risk his reputation after that whole mess with Adita's Coup."

"Right," Fox said, nodding. "I understand now. And it was well thought and very considerate, meyn kind, but you know Echo better than that."

"Well, if it had taken him about five minutes longer to figure it all out and get there, it wouldn't have mattered," she pointed out. "I'd have been on ascent already."

"Yeah, but then we'd have ALL been dead, EXCEPT Echo," Chi noted. "Because when your suit got breached, if he hadn't been there with that cool patch, you'd have died. And we wouldn't have been able to fix that mess on our own, and it was YOU who showed me how to fly that fancy spacecraft of yours, when we went to grab Echo..."

"Ooo," Fox said, alarmed. "Suit breach?! Oh! I remember Chi, here, saying something about that when you were still on orbit! Are you all right, tekhter?"

"Yeah," Omega confirmed. "Last night, when India and Romeo were feeding me and getting me ready to go to bed, I told her what happened, and made sure she gave me a quick once-over for that very thing. I'm okay. Echo got the breach patched before the pressure in the suit got too low to put me at risk."

"Ah, good, then. I brought Chi along to the Alpha Line Room to meet you because, one, I thought you'd like to see him in 'uniform,' as it were."

"Yeah, and he looks good in the Suit!"

"Aw," a grinning Chi said, flushing slightly. "It's one a' those that's cut to look good on just about everybody, I think."

"Well, it is, but she is still right, zun. And two, while Chi has briefed me on everything that happened, there's still an after-action report that needs writing, and while he doesn't know our format yet, you do, Omega, and the two of you can write it up—that way, it can be one report for you, Echo, and Chi, and have done. Easier for you to do, and easier for me to read! And three, Chi is interested in Alpha Line. He'll need a probationary period, and he's currently in training, assigned under Crutch's standard field agents, but once he's up to speed, he wants to take the Alpha Line qual testing."

"Okay," Omega said, perking up. "I'd lay money he'd pass, no problems. And that'll be fun, having an old friend in the department. Scot-er, Chi, you know I'm the assistant department chief, right?"

"Yeah, but that won't cause a problem, Poo-um, Omega," Chi averred. "You showed your abilities to me during that whole repair job an' all." He grinned. "You guys had some serious cool, assurance, and general 'right stuff' goin' on through all that. Even...well, I get that you were upset when you thought Echo had died, 'cause you love him, but even then, you never lost it. I'd follow your lead anyplace, and Echo too. An' you know me, Pook—I'm not gonna say a thing like that if I don't mean it."

"I know," Omega said, nodding.

"Pook?" Fox wondered. Chi and Omega both smeared hands down their faces.

"It's an old nickname he had for me, back when I was still in the astronaut corps," Omega tried.

"Ah. Back when you were still seeing each other?"

"Yeah," Chi admitted. "But then it stuck, and I've called her that ever since. It doesn't have a, an 'intimate' connotation or anything."

"I suppose that's acceptable, given Echo calls her 'Meg' and she calls him 'Ace' half the time," Fox decided. "But Chi... it IS a 'cutesy' name. I don't want it interfering with Omega's reputation or discipline over the department."

"No sir. I'm already trying to break myself of the habit," he admitted. "I suspect it kinda embarrassed her in front of Echo; I think she'd forgot about it, and I wasn't thinking, and it slipped out, during their EVA. He carried her kinda high over it, so I'm working hard to stop it." Chi offered an apologetic glance at Omega. "And then here I go and let it slip in front of the Director. I'm sorry, Meg."

"No big deal," Omega said with a slight smile. "I'll just beat the crap outta you, the next time you say it."

"You can try," Chi shot back with a grin.

"Trust me," Omega noted, raising an eyebrow. "I am NOT the woman you remember, in terms of martial skills."

"Believe her," Fox added, hiding a smirk. "She came to us with a black belt. We've...improved...on that."

"Oh," Chi said, sobering. "And you were never a slouch at that, as it was. Um. Duly chastened, ma'am."

"That's better. Let's see about this joint report, then."

"This is very good," Fox declared. "I'll leave you two at it."

"Thank you, sir," Chi said.

"Yeah, thanks, Fox," Omega echoed.

The Director departed, and Chi dragged up a visitor chair, sitting next to Omega as she booted her computer and opened the shift report form.

* * *

By the time they finished the report, the various members of Alpha Line were filtering in for the morning departmental meeting. Several wall panels flashed, and Omega grabbed a remote from the credenza along the back wall, beneath the giant Division One and Alpha Line logos. She pointed, clicked a few buttons, and the wall panels lit as video screens, each depicting branches of Alpha Line assigned to different Offices.

"Whoa," Chi murmured, eyes widening. "Big department."

"It is now," Omega noted. "When I first came aboard, it was just Echo an' me. We've worked hard at growing it." She gestured at the wall screens. "We only just got done setting up branches of the department at the bigger Offices around the planet."

"Um, then I guess I should...go?" Chi wondered.

"Nah, we don't have anything classified on the agenda," Omega said. "If you're really curious about the department, you can stay. Grab one of the desk chairs over here," she pointed to an empty college-classroom-type desk in the front right corner, "and listen in. You...I gotta tell 'em about...about what just happened, see...and I might...need your help, anyway."

"Oh. Okay." Chi took the indicated seat as Omega stood and moved to the front of the room, standing just in front of, and between, her desk and Echo's.

"Test one two, test one two," she said, turning to the wall screens. "How do you read?"

Variants on, "We read you loud and clear," came back from all the Offices represented, in sequence.

"Good. I read each of you five by five also. Let's get started, y'all. First off, I have someone I want to introduce to you." She gestured at Chi, who stood and turned, so that the screens and the rest of the room could see him. "This is Agent Chi. He's brand-new to the Agency, but he's an old friend of mine, just recruited from NASA. He's just starting his probationary period, training with Crutch and the Field department, but he's interested in Alpha Line, so keep it unclassified, y'all. Say hi, everybody."

A general chorus of "Hi, Chi!" came back, and Chi grinned and waved.

"Hey, guys," he answered. "Good to be here, and I hope this isn't the only Alpha Line departmental meeting I attend!"

General laughter, a smattering of applause, and murmured welcomes greeted this comment, then Omega raised her hands for silence.

"Okay, guys, I did that first because I might need his help in this next bit," she noted. "You'll notice that Echo isn't up here, and if you look around, Alpha Two isn't here either. And

Alpha Two ran the meeting yesterday, 'cause Alpha One was away." Omega drew a deep breath. "That's because we were off rescuing the space plane. Which is why Sc-uh, Chi is here now." She threw him an apologetic glance at the nigh-slip, and he subtly waved a dismissing hand. "So, um, that rescue didn't really go that well...I mean, it did, they got home safe, but..."

* * *

"...So that's pretty much what happened," Chi finished the explanation, while a pale Omega sat on the edge of her desk, silent. "It was a damn hard job, but those two," he indicated Omega and by extension Echo, "did a helluva job."

"When do they not?" Monkey murmured. "But Echo's gonna be okay, right?"

"Near as I was able to understand, from what info Fox updated me on this morning," Chi answered, only after Omega opened her mouth to speak, but nothing came out. "Meg...well, she's pretty upset, as you can imagine..."

Omega swallowed, then nodded.

"Hey man, thanks for helping 'em get back safe," Golf said, gruff. "Sounds like you're gonna make a good addition to the team, once you get done with your initial training."

"Speaking of which," came a voice from the door, followed by a light knock.

A relatively short, older female agent stood there. The nigh-legendary Crutch only stood an inch or two over five feet, with eyeglasses and grizzled gray hair in an attractive—and easily-and quickly-styled—pixie cut. Her build was lean and wiry, notable even through the Suit. Yet her entire attitude and demeanor gave the impression of someone much larger, a force to be reckoned with—and she could be, when she chose. Or when she had to be. She was not considered one of the Originals because she had not been at the First Contact, but as a young woman, she had been one of the active members of the 'pre-Agency' prior to the First Contact, so she had been around the Agency essentially since well before its official inception. Her code name, like Echo's, derived from the affectionate nickname her colleagues had given her—based loosely, Omega had it to understand, on her real name, though no one but Crutch knew what it was any more; she refused a 'standard' code name based on a phonetic alphabet or similar. But she had once told the Alpha Line assistant chief, originally the code name had been a pun, because she had been the 'crutch' on which many of the other field agents leaned, when the going got tough. And given what she knew of the older woman's exploits, Omega readily believed it. Fox had once noted that entire books could be written about Crutch's adventures alone.

"Forgive me for the interruption, Omega," Crutch noted then, with a courteous nod, which was accompanied by a friendly smile. "Fox told me where I might find my newest recruit, and the door was open..."

"That's fine, Crutch," Omega said, trying to return the smile, but it was strained...as was her voice. "We weren't going over any classified information, so the door stayed open. Sometimes Fox wants to come over and listen in."

"Do I need to go?" Chi wondered, glancing between Omega and Crutch.

"Only when Meg is done with you," Crutch noted. "It sounded to me like you were making yourself useful for your old friend, there. I do have some evaluation and training for you, but it can wait. Meg, dear, are YOU all right?"

Omega rubbed her hand across her forehead, then nodded.

"Yeah, I think so, Crutch," she decided. "I just got a damn bad scare yesterday, that's all."

"Several, all things considered," Chi pointed out.

"I can imagine," the older female agreed. "Is there anything I can do to help out?"

"I don't think so, but thanks. Do the best job you've ever done training THIS guy," Omega said, nudging Chi's shoulder, "'cause I think we're gonna draft him, if it's all right with you."

"That was pretty much what Fox told me going in," Crutch informed her, "so I'm tackling his training personally, with an Alpha Line slot in mind. If he changes his mind, or doesn't make the cut on the testing, I'll have a damn fine field agent. If he makes Alpha Line...which he probably will, from what I've already seen...then you and Echo will have a damn fine field Agent. Either way, the Agency gets a damn fine field agent."

The two women chuckled, but there was a slightly grim sound to it; the job of field agent could be very tough and very dangerous, whether 'standard' or Alpha Line, and they both knew it.

"I think I'm done with him for now," Omega decided. "I'll be glad when the very thought of what happened doesn't make me choke, though. Not having a working voice is a pain in the ass, especially when you're tryin' to run a departmental meeting. Thanks for the loan of him, and Chi, thanks for the help with the explanations."

"Not a problem, Poo-um, Omega," Chi threw in an emergency midcourse correction, flushing slightly; Omega rolled her eyes.

Then Chi accompanied Crutch out of the room, as Omega took individual status reports from the teams.

* * *

Omega sat by Echo's bedside in his hospital room, waiting patiently for him to awaken after decanting, later that afternoon. When he finally began to stir, she hit the button on the bedside, notifying Zebra; within moments, the 'family' had arrived—Zebra, Fox, Dihl, Romeo, and India. Zarnix, also in attendance, hovered just outside the door, prepared to offer assistance should something go wrong. Zebra and Dihl moved to the bedside, checking their patient's status and vital signs, then standing by to provide support. The others clustered around the room, either sitting in visitor chairs or leaning against the wall, as the tall, lean form in the black medical jumpsuit began to shift about in the bed.

"Mmh...where am I...?" he murmured, as he stretched and opened bleary eyes.

"You're in the medlab, honey," Zebra noted, leaning over him and feeling for a carotid pulse. "Omega and her friend rescued you and we got you straight here. Between us, we put you through all the proper protocols to bring you back from 'mostly dead' to normal, and here you are. Dihl and Meg between them have been watching over you, pretty much ever since, one way or another." She nodded at Omega, still sitting in the chair next to the bed.

Echo turned his gaze on his partner. He blinked several times.

"Who are you?" he wondered. "And...what's my name...?"

The room erupted.

Chapter 7

"...And more than likely, this was brought on by being 'mostly dead' a smidge too long," Zarnix decided, as he and Echo's 'family' discussed the situation in a nearby conference room, while Whiskey saw to settling Echo, who had been mildly perturbed by the crowd of—what seemed to him—strangers in the room, never mind the realization that he didn't remember his own self. "It's a simple case of temporary amnesia, and should be taken care of by gradually reintroducing him to his life, friends and family, until we hit one or more memory 'triggers,' and then it will all come back."

"But he didn't recognize Omega," Fox pointed out, casting a worried glance at a pale Omega, who, after an initial dismayed cry upon Echo's reaction, had said nothing. "Hell, he didn't even recognize his own mother. Those two, right there, should have been all the trigger he needed, I'd have thought."

"Admittedly that is disturbing, but it is all part and parcel of his condition," Zarnix averred. "What I would recommend is providing him with as much in the way of files, video, and such like from his life in the Agency as you can legitimately get to him, Fox."

"I can do that," Fox decided. "I think we should start by getting him re-familiarized with his current partner and his mother, don't you? Then, if we need to, we can provide records on the rest of his 'family,' as it were—me, Zebra, and Alpha Two. Then add in others from his less-recent past, like X-ray, Oboe, Pulgey, and the like. Is everyone okay with that?"

Nods went around the room.

"And Zarnix and I would concur on it, medically-speaking," Zebra confirmed, after a quick glance at the chief of staff. "Because you're right—those are the two people he's most emotionally attached to, and so that's most likely to trigger the memories. But make sure he's got information on his own history, too. You never know what memory will trigger the cascade."

"All right," Fox said, pulling his ever-present electronic tablet from a warp pocket and activating it. He tapped several places on the screen, typed something, then swiped across it. "There. That just sent the orders to the Boys, and they'll have Echo's and Omega's personnel files down here post-haste, with Dihl's likely right behind." He replaced the tablet in his pocket, then laid a compassionate hand on Omega's shoulder, noting its tenseness. "Hang in there, tekhter. We'll rectify this yet."

"Mmm," was all she replied.

But he noticed her shoulders relaxed, just a little bit.

* * *

"...So this file is on my partner?" Echo asked, accepting a tablet from Lima as he sat in his hospital bed in the medlab. "And she and I are engaged to get married?"

"That's right, Echo," Lima said with a smile. "It's pretty much everything about her except her detailed medical records. She's a really cool lady."

"Where did she go?" Echo wondered. "After I woke up, everybody kinda...left..."

"They were thrown off by your amnesia," Lima explained. "And you were understandably agitated, so the medics cleared 'em out so they could get you settled and start treating you. From what I gathered from Director Fox, Omega was pretty upset by it, more so than anybody else, and that's including your mom, who was the nurse."

"Oh..." Echo murmured, thoughtful. "And you're going to bring me her files next, right? My mom's? And my own?"

"Yup," Lima said with a smile. "But I'll be surprised if that right there," he nodded at the tablet, indicating Omega's personnel files, "doesn't bring everything back for you. You two are the most badass-est Agents in the Division, maybe the whole damn galaxy, and from what I've gathered, crazy about each other. You sure make the top partnership in the whole damn place, no doubt! Oh wait," Lima broke off. "Fox did explain about the Agency, and the Galactic Coalition, and all?"

"Yes, he did," Echo confirmed. "I...well, I'm still trying to take it all in. It sounds pretty cock-eyed on the face of it, after all."

"Roger that," Lima said with a grin. "I'm assuming, since

you can talk just fine, that you can read okay, too, or was that affected by this 'shtik drek,' as Fox put it?"

"No, I haven't had any problems reading shit. That doctor dude said it was one of the biggest indications they have that I've just got a simple form of amnesia." Echo huffed in impatience. "I hope he's right, and it all snaps back soon. This not knowing shit is getting old, fast."

"Good, and I bet it is. Well, let me get outta here so you can have at it. Yell when you're done—or, well, hit the red confirmation button that'll come up when you finish, and I'll have the files on the tablet updated with your and Dihl's records, then you can choose which one you wanna read next."

"All right," Echo agreed, and Lima headed out.

Echo settled down to read.

* * *

Echo spent the next hour or so perusing the files on Omega. The deeper he got into them, the more he frowned in consideration.

"Waitaminit," he murmured, brows drawing together. "She did WHAT, exactly...? Whoa."

Finally he finished the files on Omega and leaned back, into the pillows, where he stared at the ceiling for long moments, pondering. After several minutes, he shook his head, tapped the red 'button' that had popped up on the tablet's screen, then studied the menu that appeared for a moment before making a selection.

Seconds later, a new file had downloaded, marked DIHL in large block letters.

He opened it and began reading.

* * *

When he was finished with Dihl's file less than an hour later, he hit the red 'button' again, as Zebra came in to check on his vital signs. Echo showed no evidence of interest in or recognition of the assistant chief of staff, so she slipped back out after recording his vitals, and headed down to the conference room, where the others still waited.

"So far, no joy," Zebra sighed. "He's reading right along, at some considerable pace, but I see no sign of recognition in his responses, at all."

"And according to what the Boys have been feeding me, he's already through Omega's and Dihl's files, deep into his own, and has asked for the rest of us," Fox said.

"Oh man. This ain't good," Romeo grumbled. "We mighta lost 'im, even though Meg an' this new guy Chi brought 'im back."

"Shush, Romeo," India murmured, elbowing her life partner in the side.

The others glanced at Omega, but aside from a slight tightening of her face, she showed no evidence of having heard.

"Well, that's unlikely," Zarnix soothed. "Maybe, now that he's read their files, we simply need to send in Omega and Dihl to talk with him, and that will begin to trip synapses and raise the memories."

"That should work," Zebra agreed.

* * *

Zebra and Fox escorted Dihl and Omega into Echo's hospital room; Alpha Two hovered just outside the open door with Zarnix, in the corridor. Echo sat in the bed with the head raised in order to watch TV for a bit, taking a break from reading personnel files after having finished his own, and watching documentaries and the like, apparently trying to come back up to speed on things he no longer remembered. But when they came in, he picked up the remote and clicked off the television. His gaze fixed on Dihl.

"So according to the files I read, you're my mother," he stated.

"That is correct, son," Dihl said with a smile, moving to the bedside.

"According to MY files, never mind looking in the bathroom mirror, you don't look nearly old enough," he pointed out, and her smile faded. "You're a couple of decades too young to be my real mother. So who ARE you, really?"

"Did you read about my pancreatic cancer, and the regeneration process, in those files?" Dihl tried.

"Yes," Echo said, looking blank at what, to him, apparently seemed like a non sequitur. "But how could that affect your age? It was only chemotherapy, right? Like they just talked about on the science TV show? Did that affect your appearance somehow, so you only LOOK younger?"

"It did," Zebra interjected the explanation. "This is medical science that's far more advanced than regular Earth medicine, or anything you'd see on ordinary Earth-produced TV. We don't merely remove the cancer, we remove all the predispositions to it, so it doesn't come back. And there are two kinds of triggers, or predispositions: genetic, and environmental. The way the process works for cancer, you have to regress the age of the systems in order to get rid of any environmental causes. The genetic causes and predispositions are eliminated by the way we set up the fluid formula, but by the time we remove the environmental stuff, it's usually the equivalent of shaving several years, sometimes decades, off the patient's age."

"So...you don't just LOOK a couple of decades younger..." Echo puzzled.

"Right," Dihl averred. "I'm physically a couple of decades younger than my true age. Chronologically, I suppose one might say, I still have my age and experience, so I'm still in my 60s, but my body is now effectively that of an extremely healthy and fit woman in her early 40s. And I work hard to keep it like that."

"Oh."

"And believe me," Dihl added, with another smile, "it feels much better this way!"

They laughed. Echo shook his head, a wry grin on his face.

"This is all gonna take some getting used to," he began, but Fox interjected before he could say more.

"Ah! That laughter sounds very good! And we brought Omega along for the ride," Fox said with a smile, gesturing at the younger woman. "We thought you'd be happy to see the two women you care about the most."

"I'm not sure why you thought that," Echo noted, raising an eyebrow as he stared at his partner with narrowed eyes. "I'm not even sure why you kept her in the organization, after you found out what she is, what she tried to do."

Gasps went up from the room's other occupants, as well as those watching just outside. Omega made no sound, but she paled.

"Echo," Fox noted, calm and slightly stern, "she is your

partner, and your fiancée. What happened was not her fault, and was the result of an atrocity perpetrated on her when she was a minor. And we have known this since the entire thing went down. She didn't want it to happen, and she's fought tooth and nail ever since, to rectify the situation—including during the period when her subliminal, telepathically-inserted program triggered—which is why you're still here and alive, many times over. You've always trusted each other, as much as it is possible for humans to trust one another."

"Kinda hard to say that when she isn't, don't you think?" Echo observed. "I had that Whiskey fella bring me her medical files, and explain 'em to me. It's there, plain as day...'sir.'"

"What are you saying, son?" Dihl asked, shooting a worried glance at Omega, who was now nearly white.

"I'm saying that, according to what I was told, I don't think you can call her a human, because there's enough variance in her genetics that she's NOT really human. And," Echo added, "frankly, I don't think I want her anywhere near me, either, especially not while I'm asleep or unconscious. And she sure as hell isn't gonna be making decisions for me if I'm out of it."

"Echo!" Zebra exclaimed, shocked. "You can't mean that!"

"You showed me her files," Echo said with an uncaring shrug. "I don't know her. I don't know any of you. If what you put in those files is fake, then I can only draw wrong conclusions. But based on what you showed me, those are the conclusions I've reached. She's not human; she tried to kill me; she's a traitor, and I don't want anything to do with her, or her anywhere near me."

Omega, white to the lips, spun on her heel and walked out. No one tried to stop her.

* * *

"Meg? Meg!" a voice interjected itself into Omega's consciousness, and she stopped, as Chi came running up.

"What?" she asked, voice flat.

"I just ran by the medlab, and heard what happened," Chi said, concerned. "I saw you headed out as I was headed in, and you looked like hell. So I only stayed long enough to find out what happened, then came after you. Do you need to talk, Pook? I...I know I'm not...HIM, but I know you pretty damn

148

well, and you know I listen good..."

Omega shook her head.

"No, Sco-er, Chi. I just need to...to get away...for a bit," she tried, not willing to tell him what she had in mind. "I need to think. I—"

Her voice cracked badly, then stopped entirely, and she attempted to force the words out, then gave up when she realized that her body was going to ignore her orders. She closed her eyes and shook her head, even as one tiny teardrop forced its way through her lashes and down her cheek.

"Aw, Pook," Chi breathed, pulling her around a corner and into an alcove, where he tried to take her in his arms and hold her, offering gentle comfort. "I'm here. Even if he's not, I'm here, and I'll always be here for you."

But she pulled away; he blinked in surprise, then flushed.

"I'm sorry, honey; I truly didn't mean it like you apparently took it," he murmured. "You're hurting, I can see that. And I just wanted to let you know...you have friends, hon. Don't shut us out. Don't shut ME out. We want to help. Let us. Let me help."

Omega just shook her head, turned, and walked on.

Uncertain what else to do, a pained Chi stood where he was, and watched her go.

* * *

That's it, she thought, as she headed back to the agent living area of Headquarters, Chi already out of sight and out of mind. *The love of my life no longer wants me. He was right, those last words Echo spoke to me on-orbit. This was never meant to be. And now the one thing I had left, the one thing keeping me going, is gone, because this'll destroy what 'family' I have left—he was the core of it, at least as far as I was concerned, anyway. And he was the one who brought us all together, really; they all knew him way before they knew me. But he barely even acknowledged that Dihl MIGHT be his mom! It's all gonna come apart at the seams. No more life partner or husband, nor even work partner. Not now. He's repulsed by me. I could see it in his gorgeous eyes, the one expression I always feared seeing there. The one expression he'd finally convinced me I'd never see there. And now I have. And I don't know if I will ever, CAN ever, 'unsee' it. The other shoe finally dropped, squarely on top of me, and it was a damn combat boot for a giant.*

She entered her quarters and went straight back to her bedroom, pulling out her travel kit and throwing items into the special space-warp compartments. All of her mission equipment went into it, as well as several changes of clothing—oddly, most of it casual, off-duty wear—and her most treasured possessions, including an old Bible and a small pink resin cube containing a rose blossom, as well as a little Valentine card and two family portraits—one of her birth family at Christmas shortly before they had been murdered some decade earlier, the other a recent photo of her Agency 'family' made on her last birthday.

Then she threw the kit over one shoulder, looked around for the last time, and headed for the front door, closing and locking the back door as she went past it. *There,* she thought as she locked it, *at least when they let him out of the medlab, he won't be made uncomfortable by the fact that his quarters are connected to mine. That's assuming they don't retire him, I guess. I dunno what good it'd do to keep him in the Agency, when he doesn't know anything about it any more. But it's not my call, either.*

Moments later, she was downstairs in Grand Central Station, hopping a maglev train for Pennsylvania Station.

* * *

At Penn Station, Omega went to the hangar master's office and used her authority as Assistant Chief of Alpha Line to commandeer a small but powerful spacecraft—it was a corvette, one that had seen service during the Battle of the Orion Nebula—named *The Grapes of Wrath.* Deciding it was a singularly befitting name, given her situation and her life, Omega boarded it, stowed her gear, and prepped for launch.

"*Grapes of Wrath* to Launch Control," she spoke into the mic.

"This is Launch Control. Go, *Grapes of Wrath.*"

"*Grapes of Wrath* is awaiting approval for launch."

"*Wrath,* Launch Control. We don't see a flight plan filed."

"Launch Control, this is Alpha One Agent Omega with

150

Wrath. That's...classified Alpha Line information."

"Aha. Copy that, *Wrath*. We understand now. Stand by while we set up your departure."

"Huh. That was easier than it was in Chicago," she muttered to herself—WITHOUT keying the mic. "I guess they know me better here, or something."

"*Wrath*, Launch Control. You have go for launch in...wup, stand by for standard aircraft clearance...aaand...go for launch now."

Omega initiated the launch systems.

The Grapes of Wrath lifted off.

* * *

Within minutes, *The Grapes of Wrath* was aloft and on ascent, going exo rapidly, with the full cloaking and sensor-scrambling system activated, as was protocol for an Earth-based launch.

Fifteen minutes later, the *Wrath* passed the Moon, traveling at maximum interplanetary acceleration, and eight minutes after that, Omega activated the Alcubierre drive.

"Goodbye, Earth," she murmured, as the warp bubble formed. "Goodbye, old life, and new-old life. Goodbye love and happiness, and friendship, and family. Goodbye...everything."

In seconds, she was light years away.

With no one the wiser for where she went.

Which was as she wanted it.

* * *

"...Yes, that's right," Fox spoke into his cell phone. "We need a Deltiri interrogator, preferably one familiar with Agent Echo, to come by Medical and check him out, if you have anyone available, hopefully in the next few minutes. He was out of Omega's sight for a considerable period of time, you see, and is not currently behaving as we would expect, so we are concerned about the possibility of a doppelganger."

He paused, and glanced at the rest of the 'family,' plus two—Zarnix and Whiskey were sitting in—all of whom were listening closely. The last thing he wanted was to remind them all of what he was thinking: *If this IS a doppelganger, then Echo is long since dead, and may have re-entered atmosphere already, so there probably isn't even a body to recover.* It was possible they already realized it, of course, but he didn't feel like broaching the subject until it became absolutely necessary. The truth of the matter was, he preferred not to think about it, himself. He listened for a moment, then nodded.

"No, that's true, he was unconscious and oxygen-deprived for most of that time, as well, so...but no, I wouldn't...oh. Well, can your interrogators tell that? They can? Then yes, let's have a look-see as soon as we can."

He deactivated the phone and slipped it back into his pocket.

"They're sending one of their interrogators to check Echo out," Fox confirmed.

"Zz'r'p?" Zebra wondered.

"No, he's out of pocket for the moment," Fox noted. "Seems he was due some time off, and he's gone to the Tokyo Office to visit a friend there, and look all around the oriental gardens. I gather they remind him of home. He took care of scheduling Omega's counseling before he left, so that's all good. But this will be his new assistant, a young female Deltiri named Mm'l'n ag Mii'laa, and Zz'r'p assured me when she came in that she was skilled, gentle, very on top of her game, and would work readily and easily with us. I gather Omega's already met her, and they got along like bread and butter."

"That's good," India decided.

* * *

Shortly thereafter, Mm'l'n was casually introduced to Echo, with the explanation that she would attempt to locate his memories and pull them to the fore; this was something, Mm'l'n had assured the Division One Agents and medics, that was indeed within her capability to do.

"But I will also check for you, to ensure he truly is Agent Echo," the Deltiri had remarked. "I do not know him as well as Zz'r'p, but I met him when he came by with Omega for several of her recent counseling sessions, so I will recognize him, and be able to tell if it really is him or an imposter."

A somewhat suspicious Echo shrugged when Mm'l'n asked permission to access his mind.

"Either you are what you say, or that is one damn good costume of some sort," he decided. "But if you really CAN read my mind, why do you need my permission?"

"It is a matter of courtesy," Mm'l'n explained. "You will not recall, of course, but only a few weeks ago, my predecessor grossly violated your AND your partner's privacies by invading your minds without permission, and revealing what he found there to all the beings within earshot. It is one of the major reasons why I am here now, and he is not."

"Mmph," Echo grunted, considering. "Yeah, okay, I can definitely see that. Have a look, I guess. If you can pull the memories out, that would be damn good. I'm tired of being a blank slate, here."

"I cannot promise I can, but I do know the technique," Mm'l'n said. "It can be complicated. Just relax, and let your guard down as much as you can."

"Whatever," Echo grumbled.

* * *

"NO! What the hell are you telling me?!" a flushed and angry Echo yelled, patently upset. "I can do arithmetic! Look! Right there, on that page, it's basic addition! One thousand, two hundred twenty-three plus eight hundred forty-seven is two thousand and seventy! Piece of cake!"

"All right," Mm'l'n said, soothing him with her voice as well as a light mental touch. "Let us try this, then. Here is a fresh problem for you." And she wrote,

4,596
+ 7,534

Then she handed the pen to Echo.

Calming, Echo took the pen in hand, and Mm'l'n noticed a slight tremor in the top of the writing implement, but said nothing. He took the tablet and laid it on the bed table, then scrutinized the math problem. He applied the pen to the paper, pressing down, and drew a single, slightly jagged line...but did not write down a digit.

"I...I..." he stammered, then looked up at the Deltiri with wide, shocked eyes, and his voice dropped into a whisper. "I can almost see it, but...it's not there."

153

"Let's try something simpler, then," she decided, and wrote,

$$4 + 5 = \underline{}$$

"N-no, I..." Echo began, and paled slightly. "I'm just not seein' it right now, I guess."

"Well, why don't you write out the original equation as words?" she suggested. "Four thousand, five hundred ninety-six..."

He pressed the pen to the pad of paper again, but only managed another wobbly line.

"No," he breathed in horror, eyes dilating in deep dismay as he paled. "You...oh, dear Lord...you were right." Echo stared at the notepad for long moments, then flung the pen across the room. "I CAN'T WRITE! I CAN'T EVEN DO BASIC ARITHMETIC! What is WRONG with me?!"

* * *

"WHAT?!" Fox all but roared, when Mm'l'n reported to them in the conference room down the hall, half an hour later. "The boy is, and always was, at a genius level intellectually! It's why he and Omega got along and partnered so well—she's brilliant, and he understood everything she said! TELL me I misunderstood what YOU just said!"

"No, I am afraid you heard correctly, Director," Mm'l'n sighed. "It IS Agent Echo, without doubt—I recognize the synaptical pattern, and the...quantum entanglement, I suppose we may term it, from my previous encounters with him. But there are no memories left in his mind to retrieve. He is, in essence, what some of you humans call a tabula rasa—a blank slate. And he himself had sensed it subconsciously, because he used the phrase of himself just before I entered his mind."

"Wait! Then how is it that he can speak, read, and write?" India demanded to know.

"He cannot write. I ascertained that just now," Mm'l'n informed them. "He can still speak English—his principal, original language—and he can read it, but he no longer remembers any other languages—including Apache and Spanish, which, while not his primary language, were both still learned at a very young age—nor can he read them. He cannot write in

ANY language, or do even basic arithmetic, such as addition and subtraction. He can follow it when it is laid out for him, but the rest...is gone. I suppose we might liken it to the operating system of a computer, when the random-access memory has lost power, and the operator had not yet backed up. The basic operating system is there, but all the files and applications are gone."

"Has he realized it?" a distressed Dihl wondered.

"Unfortunately, he has," Mm'l'n confirmed. "In the course of my investigations, he perforce recognized the situation. I had to exert some mental effort to calm him, before I came here to report to you. I did call Dr. Whiskey to administer a mild sedative, to ensure he did not...'freak out,' as he used to tell Omega."

The room was silent for long moments, its occupants in shock.

"So he really WAS 'mostly dead' too long," Zebra whispered, horrified. "And when we brought him back, his brain did a reboot..."

"Only the core memory had already been deleted by the extended 'power outage,'" Zarnix finished the analogy for her, then put his face in his hand. When next he spoke, his voice was muffled, emerging between his fingers. "Fox, Dihl, Omega—wherever you got to—I am so sorry; there is nothing more we can do for him. This is beyond our ability to repair."

"HaShem help us," Fox said in a hoarse voice, sitting down hard. "Romeo was right. We've lost him. He's still alive, but he's lost to us."

Dihl put her face in her hands and began to cry.

* * *

"...Fox and I'll take care of Dihl," Zebra murmured to Alpha Two. "We're all older, and know how to handle each other; we've gotten to be good friends since Dihl was brought on board. We need you two to find Omega and let her know what's happened. I only realized she was gone when Zarnix said something. Where did she go, anyway?"

"No tellin', Zebra," Romeo said, and shrugged. "When Echo rejected 'er like that, so flat-out an' all, I think it 'uz prob'ly one of her worst nightmares happenin' in real life, if 'er face was anything ta go by. She cleared out. Needed some space t' deal, I expect."

"Did you guys see her expression?" India said, voice low. "It...dear God, I hurt for her so bad in that moment."

"Yeah, I know whatcha mean, girl," Romeo agreed, subdued. "I think it 'uz even worse 'n when she thought he was dead, back at The Beach in th' summer. 'Cuz, at least then, she still knew he cared. Now..." He shrugged again.

"She's not answering her cell phone," India noted, looking up from her own. "Neither text nor voice."

"Do ya blame 'er?" Romeo wanted to know.

"Well, we need to find her, and fast," Fox said, pulling his cell phone and activating it on a special direct comm. "I want one of US to be the bearer of bad news, not for her to hear it offhand in gossip or the like. She's in bad enough shape, poor girl, as it is. Ah. Lima? Get on the security system and see if you can locate where Omega is in the building; we need to pass on some news to her as soon as possible. Keep in mind she may be on the roof, in her observatory or the like. No, it isn't good, zun. No, it doesn't look like it will. He was 'dead' too long. And yes, that's classified. Yes, but I'd like for some of her adoptive family to take that job, zun; it isn't going to go down well regardless, but it's more apt to go marginally better from one of us. So just find her and tell me where she is, and one of us will go get her. Yes, I'll wait."

He watched, phone still held to his ear, while Zebra drifted over to the grief-stricken Dihl and put her arm around the other woman's shoulders. The normally-impassive female medtech promptly turned into Zebra's embrace and wept.

"This sucks," India sighed, also watching. "He's her son. She only JUST got him back a few months ago! You consider him a son. We consider him a brother. Or we did. Now...it's like he's a stranger."

"For all intents and purposes, he might as well be, tekhter," Fox murmured. "The Echo we knew is...gone. But he's still alive. And I'm not sure how to react, or what to do. I've never seen anything like this one."

"Forgive my eavesdropping," Zarnix interjected in a low voice from his seat nearby, "but I accidentally overheard. Yes, this is an exceedingly rare circumstance, insofar that as experienced as I am, I have never heard of it happening before. Evidently we hit a very narrow window during which the brain had already performed what amounted to a core dump, but before all of the organic tissues ceased to be viable. Were it not for the extremely advanced, highly sophisticated galactic medicine we use, it would all have been moot in any case—there would be no 'sort of dead' or 'partly dead' or 'mostly dead,' there would just be...dead. Unfortunately, his brain's basic functions did not...anticipate...physical resuscitation, of course, and it reacted as if...well. As if he were indeed fully dead. Which, normally, he would have been." He shrugged. "It is difficult to explain. It is even possible—perhaps probable—that Echo was already in the throes of brain death, the early stages at any rate, and the regeneration procedure reversed the organic damage... without the ability of that brain to retrieve the information thus lost. It is Agent Kappa's situation, but taken to the ultimate extreme—it wasn't just SOME data that was lost, it was effectively ALL the data."

"Tsu aldi rukhes," Fox grumbled to himself. "Of all the— wait, what? Bravo? What did you say?" Fox's jaw dropped, and he stared blankly into space for a moment. "She's not? But then where...oh, no. Lima, repeat that, please." There was a pause. "A brokh. No, this is...not good, kinder, but let me consider matters for a bit, and I'll get back with you. Oh, and I'm sending the Deltiri ambassador's assistant to you; I want the two of you to work with her to locate Zz'r'p and bring him back on an emergency summons. I have the feeling we're going to need him. And rather badly, at that."

As Fox deactivated the phone, Romeo asked, "What's wrong, Boss-man?"

"Omega isn't in Headquarters," Fox declared, and the others in the room—even Dihl—turned to listen. "She left the building not long after she left the medlab. Likely only took long enough to run by her quarters and grab a few essentials, to judge by the timing and tracking history."

"Well, she's probably retreated to the Farm in Alabama, then," India decided. "That was where she went after we had to convince her that Echo was dead, back in the summer."

"No, India, she didn't; because they've been involved with helping her get through the whole farkakte mess that she's been slogging through for the last couple of months, the Boys were worried when they realized she'd left Headquarters, so they dug into her whereabouts, " Fox corrected. "It seems she headed for Penn Station, commandeered a small spacecraft, and took it up. When asked for a flight plan, she identified herself as Alpha Line and told them it was classified. And per protocol, she activated the full cloaking systems before departure...and apparently never dropped it once exo. She's nowhere on Earth. Nobody knows WHERE she is now."

"Oh, shit," Zebra breathed. "No wonder you want Zz'r'p back here five minutes ago."

"Right," Fox noted. "She's in a bad state, emotionally and mentally—"

"And with her still undergoing counseling for the PTSD," India reminded.

"Yes, and normally, Echo would be our biggest asset in figuring out where she went," Fox pointed out. "But we've lost that advantage. Her telepathic counselor and teacher is now the best hope we have of coming up with some way to find her before she may do something...irrevocable."

"Dayum," Romeo murmured, worried.

Chapter 8

Omega took *The Grapes of Wrath* well away from Sol system, as well as the regular transport lanes—both those used for shipping and for passenger/manned spacecraft—moving up, out of the galactic plane proper, for several hundred light years—almost a full thousand light years, just to make certain. There, she dropped out of warp, placed the little corvette into stationkeeping with all shields maxxed, and studied her situation.

My life on Earth is done, she thought, despondent and trying not to cry. *There's no going back. There's no real REASON to go back. I'm not human any more, so it's not like I really belonged there anyway. And Echo was my last real link, my last hope of having a semi-normal life. Yes, there's still Romeo and India, and Fox and Zebra, and Dihl. And yeah, they'll try to convince me to come back, if they can. But there's no point. Not now.*

Dihl will take care of Echo, because she's his mom, and she'll CONVINCE him she's his mom. Good moms are like that, and she's a damn good mom. And so that takes care of Echo and Dihl. And Romeo and India, and Fox and Zebra, they have each other. I'll only be the odd man out.

And if they find something for Echo to do, given he doesn't remember his old job, or even his time growing up on the ranch, it's a lead-pipe cinch after his last declaration that I won't be welcome with him. And the only people that'll be acceptable around him comprise his mother, his adoptive father and stepmom, his former partner...they all had relationships with him long before I showed on the scene, and there's no place left for me in all that.

There's Chi, I guess. And he's delivered enough hints that I know he'd like to try again in a relationship with me, bless him. But...I already learned my lesson with Mu. I can't settle for second-best. I love Scotty, but not the way I love Echo. Scotty's a buddy to me, not a lover. No matter how much he might want it different. And that's the real reason he and I broke up, back in the day, I think.

So...yeah. I'm done there. Romeo will do fine as head of Alpha Line, and Golf and Easy—Alpha Four...I guess Golf can be the assistant chief, and Easy the backup. After all, they handled the ouster of the fake Adita and his enforcers just great. And Fox will help. It'll work okay. I just...I can't go back. Not now. It hurts way too much. And everything—EVERYTHING—will remind me.

They'll try to get me to come back, of course. Just like they did after that whole 'Echo's dead' ruse. Probably try even harder this time, and they pulled out some o' the stops last time. That ain't happenin' this go—I'm not goin' back—but if they know where I am, they'll still try. And I just don't wanna deal with that right now.

But once it gets out what happened, and that I've left the Agency—and it will, sooner or later—there's gonna be a bunch of people gunning for me. And a small but significant fraction of those are truly evil and sadistic. I'll do the best I can, for as long as I can, but I don't have eyes in the back of my head. So eventually despite my best efforts, and without Echo to watch my six, somebody'll get me—I get that. And I guess... that's okay. The last couple of years since I found out what Slug did to me have been a living hell, more than anybody else— even Zz'r'p, even Echo—can ever, EVER know. I couldn't trust my body, I couldn't trust my mind. I didn't know WHAT kinda damn booby traps Slug had left inside me, FOR me...and Echo. I THINK maybe we finally found the end of that, but even so, I can't be SURE. I had hopes of making it something better, something maybe even wonderful, but Echo was at the heart of that dream, and now...I have nothing. He doesn't even remember what I showed him Slug did. Doesn't remember realizing I was fighting for all I was worth, to keep my programming from killing him. Doesn't remember me getting toasted under the Cortians' engines, either...to protect him. Or looking after him in the wreck on the protoplanet. Or any of a thousand other things like that, big and little, that showed how much I cared. Maybe it's just as well, though. It wasn't meant to be, him and me. And I guess, if I'm honest, given everything Slug did to me, that's probably the fair and just thing; I was never really worthy of Echo; I was only the bitch dog mutt intended to be his killer. HE was the purebred, the thoroughbred, the one who got where he was on his own, without needing any damn 'enhancements.' Dear God, how I hate that word.

And I'm tired. So very tired. I just don't feel like fighting it any more. I don't have anything left to fight FOR, any more. So if they get me, if the perps get me, as long as it's a quick, good death, and maybe I can take a few of 'em with me, it'll be all right. No more fighting; no more pain, no more loneliness and feeling shut out from the human race. Yeah. I can deal with that.

But I'm not gonna let it happen before I finish my plan, she decided, squaring her shoulders and firming her jaw. *I'm tired of this shit doggin' my heels. I'm tired of it doggin' ECHO'S heels! None of this would have happened if SOMEbody hadn't hired Slug to come to Earth and take out that ambassador to begin with, dammit. Only Echo was good enough to take Slug down, an' then Slug couldn't let it BE, damn the bastard! I guess he figured he was getting revenge for his wife and unborn kids, but shit. It was his own damn fault for bringing along a preggers wife! Of course, I guess without all his machinations I would never have met Echo either, but that's kind of a moot point by this time, nohow. But Slug's long since dead, and hopefully we finally put to rest the last of his damn plans...not that it mattered in the end for me an' Echo, I guess; our relationship is dead despite my best efforts, now. And his, I guess. But there's one last perp, one final criminal in the whole big picture that's still out there, somebody that needs taking out, so that he can't take US out...even if there really isn't an 'us' any more. And that's the being who HIRED Slug in the first place. And I'll be damned if I'm not gonna find him—or her, or it, or... whatever it is—and see it gets what's coming to it! And to do that, I need to make sure nobody can find Omega after this, for as long as I can. So from this moment on, Omega...is gone. Just like Megan McAllister is gone. I'm...* She shrugged. *I'm X now. The unknown factor. So let's get with it.*

She turned to the little corvette's master computer and brought up the disk operating system. Not that it still used disks; it was rather more sophisticated than that. But the terminology was still in use, at least by the Earth-based agents.

"Let's see," she murmured, studying the directories. "Echo showed me how to do this as a just in case thing, back in the spring when he was training me during our big Orion expedition. And the first thing I have to do is to take down most of the externals—which is why I came all this way above the galactic plane, so nobody would see while I do it. So...yeah, this ought to take care of it..."

With that, she brought down the shields, cloaking, and sensor scrambler, then dug into the directories, locating specific files.

She began to hack the operating system.

* * *

The avian being with the bright yellow feathers studied his console readouts intently as the carefully-cloaked starship eased its way around the outskirts and backwaters of the big spiral galaxy. Their homeworld, in a tiny satellite galaxy orbiting the big spiral, was blockaded and there could be no respite from that source, so it behooved them and their few remaining sister ships—who now tended to travel in a paired 'buddy system'—to maintain caution and a high alert. If they were caught by the local denizens, it would be an understatement to say they would be unwelcome. It would not be an overstatement to say they would likely end up dead. So he was paying especial attention to his sensor readings, looking for anything that might indicate danger.

Just then, a soft *ding!* sounded, even as a purple light lit on the helmsman's console. His crest plume rose slightly in mild surprise, and the helmsman reached for his controls, pulling up a sensor readout. He studied it intently for several minutes, before turning to the command seat nearby.

(Captain, I have something that may interest you,) he said.

(Oh?) The captain, somewhat bored, sat up and took notice. (What do you have?)

(I have the signature and automated identification signal of a Division One spacecraft on my long-range sensor grid,) the helmsman noted. (But we are a considerable distance from the edges of Division One space. And the ship is still some little distance from us, as well; it would take us a few hours to arrive at its locus, even at high warp. And at this distance, there is no guarantee that it would still be there when we arrived. But it appears to be stationary, at least for now.)

(That IS interesting,) the captain decided. (Has the *Yiskos* taken notice as well?)

(Unknown, Captain. Do you want to notify it and move closer, in case we have an opportunity?)

(Yes, I think that is a wise notion. Considering the problems they have given us, anything from that damnable Division One group definitely has my attention. And if we have an opportunity for payback, in addition to obtaining somewhat by reaching out to take it, so much the better. Communications, notify the *Yiskos* to accompany us as we investigate the matter. Helm, maximize stealth, take your time, and lay in a course for the Division One vessel. Drop us out of warp some distance away, so that we are not immediately detected. This could be a ruse, even a trap, and I do not intend to fall for it. But if it is of value, we would be foolish not to take advantage of it.)

(Aye, Captain.)

* * *

It took nearly three hours to work down into the deepest levels of the security identification of *The Grapes of Wrath*, but Omega was determined, and kept doggedly at it.

Eventually she hacked her way into the ship's ID section of the master computer memory, and began replacing out the information already there with the identification she had worked out while in flight: She had used her Alpha Line status to bring up a list of unused spacecraft identification numbers for the galactic registry, and selected one a moderate way down the list. This number she now 'assigned' to the corvette, giving it a new name and private ownership. Henceforward it was no longer Division One's *The Grapes of Wrath*, but the *Franckenshteine*, a private vessel belonging to a female Gurgev from Dekken in Division Three, named 'Ekaturg Xelsib.' The last name was, she had decided, appropriate to her new status as the X factor in certain galactic events. And Gurgevs were sufficiently humanoid that it would be a relatively easy cover to assume.

"There," she sighed, sitting back at last, "that's done. And

163

I've got a Gurgev disguise already programmed into the solid hologram full-head mask I started keeping in my kit, so that'll become 'Ekaturg.' So I'm good there. Now I need to climb into that generic space suit in stowage...I guess it's a good thing my own space suit is in for repairs after all, 'cause it's got Division One an' Alpha Line logos all over it, and that won't do now, at all...and then I'll go outside and do a bit of cosmetic work on the skin of the ship. But I think I might need to eat a little something, first."

* * *

She didn't eat much; the entire situation with Echo had taken her appetite rather thoroughly, so she ate just enough to ensure she had sufficient energy to perform another EVA, especially so soon after recent strenuous spacewalks. This meal amounted to a couple of the Agency's full-nutrition meal-replacement bars, choked down with a great effort and plenty of water, and took all of about five minutes. It was fuel, and it would keep her going, and that was all she cared about at this point.

Then she pulled the general-use space suit from the ship's stowage, adjusted it for her size, and donned it with some exertion. The 'spaghetti suit' cooling undergarment was easy, but the torso sections of the suit itself comprised a kind of compression garment, and it took a bit of time to wriggle her way into it. Normally there would be assistants to help with the donning, or at least her partner available to assist, but none of that was any sort of option now, nor did she desire it, though it would have speeded things up considerably.

Still and all, I did it when we were crashed on the protoplanet last spring, she determined, encouraging herself. *And I had a bad concussion and a small skull fracture at the time. I can do this.*

A scant hour later, she was standing in the evacuated airlock, opening the outer hatch, and trying to ignore all-too-recent memories. Moments later, the tether was unreeling behind her, as she floated into the space around the corvette. She got far enough away from the hull to have a good look at it, then hummed to herself, considering.

"Okay, there's some fair-sized scrapes and burns, probably

164

from the Battle of the Orion Nebula," she noted, "and quite a few dents and dings, likely from the same thing. That'll do good for making it look like I've put it through a few things—even bought it used!—though maybe I need to scrub away some of the burn marks; I don't want it actually identified as a craft that's been in a battle! That might give me away fast... or get me arrested as a ship-jacker! Other than that, I think if I use some of the special enamel remover to ditch the name and ID numbers, then I can dig out the repair kit and replace them with the new ones. Should be some stencils in the repair kit, so...let's go."

* * *

Execution of her intended plan was labor-intensive, especially in a space suit, even if it was one of the Agency's; it might be easier to work in than the 'human balloon' NASA suits, but only slightly—part of the problem was simply the lack of leverage to be found in the microgravity environment. So she had to break the job down into stages, and go inside for several breaks in between those stages.

First, she used the power cleaning brushes in the maintenance kit to scrub off the worst of the burn scoring from the battle, months before. That required considerable elbow grease even with the drill-like power brushes, and anchoring herself to the hull to get the leverage needed to provide sufficient force. So when she was satisfied with the look, she ingressed through the spacecraft's airlock hatch, removed her helmet and gauntlets, and sat down in the pilot's seat, fatigued.

"Wow," she murmured to herself, sipping from the water bottle she had left there earlier while she reviewed the ship's status, "not only is this gonna take a while, I'm gonna have to grab a pretty good long break when I'm finally done with everything! Oh well, it isn't like I have a specific schedule. It's probably going to take me some time to figure out who Slug's employer was, anyway. That one was a damn cold case, from years ago. Like, glacier cold."

Her stomach rumbled, and she wandered to the rear of the tiny flight deck, pulling another food bar from the consumables stowage bin. She wolfed it down without much thought, dimmed the cabin lights, then stretched her length on the deck, not bothering to doff the space suit, or to try to get more comfortable in the tiny, cramped three-person sleeping berth in the aft, next to the head.

* * *

After allowing herself an hour to rest—managing to nap a little bit only because she was so tired from her EVA—she rose and prepped the templates for the enamel she planned to apply, arranging the letters and numbers in proper order and attaching them to each other with a few bits of gray tape. Then she donned her helmet and gauntlets, repressurized the suit, and headed back out to work on the hull some more.

This time, she brought the repair kit with her, and used essentially all the special enamel remover to thoroughly erase the ship's name and ID numbers, prominently displayed on what passed for the prow of the tiny saucer, underneath the big forward 'windshield.'

* * *

Then she took another break, this time longer; by this point, her hyped, enhanced metabolism was taking its toll, and Omega was flatly starving.

And worn slap out, she realized. *Really, really just so damn tired. I hate to take off this suit; it is SO hard to get back into, by myself! But maybe I need a couple hours' sleep, and a proper hot meal in me. And that ain't gonna happen while I'm in the suit.*

So she pared off the outer suit, leaving on the decidedly-revealing, full-body mesh spaghetti suit given that there was no one else to see, and pulled one of the prepared meals from stowage—basically a TV dinner of macaroni and cheese—and popped it in the little microwave oven built into the stowage wall among the storage cabinets.

When her meal was ready, she took it and a couple of bottles of water over to the pilot's seat; it was equipped with a small excuse for a fold-out table, for those times when the pilot needed to stay at the console, but had to take sustenance. There, she ate and surveyed the sensor data and ship's status again, determining that all was well, before she pulled out her personal electronic tablet and brought up the Agency files on Slug's first advent on Earth.

Once she was done eating, she mulled over the case history for some fifteen minutes, then yawned prodigiously.

"And there's my cue," she told herself, somewhat whimsically. "Time to get some proper shut-eye."

She glanced at the instrumentation, preparatory to setting up station-keeping status.

"Oh shit," she realized, "I never turned the sensor scrambler and cloak back on. Well, I was working on the hull, so I guess that wouldn't have been a good plan anyway. But I need it on now." She reset the devices, then programmed numerous sensor alerts and alarms into the system, cranking up the volume on the audio so that if anything above the size of a pebble came closer than a few hundred meters from the ship, she would know about it virtually instantly.

Then she headed to the minuscule sleeping berth in the aft, setting a wake-up alarm on her cell phone as she went.

* * *

As the two Cortian vessels dropped their warp bubbles several astronomical units from the newly-designated *Franckenshteine*, the helmsman scanned his sensors, then turned to his commander.

(Captain, the registry on the ship has changed. I swear upon my fathers that this is the same ship; the location has not changed by more than a few three-millionths of a lightspeed annum's path. But the registry now says it is a private vessel from Dekken in Division Three, registered to a female Gurgev named 'Ekaturg Xelsib.')

(Interesting,) the captain decided. (Someone very badly wishes not to be identified. Likely a pirate of some sort. But I wonder...)

(What do you suspect, my captain?)

(See if you can find the scan pattern records of those damned rogue slaves from Earth in Division One. The ones who destroyed the *Trindak* and the *Pindar*.)

(One moment, sir.) The helmsman delved into their records, and after several minutes of careful searching, came up with the desired records. (I have them, sir.)

(One was a female, was it not?)

(It was, sir. Omega, she was called. The male was called

167

Echo.)

(This grows more interesting by the moment,) the captain declared. (Place sensors on maximum range, highest sensitivity, and scan the vessel for occupants. Then compare any readings you obtain to the records of the rogue slaves.)

The helmsman nodded obeisance, already initiating the scan. He and the captain waited patiently while the detailed scan completed, then he pulled up the results and ran them through the pattern-matching algorithm.

(By the name of the creator gods!) the helmsman exclaimed. (You were right, my captain! There is only one entity aboard, a female— presumably this purported Dekken—but her long-range scan patterns are fairly close to those for this escaped slave Omega! Less than a third of a standard deviation difference! It MIGHT be another female, but the statistics indicate it is unlikely.)

(Mm. As I thought,) the captain said, intensely self-satisfied. (Let us—)

(What the—?! Hold one, Captain. The ship has just vanished from my sensors.)

(Is there a warp bubble signature?)

(No sir. It simply disappeared.)

(Ah. They have some nigh-magical technology, this Division One Agency. There were reports from the *Trindak* before it was destroyed, as well as several of the vessels involved in the Hunter Nebula battle, that they had devices to produce this ability. I suspect she has activated it. I should love to get my claws on it; it would prove most useful, were we to retro-engineer it and put it to use ourselves.)

(Do you think she knows we are here?)

(I suppose we will know if we are attacked. Maximum alert. All shields up. Crew to battle stations.)

(Aye, sir! Shields up; we are still in stealth mode. All hands to battle stations. Communications, please notify the *Yiskos*.)

A klaxon sounded, going off for several seconds before silencing. The communications officer turned to the captain.

(All hands at battle stations, sir, and the *Yiskos* as well. We are ready to proceed.)

(Good. Stand by to see if we are attacked.)

* * *

When long, tense moments had passed and nothing happened, the commanding officer of the *Zakai* decided they had not been spotted.

(And in that case,) he noted, (we can catch her by surprise, and take her into custody. It is a pity, I suppose, that we no longer have the means to properly harvest her genetics...though there are cruder means, but we have no guarantee that her genetics are compatible, so it may be a wasted effort...still, she will likely bring a high price, regardless. I am sure there are bounty hunters who would like this one. And there is always the cloaking technology.)

(No doubt, my captain,) the helmsman averred. (What are your orders?)

(Maintain maximum cloaking, and bring us in close, but stealthily. Take your time, and go slowly. Scan the area for any other ships.)

(Do you suspect a trap?)

(Let us put it this way: I do not NOT suspect a trap, especially where the Division One is concerned. Meanwhile, we have the upper hand; we must take full advantage of it.)

(Aye, sir.)

* * *

Omega allowed herself four hours to sleep, then rose, checked the ship's settings, turned off the alerts, alarms, and cloaking systems, and struggled her way into the compression space suit once more.

This last spacewalk should take care of it, she told herself. *I got all the letters and numbers cleared off last time. And I got the stencils arranged in templates for the ID number and the name. All I gotta do is tack the templates in position on the hull with some more gray tape, spray on the special enamel, spray on the curing gel, remove the templates, and come inside. I guess I should destroy the templates while I'm about it. I think I'll put the things through the incinerator when I'm done, then dump the ash into space, so nobody can find 'em if they get inside the ship.*

Within an hour, she was back outside, working on the hull.

* * *

(Captain! The craft is back! Sensors show she is outside the spacecraft, in an environment suit, working on the hull!) the helmsman exclaimed. (Shall we make our move?)

(Negative,) the captain decided, studying the heads-up display his helmsman had brought up. (We are still too far away, it will take too long to 'swoop' from this distance, and I still do not trust this not to be a trap. It is entirely too convenient. Consider that, if there are other ships with the sensor blocking ability nearby, they could be lying in ambush for us, just waiting for us to be drawn to their oh-so-tempting bait. No, we will wait, and do this properly, and when we do, we will have all our offensive and defensive weaponry already set at maximum.)

(Aye, sir.)

(Estimated time to engagement?)

(Approximately two standard day segments, sir.)

(Very good. That should do nicely.)

* * *

She was right; it only took about an hour of EVA work before the corvette had a new name emblazoned on its hull, in Galactic Standard lettering:

D3DK-2A1-800425 ISS Franckenshteine

A few blows with the largest wrench she could find in the tool kit, and a couple of hits with one—of twelve—targeting lasers she'd temporarily removed from the weapons bay, rendered the brand-new lettering a bit more aged-looking. Five more minutes saw the targeting laser replaced in its correct housing, properly aligned—if anyone knew how to swiftly and accurately align a pointer device, it was an astronomer—and she headed for the airlock.

Omega ingressed and stripped all the way down to skin, performing basic maintenance on the suit components before replacing it all in stowage. In the meanwhile, she didn't bother to throw anything on over her naked body, since the cabin was warm enough to be comfortable and there was no one to see. *And,* she decided, morose, *it doesn't really matter anyway.*

Taking the templates, she disassembled them and ran them,

one at a time, into the waste incinerator along with the gray tape that had held them together, then hit the 'stir' button to break up any pieces, and ejected it all overboard, into space. There was little left after the incineration, and the ash soon dissipated in the space around the ship.

"There," she told herself. "That much is taken care of. Now to go give myself a little bit of 'maintenance.'"

So she went back to the head, where she showered and washed her hair. Ducking into the sleeping berth, she pulled a fresh pair of panties and bra from her travel kit, donning them, before hauling out a pair of black jeans and a gray t-shirt and putting them on. Socks and slip-on sneakers clad her feet. The Suit she had been wearing when she left Earth had long since been shoved deep into one of the warp pockets of the sophisticated travel kit, and would later be transferred to the ship's stowage, hidden in one of the 'classified transport' compartments—effectively a kind of 'government-legal' smuggling hold.

A glance in the little mirror on the port bulkhead of the berth enabled her to quickly put her hair into its customary French braid before wrapping that into a low chignon, the better to fit under the solid hologram disguise, should it be needed quickly.

Entering the flight deck, she turned to the consumables stowage, extracting another TV dinner and shoving it into the microwave to heat, before taking the hot meal back to the pilot's seat to eat and plan. There, she re-established the alerts and alarms, but did not yet bother with cloaking, concluding that, with the new identification, she might not need it...at least for a while, until perps figured out who she really was—which, she hoped, would take them a bit. *And might not even happen at all, unless I get identified in person as Omega, sometime in the near future,* she decided. Then she turned to the problem of what to do next, to take herself forward in her chosen task.

"Mm," she decided, talking to herself around sliced roast beef and mashed potatoes with beef gravy, "yeah, I think that'll work okay. So that means now I need to work out where I am with respect to Dekken, and angle over a little, so that my approach is from the right direction..."

* * *

She had just finished working out her desired trajectory on the navcomp, when the alarm klaxon went off. She sat up straight in surprise, and immediately pulled up a heads-up display...just as the incoming-message alert tripped, shunting the communiqué through the translator.

"This is the Cortian Amalgam vessel *Zakai*, accompanied by the sister ship *Yiskos*. Our long-range sensor scans of recent hours have indicated that this is a disguised Division One Agency vessel, with probable escaped rogue slave Omega aboard. Stand down and prepare to be boarded and taken back into custody. If you do not, your ship will be destroyed."

A quick glance at her sensor display confirmed the presence and likely identity of two Cortian starships—the vessels' configurations were virtually identical, and matched the Cortian profile and design. Omega scowled.

"The hell you say," she growled, bringing up the shields and powering weapons as fast as she could go. "I am sick and TIRED of this shit."

The *Zakai* fired.

Fractions of a second later, so did the *Yiskos*.

* * *

By the time the *Zakai*'s weapons discharged, however, the *Franckenshteine* was somewhere else; no longer concerned about what anyone thought of her since the most important person in her life had rejected her, Omega threw caution and reserve to the winds, and allowed her enhanced body and nervous system—assisted by all of her Alpha Line training—to operate at full throttle. This in turn enabled her reflexes to function at maximum, and she had recognized the Cortian weapons activation and executed the maneuver even as her own shields snapped online. Within moments she had zeroed in on the vulnerable spots on the *Zakai*—the small flash-evaporation exhaust port beneath the external cantilever strut, and the critical-maintenance hatch next to the radiator field. A one-two targeting punch, and the *Zakai* was no more than an expanding cloud of debris. Before the *Yiskos* could react, Omega was upon it, and seconds later, it had joined the *Zakai*.

"I guess I'm lucky they didn't show up while I was on EVA;

I'd have been a sitting duck. And that would have ended my private little mission really damn quick. Which means I need to be a damn sight more careful, from here on out. Speaking of being careful...SOMEbody probably saw those explosions, an' they'll be here soon, to check 'em out. So on that note, I suppose I'd better cloak, sensor-scramble, and get the hell outta Dodge," Omega decided, suiting action to word.

Three minutes later, there was nothing left in the area but a small plasma cloud riddled with small bits of starship debris.

* * *

Minutes after that, the *Franckenshteine* was headed inbound, down toward the inner galactic plane, whence lay the more densely-populated regions of the galaxy. More importantly, the galactic capital, Aleancë, lay ahead.

Omega adjusted her course so that it appeared to originate from the Dekken system. Not that it mattered, at the moment—she had all cloaking and sensor scrambler technology activated on maximum. No one would see her coming until she was ready.

* * *

"...But I would STRONGLY recommend putting Omega on an extended medical leave if at all possible, once we find her, Fox," Zarnix decreed. "She's been through far too much in recent weeks for anyone's comfort, and she desperately needs downtime, and probably redoubled counseling and possibly temporary medication, after this latest blow."

"All right, I'll take that into consideration, and see it gets done...once we find her," Fox agreed.

"You're not gonna issue arrest orders on grounds of desertion, are you?" Zebra wondered, anxious. "I mean, I know it would be a fast way to get her back, but..."

"No, no," Fox demurred immediately. "After that whole verdammt meshuginah drek the Ennead did to Echo? No way in hell! I won't even chance it. Besides, we all SAW her go white as a sheet when Echo turned on her. She is not dealing with matters in a rational fashion right now, and may not even have realized she effectively went AWOL. I fully expect to find that all she had in mind was getting away, as far and as fast as she could."

"And speaking of which, has anybody talked to Whiskey, to find out what Echo saw in Meg's records, and what Whiskey told him?" India asked. "I'm thinking something got drastically misinterpreted in Echo's blank-slate mind, because I'm better than ninety-nine percent sure Whiskey doesn't consider Meg some sort of alien hybrid, let alone full-on alien."

"I would agree," Dihl interjected, having regained control of her emotions, at least for the time. "Whiskey has never given indication he thought that of Omega. Even when I consulted him about some matters, while working on her case."

"Yes, Zebra and I will be on that in just a few minutes," Zarnix averred. "Whiskey had just gone off duty not fifteen minutes ago, but we've called him back for a brief conference. He did ask for time to prepare and eat dinner, as a couple of minor emergencies caused him to miss his last couple of meals, and we agreed—there's no point in starving the poor man for what amounts to a kind of post-mortem of events. So we're just waiting for him to arrive. It'll probably be an hour or so, but it will be done."

"Good," India said.

"Meanwhile, back to what Fox was planning," Zebra redirected the conversation.

"Right, bubeleh." Fox nodded. "Anyway, whatever Omega is thinking right now, even if it's completely logical in certain respects—and I'm sure, knowing her, it is—it's definitely being motivated by the pain of that rejection. And on top of everything else, that was likely the last straw in the camel's already grossly-oversized load. I have sworn, and long made it a policy, never to load more on my agents than they can bear— I never want to even risk breaking them under that load—but with all these schemes directed AT Omega and Echo, it has been next to impossible for me to block the continual onloading! So that poor little camel of ours needs all the care and looking-after that we can give her, and as much of the burden offloaded as we possibly can...if we can figure out HOW. No, I gave Bravo and Lima instructions to issue what amounts to a 'gravely ill Agent, may be confused, please locate and detain for medical treatment' notification, up through the PGLEIA chain of command, and out to all Divisions. With permission to provide a classified explanation, if inquiries came in. I've already sent a direct communiqué with all the pertinent information to Chief Wuxullian, marked URGENT."

"Has he responded?" Zarnix asked.

"Not yet. I'm expecting—" Fox began, even as his cell phone gave an odd, peculiarly insistent *beep!* He checked it, then activated it and read something quickly. "That was his acknowledgement. He's received, read, and understands all of it, and is in concurrence on my choice of actions. He also offers his concern and distress, as well as any assistance we may need. He is forwarding the emergency alert through all PGLEIA channels."

"Hallelujah for small favors!" Zebra exclaimed.

"Amein," Fox agreed. "Does anyone here have any suggestions or general input? Are you all in agreement?"

"Yeah, man. An' good on th' classified part," Romeo noted. "We don't need ev'ry old enemy of Alpha One comin' down on 'em right now, when they's both so vulnerable it ain't EVEN funny."

"No shit," India averred. "Let alone an old enemy of Echo's from way back, that everybody's forgotten about INCLUDING Echo, and Meg might never have known about to begin with."

"Amein again," Fox concurred. "Especially including him, at this point. Which is exactly why I did it the way I did it. AND I've already arranged to set up a clandestine guard on Echo for that very reason, because despite our best efforts, information does leak, especially on a patient in the medlab. Yes, Omega's gone rogue..." he winced, then added, "in a fashion... but..." He broke off abruptly.

"You don't like the thought that she's mentally ill, or even possibly deranged," a knowing Zebra stated.

"No, I don't," Fox admitted. "That wonderful brain of hers...it just seems wrong. But HaShem only knows, she's been through the wringer lately."

"I know," Dihl murmured, pulling a face. "I feel...the same, Fox. I know that PTSD is induced, and I know that our galactic medicine can work wonders, and Zz'r'p's skilled counseling was starting to really help her..."

"I suppose, Dihl, you and I are old enough to still respond

to some of the old stigma of the term 'mental illness,'" Fox sighed. "And I know there's still a little of that around, whether we would or no, and I only want to protect her from that."

"I think you are right, and I concur," Dihl agreed. "And added to that is my son, and..." It was her turn to break off, as she struggled to keep her face from crumpling again. She bit her lip, attempting to forestall tears. "For-forgive me..."

"Shh," Zebra whispered, putting an arm around the older woman. "He's your SON. It's okay to be upset. Let's go back to my quarters for a few minutes. I'll make you some tea, and you can let it out in private, with just me, as friend to friend, not boss to subordinate, instead of trying to keep it all corked up inside, to appear professional in front of all of us. When you're up to it, we'll come back and see if there's anything we can brainstorm with the rest of the medical staff that stands a snowball's chance in Hell of fixing this, some kinda way."

"And I shall stay away from our quarters, and give the two of you a chance to vent," Fox murmured.

Dihl opened her mouth to answer, but nothing came out; she closed her mouth and simply nodded. Zebra glanced at Fox and Zarnix; both males immediately nodded permission, and the two women slipped out quietly.

Just then, Fox's cell phone bleated, and he extracted it and answered. "Fox here."

Zarnix, Romeo, and India watched as he listened. After a few moments, he raised a grizzled eyebrow.

"Oh really? You think...yes, yes, that makes a great deal of sense. All right, zun, keep me posted. Have you gotten hold of Zz'r'p yet? Lima is on the other line with him? All right. Call me back and tell me how that turns out."

He hung up, then looked up to find three pairs of eyes staring at him.

"Oh, that was Bravo," he noted. "It seems that there's been a shipwreck detection, except it looks as if the shipwreck had help, if you know what I mean."

"We do, Fox," Romeo said, as India and Zarnix nodded. "What else, Boss-man?"

"Well, the preliminary forensic readouts indicate there were two ships there, both—get this—CORTIAN, and well outside the normal shipping lanes, up above the galactic plane by nearly a thousand light years. There wasn't much left of either one except a few tidbits dispersed in a cloud of vaporized metal and plastic, and it looks to have happened rather suddenly to both, within seconds."

"Ooo," Romeo said. "Looks like, whatever else she might be, Meg is on th' ball as far as situational awareness is concerned. An' remembers how she an' Echo took those bastards out last spring."

"That's the way Bravo and I read it, too," Fox agreed. "Which means that she went out of her way to go someplace she wouldn't be observed. But why? And was she hunting Cortians, or were they hunting her?"

"Hard to say, quite yet," India decided. "Maybe we'll get more news and be able to tell. Meantime, we know where she was, recently."

"Exactly," Fox said. "I—" His phone bleated again, and he activated it as he put it to his ear. "Fox here. Yes, Lima. Oh? That is excellent news, for a change. Oh dear; he was that upset? He did? Well, I've known him for a long time, and he and I are a lot alike in many of the ways that count, and I've always found that action taken toward a hopeful resolution tends to help counter those kinds of feelings. Yes, send him straight here. Yes, I'll have Zarnix give all the staff a heads-up to direct him to us. No, that's fine. Fox out."

"Whassup now, Boss-man?" Romeo wondered.

"That was Lima," Fox explained. "It seems that the Boys reached Zz'r'p and told him everything, and Zz'r'p was extremely upset—he dropped everything to see to this, and canceled the rest of his vacation. He's headed straight here, as fast as he can get here—which means he's commandeered a spacecraft and pilot with Lima's assistance, and is taking a suborbital hop at emergency speeds. He'll be coming in to Penn Station in about five minutes, and Bravo meanwhile arranged for an emergency maglev to meet him and convey him to the Medical Emergency dock. He'll be here in about seven..." Fox glanced at his wrist chronometer, "make that six minutes."

"That seems unusual for Zz'r'p," Zarnix observed, pulling a tablet and tapping orders into it. "He is one of the most settled, what Zebra would call 'zen,' beings I know. He even rivals Doron in that respect. There, the staff has been notified to watch for him."

"Good; thank you. And yes, he is, but he has grown very close to Omega over the time they've known each other," Fox pointed out. "And in turn, has gotten close to Echo as a consequence. I rather think that, just as Pul is effectively an offworld 'uncle' to the little family unit Omega has created, so is Zz'r'p, in some measure. At the very least, he is a dear and honored friend of that 'family.' I'm sure to find his student and patient... his 'niece,' if you will...has gone ballistic and fled the planet— because her partner and intended has forgotten and rejected her—did his own feelings no favors."

"Most likely," Zarnix agreed, then offered a wry grin. "How might a busy but somewhat lonely Chesharilzi physician, most of whose genetic family members were recently recalled to the homeworld, gain entrance into this family of yours?"

"Oh, I expect a way could be found," Fox said with a smile. "If the busy Chesharilzi has the time for such matters. After all, he is, essentially, 'brother' to the stepmother, as long as they have known each other, and as well as they get along."

"I think he is apt to MAKE the time," Zarnix said, grin growing wider.

"Then he might be receiving an invitation to the next family gathering...assuming Zz'r'p can help us assure there IS one, some way," Fox said, sobering. Zarnix nodded.

"Well, I welcome his assistance; as well as he does know them, perhaps he can help us...somehow." It was Zarnix's turn to sigh.

"If nuthin' else, like Fox was sayin' earlier, he c'n help us find Meg, maybe," Romeo decided.

* * *

Scant minutes later, the tall, thin Deltiri burst into the medical conference room where the Director, the Chief of Staff of Medical, and Alpha Two awaited.

"Where are they?!" the fishlike alien demanded. "We must get the procedure under way at once!"

"What?" came the general chorus from four voices. "Calm down, Zz'r'p," Fox said, raising both hands in a *hold it* gesture, and keeping his voice low. "Tell us WHAT procedure we can possibly perform to fix this. And by 'where are they?' I assume you mean Alpha One."

"Yes, of course!" Zz'r'p exclaimed. "And how long has it been since Echo mostly died?"

"Not very long," Zarnix noted. "It's only been maybe three, four hours since we decanted him."

"But before that?"

"It has been, according to the reports I have seen, roughly twenty-four to maybe as much as thirty hours since the accident that resulted in his current condition," Zarnix filled in the other alien. "And that means that it has been slightly less than twenty-four hours since...brain death began."

"Ah," Zz'r'p said, relaxing slightly. "That is good news."

"But Zz'r'p, it's too late," India explained. "According to your assistant, his mind is already gone. Core dump down to nothing but the operating system, as it were."

"That may be so," Zz'r'p replied, "but it is not too late. My assistant is very good, but she is young, and has not yet learned all there is to know about such matters, nor does she know Alpha One as well as she thinks, quite yet. YOU four should remember, Omega carried a 'backup' of the mind in question. Granted, that backup was made when she had the telepathy chip implant, and so in the absence of that chip, the nd't'lq apparently did not automatically re-download into Echo's mind, but I can help with that. I can expedite the transfer. But it must be done quickly, else with Echo a tabula rasa, the nd't'lq will dissipate as surely as if he HAD died."

"Farkakte, verdammt, merde, glagaram, gronk, sssshttt, and argdun!" Fox cursed, with feeling.

* * *

"Oh, now that is NOT good," Zz'r'p declared, as soon as the full situation had been made known to him. "So you really have no idea where Omega is, but you know she has definitely left the planetary system."

"That's an affirmative," Fox averred. "The Lunar Farside Drydocks did report a gravitational passage within scant minutes of her departure from Penn Station, moving outbound, at a speed consistent with the maximum emergency interplanetary acceleration her ship would be capable of achieving—which is fairly hefty, given it was a corvette—and there was a warp bubble formation signature out near Mars-orbit distance shortly thereafter, and on the same trajectory. But we know that only because my executive assistants have been hard at work, trying to track her. So we know she is out of the Sol system. Beyond that, we know nothing. At least as yet. I've put out an emergency notice to watch out for an ill, confused Agent, so we have hopes someone will spot her soon."

"Mm," Zz'r'p hummed. "And Echo, her un'g't—soulmate, you might translate it—is sundered from her, and because he no longer has a past with her that he remembers, he is coming into knowledge of her as a complete stranger, and given the more...tempestuous...parts of that joint past, has evidently chosen to ignore the familiarity, the affection, and the trust."

"Exactly," Fox said with a sigh. "And she was present for that rather blunt and complete rejection. She went completely white, Zz'r'p."

"Even her lips were a pale gray," India added.

"I ain't never seen her like 'at before," Romeo claimed, subdued. "Even when she thought Echo 'uz dead. She 'uz hurtin' REAL bad, Zz'r'p."

"Romeo and I think it was essentially her worst nightmare coming true," India added. "Echo rejecting her as a kluged-up alien 'thing.'"

The Deltiri winced, then pondered this information for several moments. Finally he nodded.

"All right," he said. "Then let me ask you for a few minutes of silence, while I attempt to locate and reach her."

"You have it," Zarnix agreed, "anything you need, and more," and the others nodded affirmation.

The telepath sat in the nearest conference room chair, composed himself, and closed his eyes. His facial expression slowly blanked, and the others knew he was reaching out, seeking his pupil and their friend. More than one being present in the room was strongly reminded of similar behavior by Omega, when she was attempting to access other minds at a distance.

This went on for nearly five minutes before Zz'r'p stirred, sighed, and opened his eyes.

"I cannot locate her," he admitted. "And while, given an unlimited amount of time I might eventually locate her, the galaxy is a very big place. More, she is evidently closed down VERY tightly, and with the current strength of her mental block, combined with her emotional state—after all, remember how she took down Tt'l'k, and she is far more upset now—I submit to you that no member of any telepathic species known to the Coalition could reach her now. She does not wish to be reached, let alone found."

"Damn," Fox murmured.

"That," Romeo agreed.

"That said, it does not mean that I did not pick up...mm, echoes of her thoughts and feelings, let us term it," Zz'r'p noted. "I have known and interacted with her quite closely in the last two years, and we have come to consider each other dear and trusted friends; she has even semi-jokingly referred to me as 'Uncle Zz'r'p' once or twice. So I could sense her, very faintly, but it was not enough to locate her, nor to reach her through the positively adamantine mental wall she has erected."

"What DID you get, then?" Fox wondered. "She's fleeing, isn't she? Running away from the pain?"

"Yes, she is doing that," Zz'r'p averred, "most assuredly. But I believe she is attempting to extrapolate a purpose for that flight."

"What, then?"

"None of it is good," the telepath revealed. "If memory serves, Azeln—Slug—was a mercenary assassin sent here to kill some diplomat, was he not?"

"That's more or less correct," Fox confirmed. "You may remember the big dispute between the M'Quer and the Veldorn, nearly twenty years back?"

"Yes?"

"As best we were able to tell from the telepathic interrogation after Echo captured Azeln, the Veldorn—or, well, SOMEbody high up in Veldor's hierarchy, or supporting that hierarchy; whoever it was used a codename, and we were never able to determine an identity—hired him to locate M'Queran Ambassador Quequar M'reth, and kidnap it or kill it, whichever proved easier, in order to put paid to the negotiations that the ambassador was successfully leading. That said, by the point at which the interrogation occurred, Azeln was in shock, we now know because he was dealing with multiple levels of telepathic death feedback, and was well on the way to the madness that would claim him in the wake of his wife and children's deaths. Still and all, judging by the way things were going, we fully expected he would have killed M'reth. So yes, the term 'assassin' fits."

"Ah. And there will be mission records, and interrogation reports, and the like, from that case?"

"Of course."

"And Omega would have had access to these?"

"As Alpha Line assistant chief and partner to the Assistant Director slash Director Successor, she's got clearance access to just about anything in the Division that isn't at full Director levels," Fox pointed out. "And that stuff's not classified at Director level, so yes, she would have ready access. Goodness knows, she researched everything to do with that particular incident, before she would even agree to anything more than a partner relationship with Echo. So I'm sure she's read it all, multiple times. Most of it isn't classified at all any more, so just about anybody can look at it, because it's a cold case, and it's hoped open-source might turn up witnesses or whatnot."

"Uh-oh," a worried Romeo muttered, seeing where the Arcturan was going. "She didn't."

"I think she did, and is," Zz'r'p avouched. "I believe she has initiated her own personal investigation into who on Veldor hired Azeln."

"Oh, farkakte. She's on a vendetta, to end it once and for all," Fox realized. "To find the source and take it out, one way or another."

"It seems likely," Zz'r'p affirmed.

* * *

"Oh, HELL no," Whiskey averred, when Zarnix and Zebra quizzed him about what he had told Echo; Fox sat in the corner and listened, saying nothing. "Omega may be unusual, but I have to agree with Echo—er, with Echo before all this shit went down—and Zebra: she's not an alien in any sense of the word. She's had alien genetics spliced in, but the fundamental unit—her 'base model,' if you will—is and always has been human. And I never said otherwise. He did ask some questions about the differences, and I explained them. And I showed him some papers on identifying species via DNA sampling, but there shouldn't have been anything in there to indicate that Omega was anything other than a grossly-abused human, with what he and she used to term 'enhancements.' Unwanted enhancements, but hey."

"Which is as I thought," Zarnix noted. "We knew you did not think that of Omega, but were concerned that you had said something that might be INTERPRETED..."

"Well, evidently I did," Whiskey pointed out. "But not intentionally, and in fact I kinda tried to go the OTHER direction with it. Maybe I overdid it and raised his suspicions; I dunno."

"Or maybe it's an indication of what Zz'r'p was talking about," Zebra noted, deliberately oblique.

"I suppose it is likely," Zarnix agreed. "Perhaps we should discuss it with him."

"You got anything else for me?" Whiskey wondered.

"No, zun," Fox said, sitting up and finally speaking. "Go home and get some rest. I have the feeling that commodity will be in short supply soon."

Chapter 9

Omega, now clad in casual clothing, her Suit hidden deep in the classified stowage compartments, a solid hologram headset disguising her features, took the equally-well-disguised *Grapes of Wrath*, now dubbed *Franckenshteine*, via a roundabout route, to Aleancë. As she neared the planet, the comm snapped on and annunciated.

"Spacecraft *Franckenshteine*, this is Aleancë Spaceport Tower. Please respond."

"Spaceport Tower, this is Ekaturg Xelsib of Dekken, aboard *ISS Franckenshteine*. What do you require?" Omega replied, trying to swallow and force her heart out of her throat.

"We have high traffic levels today, and are attempting to work out gates for landing craft; your incoming automated signal indicated a desire to land. Do you or your craft require any special attention in this regard?"

"Negative, Tower, a standard landing berth will do. My craft is small, and will not take up much space," Omega noted. "And I am Gurgev, which as you know is a fairly standard bipedal humanoid species of the Opdip morphology."

"Very well; thank you. Please tune your navcomp to Band 12 and follow the signal to planetfall, utilizing Gate 114 Bet."

"Band 12, Gate 114 Bet. I copy," Omega murmured, adjusting the settings on her command console. Moments later she was descending through the pristine atmosphere of Aleancë, toward the massive general-aerospace port visible on the outskirts of the capital city.

* * *

'Ekaturg Xelsib' landed and secured her spacecraft at Gate 114 B, passed through the small-craft concourse and successfully transited Customs with her disguise intact, then hopped a mass-transit maglev shuttle into the city proper, exiting the shuttle at the Hall of Records.

"Greetings," she said to the being at the front desk, adopting her crispest Galactic pronunciation; as had been generally true on Earth, somehow English had become one of the *linguae francae* of the Coalition, despite the fact that Earth generally had no idea about the Coalition. "I wonder if you could help me..."

"What do you require?" the Ulyffon behind the desk asked; it was a Vandana, and its ratlike nose twitched in the species' expression of friendly interest.

"I am working on my graduate degree in law," the disguised Omega said, careful to maintain a more formal speech pattern, free of most contractions, "and my instructor has assigned me a particular case study to review and report. But it is not in the same Division as Dekken, and after recent events in the news, Earth has rather a lot of security to go through for a visit, so she recommended I attend this facility."

"Is it a PGLEIA case, then?"

"Yes, it is," she said. "I believe it is..." Omega pulled out her cell phone and consulted the memo app, "case number D1-047836-032601."

"Ah," the Vandana said. "Division One, some seventeen, perhaps eighteen Earth years ago, if my memory of the conversion rates serves..."

"That sounds correct, based upon what Professor Altayli said when she gave me the assignment," the Agent noted; Omega had even carefully looked up the names of the law professors on Dekken, to ensure that she sounded legitimate.

"Some of the records are printed; is that an issue?"

"No, I do not think so. Would you mind if I imaged them on my outboard brain? That way I can take copies with me and ask questions of the professor, if need be."

"Mm. Let me check the register," the bibliognost murmured, and turned to the nearby computer terminal. After a few moments of searching, it replied, "Not at all. There is no requirement for rights management on them, and the case is what is sometimes known as a 'cold case,' in several respects, so it would be desired that the information should be spread, in hopes of solving the case. Nor have any victims set a requirement for sealed records. It is interesting, however. Those records, at least in printed form, have not been accessed in many a long annum...though there is indication the electronic records have been accessed from Earth in recent months."

"Good. Then that will be fine. And Professor Altayli said she looked for some unusual cases for the class this annum."

"It sounds like an interesting class. Very well. Follow me, please, and I will show you to the file records for that case. My name is Tylmn; should you wish assistance, simply hit the call button on the workstation I will assign to you..."

* * *

Five minutes later, Omega was alone in the depths of the records hall, sitting at a table and poring over the files on Echo's fight against Slug.

"Hmph," she grumbled, after an hour of slogging through printed paperwork, "there's nothing here I haven't already seen back at Headquarters. That's disappointing. Well, maybe the electronic files will have something new." She shuffled through the various printed files, verified that indeed there was nothing in them she had not already perused weeks prior, and carefully re-filed them in the case container, then turned to the electronic files, opening and scanning the directory on the nearby workstation computer screen.

"Ohh, now THAT looks interesting," she murmured, grim. "They didn't have any telepathic interrogators on Earth at that time, because Zz'r'p didn't have his certification in interrogation yet, and he was just about the only Deltiri there except some basic reception and secretarial staff, so they must have done the interrogation here, on Aleancë. Let's have a look at that."

* * *

Report on the Interrogation of Gastropoid Prisoner Azeln AbdohNeléKein of Delta Scorpii

Captured by PGLEIA Division One (Earth) Law Enforcement Agents

Interrogator Ss'v'n ob Waa'kii of Deltir/Arcturus VII, presiding

PGC Custody Date 02/249/114310

PGC Reporting Date 02/273/114310

Rationale for Delay between Custody and Report: Medical condition/treatment of prisoner

CASE: Gastropoid perpetrator Azeln AbdohNeléKein of the Delta Scorpii system, recently arrested by Division One agents of Earth, Sol System, after an attempt to kidnap and/ or assassinate M'Queran Ambassador Its Excellency Quequar M'reth, was brought to PGLEIA galactic headquarters on Aleancë for a full interrogation, there being no duly-certified telepathic interrogators on Earth at this time.

BACKGROUND: Delta Scorpii B VI, as it is known on Earth (though not to the general Earth population), is NOT a member of the Pan-Galactic Coalition; it is, rather, a seclusive, separatist system, about which very little is known to the Coalition at large, including the indigenous name of the homeworld. Only a scant handful of gastropoids are known to the Coalition, and all of those are of dubious reputation, though that is likely a selection effect—it is expected that the peaceful, law-abiding members of that species would remain in-system and unknown to the Coalition as a whole. Apparently only those few who are more adventurous and less scrupulous are therefore willing to be hired out as mercenaries, to leave the planet on various less-than-lawful assignments.

There are, however, a few races in the Coalition that carry on independent trade with the system, such as the Hypothenemoids of Loterus V. These races are generally the source of what little we know of the system, which is still rather less than we should like, as the trade partners tend to be sworn to secrecy in order to maintain the agreements.

The majority of the system is obscured from detailed observation by the irregular and constantly varying decretion disk thrown off by the primary star, Delta Scorpii A, due to its rapid axial rotation. In fact, it was only recently that the number of planets in the system, and their distribution about the parent stars, was reliably determined; the interrogation which comprises the body of this report confirmed that number and distribution. Native names of the stars and planets were probably within the information gleaned from the subject's mind, but due to the subject's severely mentally-injured condition and subsequent and considerable mental confusion, could not be identified for certain.

THE SUBJECT: Azeln of Delta Scorpii B VI is a powerful

short-range telepath, capable of killing via telepathic attack if so desired; considerable care was taken that no interrogators or guards should be harmed or in danger during the course of the interrogation. However, subject is currently severely mentally incapacitated as a result of telepathic feedback apparently consequent to the death of its symbiote shell in the firefight that resulted in subject's arrest. Amount and quality of information obtained during this interrogation is therefore, and of necessity, somewhat muddled, though care has been taken to sort out the tangled narrative as it currently exists in the subject's mind, to the best of the interrogators' abilities. The interrogators assigned to the case therefore believe the information is fully accurate; however, interpretation has been difficult due to the unbalanced mental disorder of the subject in the wake of the telepathic feedback.

Azeln was contacted some six standard lunations ago on his homeworld, via means we could not understand, by a Veldorn opposed to the treaty then being negotiated between Veldor and M'Quer. There are indications in Azeln's mind that this Veldorn was a member of the ruling party, but this is uncertain, as it may be that Azeln himself did not know. In any case, the Veldorn in question was likely either very wealthy or an experienced scam artist, for it offered Azeln substantial funds—half of which was to be paid in advance—in exchange for removing Ambassador Quequar M'reth from the negotiations, whether by kidnapping or assassination was apparently immaterial to the Veldorn. The total fee was such that Azeln considered he would be a very rich gastropoid, with no need for further mercenary work. He apparently intended to return to his homeworld afterward and marry; there was considerable, and very bitter, mind-chatter about a wife and family, but the details were confused and confusing.

Azeln therefore negotiated a substantial fee for an open contract, allowing him to handle the matter in whatever fashion proved easiest in the circumstances. The Veldorn, going by the pseudonym or codename of Uesleion, his true identity thereby unknown to Azeln—and by extension, us—agreed to the contract, and as previously stated, paid half of the substantial fee in advance. (The meaning/translation of Uesleion is also not known; we do not know if the word is some declension of a Veldorn word; a word in whatever passes for a gastropoid language, given they are totally telepathic and have nothing anatomically corresponding to a voice box; or a twisted version of an M'Quer phrase. Given it is not recognized by any member of our investigatory team, including the linguists, we lean toward the notion that it is a gastropoid word. Unfortunately, since so little is known of that race, and that part of Azeln's mind appears most damaged, we are unlikely to ever know what it means. This is unfortunate, as it could have proven a telling clue regarding the identity of Azeln's employer.) In any case, the deal was struck, and Azeln prepared for his mission and set out for Earth in his personal spacecraft.

This interrogation supports the conventional Agency report from Division One Headquarters in all points: Azeln made landfall on Earth somewhere in the vicinity of the New York City metroplex, then set about determining where the negotiations were being held. Unfortunately, he was not as subtle as he should have been in the doing, likely as a result of a general sense of superiority as well as underestimating the humans' skills and abilities, and the Agency detected his activity relatively quickly. Wisely, it promptly sent Quequar M'reth and the rest of its envoy into hiding, and initiated a 'manhunt' for Azeln. However, given the fact that humans are not telepathic, nor can they erect more than the most rudimentary mental blocks and that rarely for a strong mind, Azeln found it incredibly easy to telepathically attack and destroy their minds, killing several and leaving even more physically alive but 'brain-dead,' as the colloquial Earth terminology has it. In addition, numerous civilians died as collateral damage, caught in the attack. Azeln does not appear particularly remorseful for any of this; in point of fact, he seems to have found it generally amusing, noting how easy it was to do.

The Division One Agency's youngest agent, codenamed Echo, performed what appears to have been an excellent job of detection, especially noteworthy given his age; it is recommended that he be watched closely, for his career should be a stellar one, in our estimation. Fortunately, it seems he took to the mental block training rather better than most hu-

mans, and it provided just enough protection to hide him as he slipped up on the somewhat preoccupied gastropoid, then enabled him to survive Azeln's mental attack long enough to respond with a laser pistol. This response resulted in the death of the shell symbiote, which Echo claims was accidental, and likely caused by Azeln's interference with the agent's nervous system and musculature as he fired. There is some indication from our telepathic interrogation of the perpetrator that Azeln was indeed playing what the young agent calls 'mind games,' and Echo himself submitted to voluntary interrogation, with the result that we firmly believe he is telling the truth as best he understands it.

In any event, the mental symbiosis was apparently a sufficiently profound link that the symbiote's unexpected death and link-severing generated a severe telepathic backlash, and Azeln went down. Azeln is not aware of any events past this point, as the backlash rendered him unconscious for over three Division standard days—essentially a standard Earth 'week,' or one-quarter of a lunation—during which the medics believe he was the gastropoid equivalent of comatose. During this period, the physicians stabilized him as best they could, given their limited knowledge of his species. After that time, he gradually regained consciousness, but his mental state was drastically and apparently permanently affected. It was some considerable time after that, however, before he re-attained mobility and control of his body.

At the current time, he is conscious and semi-alert, but it cannot be said that he is coherent, by any means. Attempts to carry on a standard, conversational-questioning pattern have only resulted in disjointed ramblings, the occasional angry rant, and a kind of jumbled babble, all of which quickly strays from the topic under discussion. He seems fixated with the notion of marriage and family, though the reason behind this fixation is unclear.

CONCLUSIONS, PROGNOSIS AND RECOMMENDATIONS: It is the joint, considered opinion of this interrogation team that Azeln AbdohNeléKein is permanently mentally injured, and is unlikely to fully recover. His mental capacity is significantly diminished, in our joint assessment, and the prob-

ability that he will be a continued danger to any other than himself is, we believe, low.

We therefore recommend he be designated fully mentally incapacitated, and handled appropriately henceforward.

* * *

Omega finished reading, and let out a lone bleak, almost mocking, bark of laughter, even as her face twisted in disgust. "Damn, they couldn't have been more wrong," she muttered to herself. "Permanently brain-damaged, yes. Not a danger to others? No way in eighteen and a half levels of hell."

She continued to dig through the electronic files, looking for anything she didn't already know from studying records of Echo's missions, especially after Slug's attack some year and a half earlier.

All at once, she sat upright, staring at the screen.

"There," she breathed, staring at a name. "Xoreplirg Erushin of Veldor. He was twelve kinds of demanding for Slug's apprehension, and pretty high up in the political structure, but... lessee. His name means..." She thought hard, trying to pull up a memory, unaware it was not her own, thanks to recent events leaving her too agitated to focus on more than one problem at a time—and the current problem was 'Who hired Slug?' not from whence the expert linguistics knowledge was coming. "Xoreplirg is Veldorn for...'highly favored.' Pretty typical for doting parents, I suppose, especially for a first child, and it looks like he...or it...is the eldest of several kids. But Erushin means...it means...what the hell does it mean?!" she grumbled, frustrated, as the information just eluded her conscious mind; she concentrated, trying to dredge it up to the surface. "Ah! 'One who lies in wait.' Now THAT is an interesting name. And I'm getting an unpleasant sort of vibe off it, too, like 'one who lies in wait' is NOT sitting in, say, a doctor's office, waiting to get called back. Wonder what it represents. Nothing good in the family tree, I'll bet. Hm. Lemme see what I can find on HIM. Er, it...or something. I guess I need to find out about the Veldorn genders while I'm about this. 'Cause that might be my next stop."

Omega pulled her own tablet, linking it into the Aleancë records system, and did a quick search on Xoreplirg Erushin.

She studied the file that came up.

"Okay, it's a 'he.' Old, very wealthy Veldorn family," she murmured, blue eyes flicking down the file. "Heavily into planetary politics. Currently mostly retired from politics; family patriarch now. Hm. Well, that rather fits the profile the interrogators came up with. But that's not proof, by any means. I need to KNOW I've got the right being, before I do what I have in mind."

She raked a distracted hand over her hair, and shoved down the memory of Echo's face when he told Fox to keep his partner away from him. *Stop it,* she told herself. *You already know it's over, and your life with it. You've lost him, for good and all. If it's going to ever mean anything, be worth anything lasting, you have to solve this one and take care of the bastard who's ultimately responsible. And do it before you get taken out, yourself. Because if this dude ever finds out you're after him—whoever he turns out to be—you can bet he'll do whatever it takes to take you out before you can get too close. And I expect he has the money and the power to see that that happens, too. Now, once I get him, eh. Whatever. I don't guess it matters much, after that; I'm too tired and beat-down to care any more. But I have to get him first. And take him out. One way or another.*

She considered for long moments, then picked up her tablet again.

"Let's try a search on that pseudonym," she decided, "and see if I pick anything up. After all, it's been almost two decades, and just because they didn't recognize it then, doesn't mean it's not someplace in the system now."

So she plugged 'Uesleion' into the search engine and initiated a search, then waited.

It took nearly five minutes before a response popped up.

* * *

Uesleios, [WHES-lee-os] n. sing.—*chief assassin, chief executioner; from the archaic Veldorn uesleion, antagonist, executioner, attacker, usually connoting long planning; synonym erushios, -on.*

* * *

"Oh shit," Omega whispered, sapphire eyes widening.

"Erushion and Uesleion are synonyms. And a variant of erushion—Erushin—is that guy's last name. Which means 'one who lies in wait.' There's GOTTA be a connection. I need to dig into the Erushin clan."

* * *

Several hours later, Omega finally found the file she wanted—in, of all places, the Predecessors Dot Com website, whose Earth spinoff had proven quite popular among humans—pulled it up, and read it in detail.

"'The Erushin family is a very old, patriarchal family of the Veldorn,'" she read aloud to herself, having discovered that she was still sufficiently perturbed by recent events to need that auditory aid to concentration, but keeping her voice to a bare whisper. "'Their wealth was obtained in antiquity, when there were fewer laws—and fewer who were law-abiding—than today. What rule of law there was tended to occur at the whim of the local warlord, whose word was the only law extant. Clan Erushione, as they were known then, provided many of the formal executioners to the various warlords, as well as covert agents and skilled mercenaries, specializing in ambush, infiltration, espionage, sabotage, assassination, and other clandestine forms of guerrilla warfare. So skilled were they at matters of dealing death, obtaining information, and generally subverting activity, that they commanded high fees, often higher than any other such agent, and thereby enriched the clan—and many personal—coffers. Special skills and secret tricks of the trade were passed on from parent to offspring, along with intensive training from the time the child could walk; by the time the child reached the age of majority at 15 annums, it was a fully-fledged erushion. This is, of course, the origin of the familial surname.'"

Omega's head shot up.

"That's it," she muttered. "It's gotta be. I wonder..." She dove back into the ancestral history file.

"Mmm," she hummed. "Lessee, here, now...ah! 'Legend has it that the Erushins continued the training, passing on family techniques, until relatively recent times. However, four generations ago, the famous patriarch of the house, Zaxrakalich Erushin, decreed that this would cease, declaring that it was a barbarous practice, which should be limited to the old days. More recently, prominent members of that family, including the current patriarch, Xoreplirg, have bemoaned the loss of the skills which made the family unique.' Aha! And that explains why he had to hire Slug," Omega concluded. "Because he couldn't do it himself, or order anybody else in the family to do it for him—they lost the ability to do it for themselves, when their ancestor outlawed passing on even the training in the family practices."

She continued to read through the article, absorbing as much information as she could, especially about the family seat and home, until the Ulyffon bibliognost returned.

"Gentlebeing," the little rodent-like creature piped in a soft tone, "forgive my interruption, but the Hall of Records will be closing soon, for the day. Do your studies progress?"

"They do indeed," Omega, still in guise as Ekaturg Xelsib, replied. "In fact, I believe I have either scanned or duplicated all of the files I need for my assignment into my hand tablet, so I think I can help you replace the hard files before closing, and be on my way."

"Oh! Very good! That is much appreciated," the bibliognost declared, pleased. "It is not often we are helped in the tidying away..."

Omega rose from her chair and began helping the grateful bibliognost clean up her workstation, refiling folders and papers and generally putting all to rights.

Fifteen minutes later, she was on the maglev shuttle headed for the aerospace port.

Half an hour after that, she was outbound from Aleancë...

...Headed for Veldor.

* * *

Peter Dianus, astronaut, sat in the office of the Chief Astronaut, Morgen Kirby.

"What I want to know is, was it deliberate?" she asked then. A shocked Dianus paled.

"Wha-? Deliberate?"

"You jumped the gun on the hotfire test...while Scotty was still on EVA," Kirby pointed out. "And Scotty didn't make it back. You've had a problem with him from the beginning. He sacrificed himself to get your ass home safely, along with the rest of the crew. Did you ensure he had no other choice?"

"I-I didn't...It wasn't like that, Morgen," Dianus protested, shocked.

"Did you or did you not jump the gun on the test?"

"I...I did, but...it wasn't deliberate! I swear, it wasn't deliberate! With all the adrenaline going, I was crankin', you know? I just mistimed it!"

"Mmm," Kirby said, noncommittal. "Well, you're done."

"Huh?"

"You had a major, nearly catastrophic malfunction on YOUR watch, on YOUR command. Because of YOUR actions. The only reason the spacecraft came home at all was thanks to massive prep in the aftermath of the *Columbia* disaster, and the heroic, sacrificial actions of...your PILOT. Not you, your pilot. You didn't even suit up! Or, as nearly as we can figure, allow anyone BUT Scotty to suit up...which lays suspicion back on you, no matter what you may say."

"But-but..."

"Don't give me that! You know the protocol! TWO crew on EVA, ONE on backup-slash-IVA. You had ONE crewman on EVA, and NO backup. As a result, you lost a crewman... on your watch, under your command. The crew is unified in stating that you were a major negative factor in the entire sequence of events—including your failure to follow the checklist, which led to the catastrophic failure mode to begin with. BOTH payload crew members AND the MS-2 state categorically that you systematically REFUSED to properly follow ANY of the procedures for the Atom engine! They want your hide. Preferably peeled off your body, dried, tanned, and nailed to the wall. The whole damn crew. Every one of 'em, including the Teflon Astronaut. Do you KNOW how much it takes to piss off the Teflon Astronaut?"

A horrified Dianus was speechless. Kirby continued.

"The entire cadre of flight directors that sat console during the mission wants your hide. The mission managers want your hide. The advanced prop project managers want your hide. And this morning, the NASA Administrator called me for a long talk...about you. Given the general trend, you can guess what

SHE wanted." She stared at the astronaut, gaze cold. "You're done, Dianus. Not even your father can save you this time; he's scrambling to save his OWN hide, because the backsplash from your shit has landed on him. As of this moment, you are officially no longer a member of the astronaut corps. You will never fly again."

"But...I've got tenure! I'm a GS-13 step 9!"

"Yes, you do. And yes, you are. And because of that, you will be given a lead position."

"Well, that's better, at least." Dianus grinned, thinking he might be able to negotiate a promotion out of the situation, or at least a lateral transfer. *And a lateral transfer from astronaut commander won't be shabby,* he thought. *And Dad can help me move up from there, once things settle out a little.*

"Therefore, you will have your choice of one of these four positions," Kirby continued. "You will be the NASA lead—NOT the overall person in charge, just the NASA lead; any contractors responsible for constructing the facilities own it, and may run it as they see fit—for one of the following: the ground tracking station on Guam, with PERSONAL, on-site responsibility for maintaining the backup site on Diego Garcia; the ground tracking station at McMurdo; the ground tracking station outside North Pole, Alaska; or the ground tracking station at Dongara, Western Australia. If you refuse to choose, a choice will be made for you." She watched as a very pale Dianus licked dry lips. "So. Which will it be?"

* * *

"Wait a minute," Echo protested, outraged. "You're telling me that my mind is in her head?"

"That is precisely what I am telling you, Echo," Zz'r'p averred. "Or a copy of it, at any rate. Once we get her back here, we can retrieve your nd't'lq, letting it 'download' back into your own brain, and you will have your memories and abilities back."

"How the HELL does somebody STEAL a guy's MIND?!" he demanded to know.

"Omega didn't steal it," Fox declared, stern. "You GAVE it to her, voluntarily, because she was trying with all her might to protect you from being brain-bleached as a result of an unfair accusation! That young woman would DIE for you, and nearly has, on a couple of different occasions! She LOVES you, Echo!"

"Wait— what?" Echo said, voice flat, as what Fox said registered.

"It is true," Zz'r'p confirmed. "Part of the reason why she is suffering from PTSD is because she was nearly forced to kill the man she loved—you—because her body had been essentially commandeered by an interstellar criminal, and was beyond her control. I can speak to this directly; I have been in her mind, and know it for a fact. You know I speak the truth regarding my abilities, because I spoke directly with you, mind to mind, when I entered the room."

"I thought...I thought she'd just managed to sucker me in," Echo murmured then. "You know, seduce me and convince me...for her own purposes, or this Slug dude's...I mean, she IS gorgeous, I'll admit that..."

"No," Fox noted. "I know for a FACT she hasn't seduced you, because she's old-fashioned, and still waiting for the two of you to get married."

Echo's jaw went slack.

"You're kidding."

"No. The lady...AND the gentleman, because you are one, zun...is honorable. ARE honorable. Both of you."

"Then why has she run off, when she knows she's got my mind, and it has to be downloaded real soon quick?" Echo challenged.

"Several reasons, but one main one, I suspect," Fox decided.

"Indeed. And I will confirm it: that main reason was because you did the one thing that she could not bear, Echo, the one thing that undid everything I have been working to overcome in her counseling sessions," Zz'r'p said. "The thing she feared more than death itself."

"And just what the hell was that?"

"You rejected her, point-blank to her face, on the basis of what was done to her. Because Slug attempted to degrade her into a murderous beast...never mind the fact that he failed to do so."

"Huh?" Echo whispered then, shocked, and the two males adjudged that he had not been expecting the answer he got. "Failed? Feared more than...than death?"

"Zun, I'm thinking that perhaps you skimped on reading your own files, after going over your mother's and your partner's," Fox observed. "You only skimmed over them, didn't you?"

"Um, well, I was gettin' kinda tired," Echo confessed. "I thought, when I saw all that stuff in Omega's files, that you were tryin' to warn me, and...uh...you know, maybe I oughta try again...?"

"I have a better idea," Fox decided. "Let me see what I can pull up in the way of security and surveillance video of the two of you together, as well as some of Alpha One's training sessions, and let you WATCH them. I want you to see the two of you interacting, working together. I expect you need to understand your partner, the woman who loves you more than she loves herself, in order to allow the download process to proceed properly, once we manage to find her and get her back."

"Indeed," Zz'r'p confirmed.

"Uh, well, um, o-okay," Echo agreed, seeming uncharacteristically uncertain.

"Let me help," Zz'r'p told Fox. "I have some ideas about what he needs to see, I think. Echo, we will be back shortly."

"I ain't goin' anywhere," Echo pointed out. "'Cept maybe to the bathroom, and it's right there." He pointed at the tiny toilet.

"All right, just wait for us, and try to rest in the meantime," Fox ordered.

* * *

"I can't think all that was good," Fox murmured to Zz'r'p, once they were back in the conference room. "Anything about that whole exchange. It spoke to an Echo who was not nearly as alert and aware and...COGNIZANT...as the man I am used to working with, socializing with."

"No, I am forced to agree, it was not good," Zz'r'p allowed. "I think you are right—that was evidence of a certain lack of cognition. So it is not merely his ability to write, perform mathematics, his memories, that are in absentia; he can no longer reason with his usual aplomb. More, it strikes me that what cognition with which he awoke...may now be deteriorating. Worse yet, this may bode ill for his continued existence, if we cannot get Omega back here in time."

"What do you mean?"

"I mean that, if the nd't'lq dissipates, his cognition, his coherence, perhaps even his very consciousness, may dissipate shortly thereafter. The body may still live, but the brain—the mind, the personality, the intellect, Echo's very psyche—will be entirely gone. No matter what we may do. More, it is possible that, due to the separation, this will happen with greater speed than nd't'lq dissipation. Possibly by an order of magnitude."

"Oh, verdammt," Fox breathed, horrified.

* * *

Moments later, as the two males worked together on developing a selection of videos for Echo to watch, Fox's cell phone bleated in a certain tone. He jerked it out of a pocket, activated it, and held it to his ear.

"Fox here."

"Fox, this is Lima. We just got an interesting automated notification."

"Oh? About what? And from where?"

"It came from the Hall of Records on Aleancë," Lima answered. "It was—"

"No, wait, don't tell me," Fox said, putting his free hand to his forehead, as Zz'r'p watched. "It was the records of our first encounter with Slug, wasn't it?"

"Nailed it in one, Boss," Lima verified. "But it wasn't Omega who accessed it."

"It wasn't?"

"No. It was one Ekaturg Xelsib of Dekken, a law student doing a case study, according to the automated notice."

"Hm. No, it was Omega."

"Huh?"

"Look at the facts, zun. Omega goes missing, apparently on a rogue mission of her own, which Zz'r'p strongly believes is an attempt to learn and bring to justice whoever hired Slug to begin with. Her last probable location, based on the destruction of the two Cortian pirate ships, was in the general direction of Aleancë from Earth, though well out of normal shipping and traffic routes..."

"Okay..."

"And she is no longer there, per the search that took place when the debris was discovered. Then someone checks on the records of that very case on Aleancë, and the records on Aleancë are more complete than the ones here at Headquarters, because we did not, at that time, have a certified telepathic interrogator on Earth."

"Okay, Fox, go on; I'm following you."

"So the person who accessed those records was this 'Ekaturg Xelsib of Dekken.' Gurgevs are the principal sentient species in the Dekken system, and they look enough like humans that visiting Gurgevs can pass on Earth without any disguise necessary. More, 'Ekaturg' is a feminine name; if memory serves, it's the equivalent of Cathy, not that that means anything. The point is, whoever accessed those records was female. And appeared young enough to be taken for a graduate law student, hence the cover story. And Omega is generally mistaken as considerably younger than her actual age...and undoubtedly knows that we—and others, given the Cortian attack—will be looking for her..."

"Oh shit," Lima said then, sounding blank. "Yeah, it was Omega, wasn't it? Undercover, in a disguise?"

"He's got a point," Bravo's voice sounded in the background. "I'mma dig into the admissions records for the law schools on Dekken. I'm betting there's no such a student as this Ekaturg Xelsib."

"I'd lay a significant amount of money on it, zun, yes, and good idea," Fox declared. "Can you tell if she is still there? On Aleancë?"

"No, but I can find out real quick."

"Do it. And keep me posted."

"Wilco."

* * *

Fox deactivated the phone and put it away, then looked up to find Zz'r'p watching.

"So she has begun her quest?" the Deltiri wondered. "Dig-

200

ging into records on Aleancë?"

"Yep," Fox said, succinct.

They resumed selecting video records.

* * *

Moments later, Fox's phone rang again with the same special identifying ring tone.

"Fox. That you, Lima? Bravo?"

"It's Lima, Fox. Bravo says there's no such student as Ekaturg Xelsib in any of the law schools on, or affiliated with, Dekken; and I did a quick ping of the Hall of Records on Aleancë. Other than the facial features, the Dekken did match Omega's general description, and didn't you tell me one time that she'd added one of those solid hologram disguises to her field travel kit? Like, after we got in the special kits with warp pockets, so they could pack all kinds of field equipment in 'em?"

"That's right, now you mention it; she did."

"Then I'd say you nailed it—it was almost certainly her."

"Is she still at the Hall of Records?"

"No, she left a while back, when it closed for the day. So I pinged the general aerospaceport. A Dekken matching that name landed there in a small spacecraft named *Franckensh- teine* several hours ago—"

"Of course! A variant on the name Frankenstein, when she considers herself a monster..."

"...But departed Aleancë within the last hour. I double- checked on the make and model of spacecraft, and it does match our corvettes, but she must have messed with the auto- mated ID, 'cause it wasn't that of *The Grapes of Wrath*."

"Well, that would almost certainly be well within her skill set; X-ray, Echo, and I once had to do that when we dropped undercover in an emergency situation during one of my diplo- matic missions, so I'm sure Echo's showed her how. Did she file a flight plan when she left Aleancë?"

"Yes. She left a flight plan to Dekken, but there doesn't seem to be any indication of a ship that's actually following it."

"No, that was a wild hope, and I knew it. All right, zun, here's what I want you to do."

"Waiting to copy, Fox."

"Good. I want you to go back and get the automated identification information on the *Franckenshteine* if you haven't already—"

"I have."

"Good, zun, and I want you to append it to the bulletin we put out on Omega, as being...let me see...make it an alternative ship she may be using. I don't want to get her into trouble for stealing a spacecraft or something. She may seem rational enough, but I'd say she's obsessed at this point, and not in a healthy way."

"Understood."

"Then get me on Gwag Wuxullian's schedule for a vidcall meeting later today," Fox said.

"The galactic chief of PGLEIA?"

"The same. I want to make sure he understands exactly what's going down, in excruciating detail. After the debacle with Echo's arrest a few weeks back, I don't want a repeat performance with Omega. I know I sent him a special communiqué already, but the way this is developing, I think it warrants a face to face. Or at least an electronic one."

"Roger that, Fox," Lima said. "I'll get on all this ten minutes ago."

"Good man. Fox out."

"Lima out."

* * *

"...So these videos are gonna show me an' this Omega in action as partners?" Echo verified.

"That's right," Fox confirmed. "I'm hoping you'll begin to see that she's someone you trusted with your life...because she always came through for you."

"Can..." Echo paused, seeming undecided, then continued, "can I ask you something?"

"Of course, zun. I understand that, what with no memory of events, all this is immensely confusing for you," Fox said, sympathetic. "About the only thing I'm not going to tell you at this point would be classified matters for which you don't currently have a need to know."

He neglected to say that Echo's clearance had been significantly downgraded as a result of the current situation—essentially to that of a new recruit, which was only one step up from a complete civilian; Fox hoped against hope that the entire matter would be rectified, and Echo back to normal, before it was necessary for Echo to even know about THAT. He already had the matter set up as a temporary downgrade, and if what Zz'r'p had planned actually worked, the downgrade would be immediately revoked.

"Okay, and I get that," Echo agreed. "So, um...you said the MAIN reason Omega left was because I...rejected her. But you and this Zz'r'p fella both said there were OTHER reasons why she left, even while knowing my mind was in her brain. What were those other reasons?"

"Well, nobody remembered she even had it until Zz'r'p came back from his vacation, after getting an emergency summons over this whole farshtinkener mess, because he's her psi trainer and counselor," Fox explained. "Therefore, nobody's actually talked to her about it, so this is...eh, it's a bit more than speculation, but not as hard as verified knowledge. Call it an educated guess, based on my knowledge of my agents."

"Okay, fair enough. Keep going."

"All right. So. The rest of us forgot; it's possible she forgot, herself, that she had it—the transfer was done while she was using an experimental chip implanted in her brain to give her full telepathy. But she had a severe immune reaction to the blasted thing, and the chip had to be removed before it caused brain damage—though she refused to allow that to be done until AFTER you were out of danger of being brain-bleached, let me note."

"She-wha? Holy shit."

"Exactly. But THAT...is how much she loves you, zun. She was willing to suffer brain damage in order to keep from losing you. Because she already knew, due to a skull fracture and concussion she suffered last spring, that YOU would stand beside HER, even if she no longer had her full intellect..."

"I...wow. Um, okay. Keep...keep going."

"All right. So. Since then, I've gathered from some offhand comments you both made, that neither of you were strong enough in telepathic...shit...to maintain a full nd't'lq-type connection. I think, had it been hers in you, there would be a connection, because she IS a low-level psi, due to Slug's 'tinker-ing,' she calls it...with considerable disgust, let me add. But you're NOT a psi, and it's yours in her, so you can't reach it and she can't help you to reach it."

"In other words, it's there, but it's kinda...inactive, sorta."

"Right. More than 'kinda,' I think, though I might be wrong about that. So she might have forgotten about it," Fox continued. "Especially as upset as she was. Another possibility is that, since it didn't automatically download this time, like it did when you got brain-bleached during Adita's Coup—do you remember reading about that in the files?"

"Yeah, I do, now you mention it," Echo said, thoughtful.

"So it may be that, since it didn't download automati-cally and instantly this time, if she even remembered, she ei-ther figured it never would, or possibly that she'd somehow lost the nd't'lq, that it had dissipated, or the like, when you went through being 'mostly dead'...or even that it started dis-sipating when she had the chip removed," Fox finished. "By the way, just so that thought doesn't upset you, I've already asked Zz'r'p, and he says that the chip removal would not have caused it to dissipate, and it takes much longer to dissipate than you were 'mostly dead.' Like, several weeks to months. So it should be fine, just...dormant. In any event, the probabil-ity is high that she is so upset that she is not thinking clearly. She may believe she is being quite logical; she may even pres-ent the appearance to a disinterested observer that she is. But those of us who truly know her? We know she is NOT thinking clearly, simply because of her actions."

Echo sighed.

"And that...would be my fault," he noted, shoulders slump-ing.

"Well, we none of us are blaming you, zun. I honestly have no idea what I would make of my own life, were this to happen to me. I probably would not believe my own history...which is fairly unusual in its own right, even relative to other agents."

Echo just shrugged. His face and overall demeanor indi-cated a certain degree of despondency to the Director, who bit the inside of his lip in concern.

"Well, let's have a look at these videos," Fox said, voice

gentle. "This first one is relatively recent, just a few weeks old, and it's a training video. It shows the two of you in action in the training room simulator, working your way through a problem I set for you, to demonstrate to department candidates how an Alpha Line team should work, from start to finish of a mission, no matter how unexpected..."

* * *

"Holy shit," Echo said, nonplussed, as the video ended. "That...that was ME?! And her? Damn!"

"Exactly, zun," Fox said with a slight grin. "I'm not joking when I say that the two of you are my premier team."

"Shit hellfire damnation," Echo replied instinctively. "What the hell has this done to me? I've noticed in the last few hours that I'm doin' good not to trip over my own feet when I get up to go to the can! But I was mopping up the ground with the bad guys on that!" He jabbed a finger at the television.

"Well, we think this may be a side effect of the whole memory-loss thing," Fox tried, tap-dancing around the magnitude of the 'side effect' so as not to upset Echo; he was already agitated enough at the realization of the discrepancy. "When we can get the nd't'lq re-downloaded into you, everything should come back."

"So this Omega—this 'Meg'—she's still missing?" Echo wondered.

"So far, yes," Fox admitted. "But we're all working on that. Even when I'm here, my assistants are searching, and keeping me apprised of matters. She IS good, very good...but so are we."

"Okay. Meanwhile, show me more about her, about us," Echo decided. "You got my curiosity up, big time. Keep going."

"Onward," Fox said, secretly pleased, initiating another video sequence on the television.

* * *

A patient and secretly hopeful Fox spent several hours showing an attentive and highly interested Echo assorted recorded feeds, most of them pulled from various security/surveillance systems at Agency facilities around the world: Headquarters, the McMurdo Office, Chicago Office, London Office,

Sydney Office, and more. He also showed Echo recordings of the recent hearings in the Ennead, where he had been charged with criminal insubordination. Echo was silent for long moments after that sequence ended.

"She really did save me," he whispered. "And I saved her—she'd be dead, if I'd left her on the Premier's flagship. And we'd be at war."

"At the least," Fox agreed. "If not outrightly conquered already."

"And the kiss...wow."

"Yes, but that isn't even the most passionate kiss I've seen between the two of you. That one was pretty tame, because you both knew everyone was watching. Let me see if I can find the security video from your cell on Aleancë..."

Moments later, the pair watched as a recorded Fox explained the nature of Omega's 'modifications' to an imprisoned Echo, and the ramifications thereof. Then the video image of Fox confessed to providing the information to Echo on Omega's behalf, since she was too ashamed to tell him herself. When Echo's documented response indicated he didn't care about the 'modifications,' the recorded Omega burst into the cell and ran straight into Echo's arms, kissing him as if it were some form of life support for both of them, as Fox slipped out of the cell.

A slight gasp escaped the amnesiac Echo in the hospital bed. Fox glanced at him, to see him wide-eyed, gaze fixed on the screen, watching every nuance of that kiss, even as his eyes dilated, his nostrils flared, and his respiration increased.

And there's the indication that she still holds attraction for him, the Director realized. *Regardless of what reasoning he came up with for rejecting her, somewhere deep inside, he still loves her. And that...will help this situation. Assuming we can find Omega in time. Otherwise...he'll end up brain-dead.*

At last that particular video came to an end, and Fox turned to the man in the bed.

"I have one last sequence you need to see," Fox said, "but this one isn't going to be easy to watch, at all."

He turned and initiated another recording. The imagery opened on a cavernous hangar, with a large black vessel sitting in the docking clamps. The caption in the bottom right corner read, *Chicago Station Spaceport, Hangar 16, 16.05.02.08.45D1.* A large group of agents formed an honor guard along the walkway to the black spacecraft's hatch, even as a group of yellow-feathered avians led Echo toward it. Omega and Fox stood at the head of the honor guard, watching; Omega's face was grim.

Abruptly Echo's distant voice sounded over the television's speaker, just as he reached the alien vessel's hatch.

"Meg! DANTE!! DANTE, baby!"

Scant seconds later, Omega's voice, clear and commanding, rose over the thrumming sound of a spacecraft warming up for launch.

"ALPHA LINE! Commence Operation: Dante! GO!!"

Echo's jaw dropped as all hell broke loose onscreen.

* * *

Fox made him watch all the way through to the emergency medical evacuation. When the medical team loaded Omega's charred—but still living—form into an antigrav stretcher, Fox ended the playback and switched off the TV. Then he turned to Echo.

A horrified Echo sat in the bed, rigid, face so pale it was nearly white, brown eyes dilated and still fixed on the television screen, lips parted as if to say something, but nothing would come out. After long moments, he turned to look at Fox, and licked dry lips.

"I," he began, then broke off.

"Yes," Fox agreed, keeping his voice soft. "Exactly."

Echo swallowed hard a few times, then a dry heave escaped him, and Fox quickly reached for a bed pan. Echo grabbed his belly with one hand and turned away slightly, holding his other hand out in a *wait, I got this* gesture, and Fox obeyed, watching...but with the pan still in hand, just in case. After several seconds, Echo regained control of his stomach and his emotions, panted a few moments, then looked back at Fox, who reached for the patient's water bottle on the bedside table. He offered it to Echo, who sipped from it for a little bit, settling his belly. Then Echo set the bottle aside and returned his attention to Fox...who only then discarded the pan.

"This is the mission where she...saw part of it coming, wasn't it?" the younger man recalled. "I remember reading that in the report."

"Yes," Fox confirmed.

"I don't remember if it said...did she know she was going to survive?"

"I don't think it's in the report, no. But you asked her that specifically, in a conversation during her recovery period, in front of the rest of us," Fox noted. "I recall that EXTREMELY clearly. And she told us that she didn't have any information past ending up on the hangar deck with you, as the engines came online, with her leg broken. She went into it expecting to die...in order to save you."

Echo put his face in his hands.

"What have I done?" he breathed through his fingers.

* * *

"...Yes, that's right, Wux," Fox said to the being on the large wall screen in his office. The bay windows were opaqued, and Fox had just finished explaining the detailed situation, including all of the latest information and probable surmises, to the Erikian who headed up the Pan-Galactic Law Enforcement and Immigration Administration and reported directly to the Ennead; Gwag Wuxullian's current official title was 'Chief Administrator of Pan-Galactic Law Enforcement and Immigration,' but Fox had known him back when he was the Director of Division Two. "It's really rather a sad situation, I think, and I'm very concerned we might lose BOTH of them, at this point... one way or another. Omega is emotionally distraught, because this was the final straw, especially after everything she's been through in the last two or three months—you've seen all my reports in the last, oh, four to six months or so. You've seen how it all kind of ramped up."

"Yes, I have," Wuxullian averred. "The fact that she and Echo were able to continue so efficiently for as long as they did was a testament to their determination and strength of will, I felt."

"Yes, but it's gone over the top now, and it looks to be headed straight to hell in the proverbial handbasket, unless we have a little luck. Maybe a whole damn truckload of luck.

So anyway, she's out there someplace; we're pretty sure she's trying to track down whoever hired Slug on his first 'visit' to Earth, back when Echo first took him on. I can't say what she's thinking, or what she's planning to do, if she finds that being. I don't think she's the type to simply take him, her, or it out without due process, but if the perp does something stupid, like draw down on her, all bets are off."

"And that would be normal procedure in any case, and well within her prerogative, were it to do so," Wuxullian agreed. "But she's already taken out two Cortian pirate ships, you said?"

"We can't prove it, but I'd lay money on it," Fox noted. "Judging by the pattern of damage to the debris, I think she used the same tactic she and Echo developed last spring during the altercation that led to the Battle of the Orion Nebula, and then showed Coalition forces how to perform, during that same battle." He shrugged. "That said, the reports I'm getting back also indicate that there may be evidence that she was provoked into attacking—the investigators found the remains of a partial bank of the Cortian main guns, and forensic reconstruction indicates they'd been fired in a timeframe roughly concurrent to a time several seconds before the spacecrafts' destruction. And frankly, back when the Cortians made 'first contact,'" he quirked his fingers in air quotes, "they gave evidence of wanting to take her captive as well as Echo, and the nebula search parties were after BOTH of 'em, without doubt—the Cortians even referenced Echo AND Omega as, get this: 'escaped slaves.' Like they'd ever belonged to the Cortians, or anybody else!"

"Ag ogdun rag gargun!" Wuxullian snarled.

"Those sons of bitches? You betcha. And Wux, that lot was flatly willing to kill Alpha One if they couldn't capture 'em. So if they thought they'd found Omega, and she didn't stand down when ordered—and I know she wouldn't, BECAUSE OF what's been done to her, 'cause she's told me so—well, they probably made the first move in THAT standoff."

"And then Omega made her first, last, and only move, taking them out," Wuxullian added.

"Exactly. When she really turns loose, she can be amazingly formidable...as is Echo, when you get down to it, even without his having 'enhancements.' Which, when combined with their high intelligence, is why they make such a damn fine team! And Echo says—well, said—that if she opens up those enhanced reflexes without stopping to think about the fact she's doing that, it can be a little like watching a science fiction film. Not quite, 'cause this is real life, but still." He shook his head. "And as upset as she is, if she channeled even some of that into her response to their attack...well, 'those sons of bitches' probably never knew what hit 'em."

"Interesting. Yes, that sounds reasonable. So she hasn't really done anything wrong, as such, except she did not have permission to leave Earth?"

"Well, no, but I'm not about to get her into trouble over it," Fox declared. "I think that, in those moments, all she could probably think of was getting away from the look in Echo's eyes, as far and as fast as she could—and offworld, maybe even to the far side of the galaxy, MIGHT have been far enough...maybe. Goodness knows, that poor child has had enough dumped on her in the time since she's been with us for any two dozen Agents. You know she was getting counseling from Ambassador Zz'r'p, yes?"

"Yes, I remember reading your report that included the matter," Wuxullian averred. "And if memory serves, the report said that, once the 'programming module' inserted by the Deltiri assistant to the ambassador—who no longer has that position, being now in a mental institution on Deltir..."

"Right," Fox confirmed.

"Once that was removed, her job performance went back to normal, correct?"

"Entirely correct. Else Echo and I, as her two supervisors, would have worked out a way to keep her off the active roster..." Fox shrugged, "without actually taking her off the active roster, if you get me. We felt that openly removing her from duty would have been highly detrimental to her mental state at that point, or we'd have already done it. And let me note that Zarnix, Zebra, Whiskey, India, Rglfrz...oh hell, basically our entire Headquarters physician staff, plus one, namely Ambassador Zz'r'p in his capacity as a counselor...were in solid agreement. No, at this point, the issue is simply the stress, combined with her PERSONAL view of herself...and Echo's out-of-character reaction. She's entirely capable in the job, and more importantly for this situation, she KNOWS she's capable—it was Tt'l'k's little programming module that caused THAT problem, without doubt."

"Understood," Wuxullian said with a nod. "All right. I grasp the situation, and I concur in every respect. Quite aside from benevolent considerations, she is much too valuable an asset not to attempt to rescue in whatever means is needed, and rescue Echo in the process, it sounds like. I fully comprehend that our agents sometimes get put through a lot, and while I might be a tough sonovagarg in some respects, forcing our people past their limits is just wrong. You and I see eye to eye on that, Fox, and always have. And as between us, while there are a few Division Directors who do not see things that way, I am working hard to ensure they...retire. Soon."

"That sounds like a plan," Fox said with a smirk. "And I heard nothing."

"Good male."

"I try."

"Yes, you do. So...you want an 'ill agent—please detain' alert to go out?"

"Oh, I've already SENT one out, Wux. I just wanted to make sure, after that little debacle with the Ennead and the Persans, that I got you on the same page with me before anything had to go down. And if you choose to, say, put some gentle top-level emphasis on it, across the Divisions, I surely wouldn't complain."

"Ah. Right. Consider us on the same page, then," Wuxullian said with a smile. "And consider the emphasis done, because I will do it as soon as you and I are finished here. So how is Echo handling matters?"

"Not as well as we'd like," Fox admitted, sobering. "In fact—okay, you understood why we need Omega back, and soon?"

"Yes..." Wuxullian frowned. "This does not sound like it is going to be good."

"It isn't," Fox sighed. "It seems that the...'operating system,' we've been calling it for want of a better term, in Echo's brain may be degrading. If we lose the ability to download the nd't'lq from Omega back into Echo to effectively 'reboot the system,' then it's probably only a matter of time before we have to declare Echo brain-dead."

"Oh no," Wuxullian whispered, shocked. "That is anything BUT good." He paused. "Does Echo...know?"

"I don't know," Fox admitted. "I know he's aware that he's...not what he was. And that certain abilities have gone away. But I don't know if he's realized the level of the deterioration or not, nor that it's ongoing, let alone recognized the ramifications. It's slow, as yet. I don't know if it'll accelerate or not. I'm not sure this has ever happened before. We evidently hit the 'not-quite-dead-yet' window just so. And of course, humans don't normally exchange mind clones..."

"What do you think Omega will do if...that happens?"

"I don't know that either, and I'd rather not think about it," Fox said, sigh even deeper than before. "But it wouldn't surprise me if we were to end up losing Alpha One altogether. And not in the good way. Not in any kind of good way. Romeo and I have discussed it in private, and he fully expects she would 'kamikaze out,' as he put it." Fox shrugged. "And probably take some perps with her, but still." He paused, then added, "Frankly, as between us, THAT is what I'm worried about now, as it is."

"Not to be callous, but who would run Alpha Line in that event?"

"The Alpha Two team is composed of Romeo and India; you met them during the whole Persan fiasco," Fox reminded him. "Alpha Three isn't really a field team, being a highly-skilled code-breaking and SIGINT team, but Alpha Four commanded the forces that ousted the fake Adita, and they'd probably be set up as the assistant chief and the third—notably Golf and Easy, in that order. So Romeo would be chief, Golf assistant chief, and Easy, the shift relief, as it were."

"But would not the Alpha Two partnership become the chief and assistant chief?"

"No, because India specifically does NOT want to be in the chain of command. In addition to being a fine Alpha-level field

Agent, India is the department's field MEDIC—and if ever a department needed its own medic, it's that one! Romeo has extensive clandestine military experience; he's just young. But right now he's also number three in the department chain of command, and often fills in when Alpha One is in the field, usually with India's help—functioning along the lines of a very experienced executive assistant-slash-advisor, I guess—but still." Fox pulled a face. "We'd hoped to get him some additional leadership experience under his belt before he has to take over, but we've come close on a couple of occasions already, when Alpha One got themselves badly bashed up and it initially looked to be permanent. He'll do fine. And I'll help guide and mentor him, if it comes to that." He broke off, swallowed, then added, "Mind, this is no reflection on him, but...I hope to hell it doesn't come to that. Echo is an old and trusted friend, my protégé and the closest thing I have to a son, and..." He sighed.

"What is it you usually say, my old friend? Ah. 'Amein,'" Wuxullian said.

"From your lips to Adonai's ears," Fox agreed.

Chapter 10

Echo was dealing reasonably well with whatever was going on; he was disturbed on several levels at what seemed to have happened, and he was beginning to realize he may have made a serious mistake where Omega was concerned. But he was keeping on keeping on, because not only was that what he apparently did, he saw little other option. 'Keeping on' included trying to review various files, videos and the like, and trying to keep himself in as good a physical shape as he could, under the circumstances. This latter, in turn, included keeping himself rested, fed, and hydrated.

So when the bladder decreed it was time to give back, he flung aside the covers, scootched to the edge of the hospital bed, and stood up, headed for the tiny bathroom. He wobbled a bit as he stood, but regained his balance and headed through the bathroom door, closing it behind himself.

There, he took care of business, washed and dried his hands, opened the door, took a step forward...

...And suddenly he staggered badly, as his legs abruptly tried to go every direction except the one he wanted. He stumbled, grabbing for the door frame, but his hands shook, his fingers loosened, and his grip failed. Echo lunged for the bed, but didn't come close. His full six-foot, three-and-a-half-inch, muscular frame toppled like a freshly-cut tree, smacking loudly—and painfully—into the floor.

He lay on the cold tile flooring, stunned, for long moments. Finally he made a firm effort to push to his feet.

Only to find that his body wasn't obeying his commands.

And the call button was on the bed, completely out of reach.

"Oh shit!" he exclaimed, as he flailed for a moment. "What the hell's wrong with me?! Hey! Somebody! I need some help, here!"

No one answered immediately; he tried again to rise on his own and failed. He raised his voice.

"Yo! SOMEbody! I need a HAND, here!"

He was unaware that the 'family members' and most of the top medical staff were all closeted in the conference room nearby, brainstorming his very case, except for Alpha Two, who had gone off to run the departmental meeting; Zz'r'p, who was researching techniques to delay Echo's deterioration; and Fox, who was finishing up the teleconference with Wuxullian. So when that cry still didn't garner a response, and he was still unable to get to his feet despite the most determined effort yet, he let out a bellow.

"HEY! HEEELP! I NEED SOME HELP IN HERE!"

Running feet sounded, and suddenly the room was filled with physicians and medtechs.

* * *

"What the hell?!" Zebra exclaimed, as she and Zarnix knelt beside the fallen Agent and ran medscanners over him. "What happened, Echo? Are you all right? Did you hit your head?"

"I'm not real sure, I'm not real sure, and sort of," a patently-shaken Echo noted, as they examined him from head to toe, palpating gently, checking for serious injury. "I hadda take a leak, so I got up to go to the bathroom. My legs felt a little wobbly, but they straightened out, so I went on to the can. Only when I came out, it's like...like everything kinda frazzed. My legs...just went. I lost my balance, grabbed for the door frame, couldn't hang onto it, and splatted the floor, pretty much face-first. I thought I was gonna leave a faceprint on the tile!"

"Well, not quite," Zarnix said with a slight smile, gingerly rubbing a reddening bruise on Echo's cheekbone, "but I bet it felt like it."

"No shit. Ow."

"You didn't lose consciousness, did you?" Zarnix added. "At any time, before or after you hit your face?"

"No, just my balance an' coordination."

"All right, let's get you back upright," the chief of staff added, taking a firm grip on Echo's torso, even as Zebra took hold of his opposite side. "Ready, Zebra? One...two...three." And they hoisted Echo to his feet.

"You still seem a little wobbly," Zebra observed, as she and Zarnix supported the ailing Agent, and Dihl and Yorker quickly straightened out and turned down the bed sheets, in

215

preparation for returning Echo to bed. Whiskey grabbed the controls and quickly lowered the bed, to aid in getting Echo back into it.

"Yeah, I can tell," Echo said, attempting to step forward, apparently hoping to cover the remaining ground to the bed himself. But his knee refused to lock out as his leg tried to buckle under him, so Whiskey had to add his strength to the mix, as Echo's greater mass threatened to take Zebra down with him. "WHOA!"

"Easy, here," Whiskey advised, helping lift Echo back to an upright position. "Hey, everybody, move outta the way, and let's see about getting Echo back in bed, here, before somebody falls down again—him, me, Zebra, Zarnix, or some combination of us—and something more than pride winds up getting hurt."

Everyone pitched in, and soon Echo was more or less cozily ensconced in the bed, while Zarnix explored his reflex response, Whiskey applied a Rejuvic-soaked swab to the obvious bruises—including his cheekbone and eye socket, hoping to prevent a black eye—and Zebra studied her medscanner readouts. Meanwhile, Dihl worked on making her son more comfortable, tucking covers and adjusting pillows, and Yorker took away the patient water bottle, bringing it back refilled with ice and fresh water.

"Echo, do something for me," Zarnix said, after several moments of his examination.

"Sure. Whatcha need?"

"Grab my hand and squeeze it for me. I want to test your reflex strength."

Echo did as he was told, but there was a slight tremor to his arm; the others watched as Zarnix' fingertips reddened only slightly.

"Harder," the physician ordered. Echo bore down; Zarnix's fingertips darkened a little, but were still hardly more than pink.

"Okay, that's good, that's fine," the Chesharilzi physician noted. "Are you okay? Any bumps, bruises, or abrasions that we still need to treat after that fall?"

"I don't think so, not now," Echo decided after a moment to consider. "Oh, I might have a bruise or two on my hipbone or knee or something, but nothing that needs worrying about. And I'm not sure about that, even."

"No bruised elbow, sprained wrist? Wrenched shoulder?"

"No, I'm good. I did try to catch myself, but my hands slid out from under me, and I splatted the floor. And almost planted my face while I was at it. But that means my arms didn't really take a hit."

"Mm," Zarnix hummed to himself.

"Okeydoke hon, you sit back there and kinda catch your breath, and we're gonna go keep working on your situation," Zebra told him.

"Okay. Anything out of Omega yet? Have you found her?" Echo asked, his spirits obviously lifting.

"I haven't heard anything, hon, but then, I haven't stayed in the loop on it," Zebra answered. "Fox went off to see about all that."

"Oh." His face fell. "All right. Y'all lemme know when you find her, ya hear?"

"We will, son," Dihl murmured. "Do you want me to keep you company for now, or had you rather rest?"

"I think I wanna take a nap right now, if it's okay, Dihl," he responded, seeming apologetic. "I'm not pushing you away, it's just...I'm kinda tired after all that." He waved at the floor where he had fallen. "It was...I didn't expect it. And I couldn't get anybody's attention; it was..." He shook his head, confused. "I dunno. I just need to lie down and BE for a few minutes, I think."

"All right, son, rest. I will be close, if you need me," Dihl said, and Zarnix waved everyone out of the room as a shaken Echo settled down in the bed and pulled up the covers.

* * *

"...Oh no," Fox said in dismay, when he and Zz'r'p had been summoned in order to be informed of this latest incident. "And he couldn't even get up by himself?"

"No, nor walk," Zebra said. "After Zar and I got him vertical, he tried to walk over to the bed, and nearly took me down with him 'cause he's just that much bigger than me."

"His entire somatic, and possibly parts of the autonomic, reflexive nervous system was..." Zarnix said, then broke off,

217

searching for the right terms. "Shorted out, perhaps? Misfiring? There was a definite malfunction there, in any case. Even the musculature was weak. When I asked him to squeeze my hand, he barely had any serious grip strength at all. Being Chesharilzi, my overall strength is somewhat greater than most humans, and that includes my grip strength. Except normally Echo can give me a run for my money in grip strength...but not just now." He paused, then added, "And if the entire autonomic systems go down, it will be very difficult to keep him alive, even if he has not yet suffered full brain death."

"What?! Why?" Fox demanded.

"Because that neural system governs the body's automatic behavior, Fox, such as pulse and respiration," Zarnix explained, and the Director paled slightly. "At best, we would have to install a pacemaker, and place him on a ventilator. Intravenous feeding would likely follow. And despite the damage to his pride, we may need to look at installing a catheter soon, if he can no longer walk to the bathroom."

"Farkakte, verdammt, merde, glagaram, and argdun!" Fox breathed.

"Could your scanners tell from whence the problem originated?" Zz'r'p wanted to know.

"Yeah," Zebra declared, before Zarnix could say anything. "His brain. It was acting like, almost like he'd had a mild stroke or something, but with no physical pathologies presenting—in other words, no sign whatsoever of anything physically wrong with the tissues. No clot, no plaque, no bleed, no damage... nothing."

Zz'r'p put his hand to his face and sighed.

"I was afraid of this," was all he said.

"It's the deterioration, isn't it?" Fox queried, face tight. "Echo's 'operating system' has begun the downhill slide."

"That is how I interpret it, yes," Zz'r'p averred. "You will need to ensure someone sits with him to help him from now on, until this matter is resolved...one way or the other. Because it is likely it will only get worse, unless and until we can 'reboot' his mind."

"Aw shit," Zebra grumbled.

* * *

Omega's next stop was Veldor. It would be a bit harder to slip onto Veldor unnoticed than it had been to operate on Aleancë, though not as difficult as if it had been the other side of the historic dispute that had brought about Slug's involvement; the M'Querans were Megophiuroids, looking much akin to six-foot brittle starfish, with a central eye on one side and central mouth on the other; sometimes they used the ends of all five arms like long legs, and sometimes they scuttled along low to the ground. There was no way the most sophisticated solid hologram disguise was going to make her bipedal humanoid form look—let alone move—like THAT. However, the Veldorn were at least bipedal humanoids of similar size and height, though their eyes were three times the size of human eyes, and they had bright fuchsia skin, with hair that ranged from various shades of purple to the brighter blue tints.

But if I wear gloves or body makeup on my hands, and program the hologram disguise right, I can pass, she decided. *And I have all the information on where Xoreplirg Erushin lives from the files I got on Aleancë. Let's see what I can dig out on him with a more direct approach.*

So, while leaving a flight plan at the Aleancë spaceport that indicated a 'return' trip to Dekken, as soon as she brought up the warp bubble and exited the Aleancë system, Omega activated the full cloaking and sensor-scrambling suite, vanishing from any ability to track her...

...And altered her course for Veldor.

* * *

Given the *Franckenshteine*'s effective invisibility of sorts, and the fact that her course was not recorded anywhere, Omega did have sense enough to max out her proximity alert systems; it would not do to collide with another craft simply because it didn't know she was even there. But she encountered no interference and no further attention—from Cortians, PGLEIA, or anyone else—during the trip to Veldor, much to her relief. And by the time she had arrived close enough to her intended destination to drop her cloak and sensor scrambler and approach like a 'normal' spacecraft, she had devised a new backstory for Ekaturg: travelogue writer.

The Erushin estate lay in a suburb of one of the main cities,

219

Chokiin in the nation of Turheg, on the southern-hemisphere continent of Ketzir. So en route, she researched the interesting points of the city from a tourist perspective, making sure to memorize the salient points, in order to enhance her cover story. Upon close approach, she requested permission to land in the spaceport of that city, and the orbital traffic control shunted her into a suitable approach path.

Within minutes the *Franckenshteine* was safely birthed in its own docking clamps at a small-craft gate, and Ekaturg Xelsib debarked into the concourse from that gate, a small travel kit under her arm. Once through customs and in the main concourse of the spaceport, she moved to the nearest information kiosk, requested and obtained a map of the city, as well as cheerful instruction on the most interesting sites, and headed for the mass-transit station.

It took her several hours of exploration—periodically extracting her personal tablet to record jotted notes and photographic images, to help provide cover—to be sure that she was neither watched nor followed, and that anyone who might have taken notice of her would be convinced she was nothing more than the travelogue reporter she claimed to be. The sites she visited included numerous historic monuments, cathedrals, and old houses...several of which belonged to famous and/or wealthy families of the city. This, of course, included the Erushin family home, a large brick-equivalent structure which an Erushin ancestor had dubbed Pavonuub sometime in antiquity. The name reportedly meant, 'Executioner's Lair.'

'*Close enough, I guess,*' she thought...in Echo's voice. Then she tried not to wince at the pain the memory of that familiar and much-beloved voice evoked.

After she was convinced she was not being watched, Omega began nosing about a bit more, and discovered that Pavonuub, being such an old and large dwelling—it was, in fact, a sprawling, multi-story mansion with several wings, most of which had been constructed in different historical periods—not only still had considerable family of several generations living in it, but an active tourism trade, with tours through the more public parts of the house, including all of the different eras of occupation. The family business had once operated out of the manor home, but was now located in an office building also owned by the family, just down the street.

And all that's perfect, she thought. *Not only does it fit in with my cover story, it enables me to get into the house and get a feel for it while most of the adults will be away from it. I don't have any illusions that I'll be allowed anywhere close to 'milord Xoreplirg,' who is apparently something of a recluse, but you never know; I might be able to slip away from the tour group, especially given the other disguise I have programmed into my solid hologram. Or, I might find a way I can get in, if I come back late tonight.*

So she paid the fee with an app she had set up under the Xelsib persona, and joined the tour.

* * *

One of the family members led the tour; it turned out that they took turns, and today was Xychaffa Erushin's turn. Xychaffa was a friendly sort, if rather reserved, and apparently much amused by the family history; she told numerous stories about her ancestors, not all of which were necessarily flattering, and some of which cast them in an outrightly humorous or even unfavorable light. Omega found herself laughing despite herself on a couple of occasions.

As the tour progressed, Xychaffa eased closer to Omega, and cautious, Omega became moderately reserved, appearing shy as the family member paid her subtle attentions. *Either she suspects something, or she's attracted to me,* the female Agent decided. *Either way, I need to be careful; I don't go that way, and I don't want to accidentally lead her on or something.*

But Omega's observing skills were still in full sway, and she noticed many things about the house that gave her pause to think—the highly-regular and repetitive layout of the floors, the way the doors locked, the direction the doors opened, the height of windows, how they were latched, and more. There were myriad ways she could see of getting into the house, though bypassing the unobtrusive but omnipresent security system might be somewhat difficult—she had not thought to acquire certain items of equipment which had been available back at Division One Headquarters, and which would have rendered the matter moot. But the whole idea bothered her: any such means would effectively require breaking and entering, even had she possessed the specialized equipment, and this was an action that she was hesitant to make. It was one thing to take out a perp who was trying to kill her, but it was another thing entirely to burglarize the house of a man that she wasn't completely sure yet WAS a perp. *Especially given it's not just HIS house, but it's home to his whole extended family,* Omega thought, watching Xychaffa point out an historic painting.

As the tour came to an end, the small tour group reached the front door and dissipated, the tourists moving to the street and vanishing. Omega felt a light hand on her arm just as she reached the threshold. She turned.

"Might I speak with you for a moment?" Xychaffa asked. "I promise it will not be...untoward. And it may assist you."

Omega blinked.

"I am not sure how you can assist me, milady," she said. "Other than perhaps allowing me to take a few photographs for my travel book."

Xychaffa smiled.

"I think we understand each other better than that," she murmured, turning and gesturing Omega to follow, as she headed back into the mansion. "Surely you know the occupation my family members took up after Great-great Grandfather made the historical occupations anathema."

Oh shit, Omega thought, dismayed, as she recalled the dossier she had compiled, back on Aleancë. She bit her lip. *They took up investigation and detection! It was a logical segue; as former assassins, they understood better than anyone what to look for. But is this woman a detective? Have I given myself away?*

"Not really," Xychaffa answered her unspoken question, apparently seeing and interpreting the bitten lip, as she entered a small office and closed the door behind Omega. "And yet, you did. Or rather, that did." She pointed at the wrist chronometer Omega still wore and had forgotten, in her distraction, to remove. "You are PGLEIA. More, that is the style worn by the bipeds of Division One. You are most likely either from Va'du'sha'ā, or just possibly Earth. But I know there were... mm, issues...with Va'du'sha'ā, only recently...so that would be my deduction."

Omega blinked in shocked dismay, and felt her face heat beneath the solid hologram, but she said nothing.

"Good. You do not deny it, but you do not confirm it, either," Xychaffa noted. "That will help me, as well, by allowing me a certain deniability. Stand by for a moment." She pulled out a small gold rod—of distinctly familiar make—and swept it around the room. "Good. We are still in the clear. I fully expected we were; I have a small application in my own chronometer which would have warned me if there were a problem, but it was best to make certain, given what I am about to broach. Come here, sit down, and listen to me closely." Xychaffa pulled two visitor chairs around to face each other, sitting in one and pointing to the other. Omega sat.

"Now, I am going to presume that you are searching for somewhat on my great-uncle Xoreplirg," she said in a low voice. "I think it is high time. While he was an important man, and did much good work for the PGLEIA, there have been...rumors...for years that not everything he did was...above-board." Xychaffa paused and licked her lips, glancing around her, then she sighed. "If I had to say, I think he was far too involved in interstellar politics, possibly—most likely—of a partisan nature, though I cannot tell for certain myself. I fear I do not know a great deal; in fact, and probably surprisingly to you, I know very little. I do know my grandfather was thoroughly disgusted by his brother's behavior, and flatly would not talk about it. I am certain that my father knew more than I, likely a very great amount, perhaps all; I do know that he knew everything that Grandfather knew, for they used to discuss it in private. But my father was killed three years ago when the perpetrator he was attempting to follow for the PGLEIA local Office...well, let us just say that matters went badly wrong, and Father did not survive the night." Xychaffa pressed her lips together, even as her large eyes sparked in anger and grief. "I made as certain as I could that my great-uncle had nothing to do with it, however."

"Did he?" Omega breathed, shocked. "Are you positive?"

"Not that I was ever able to tell, and I applied considerable of my abilities to the question," Xychaffa averred. "Though to this day, I have my suspicions; there were certain things that I could NOT verify, you see. But I think Father knew too much, and I think that is why I—and my brother—do NOT know very much; he and Grandfather wanted to protect us."

Omega nodded, then gestured for the other woman to go on.

"I believe Uncle Xoreplirg to have disgraced the family, probably several times over," Xychaffa said, "likely again and again and again, and I would like to see him brought to justice so that the rest of us can function well in the family agency."

"Ah. Erushin and Associates?"

"The same. It is a GOOD detection agency," Xychaffa declared, "an honest one, and I want the shadow of illicit behavior which Uncle Xoreplirg has cast on it to be erased. It has...come back to haunt us...over the years. It is time that was ended."

"What do you think I can do about it?" Omega wondered, careful never to say that she COULD do anything about it. *Because, when you get down to it,* she thought, *I don't really know that I CAN. But damn if I'm not gonna try. It sure sounds like I might have hit the target, too.*

"Uncle Xoreplirg is not here," Xychaffa explained. "Something over a standard annum ago, news came to him, news which he did not share with anyone else, and he left the planet, taking most of his belongings with him, apparently never to return. Ostensibly he is still the family patriarch, but he has never been back to Veldor; for all practical purposes, my twin brother and I run the family now. Well, really me; I was born first. But he—my brother, Xorzan—agrees with me about Uncle Xoreplirg."

Omega's heart sank. *He's not here,* she thought. *And he took his things with him. I'm not going to find anything.*

"Now, now," Xychaffa said with a slight smile. "I saw your shoulders wobble a bit, there. The Erushins are VERY good at observation, believe me. Just as the stories of that fictional detective from Earth, observation and deduction are our métiers. Just because he took MOST of his belongings does not mean he took ALL. His case file chest is still here—I insisted upon that remaining, so that we might have any and all records necessary for operation of the agency. He was not at all happy about it, and we exchanged many heated words, but I would not be dissuaded. I am sure he likely took SOME files with him, nevertheless, and others have probably been altered, but there may be somewhat in there that could help you." She drew a breath. "So here is what I propose. You will have noticed that the floor plans follow a pattern."

Omega nodded.

"Two floors up, directly above this office, is HIS personal office. Tonight, after the family retires, come to the door I will show you shortly at 24:00 local time. Make your way to the stairwell and up two floors. His office suite will be unlocked, and the file chest will be in the inner office, with the key on top. I will see to all of this. Should you need to confiscate evidence, you have my express permission. I will also do my best to ensure that the office suite is undisturbed until at least mid-morning tomorrow, so you can stay and peruse files if need be. I will have to divert the household servants, who want to clean the place from top to bottom every single day, but I believe I can handle that." She offered a rueful smile. "Then you can blend in with one of the tour groups—there is a sanitation room intended for public use just down the hall from Uncle's office; you can duck in there and wait until the tour takes its hygenic elimination break—and slip away after."

"How do I know you are not just trying to set me up?" Omega wondered, mentally reminding herself to use a more formal English.

"Do you know of Gwag Wuxullian, Chief Administrator of the PGLEIA?"

"...I have heard of him."

"He is a good, trusted friend of mine. I will be on a video-call with him in a few minutes; I will hide you in the room—it is not business we will be discussing, but some personal matters, so there is no clearance to be negotiated; I had invited him to a ball we are having in two weeks, with an offer to introduce him to some of our newer, non-family investigators. We often contract with the PGLEIA on Veldor, as the local Offices are somewhat under-staffed, you see; we even occasionally work across Divisions. So he knows us. And he and I have been friends since he was first promoted to Chief Administrator; my work as a young investigator garnered his attention, as it turned out. He has been a mentor of sorts for me, especially after my father's death, and I admire and respect him deeply. In any case, you know that he is what the Earthers sometimes term 'a straight shooter.' And you know that he would not work with me if I were not, also—he refused to work with Uncle, though he HAS worked with Grandfather, Father, and Xorzan, many times. He has told me several times in private that there was 'something not quite right' about Uncle and his way of doing business. And I was in assent. We neither of us were ever able to quite put our fingers on what, though."

Omega considered the matter for long moments, then nodded agreement to the plan.

"Then let me hide you, out of sight but not out of the ability to see and hear, in a special safe room I have—I have received death threats from certain organized groups, and it proved useful to have—and then after you verify my bona fides in the video conference, I will show you out in the way you should enter tonight," Xychaffa said.

* * *

Twenty minutes later, the casual video conference had ended, and Omega was being shown out a rear door near the kitchen, which let onto an alley to the main street, normally used for deliveries. Omega waved in a friendly fashion in case anyone was watching, waited for Xychaffa to close the door, then she eased casually down to the street—which she had earlier noted was named Uesleion Way; aptly named, Omega thought, in the circumstances—and walked away.

This might work, she decided, as she strolled nonchalantly down the street, away from Pavonuub. *She and Wux, as Fox sometimes calls him, seemed to be on very good terms, almost the same way Fox and I have been. And she was right in that he doesn't put up with shenanigans...which was why he was so stand-offish with me and Echo during the whole trumped-up accusations mess a few weeks back. And this way, it isn't breaking and entering; the head of the family is allowing me in. Inviting me, even.*

She turned off Uesleion Way onto Chokiin High Street, headed back in the general direction of Chokiin's downtown district. *Now I need to see about getting a bite to eat, and hang-*

ing out until later tonight.

* * *

Over the course of the remaining afternoon and evening, Omega had changed the solid hologram from the Ekaturg disguise to that of a nondescript Veldorn. She also added different outer clothing from a convenient second-hand store to enhance the disguise, and shoved her wrist chronometer high up her forearm, where it would be hidden by her sleeves.

She had not wasted the rest of the time. Not only had she acquired a different disguise, she had stopped off in a café—coffee was almost as popular on Veldor as it was on Earth—hooked into available net services, and researched the other members of the Erushin clan through the planet's news and social media sources. While she researched, she also nibbled a little in the way of nourishment and washed it down with coffee, to keep her metabolism active.

She had found that indeed, the great-niece and -nephew of the family patriarch were currently in charge, as the eldest surviving family members, being surprisingly old for their appearance; there were reports of some aesthetic surgery, some five years earlier. More, they were excellent investigators, considered the top detectives on the planet, and the title 'Sherlock Holmes' had been applied to both at various times—the Holmes character being as popular offworld as on Earth. They were also placed in the highest trust by local, regional, national, and PGLEIA law enforcement.

There were, however, old and longstanding rumors about the politics and morality of their somewhat-less-than-illustrious uncle, who was, if not obviously involved in interstellar politics, certainly had plenty of friends in that milieu. In fact, there were some who thought that old Xoreplirg Erushin had sold his considerable talents as it proved convenient, up to and including organizing hits on politicians he opposed. No one had ever been able to pin anything on him, however, and he was considered an excellent detective in his own right...when he was motivated to so apply himself. He had only retired recently, when aging mental faculties had apparently begun to tell on his skills...or so he claimed; the retirement occurred at the same time he had vanished from Veldor.

Upon ascertaining these things and copying the more interesting articles to her tablet, she disengaged from the network, shut down, tucked the tablet into a hidden warp pocket, and left the cafe in enough time to show up in the side alley beside Pavonuub at precisely 24:11 local time.

At Pavonuub, she found the back door open and unattended. She slipped in, not content to trust to the Agency technology which had erased her handprints to ensure she left no significant latents; she had also donned thin latex gloves to ensure she also left behind no oils or skin cells which could be used to identify her. She pulled out her highly specialized Agency cell phone and activated the anti-surveillance app, checking to see if she were being watched or otherwise observed. One small blip came up in the doorway she had just entered, indicating that the security system knew someone had passed through, but the app declared that the surveillance system had not set off any alarms, nor triggered any 'unauthorized intruder' type alerts. *Which means,* she thought, *I was expected.*

Inside, the hallways were deserted, with small nightlights here and there to light the way. Interestingly, she noted, those nightlights were not in all the passages, and appeared to be newly-placed. Even more noteworthy, they seemed to be lighting the way Omega was intended to take.

Hm, she thought. *Either they're trying hard to help me because they REALLY want Uncle Xoreplirg caught, or it's a trap. Either way, I'm ready.* She subtly patted her jacket near the belly. *This miniature sensor scrambler I ginned up outta the one on the ship ought to enable me to 'cloud some minds' if I need to. Eyes are, after all, sensors, just of a biological nature! Of course, then I gotta figure out how to re-install the thing back into the ship before I go out-system again, 'cause it's tied in with the cloak, and if I ain't got one, I ain't got neither. Which isn't a good system, in my opinion. But hey. It's not like I'm gonna be talking to the boys and girls in R & D any time real soon.* She shrugged. *I'll just plug it back in, and if I can figure out how they have 'em tied, maybe I can decouple 'em in the ol' Franckenshteine. That'll at least set me up for future events. And maybe I can even manage to scrounge parts to make one of these babies without having to cannibalize it off the ship, next time.*

She followed the instructions Xychaffa had given her that afternoon, and discovered that the nightlights did indeed direct her straight to the desired office...which was unlocked.

* * *

A relatively young—as such things went; he was older than he looked—male Veldorn sat at the desk in his study, which was just off his bedroom and a part of his personal suite of rooms within the mansion, reading on his private tablet. Just then an alert came into that instrument; he pulled it up and studied it briefly, then reached over and touched a toggle box on a corner of his desk.

"Xychaffa?"

"Yes, Xorzan?"

"Someone has entered through the cook's entrance. I am uncertain if it is your friend, but the report says it is a female of about that build. The indications are that it is a Veldorn, however."

"PGLEIA has extensive clandestine equipment, brother," Xychaffa reminded him. "The timing is right; I did not expect her to arrive precisely on the dot of the hour, for I would not have done, in her shoes. The security system does not indicate an intruder in any other part of the mansion?"

"No. Thanks to our work earlier this evening, it does not indicate anyone is here who is not supposed to be here."

"Because no one IS here who is not supposed to be here."

"This might just work, then."

"If Uncle finally erred and left anything significant, I am sure it will," Xychaffa said. "Personally, I am quite, quite tired of it all. Revelation of what he has done will be unpleasant for us in the short term, certainly, but once we manage to clean up his mess, and prove that it has not tainted the rest of the investigative agency, I think we will end up with a much better situation."

"Let us hope, my sister. Let us hope."

* * *

Omega headed straight for the file chest in the corner of the office, and to her pleasure, one of the tiny night lights was set into a power socket right beside the chest. The key lay on top.

Entry, and light to see and tell what I pull out, she thought. *No alarms or alerts, my app shows clear, and I have complete access to the records vault. Hm. Looks like she was legit. And damn helpful. She's honest as the day is long, if she really wants her uncle taken down this bad. Or...she wants to replace him, one. But the evidence doesn't point that way. And she already has control by default, so there's no motivation in that direction.*

She knelt and unlocked the large chest, opening the multi-hinged lid to reveal something akin to a small bureau or chest of drawers.

Okay, she thought. *Let's see what I can find out.*

* * *

Nothing, Omega thought in disappointment, well over four hours later, as she dug through the next to the last drawer. *Could I have been wrong? Was it someone else? But the clues all pointed to him! What do I do now?*

'*Keep looking,*' came the remonstration...in Echo's voice. '*He may have scrubbed his files, to avoid anybody doing exactly what you're trying to do. But there might be something there he overlooked.*'

Well, that makes a certain sense, she decided. *And it's what Echo really would do. Back when he could remember how to do it, I guess.*

She kept digging through the files.

* * *

After another solid and anxious hour of searching, all while hoping she would not be found out—it had been late into the night when Xychaffa had told her to return; now it was nearing dawn, and she could hear the household servants beginning to stir outside the office suite, as the daily top-to-bottom cleaning began—Omega closed the next-to-the-last drawer of the massive file chest and opened the last one...or tried to do so. The drawer pulled out partway and abruptly hung up with a soft *thunk!* Then it refused to open any farther. She wrestled with it, trying to keep it quiet and still force it to open, and finally decided that something was hung in the rollers.

Just then, footsteps in the hallway outside came closer, stopping in front of the outer office door. Omega froze as the antique door knob rattled, thankful she had thought to lock it behind herself as a diversion, just in case—after first ascertaining that she could also unlock it and let herself out again. A knock came on the door.

"Madame?" a female voice called from outside the door. "Madame Xychaffa? Are you in there? Is there anything you need?"

Omega carefully eased all the drawers closed, and silently moved everything back into the positions they had been when she had arrived in the room, then rose, moved to the corner, and prepared to activate the sensor scrambler. More footsteps came to the door.

"What is it, Kureef?" a male voice asked.

"I am not certain, Xopal," the first voice replied. "I thought I heard someone in Master Xoreplirg's office, but the door is locked, and no one answers. I thought perhaps Madame Xychaffa was looking for a case file or the like, and might want a hot cup of zorlan, this early in the morning."

"What did you think you heard?" Xopal queried.

"I...am unsure," Kureef decided. "A couple of bumps, soft, like...like perhaps a drawer being closed, or something of that sort?"

"Mm," Xopal hummed. "And you heard this inside Master Xoreplirg's office?"

"Well, yes."

"You are sure it was from INSIDE the office?"

"Very sure!"

"Come with me, Kureef," Xopal said, lowering his voice. "You are new here, so you do not know, but it does not do to be too curious about what goes on in Master Xoreplirg's office. Even when Master Xoreplirg appears to be away."

"Ohhh..."

"Exactly. I do not know...nor do I particularly WANT to know...but what I DO know is that you and I need to leave this hallway. Right now."

Two sets of footsteps headed away from the office door at a swift walk, fading into the distance.

Omega sighed and relaxed slightly, then raised her eyebrow as the import of the servants' conversation hit her. She drew a deep breath and returned to the file chest, knelt and opened it again, then returned her attention to the recalcitrant drawer in the file chest.

She opened the bottom drawer again, being even more careful to keep it quiet, and silently explored the limits of its motion, testing, trying various things to ease it farther open than it wanted to go. She remained unsuccessful.

Finally she closed that drawer and opened the previous one, pulling it out as far as it would go, before sliding her hand in around the lip of the opening, over the back of the drawer, and deep into the chest. *Whatever the bottom drawer is hanging up on has to be in here,* she thought. *If I can find it and move it, maybe I can get the thing unstuck.*

There, she felt a sheaf of papers surrounded by a tough envelope or folder. It had evidently come out of the overstuffed drawer bin, then gotten stuck in the roller slot as drawers were being opened and closed. Delicately feeling around the periphery of the sheaf, she determined the extent of the paper parcel and how it seemed to be trapped in the rollers of the lower drawer. Then she nudged a few things aside with her knuckles, pushed the rollers forward, wrapped her fingers firmly around the entire sheaf—ensuring she had a firm grip on whatever the wrapping was—and tugged, slowly and gently but with steady force. Gradually the packet eased free of the bound rollers, and after several tense minutes, she brought out a relatively intact and fairly old, faded, blue manila file folder, containing a stack of wrinkled papers easily half an inch thick. It was all quite battered and bore signs of having been there for a long time, but while there were a few torn pages, the folder was beaten to within an inch of its faux life, and the whole was crinkled and either faded or yellowed, the contents were still readable.

Omega flipped through it, then stopped dead, staring.

"Ohmigosh," she breathed. "Ohmigosh."

Quickly she stuffed it into her kit, then eased open the last drawer—the one that the confiscated folder had jammed, which now slid open readily and quietly. She flipped rapidly through it, finding nothing.

So she closed the drawer, replaced everything as she had found it for the second time—save for the confiscated file—activated the sensor scrambler and slipped out of the house, with none the wiser she had ever been there, except for her familial benefactors.

* * *

Omega maintained the personal sensor scrambler until she was out of the immediate vicinity of the house, but given that it was now daylight, she did not want to keep it up too long, lest secondary effects, such as a shadow with no obvious body, gave her away. So she ducked into a close halfway down the block; as soon as she was well into the buildings' shadows, she switched off the device, then strolled out as if taking a shortcut, and headed away from the Erushin mansion.

Once she was well away from the neighborhood which held Pavonuub, she searched for a busy mass-transport station and hopped the small elevated train, aiming in the general direction of the spaceport. However, she got off one borough past it, ducking into the public restroom at the station and closeting herself in a stall. She swapped out a few items of clothing, to include the gloves that disguised the skin of her hands, and adjusted the solid holographic disguise from 'nondescript Veldorn' to 'Ekaturg Xelsib' once more. A quick spritz of a special breath spray gave her the immediate smell of a being who had had too much to drink—with a few notable exceptions, ethanol was an intoxicant the galaxy over. Then she took a quick glance at her wrist chronometer, still hidden deep inside her sleeve—she had learned THAT lesson from Xychaffa Erushin. She shook her head in disgust at herself; she had never forgotten so obvious a giveaway before. *Then again,* she decided, rolling her eyes, *it isn't like I haven't had a few things to upset me lately. I gotta be more careful, or I'm not gonna get this finished before somebody takes me out.*

She timed off nearly fifteen minutes, hidden in the stall, pretending to be sick whenever anyone tried to enter it, or complained about the duration of her occupation. In order to assist in this ruse, she took several large swallows from a bottle of a particular herbal tea, local to the region, which she had acquired at the coffee shop earlier that evening for the express purpose, then turned and spewed it into the toilet, allowing the slightly sour odor to waft through the public restroom and even encouraging it with a few hand waves, while making some loud gagging sounds. This inevitably had the effect of causing the impatient being outside the stall to choose another stall... usually at the opposite end of the restroom from the one in which Omega hid.

Finally, a 'drunk Ekaturg' eased out of the bathroom stall, wobbled out and down to the elevated platform, and caught the train to the spaceport.

* * *

By the time she got to the spaceport, 'Ekaturg' appeared to be feeling somewhat better, and she took the opportunity to freshen herself a bit at one of the public kiosks placed for the purpose, popping what looked like a DeTox tab and a mint—in reality, both were breath mints, of different varieties. Then she headed for the gate where the *Franckenshteine* was berthed, and boarded it.

Omega locked the hatch, closed the protective shutters of the windshield—thereby presenting the appearance of having gone to bed for at least a brief nap, since she filed no flight plan, nor request for departure—and sat down in the pilot's seat, dumping her kit onto the deck in front of her. Then she pulled out the battered file folder and opened it, beginning a detailed perusal.

It was a comprehensive, in-depth, and well-organized dossier on gastropoids. And it was just the sort of thing that a logical, systematic mind would be expected to create when researching the species. Everything about them, even items that had not turned up during the research she and Echo had done recently in their efforts to determine if it was finally safe for them to have a romantic relationship, were included in this file.

Things that no one else in the Coalition knew.

Or at least, no one in an official capacity.

"Holy shit," Omega murmured as she read. "The homeworld's name is Wontwuun; they call themselves the Bozheen! They're largely fungivores, though they'll eat mostly-decayed animal tissues...even those of other Bozheen...so they're essentially scavengers. Interesting. I don't even want to think about how they became a civilized people, with that kind of natural history! Ooo. Now THIS is fascinating. He collected detailed information on their strengths and weaknesses, and more specifically, what could incapacitate 'em...and what could kill 'em." She leafed slowly through the compilation. "'Lethalities include: Telepathic backlash, overwhelming telepathic attack, the destruction of the heart, brain, or liver-equivalent...' I know about THAT one...'destruction of the antennae greatly diminishes telepathic ability;' that's good to know...oh, that's almost funny, it's so ironic. Ergotamine is poisonous to 'em—ergot, the same fungus that kills humans—because it blocks the specific neurotransmitter receptors required for their telepathy." Omega gave a grim chuckle. "It literally bollixes up their brains in a way they can't survive. Heh. Does pretty much the same to humans, when you get down to it." She shook her head. "Looks like it maybe hits them a lot faster than humans, though..." She paused to consider.

"Well, this definitely needs to find a home someplace in PGLEIA," she decided, "if I can find a way of getting it to 'em without getting caught myself. But how the hell did he find OUT all this shit?!"

She dug deeper into the stack of papers, and toward the back, she found a single sheet of paper with names and contact information scribbled...in what she had determined, through studying several of the files in the Aleancë Hall of Records, was Xoreplirg Erushin's own handwriting. *Which,* she immediately decided, *is telling. And not a little damning.*

But the names were not typical of gastropoids, and abruptly Omega seemed to recognize the language...though oddly, the mental voice she heard pronouncing the names sounded like Echo's.

"Rykatkin, Suslikin, Chysid...these are Hypothenemoid names!" Omega declared. "And Irokin and his colleagues in the Hypothenemoid embassy were our information source on gastropoids when we were battling Slug more than a year ago! Xoreplirg got his information from the Hypothenemoids!"

* * *

'Ekaturg' contacted spaceport control with a 'family emergency,' and lifted off within moments, headed out-system at maximum interplanetary speed. Once the *Franckenshteine* was far enough away from large masses, Omega raised a warp bubble and shot off into interstellar space, headed in the general direction of Loterus V, the Hypothenemoid homeworld. Fortunately, the system adjacency was such that no one was likely to tell the difference between a course to Dekken, and a course to Loterus V, even though they were in different Divisions.

As soon as she was well into interstellar space, she dropped out of warp and activated the comm. Then she dug through the file folder once again, looking for the specific names associated with contact information. It was a long shot, since the contact info was almost two decades old, but it was worth a try, she decided.

"Division Eight Headquarters on Loterus V, this is Agent Chenteb Dasseer of Division Five," she called over the comm, mimicking the slight sibilance of a Reptoid. "Division Eight Headquarters of Loterus V, this is Division Five Agent Dasseer..."

* * *

In the end, out of five Hypothenemoid names on Xoreplirg's list, two were deceased, one could no longer be located, and one was in the Hypothenemoid equivalent of a nursing home and no longer coherent. The fifth, however, was located.

"...Yes, I remember," the agéd Chysid Orkhon recalled. "It was many star cycles ago, but yes. The Veldorn wanted to hire a gastropoid some...eh, perhaps two of your octads ago? Maybe a bit more, maybe a bit less, but not much, either way..."

"For what?" Omega pressed on the comm.

"Some sort of service rendered," Orkhon answered, vague. "I am afraid I do not know more than that. I was one of a handful of merchants who traded with the Bozheen in those days, and I do not think there are many more than that who do so even now—the Bozheen are simply too restrictive, and too reclusive. And the rules required to conduct trade with them were, and are, very...limiting. Prohibitive. So the Veldorn...I do not even recall his name...oh wait! I think it was Uesleion...no, not quite...Reshion? Something like that...oh! Rushin! Ueslei-on Rushin! In any case, he wanted me to put him in touch with any Bozheen who might be willing to leave Wontwuun briefly on a lucrative contract. So I did."

"Contract? What sort of contract?"

236

"Oh, that gets complicated with the Bozheen," the old Hypothenemoid chuckled. "How familiar are you with the race?"

"I am...moderately familiar," Omega noted, controlling the irony with an effort. "I have...encountered one."

"Then you will likely know that they do not have limbs as such," Orkhon explained. "So they cannot sign a contract. And they do not have eyes, nor vocal boxes. Their communication is entirely telepathic. So contracts with them...among other difficulties...are verified with a genetic sample."

"Oh," Omega murmured. "So the hiring party creates a document, has the document 'read' to the gastropoid, and..."

"And once satisfied with the terms, the gastropoid provides two small tissue samples in a stasis container as a proof of identification and means of 'signature,' as it were. A verification that the contract is legitimate—retaining one sample for his copy of the contract, and giving the other to the other partner in the contract. And the hiring or contracting party, in turn, provides two small tissue samples as part of his or her own, and the contracted gastropoid's, legal records, as well."

"Mm," Omega hummed. "Interesting."

"Yes, it is a very interesting means of doing the thing," Orkhon agreed. "Though it can get incredibly complex, as I am sure you can see. So if you wish to determine what the Veldorn wanted with the Bozheen, I am afraid you will have to find the contract and determine the terms."

"But what if the original parties do not have the contract any longer?"

"What do you mean?"

"Where would they keep those?"

"Where would you keep your most important legal documents?" the Hypothenemoid queried, mildly puzzled. "Besides, it is Bozheen law that the contracts must be with the contracting beings. If the Bozheen desire to end a contract, they sell or otherwise trade it to another being, whether Bozheen or other. This automatically invalidates the contract. Was the contract invalidated or ended?"

"Not to my knowledge, no."

"Then find the contract, and you will find one of the contracting parties."

* * *

I wonder what ever happened to Slug's copy of the contract, Omega pondered, after she broke the communiqué. *If that guy is right, and they had to have the contract in hand to be legal, then Slug had to have brought the contract with him to Earth. But the Agency never found any sign of such documentation, even after fairly taking his ship apart. And that, despite finding a couple of secret compartments on his ship, according to the reports I saw. Then again, one of those compartments was clean as a whistle, with the surfaces looking almost brand-new,* she recalled. *I bet he had some sort of dead man's switch set up, so that if anything happened to him, any incriminating evidences were destroyed—disintegrated or the like. That would also explain the shiny interior surfaces, and if the contract and signatory tissue samples were in there, they'd be all gone now. Damn. I was sorta hoping for a corroborating piece of evidence. So that takes me back around, full circle, to Erushin.*

And therefore...the remaining contract, and the DNA samples, are going to be with Erushin, assuming he didn't destroy them after we killed Slug, Omega considered. *Which, if he did, means I may be on a wild goose chase, but still. So now I need to find Erushin. Well, at least his niece provided me with a few clues, as much as she had, anyway.*

So she pulled out her tablet and began to study the notes scribbled into it.

Okay, she considered, *it looks like he's got some sort of private world going, here. I'm not sure how he managed THAT. That would be one hell of an expensive proposition. Oh wait, it isn't HIS...well, it is, but it's a corporation that he set up. How much you wanna bet it's a money laundering operation? Whatever ill-gotten gains he's made over the years got invested into what looks like a legitimate business...namely, a resort. An EXPENSIVE resort, by the look. And now he's retired there, in a nice big penthouse suite—or the equivalent, whatever he prefers—just like a mob boss in Vegas, back in the day.*

But where the hell IS...? she wondered, pulling up a search on her navigational computer. *Aha. Huh. Way out near the galactic south pole. And that's a good ways away from...much of anything, really. Especially, oh, Earth, Delta Scorpii, and*

Veldor. Interesting. I bet it's got a great nighttime view of the galaxy, though. Never mind intergalactic space.

And it's gonna take me a little while to reach it, too. It is WAY the hell out there! I might need to look at a little maintenance on the ol' Franckenshteine, *here, first. If nothing else, it probably needs a good fill-up before heading all the way out there.*

She began to study the nav charts to ascertain where she might ensure her spacecraft was ready to travel such large distances.

* * *

"Whoa," Chi said aloud, as he looked at the day's newspaper over breakfast. "Huh. Dianus has 'retired' from the astronaut corps, and taken a position heading up a ground station in...holy shit! Guam? He's heading up that new little field station? The one that has MAYBE four other people? Never mind Diego Garcia!" Suddenly a memory hit, of a certain org chart. "Waitaminit...NO! They didn't! It isn't really GUAM he's heading—it's Diego Garcia! He's the only NASA rep for the ground station on Diego Garcia! And he's being transferred there!" He shook his head. "Diego Garcia. Land of earthquakes, tsunamis, steam heat, occasional typhoons, jungles, monster crabs, and sea snakes, an island out in the middle of nowhere, literally thousands of miles from anywhere; four hundred an' fifty or five hundred people per square mile, all crammed on a strip of land forty miles long an' averaging a little more than a quarter of a mile wide. Damn, do I remember THAT duty station!" he chuckled, wry. "Oh man! Talk about getting sidelined! Dianus won't EVER dig his way outta THAT hole! Not even with daddy's help! Wow. 'Cause they think I died on his account, I bet. Not that Echo essentially DIDN'T, I guess. And might be dyin' all over again, by the sound of it, according to what I weaseled outta Fox. But Dianus? So as far as I'm concerned, it couldn't have happened to a nicer guy. Pity they couldn't have done it sooner. Echo and Meg might still be together and happy, instead of him dying and her running off into space someplace, tryin' to escape her pain."

He sighed and tossed the paper aside, then scooted his mostly-empty breakfast plate away.

"Damn. I feel SO bad for Meg," he muttered to himself, raking a hand through his hair, worried. "I wonder if anybody's heard from her yet; I think I'll try to ping Fox once I go on shift, and see. I woulda hoped she would turn to me, as a friend, at least. But she didn't, and hasn't. Shit. I'm WORRIED. BAD worried! She is NOT in good shape. I wanted to help; I care so much about that gal. Maybe eventually she and I can get back together, but that's neither here nor there, right now. She's gonna need plenty of time to grieve and get over him, 'cause it sure doesn't sound like he's gonna make it after all. And maybe I'll be able to help with that, a little bit, just by being there—an old friend, to be there for her, and help her get her mind off things. And honestly? That's all I wanna do. IF we manage to reconnect in other ways, down the road, that's fine, I guess. I only wanna HELP her!"

He broke off for a few moments, thinking, before continuing his monologue...which was intended to allow himself to vent.

"...But I guess she hasn't gotten used to the idea that I'm in the organization yet, and it just never occurred to her that I was somebody she could turn to—somebody who knew HER, but not so much HIM. Somebody who, maybe, doesn't bring back his memory every time she looks at me, like I expect most of the other folks around here do. I really don't think she even saw me when I stopped her after running outta the medlab, poor baby. Her eyes never really focused on me, and the look in 'em...damn." He hung his head, pained.

"I only hope somebody finds her before she does something either stupid...or irrevocable." He shook his head. "What a mess. All the way around. Thank you, Peter Dianus."

He sighed again, raked a worried hand through his hair a second time, then rose and stacked his dirty dishes in the sink, heading for the bedroom to finish getting ready for shift.

Chapter 11

As time progressed, Echo's condition grew worse, and he could no longer ignore the fact. When he automatically reached for his water bottle and brought it to his mouth in order to drink from it, his grip slipped, the bottle tipped, the lid flew off, and the bottle dumped ice water all over him and the bed. Echo gasped loudly, as ice-cold water landed in places that usually did not encounter it, and he jerked away instinctively. Unfortunately, this reflex was also affected by the deterioration, and after briefly flailing for balance, he ended by going over the side of the mattress and hanging halfway off the bed; it was sheer coincidence that the medical jumpsuit in which he was clad hung up on one of the bed rails, preventing him from falling out of bed and landing head-first on the floor. But it did leave him hanging upside-down.

He reached down and put his hands on the floor to stabilize himself, but thanks to the bed's height, did not have a way to push himself back upright. Given trembling, uncertain arms, it was doubtful he could have done so even had the bed been lower to the floor.

Dihl had been sitting with him all morning, helping him with any matters that required high coordination, and calling for Yorker or one of the bigger male medtechs to help with matters of bathroom breaks; the medical staff was unready to catheterize him as yet—unwilling, if the truth be known; they fully realized it would humiliate the proud Agent—though that was likely coming very soon. But she had stepped out herself for a few moments in order to fetch a bite to eat—making Echo promise to stay in bed or hit the call button if anything came up. Given her prepared lunch was in the refrigerator in the medlab break room and did not require heating—it was a southwest-style grilled chicken salad—she did not expect to be gone long.

Fortunately for Echo, before the cloth could tear or any hook-and-loop strips rip loose—or he could pass out from hanging upside-down—Whiskey came in to check on him.

"Holy shit!" the physician exclaimed, and ran to the bedside, hitting the call button. "YORKER! Get your ass down to Lab D, Room 12, STAT! I need some help here!"

There was a beep that acknowledged the call, and Whiskey grabbed Echo's shoulders, stabilizing him until Yorker could arrive. Moments later, the big medtech arrived, and together they manhandled a red-faced and slightly dizzy Echo upright. He gasped in relief as he resumed a normal vertical orientation.

"Whoa!" Yorker exclaimed, as he tried to get Echo all the way back into the bed. "Everything's soaked, and it's cold! Did you spill your water bottle?"

"Yeah, all over the place," Echo murmured, trying unsuccessfully to hide the humiliation, even as his already-flushed face darkened. "Evidently my reflexes suck now. Anyway, Dihl went to get her lunch outta the fridge; wasn't gonna take but a couple minutes. While she was gone, I grabbed the water bottle off the side table, but when I tried to bring it to my mouth, I lost hold of it. The mouthpiece an' lid flew off, and the water went everywhere. It was ice-cold, so I jumped kinda bad when it hit my crotch. Only I didn't seem to have much control of THAT either, so I kinda flopped around and ended up going over the side of the bed, except this thing," he tugged at the jumpsuit, "hung up on the railing. Which I guess was good, otherwise I'd 'a landed on my damn head." He looked up at them, somewhat plaintive. "I'm not sure why I seem to have lost all the coordination that Fox's videos plainly showed I HAD, but I'd appreciate it if somebody would tell me what's happening to me. I mean, I know Omega has my mind, sorta, but I wouldn't 'a thought that would do...all THIS." He waved a hand down the length of his body for antecedent.

Yorker and Whiskey exchanged glances; Yorker bobbed his head over his right shoulder.

"Yeah, good idea," Whiskey answered the unspoken communication. "Echo, I'm going to go fetch Dihl, and she and Yorker can get you out of the bed and put on dry bed linens... and maybe a dry patient jumpsuit, too...and then I'll see if Zebra or Zarnix can come talk to you about stuff, okay?"

"Okay," Echo agreed.

* * *

Once the medtechs had gotten Echo into a dry medical jumpsuit and clad the bed in fresh, dry linens, Yorker departed and Zarnix and Zebra entered, along with Ambassador Zz'r'p.

"Heh," Echo chuckled, "the three Z's have arrived. Zarnix, Zebra, and Zz'r'p."

A nervous laugh went around the room.

"Apparently so," Zarnix agreed, offering a slight smile. "All right, Echo, Whiskey says you have been having some more coordination problems..."

"And then some," Echo declared. "It seems to be getting worse, but nobody's saying anything, so I wanna know what the hell is going on."

The three exchanged glances, then all three adopted 'thinking' attitudes.

"Awright," Echo grumbled, watching. "Stop that shit and TELL me! WHAT the hell is HAPPENING to me?"

"You owe it to him to tell him," Dihl said in a very, very quiet voice.

"She's right; we do," Zebra sighed. "I just dunno HOW."

"Neither do I," Zarnix admitted, to everyone's surprise.

"I suppose that leaves it up to me," Zz'r'p said, doleful. "All right, Echo. Let me try to explain..."

* * *

As Zz'r'p proceeded with his explanation, Echo grew paler and paler. Finally he held up a hand.

"I get it," he said in a low voice. "I'm gonna lose more an' more of my muscle coordination, more an' more of whatever's left of my ability to think, an' when that's all gone...I'll die."

"Maybe," Zebra said, watching as Dihl surreptitiously bit her lip in an effort not to cry.

"'Maybe'?" Echo reiterated. "What the hell does that mean?"

"It means that your body may remain alive," Zarnix offered, trying to find a way to soften the words and failing, "but you'll be brain-dead."

Echo gaped at them in horror.

* * *

As was typical of the man—his family-by-choice had discovered that, despite the loss of memory, certain personality traits remained, apparently part and parcel of the 'operating system'—Echo said little in reaction to the bad news, but he was decidedly more subdued than usual. His family members did not press him, but remained close, especially Dihl, in case he found he needed to talk.

But the normally-reticent Echo remained quiet, save for asking Fox if he had yet located Omega.

"No, zun, not yet," Fox sighed. "But we're working hard on it. I've got the entire law enforcement agency, all the way up to the Chief Administrator, looking out for her at the galactic level. Unfortunately, you taught her quite well, it seems—she's gone undercover, and while we're gradually tracking her in her wake, we have yet to be able to predict where she's going to head next, so we can be waiting."

"Damn," was all Echo said.

But his frame slumped in the hospital bed.

* * *

The *Hsshthh*, or *Winged Serpent*, the flagship of Galactic Coalition President Pulgey Entiyti, was en route to his favorite vacation destination, with a full crew and guard complement aboard.

Dr. Werfer Eretigen, Entiyti's personal physician—who was also aboard, to see to the recovering assassination victim's medical condition—had recommended an extended vacation to recover some strength. The physician was concerned at how much—and how soon—Entiyti was throwing himself back into the galactic work, and how much work was therefore being sent his way from Aleancë; he was unready to certify the Draconan as ready for that kind of work load, as yet.

* * *

"Because you are still weak, Pul," the other Draconan had told the galactic leader at the time. "Remember, you very nearly died. You had a wing amputated. And you have only recently replaced it with a cybernetic one. You are doing quite well, physically and mentally, but do not push it."

"I will be fine, Werf," Entiyti protested.

"If you do as I say, yes, you will be," Eretigen pointed out. "You have had a great deal of physical and mental stress, and you were in a depression before Omega and Madrid brought the new wing. There are matters that still need resolving, and if you do not do so voluntarily, I swear as Maker is my witness, I shall intercede...and I will NOT do it politely." He eyed the other male. "I have already been in touch with Lady Teela, who was shocked and surprised—it seems SOMEone told her that you were within a week or so of returning to duty on Ale-ancë. I certainly did not give that prognosis! I wonder who did that...?"

Suddenly Entiyti was looking around the room, taking in this or that detail...looking anywhere but at Eretigen.

"Mm-hm," the red-scaled dragon hummed to himself, knowing. "It will not do, Pul. I have no objection to your re-suming a moderate level of activity, but your work is stressful, and you are not ready yet. Even Zarnix was in agreement on that before he left."

"What would you have me do, Werf?" Entiyti grumbled. "There is work to be done, and some of it is best done by me, because I have the history of the thing already in my head."

"Postpone those things that can be set aside, let Teela handle the rest, and come with me on vacation," Eretigen pro-posed. "We will go flying together, we can hike, swim, we will eat well and healthily, and together we will build your strength back to what it should be, mentally and physically."

"On Emdali, or on...?" Entiyti began.

"You are exceedingly fond of that resort on Kenlinki, are you not?"

"HA! You have a deal, my friend! But what will you do with your other patients?"

"That was taken care of, long since," Eretigen noted. "When I realized in the wake of the assassination attempt that I should be spending a great deal of my time for the foreseeable future in taking care of the galactic president, the two other physicians in my clinic stepped up. We hired several more medtechs, another young physician fresh out of her residency, and they have taken the running of the office in hand. We can-not do it indefinitely, but you are growing stronger fast, now—not as fast as you would like, I know, but still—and by the time we return from Kenlinki in a lunation's time, I expect to begin to spend part of my time back in my office at the clinic! Half a lunation after that, I may—MAY, because you will have to do as I say, and behave yourself—certify you ready to return to work. But," he said, holding up a hand as Entiyti prepared to enthuse, "you will have to start slowly. I want no more than half time when you first begin, and work up gradually. I WILL set a schedule for you." He eyed Entiyti again. "And I intend to sic Teela onto you, to see that you follow it."

"Oh," Entiyti said, somewhat blank. "Aw. All right. We will do it your way."

"Unless you had rather me slap your buttocks back in a hospital room a week after you resume work?"

"No, no, I am heartily sick of that place for the time," Entiyti grumbled. "And I had it built."

"Well, it certainly saved your life, along with a handful of highly-skilled friends to work in it," Eretigen pointed out.

"Without doubt, but there ARE limits," Entiyti averred.

"Precisely my point," Eretigen riposted. Entiyti eyed the physician, suspicious.

"You have gotten very good at verbal jousting in recent years," he noted. "As good as any of the Coalition representatives, and better than most."

"I deal with you," Eretigen shot back.

Entiyti decided to leave be, for the time.

* * *

So the *Hsshthh* was en route to Kenlinki, with a full bridge crew complement's eagle eyes watching out for anything untoward. This meant that Entiyti could remain in his stateroom, resting, talking to Eretigen, and making plans for their resort stay...which in turn meant he was NOT on the bridge. So the captain, new to the *Hsshtthh*, was in full control.

The helmsman studied his readouts, then looked up.

"Captain, I am showing a craft ahead, and it looks...familiar."

"How so, youngling?"

"Before I transferred to this vessel, I served on the *Sssshhssst*, which was in the Battle of the Great Hunter Nebula," the young Reptoid noted. "And the vessel ahead rather closely resembles one of the craft from Division One, which

246

was involved in that altercation."

"In what way?"

"Well, it was one of the smallest craft, swift and maneuverable, that Director Fox—er, excuse me, Lord Levy, um, whatever he is properly called, these days—was using for sniping and covert attacks; they would use all cloaking means at their disposal, zip behind the enemy lines and attack, then zoom off somewhere else before they could be targeted. It was an effective strategy, though dangerous, so they had to know how long to stay and fire, and when to shoot and depart, and sometimes they misjudged. The particular ship which I recall took an oblique hit which damaged its cloaking systems, rendering it visible, and was promptly pinned down by fire from several Cortian vessels, in danger of being destroyed as a consequence. So we came to its aid. Sensor imagery of the ship ahead of us now indicates that it still has some of the minor hull damage and markings from that battle, though the worst have apparently been repaired, and the burns scrubbed away..."

"So?"

"Well, after being repaired, it seems to have been removed from the fleet roster and sold as surplus, I suppose," the helmsman said, mildly confused. "Because the identification and name that the navcomp is displaying is not the same, and it shows registry from Dekken, not Earth, and to a private individual..."

"But I thought that Division One, especially the Earth departments, kept their surplussed fleet spacecraft and repurposed them as part of their off-duty personnel transports."

"Exactly my point, madam."

"Hm. What did you know the craft as?"

"The *D1 Grapes of Wrath*, sir."

"And its call signal now says?"

"The *ISS Franckenshteine*, sir. A privately-owned vessel out of Dekken."

"Which is in Division Three, yes. Interesting. Comm, hail it, please," the captain decided with a slight smirk. "I think we shall see if it is available for escort duty."

* * *

Omega was making her way toward the nearest 'interstellar gas station' when the hail came in over the official galactic comm frequencies.

"*ISS Franckenshteine*, this is *A1 Hsshthh*. Do you copy?"

"*Hsshthh?*" Omega murmured, startled. "How can they even see me? And where do I know that name from...?"

"*ISS Franckenshteine*, this is flagship *A1 Hsshthh*. Do you read us?"

Omega's jaw dropped in horror as she remembered a major omission...and recognized the other spacecraft.

"Oh shit! I never reinstalled the sensor scrambler, and I was so agitated over the files I found that I never even TRIED to turn on the standard cloaking! And THAT...is PULGEY's ship. Oh geez oh geez! If he's on the bridge, I'll never pull this off." She thumbed the comm, then feigned a 'galactic' accent. "*A1 Hsshthh*, this is *ISS Franckenshteine*; what do you require?"

* * *

Just as the strange ship was hailed, Entiyti called the bridge. "Bridge, Entiyti here."

The startled captain scrabbled rather desperately for a moment.

"Is it an emergency, Pul?" Captain Chassav Ssiimiilav asked, managing to pull up the internal comm without inadvertently rerouting to external comm. "I have an odd situation up here..."

"No, no, dear girl, it will wait. Is it serious?"

"I hope not, but it could be a ship stolen from Division One. I was about to attempt to glean a bit more information."

"What?! Let me listen in, then."

"Of course."

"*A1 Hsshthh*, this is *ISS Franckenshteine*; what do you require?" came the response over the audio.

"*Franckenshteine*, you may be aware of recent events regarding Lord Pulgey Entiyti, Pan-Galactic Coalition President?"

"Um, to what, specifically, are you referring?" came the mildly-flustered response from the other vessel.

"The assassination attempt, aboard the transfer station at Emdali? The one that injured him?"

"Oh, um, yes, I did hear about that..."

"Chassav," Entiyti breathed over the internal comm, "can you hear me? Can SHE hear me?"

Captain Ssiimiilav held up a hand to the comm officer, then made a slashing motion. The comm officer nodded and put the external communications band on mute, then held up one taloned thumb.

"Not at the moment, Pul," Ssiimiilav noted then. "What is wrong?"

"I recognize that voice. Who do you think is aboard the ship?"

"According to the registry beacon, it's supposed to be..." Ssiimiilav waved at the helmsman.

"Ekaturg Xelsib, a Gurgev of Dekken," the helmsman read off his display, as the mic picked up his statement.

"And the ship?" Entiyti pressed.

"Helm believes it was once the *D1 Grapes of Wrath*," Ssiimiilav noted, "but it is currently the *Franckenshteine*, registered on Dekken, in Division Three."

"It hasn't anything to do with Dekken," Entiyti insisted. "I recognize that voice, though she is attempting to disguise it. That is Agent Omega of Alpha Line. Find out if she is alone, or if her partner is with her, if she has an escort, and if she is on a mission."

"Sensors indicate only one being aboard the vessel, sirs," the helmsman said, double-checking his readouts. "Nor do I detect any other vessels—aside from our own escorts—in the vicinity."

"Then something is badly wrong," Entiyti averred. "She is very unlikely to go anywhere without Echo at this point in their lives, in their partnership. If he is not there, then she is in trouble of some sort, and likely needs aid."

"Are you certain, Pul? It may only be someone who sounds like—"

"*ISS Franckenshteine* to *A1 Hsshthh*; do you copy? Is everything all right?" the other ship hailed; the voice hailing the flagship now sounded anxious. "Your communications have ceased...please respond..."

"And that is my confirmation," Entiyti declared. "A pirate or ship-jacker would have seized the distraction to get away, or concoct a cover story, not press to make sure all was well with US. No, Chassav; I know that young woman as my own family. I know her voice, and I recognize the concern for our welfare that causes her to press to make sure all is well before she moves on her way. Bring her and her spacecraft aboard—but allow her to maintain her cover—then bring her straight to me. I care not what you have to do to make it happen; simply make it happen."

"Yes sir," Ssiimiilav responded, then gestured to the comm officer, who opened the external frequency. Then Ssiimiilav smoothly lied through her extremely sharp and well-maintained teeth. "*Al Hsshthh* to *ISS Franckenshteine*, forgive the delay; I had somewhat come up with a crew member. And forgive what I am about to do: Lord Entiyti is currently short several guard units, after a recent attack by a crime syndicate on Emdali. He may still be in danger—he left Emdali to escape the last of the organized crime syndicates. I am afraid I must press you into service to help protect milord. Please bring your vessel into the hangar bay in the aft. There, your ship will be safely stowed until we arrive at our destination. You will be met and escorted to the guard barracks, where you will be issued a uniform for the hopefully brief duration of your service."

* * *

Omega stared at the communications speaker on the control panel in horror.

"Oh, shit," she whispered.

* * *

Omega did as she had been ordered; it was unusual but not unheard-of for a vessel to be temporarily conscripted in what was considered an emergency situation, and was akin to a police officer on Earth temporarily commandeering a car to catch a fleeing criminal. The *Hsshthh* was a big, powerful starship, even bigger than Fox's flagship, the *Genesis*, and had she tried to flee in her little vessel, the results would have been dire—especially given her failure to replace and engage the sensor scrambler, which was linked into the standard cloak—it was both, or neither, so she had no way of hiding her spacecraft, or 'disappearing' readily. Besides, the fact that she was being conscripted, and the tale the flagship's captain had given her, caused her to worry about 'Uncle Pulgey,' as she had begun thinking of him after Alpha One's recent sojourn.

So she aimed for the aft of the big ship, where hangar doors now yawned wide. As soon as the *Hsshthh*'s docking app connected with the *Franckenshteine* navcomp, however, the entire process became automated, and she quickly grabbed her solid hologram disguise, activating 'Ekaturg Xelsib.'

* * *

Once the *Franckenshteine* was safely in the locking clamps, 'Ekaturg' opened the hatch and exited. There, several security officers awaited. She approached the obvious leader.

"Hello," she murmured. "I am Ekaturg Xelsib of Dekken. How may I be of service to milord Entiyti?"

"Come with us," the Zardran said, her yellow eyes fixing on Omega, even as the soft blue antennae protruding from her white hair waved gently. "We will show you where you need to go."

Omega fell into step with the others, and followed them out of the hangar bay.

* * *

She was taken deep into the ship. The party stopped in front of a door, and the Zardran gestured. Omega knocked. There was a soft scuffling sound within.

Abruptly the door opened. A big, red-scaled Draconan stood there. He looked vaguely familiar, but before Omega could identify him, he turned and waved her inside, even as he gestured to the security escort to depart. 'Ekaturg' entered the stateroom, as the red Draconan closed the door. Then she stopped dead.

"Ah," boomed Pulgey Entiyti, smiling, "you may drop the disguise, Omega, my dear girl. I know it is you. I recognized your voice on the communications."

'Ekaturg' gaped.

* * *

"No, child, it will not do," Entiyti noted, growing stern when 'Ekaturg' insisted on her Gurgev identity. "If I have to, I have the means to disrupt your disguise. It must be a solid hologram, for it is too smooth to be anything less. I have heard your voice, I see your build and posture; one of our bridge crew recognized the pattern of residual scoring and hull damage on your spacecraft, from the Battle of the Great Hunter Nebula, despite efforts to repair it. We have maintained your cover for your safety, but you are safe here, with no one the wiser outside myself, Werf here, and our principal bridge crew. Drop your disguise and TELL me what you are doing, and where Echo is. I am trying to HELP."

'Ekaturg' sighed.

Then she produced a small remote control strapped to the wrist opposite her hidden chronometer, and punched a sequence of keys. 'Ekaturg's' head disappeared, to reveal Omega, a small electronic ring around her throat, nestling against the contours of her shoulders.

"I don't seem to be handling this undercover thing as well as usual," she murmured.

Abruptly she was enveloped in a gentle bear hug.

"There you are, my dear adoptive niece," Entiyti whispered, as Dr. Eretigen quietly let himself through the door connecting to his adjacent suite. "Now tell me. What is going on? Where is Echo? Is everything all right, and may I help you with anything?"

* * *

"...And so Echo is at home, recovering from a mild injury, while you continue the mission?" Entiyti verified, once Omega had given him an explanation...of sorts. This was, after all, the sort of situation likely to result in her being packed off back to Earth, whether she would or no. She intensely disliked lying to 'Uncle Pul,' but she saw no choice in the circumstances.

"Right," Omega continued the deception. "And so I'm ninety-nine percent certain I've found the guy who hired Slug in the first place, but getting to him in his little money-laundering planetary fortress might be kinda hard." She shrugged. "If you can think of any way to help me there, I'd appreciate it, but don't worry. I'll manage. You know me. And on this one, I'm pretty determined, as you can imagine."

* * *

"Yes, I can," Entiyti murmured, thoughtful. In point of fact, something seemed off about her story, her attitude, and in fact, the entire situation. "But tell me, have you managed to communicate with Fox on the matter?"

"Um, no," Omega replied, hedging delicately. "He's, uh, I think he said he was busy with some trade negotiation coming up...?"

"Ah. Well, what about Gwag Wuxullian?" Entiyti pressed gently. "He is definitely in a position to give you some assistance. Even to take over the investigation, given Echo is not available to back you up."

"Oh, well, I was kinda...I didn't want him to think Alpha One wasn't capable, after everything that went down around Adita's Coup," Omega tried.

"I see," Entiyti noted, all while thinking, *No, I do NOT see. This makes no sense. Franz would never send out Omega alone, with Echo injured at home, and provide her no backup; he would send Alpha Two with her. And I would have thought Omega unlikely to leave Echo's side if he were injured, as much as they love each other. Never mind that I thought Gwag had settled his mind about the two of them as Agents, before ever they left Aleancë, by the time Ambassador Zz'r'p was done with him. At least from what I was told...and that by Teela, Fox, Gwag himself...* He mentally shook his head. *No, something is not right here. And Omega is a much better actress than this; she is not fooling me. And that in itself is not normal.*

Finally he spoke aloud again.

"Well, why don't I see to it that you have a stateroom, so you can rest a bit while we service your ship, and you can accompany me to Kenlinki. That will put you a little closer to the Mu Phoenix system, and this planet Doukeed you believe him to be hiding on, will it not? And meantime, we can see if we cannot come up with a way my people and I can assist you in your mission."

* * *

After one of the stewards saw Omega off to a private stateroom nearby, Entiyti sat back in his chaise longue, raising his feet and staring at the overhead, as Eretigen entered the room again.

"Werf," he addressed the physician, "something is wrong."

"How so? Are you unwell, Pul?" Eretigen said, alerting.

"No, no, I am fine, my friend. No, something is wrong

with Omega. I would bet my other wing that she lied to me through teeth and claws just now...and she has NEVER done that before. She also seems...rattled, unsure, which is unusual in itself, and it is affecting her considerable abilities in a very negative fashion. She is a good Agent, Werf, not prone to mistakes, and if she needed to lie to someone to set up a scenario, she is a consummate actor. But she was not, today. And she had no need to lie to me, in any case...unless she does not wish what she is doing to become known to her friends, family, and colleagues. And that does not align with the woman I know." He thought for another moment, then sat up. "I need to contact Franz."

"No, you do not, my friend," Eretigen declared. "You need to rest."

"I need to find out what is wrong," Entiyti insisted. "If, say, she and Echo have broken up for some bizarre reason, that could explain her unusual behavior...AND it could put her at risk, and not just in what she is trying to do. And Franz will know, either way."

"Have you had your nap yet today?"

"Um, no..."

"Have you eaten your midafternoon meal? Taken your medications?"

"Uh..."

"Then you are not doing anything in the nature of 'business' until you have eaten, taken your medications and nutrient tablets, and napped," Eretigen declared, stern, folding his arms even as his own wings flexed. "You have the woman aboard your ship, and she is not going anywhere until you say otherwise, so the matter will wait. Do I make myself clear?"

Entiyti sighed.

* * *

Omega looked around her excellent stateroom, then asked the steward if she might return to her ship and obtain her travel kit, for matters of taking care of personal hygiene. The steward pinged Entiyti, who gave permission, and Omega was escorted back to the hangar. There she lowered the security on her craft, entered, found the kit in the corner of the flight deck, exited, and raised the security once more. The ship could be maintained without access to the interior, and Omega did not want to risk someone seeing her travel itinerary log in the navcomp and figuring out too much...let alone finding the onboard security video of her fight with the Cortian ships. In her current distracted state, it did not occur to her that the debris field the battle had left was telling enough in its own right, and the video would prove that her actions had been self-defense.

The steward escorted her back to her stateroom, and she entered, giving the steward a wan smile and a thank-you before closing the door.

Alone in the big room, she sighed in pain; normally she and Echo would have been together, and the emptiness and the silence only served to reinforce her loss.

He's not here, and now he never will be, she thought.

Then she flung herself on the bed and fought back tears.

* * *

Dihl was sitting beside Echo, who was watching television, when Zebra came in to check his vitals.

"How are you doing now, hon?" she asked him, while checking his pulse. Echo shrugged.

"Simple whispering arise, gleaming s-siffy. Earthy necessary fumbling boobekle. Resell furry love, clean clover a-a-agonizes g-glorph," he said.

Zebra's eyes widened, and she and Dihl exchanged worried glances. She gave the afflicted Agent a quick but thorough scrutiny, and suddenly noticed that his eyes were not properly focused. *Uh-oh,* she thought. *This ain't good. Not at ALL.*

"Do what, Echo?" the physician tried again.

"Simple whispering," he repeated, then, "curly acoustics inflame milky shrink abdel. I th-think uninterested goat saddened manager, sniff up."

"Try again, hon, please."

Abruptly he shook his head, and his dark brown eyes finally focused on her face. "I said I think I screwed up with Omega," he vocalized plainly this time. "I shot my mouth off, and she...wait. That's...that wasn't what I said, was it?"

"No, my dear, it was not," his mother noted, voice quiet.

"What the hell DID I just say?"

"I...don't think I can remember it well enough to repeat it,"

Dihl murmured, distressed.

"The colloquial term is 'word salad,'" Zebra explained then. "It's a form of something called aphasia. Your mind temporarily sorta scrambled the index to the dictionary in your brain."

"SHIT! More deterioration?"

"Possibly," Zebra said, noting Dihl biting her lip hard. "Dihl, would you run fetch my stethoscope, hon? I went off and forgot it, and it's ALWAYS been my feeling that a trained physician's ears are better than any medscanner." Dihl rose, and gave her a questioning glance. "Oh, it's lying on my desk in my office."

"I will be right back," Dihl said, escaping before her professionalism broke and she showed her emotions in front of Echo...who sat and watched the interaction wordlessly.

Until Dihl left the room.

"Okay, I get that," he noted, nodding after his mother. "You gave her an excuse to get out before she could get upset in front of me." He paused, then added, very quiet, "I'm not gonna make it, am I?"

"If we can get Omega here pretty quick, I think you'll be fine," Zebra averred.

"Is she on her way? Have you found her?"

"I don't know," Zebra admitted, honest. "I don't think so, not yet. They're tracking her closer and closer, though. They'll catch up to her soon, I'm sure."

Echo sighed.

* * *

"My dear girl, you seem almost obsessed," Entiyti noted, several hours later, when he had awakened from an enforced nap and realized Omega likely had not eaten. He had called the ship's mess for a quick human-suited heavy snack, then summoned her to his stateroom to eat and converse. Unfortunately, he did not like the trend of the conversation, and he had yet to be able to contact Fox. "Set this aside. Come with me. You need time to relax and let matters go. Even Werf, my physician, thinks that, and he is not used to treating humans."

"I can't let this go, Pulgey," Omega pointed out, earnest. "It's a cold case to begin with, and needs solving. And if this guy decides he wants to take Echo or me out, as kinda the last witnesses, never mind that Echo can't— uh, that Echo wasn't the main target of HIS attack, then this shit will never end until he's behind bars or dead, even if we managed to circumvent the last of Slug's plans."

"So show me," Entiyti declared, pretending to have missed the 'midcourse correction' in her statement; in reality, he was growing more and more worried about exactly WHY Echo was no longer with Omega. "Show me your clues, and put it together for me. Convince me this is the being we have sought for so long."

"Will you help if I do? Not try to sideline me?"

"I swear on every scale of my body, by the writings of the holy Maker," Entiyti said, clawed hand upraised.

"Then let me go get my kit," Omega said, gesturing at the door. "My stuff is stashed in it. It won't take a second."

"Go fetch it," Entiyti agreed, waving at the door.

* * *

Omega ran down the passageway to her stateroom, excited about the possibility of having Entiyti and his people helping her bring Slug's employer to justice. *And that, without having to involve PGLEIA,* she thought. *And it'll still be legal and everything.*

She opened the door, ran over to the 'dresser'—it was built-in stowage, with the top serving as a vanity/dressing table, and a mirror facing—and caught up her travel kit from its top, then turned and headed back the way she had come.

* * *

"Here," Omega said, pulling out her tablet first. "Let me take you through it step by step, as I found stuff out and worked my way through the logic."

"That is an excellent plan," Entiyti said, leaning toward her as she sat beside him and showed him the files she had downloaded from Aleancë, explaining as she went.

* * *

Entiyti leafed through the folder Omega had obtained on Veldor, studying the information within, while she watched. Finally he looked up at her.

"Yes, I see what you mean," he averred. "I think you have

something here. Yes, you definitely have some strong evidence. And you say you talked to the Hypothenemoid who arranged the contact between him and Slug?"

"Yes! He claimed the guy's first name was the codename that came from Slug's telepathic interrogation, and his last name was a variant on the guy's real surname, so there's the whole thing connected: 'Uesleion Rushin,'" Omega explained. "And I got that recorded, on my ship. And he said that there would have to be a contract, but that there would be, like, DNA samples instead of signatures. So you KNOW Erushin wouldn't leave THAT behind on Veldor. He'll have it with him. Besides, it turns out it's only legal for gastropoids if he keeps it with him. So...IF we can find it, then verify it's his and Slug's DNA samples, it's the nail in the coffin. It's hard proof."

"What about Slug's copy? Would that not finish off the matter? And surely all of his items from that assassination attempt would have been impounded by Division One?"

"Yes, but they found a hidden chamber in his ship," Omega informed him. "Well, they found several, most with various forms of contraband in 'em. But one was very interesting, in that the inside of that compartment was completely pristine... shiny, fresh metal. And entirely empty. I went back and re-read the section of the report about it, and there was, basically, not one extraneous atom in the whole compartment...which had been vented, by the way. It wasn't a vacuum, but it WAS—get this—a pure nitrogen atmosphere inside."

"Ah. So he had some device set to eliminate evidence within that particular smuggler's compartment, were he to be captured, injured, or die. Then it vented the 'remains' and replaced it with canned gas."

"That's the way I read it now, yeah. Absolutely no way to prove anything from what little was left inside the compartment."

"Mmm. Yes. You have done some excellent detective work here, youngling," Entiyti murmured, considering. "Never mind your ability to handle clandestine matters. If you are ever... available...career-wise, you need only let me know, child, and I will hire you as one of my lead bodyguards in a heartbeat."

"That...might be a good thing," Omega decided. *And it*

beats playing vigilante around the galaxy until someone takes me out, I guess, she thought, morose. *At least I know I'd be useful. And out of the way of things back on Earth.*

"No, no. This will not do," Entiyti noted, watching her face intently. "Clandestine activities seem to be fine...if the person with whom you interact does not know you. But if we are 'family,' child, your heart is practically on your sleeve right now. No, it will not do. If I promise I will give you all the help required to bring this being to justice, will you tell me what has really happened on Earth? The real reason Echo is not here beside you?"

Omega felt her face pale as her head spun.

Entiyti jumped to catch her and get a chair underneath her.

* * *

"Oh, no, no, no, surely not," Entiyti whispered in dismay, when Omega finally finished explaining. "So he no longer remembers you, nor wants anything to do with you?"

"That's pretty much it," she said, voice so low he could barely hear it. "He's decided I'm not human after all, that I'm really just an alien kluged-up...thing, that I'm an assassin—HIS assassin—and not trustworthy, so he thinks he's not safe around me any more." She turned away, attempting to hide her face. "Dear God help me, Pulgey! If you'd seen the look in his eyes when he said that..." She shook her head. "I swear, it felt like he was ripping my heart out."

"Hush, hush, dear girl," Entiyti murmured, rising and coming to stand beside her, putting a gentle arm around her slumped shoulders. "Surely by now they have managed to return his memory, and he will want you beside him again! Let me call Franz—"

"NO!" Omega spun to face him. "You don't understand! He doesn't WANT me any more, Uncle Pulgey! I'm a THING to him! If you call Fox, he'll only try to get you to bring me back, one way or another, and I can't go back to THAT! Everything will only remind me of that moment..." She cringed despite herself, remembering the cold look on Echo's face, in his eyes. Entiyti winced as he watched that expression of pain.

"But child, what if he is well by now?" he tried. "What if his memory has returned, and whatever conclusion he reached by reading those giissht files has been overcome by his old feelings for you? We MUST at least find THIS out!"

"I...I..." Omega broke off. Then she looked up at him, her wobbly expression piteous enough to catch at the Draconan's heart, as she fought to maintain control of herself, of her emotions. "Do...do you think it...it might be possible?" she breathed, and Entiyti realized she was afraid to hope for it. "That they fixed it? Fixed...HIM?"

"Omega, my dear adoptive niece, look at this," Entiyti murmured, keeping his voice soft and soothing as he flexed his wings and partly unfurled them. "Do you see the cybernetic wing that you designed, that you and Madrid built, and Zarnix 'installed' on my back? The wing that I cannot tell from my original, flesh and bone wing, because it is so delicately tied into my nervous system?"

"Ye-yes?"

"If, together, you and your colleagues can do THIS," he lightly flapped his wings, "how can you doubt that they could not return Echo's memory to him? The remembrance of how much he trusts you, likes you, loves you?"

* * *

"I...I just dunno," Omega murmured, uncertain, dropping her gaze to the floor. "Look, okay, yeah, I gotta know. But...but don't let 'em know I'm here, all right? I...I don't want them to try to talk me into coming back if, if..."

"Did Franz know how it affected you? Did you desert? Are you in trouble?"

"I dunno, sort of, and..." she shrugged, "probably."

"What happened?"

"I...when he said all that, Echo said all that," Omega tried to explain, "I-I just...I left. I had to get away. As far and as fast as I could. Initially I didn't even think; I just...went. Then it occurred to me that, that since Echo couldn't remember anything, he'd be blindsided by anything of Slug's plans come back to haunt us. But we THINK we got the last of those knocked out. I hope; dear God, I hope! Then it hit me: what about the guy who HIRED Slug to begin with? Echo doesn't even remember it! So he can't even look out for it! And I figured, well, I could do that, even if I died in the doing—by the sound of it, this guy is gonna be dangerous, see. But at least THAT would be over and done, if I could take him down, one way or another. And Echo would be safe from it. AND...it would get me away from that look in his eyes." She shrugged. "I...I never even thought about...that it would look like..." She sighed. "So...yeah. I'm probably in trouble, by now."

"Mm. How about this, then?" Entiyti determined. "Let me discuss a few medical matters with Werf, to ensure I understand some ramifications, then I will check to see if there is any sort of bulletin out about your situation..."

"You don't already know?" Omega all but gaped in surprise.

"No," Entiyti sighed, "I do not. Werf felt I was trying to get back into harness too fast, after everything that happened. That is why I was—am—headed to Kenlinki; as between us two, it is my favorite offworld vacation resort...though obviously the galactic president cannot admit to it, or show obvious favoritism in public. But Werf has informed the captain that, unless it is a galactic emergency, this ship is a vacation vessel, and we are not to participate in galactic business on pain of..." Entiyti gave a wry bark of Draconan laughter, "somebody's death, though I am uncertain whose."

"Oh."

"Yes. So let me find out how much trouble you are in, first. Once I know that, I will approach Franz, delicately, without stating that I have you here, aboard my ship. I will say that I have heard about...whatever kind of bulletin may be out about the situation, because I cannot imagine that there is NOTHING out...ask what is going on, and see about getting a medical status on Echo for you. And if things have not improved, and do not look like ever improving, perhaps I can arrange to have you transferred to my bodyguard corps. Permanently."

Omega stared up at the big Draconan, blue eyes wide.

"You...you'd do that? For me? Even if I was in trouble for desertion or whatever it's called?"

"You are family now, dear girl," he murmured, keeping his manner gentle and earnest. "And I think you do not give Franz enough credit, if you truly believe he would have issued an arrest order upon you. You said the others saw what happened, yes?"

"Yeah..."

"Including him?"

"I...I think he was there," Omega admitted, scrunching her face in thought. "I was so upset, I..."

"You do not remember for certain."

"...No."

* * *

Entiyti cocked his head, studying her, and she added, ashamed, "I know it's not like me, not to notice details like that. But just at that moment, it was...it was like my world blew up. Collapsed. Imploded. Something like that, I guess. That's... the only way I know how to describe it." She shook her head. "To be honest, I couldn't tell you ANY other detail from that moment...except the look on Echo's face, in his eyes."

"Even if Franz was not there, the others would have seen," he pointed out. "And would have known how much pain it gave you. And likely would have told him so. In considerable detail, knowing Alpha Two."

"Now that's probably true," she sighed. "I expect I went completely white. My head took off into orbit, I know that. I was light-headed an' everything. For a few seconds, I thought I might pass out. Instead, I just scrambled out the door. All I knew was that I had to get as far away as I could, as fast as I could. I couldn't...I just..."

"Did no one try to stop you?"

"I..." Omega broke off, thinking back. "Somebody stopped me to talk. I can't remember who. I don't even remember what I said." She shook her head. "I don't even know how to tell you, Uncle Pul! It was...was so...I swear, I think he hated me..." Her entire body slumped. "How can I ever...I wish I could be brain-bleached!"

"Hush, hush, youngling; I understand. Let it go, if you can."

"I...I'll try."

"All right. I think I know how to handle this. Do you trust me to do so?"

"I...yeah." She nodded. "Yeah, I do. And...and thanks."

"Hush that, young one. You are my niece in every way that counts, and I care for you as I would for blood kin; I intend to look out for you as for family. Now run back to your quarters. I will have another small meal sent; you look as if you could use it. I suspect you have been too upset to eat as you should, since this whole matter began. Am I correct?"

"Um, yeah."

"So for now I want you to try to relax, eat and drink, and rest if you can. I understand if you cannot sleep, but at least rest. If you simply cannot lie still, go ahead and get up, but do something peaceful instead. Read a book, watch a video, play a game, something of this nature, that will give your mind a break from painful thoughts. Will you promise me you will do this?"

"Y-yeah." She looked up at him, and offered a wobbly smile. "I'll do my dead-level best. To alla that."

"Good. Run on, then. I shall see what may be seen, while you do that."

Slightly heartened, Omega headed out of the room.

* * *

In her wake, Eretigen came through the connecting door.

"How much did you hear, Werf?" Entiyti wondered.

"Most of it," Eretigen admitted. "After you and I spoke, I thought it might be good if you had a professional opinion of her state of mind."

"Excellent thought."

"But I considered she might not be as...forthright...with you if she knew I was listening, so...eavesdropping notwithstanding, I stayed out of sight."

"Yes. I knew you were there—I saw your signal—but she did not. Under the circumstances, I am not going to tell her, either; I fear she is not doing well, and I need an assessment."

"Which I am now prepared to give, to the best of my knowledge of her, her circumstances, and her species."

"And?"

"She is...distraught. Professionally speaking, I should go so far as to say that she is medically in need of counseling, possibly medication. Clinically depressed, and more." He cocked his broad, flat head. "Given the history of recent months, based on what you have told me, I am not surprised. This latest matter was likely the last twig on the poor, overworked frasstid's back. I think however, in offering her a position in the body-guard corps, you may have offered her a solution that enabled her to avoid inevitable death...and she knew that death would be the end result of her plan, one way or another. May have counted on it, up until that point when you offered her an alternative."

"You noticed that too, eh?" Entiyti sighed. "My girl, my other-world niece, is not in the best of shape, Werf. And that does not bode well for things on Earth. Nor for her future, if we cannot find a solution for her."

"No, it does not...for either. And because of this, I will not only let you do this thing, I will do what I can to assist," Eretigen relented. "From all I have heard of her from you and Suud, I cannot stand firm and see her go to the abyss, when we might intervene and prevent such things."

"Thank you, Werf," Entiyti murmured, grateful. "The being she is...was...betrothed to marry was the young human I encountered during the negotiations to bring Earth into the Coalition; you have heard me tell that story?"

"I have," Eretigen said with a nod. "Agent Echo, then? And he is the one whose memory appears...gone?"

"The same," Entiyti confirmed. "And he has been a good friend ever since that time. And like a son to Franz, though Franz has been loath to admit it...until SHE showed up, and created her little adopted family, of which I am now a part. Of the extended family, admittedly, nevertheless a part of it. I would not see things end like this, if there is anything in my power which I can do to prevent it. All right. So the first thing that wants doing is to find out if there is an alert, or a warrant for her arrest, or the like, floating around out there. And for that, you must raise your embargo on my obtaining galactic information."

"I will go now, and personally speak to the captain," Eretigen noted.

"No flirting, now," Entiyti warned. "I have my eye on that one, myself!"

"Ah! Finally!" Eretigen noted with a laugh, as he headed for the bridge.

* * *

"...Mm," Entiyti hummed, almost an hour later. "So there is an 'ill Agent' alert out for her."

"That is correct, Pul," Captain Chassav Ssiimiilav said, as she, Dr. Eretigen, and Entiyti stood in Entiyti's stateroom and deliberated the matter. "Werf requested a private discussion in my command cabin to inform me of matters, in order to preserve Omega's privacy and cover. So I checked the alerts and the like from there. No one else on the ship knows this but the three of us."

"And it is what we feared, and you expected, Pul," Eretigen verified. "Director Fox was aware of her poor emotional and mental state, and it sounds as if he wishes to help, not cause problems, for the young female."

"Well, that confirms the poor mental and emotional state, true," Entiyti decided. "But it also confirms my opinion of Franz, who is a good male. We need to take excellent care of this girl; she has earned it, many times over, even were she a stranger to us, to me."

"This is the one who designed, then helped construct, your wing, yes, Pul?" Ssiimiilav asked. "And the one who saved her partner from the Cortian slavers, and thereby revealed the Cortians' true plans to us?"

"The same, Chassav, to both. As to the Cortian incident, Franz kept me apprised of matters as soon as he became aware of them himself. I was not Coalition President at that time, having retired—as I thought—a few years before; the hiigiissht way the Coalition President at the time hoosssed the situation was inexcusable, and by the time I was finished..." he sighed, "I was back in the position I had thought I was done with. Not, I suppose, that that was a BAD thing, as matters turned out." He cocked his head to one side, then gave them a wry grin. "And here we are." He turned to the desk. "Now, the two of you sscooot, while I place a classified call to Earth."

"Drinks tonight, Pul?" Ssiimiilav wondered.

"I should like that, but it will depend upon what comes of all this, Chassav. Ping me later."

"Copy that."

* * *

But Fox was unavailable, and Entiyti was unwilling to tell

265

Fox's assistants the reason for his call, opting to inform them that it was 'just a friendly chat,' and he would call back at a later time.

So in the interim, he decided to throw a small dinner party in his quarters. And he had Omega come by early, so he could present her with what news he had, in private.

"No, Omega, I am sorry; I can say with certainty that you are not in trouble, in that evidently Franz was aware of your... upset," Entiyti explained, deciding not to tell her about the 'ill Agent' alert. "He has issued no warrant for your arrest, nor other such order to take you into custody, though he has asked for people to be on the alert for you, in case you need help. But as yet I have not been able to reach him to determine Echo's status, and given your preference that no one know you are here, I was loath to tell his assistants very much."

"Oh," Omega murmured. "So...I'm not by way of being arrested, and nobody knows I'm here—at least, in PGLEIA—but you don't know if Echo's better, worse, or the same."

"Exactly. But I am not done trying," Entiyti declared. "In fact, I will try again later this evening. I simply thought that some quiet, congenial socialization might be good for the both of us, in the meanwhile. I hope you are all right with that idea."

"Well, I do need to eat some more, I suppose," Omega noted. "I managed most of what you sent me this afternoon. But thank you for keeping it a bit small, and...and bland. Every time I think of...well, my appetite is just a bit off."

And it shows in the fit of your clothing, child, the Draconan thought, in deep concern. *You have already lost a surprising bit of weight, and it has only been a few days since the 'ill Agent' alert was issued. I suspect your hyper metabolism is not helping matters.* What he said was, "And I do understand that. I remember what happened to my appetite when I realized my wing was gone. I expect you feel as if a part of you is missing, as well."

"That's...a good way of putting it, yes," Omega said, then deliberately changed the subject. "You look very nice. Very... elegant. So...who are the other guests at your dinner? And am I dressed okay?"

"Thank you! Oh, it is very exclusive, my little dinner party," Entiyti said with a smile, allowing the change of topic. "There are only three guests. You; Werfer Eretigen, my physician, whom you have heard me call 'Werf'; and Captain Ssi-imiilav."

"Two males, and two females."

"Indeed. I thought it was more appropriate that way. As Franz used to say, 'Boy-girl, boy-girl.' Though I think he picked it up from some Earth film. Chassav will be in her uniform, of course. And you look fine. You are not in your Suit, but as no one outside the primary-shift bridge crew knows you are an Agent, and you are effectively undercover, it is understood. And you are wearing a very nice pair of trousers and shirt. Um, blouse."

"Oh good. Yes, I cleaned up and changed as soon as I got your invitation; these are the nicest clothes I have with me that aren't a Suit. And so which of you gets the captain?" Omega said, the hint of a twinkle briefly appearing in her eye.

"That would not be me," Eretigen said with a grin, as he entered through the connecting door, attired in what passed for a suit on Emdali; it was a deep-burgundy, silk-like tunic and draping vest, with slits for wings and arms, and matching trousers underneath; it looked well against his red scales and vivid green eyes. Entiyti wore a similar ensemble, save his was a bright copper shade, which emphasized his flame-colored eyes and contrasted his white scales. "Forgive me; I was not eavesdropping. I merely heard your comment as I came through on the way to dinner."

"Not a problem. So the good captain is Uncle Pulgey's date?"

"Something like," Entiyti said, even as his silver-white scales grew a dusky gray.

"Oooh, somebody likes her. There's hope for you after all," Omega declared, and Eretigen laughed.

"There is, indeed," the physician agreed. "Hush, now, someone is at the door. We don't want to embarrass the love-birds."

Entiyti, facial scales still dark, headed for the door of his stateroom to let the captain enter.

* * *

Dinner went surprisingly well. Entiyti and Ssiimiilav flirted discreetly, and Eretigen and Omega exchanged equally-discreet, gently amused, nonverbal commentary on the flirtation, discovering they understood each other and got along quite well. While they had seen each other from time to time during Alpha One's sojourn on Emdali, they had had little interaction, as the medtech assigned to Entiyti had provided most of Omega's information on medication and what to watch for in the Draconan's condition.

Meanwhile, Entiyti had ordered four courses from the ship's mess, all suited to the digestive systems of both Draconan and human, and all intended to be readily digested and assimilated by an emotionally-upset human. All three Draconans subtly encouraged Omega to eat as much as she could; Eretigen had filled in Ssiimiilav on the whys and wherefores of Omega's mental state while Entiyti was trying to reach Fox late that afternoon, so the captain understood the need.

Thisssslan soup was succeeded by arsssluuk salad, which in turn was followed by roast ooog served with a delicately-seasoned duusst soufflé on the side. Dessert was a kind of flan or custard made from kooss milk, and topped with a hard caramel, not quite a crème brûlée. More, the thoughtful ship's mess had prepared different-sized servings for Draconans and human, ensuring the larger beings had sufficient to eat without overwhelming the smaller human. The Reptoid server who came along with the food cart was courteous and solicitous, ensuring everyone had what they needed, and no one felt pressured.

The others were pleased to see that Omega was able to make significant inroads on her delicious meal, finishing the soup and the salad handily, and managing all but a couple of bites of the roast ooog. The soufflé was light enough that she polished it off entirely. But initially she tried to decline dessert.

"Oh, guys, I'm stuffed," she protested, when the waiter came around with individual plates of the dessert dish. "This is more food than I've had time to eat in several days!"

"All the more reason you should eat now, young lady," Eretigen noted. "Pul has told me all about you, you know—that enhanced metabolism of yours, and your skills and degrees, and whatnot. You MUST keep yourself properly fueled if you want to finish your intended...project."

"And the custard...I think Franz used to call it a 'flan'...is very good," Entiyti added. "And not too heavy. Will you not at least try it?"

"We have the best chefs aboard the *Hsshthh*," Captain Ssiimiilav declared, throwing Entiyti a brief, meaningful glance. "We always eat VERY well."

"I would not have it any other way, Chassav," Entiyti explained. "For all that this crew does for me? Practically at my beck and call? Protecting me and carting me all over the galaxy? Of course I intend to assure that you are all fed well, treated well, with excellent quarters and pay. There is a reason assignment to the *Hsshthh* is considered so plum, even if it does place you in danger when I am aboard."

"Nonsense, Pul," Ssiimiilav declared, as Omega accepted the dish and tasted it, then commenced eating with surprising enthusiasm, failing to notice the exchange of pleased glances that went between the other three. "Granted, I am somewhat new to your bridge, after your old captain finally retired, but I think there is no more danger here than there is aboard any other fleet ship. We are not without armed escort, after all."

"Aha. That explains the other blips that kept winking in and out of my sensor scans," Omega murmured, as she tucked away the flan alongside the others. "I wondered about that."

"Most likely," Ssiimiilav agreed. "Your ship is a disguised Division One craft, is it not? So you would have the sensory capability to detect your sister ships in our escort."

"I take it, you like the flan-stuff?" Eretigen asked, as the last of her smaller portion disappeared into Omega's mouth. "We call it 'koosstik.'"

"'Koosstik.' Got it. Oh, that was great!" Omega said with a sheepish smile. "I've always liked flans and crème brûlée and the like, but I've never had one that tasted like that. Did it have any flavoring, or was it just the particular animal milk?"

"The chef uses the highest-grade kooss milk for the custard," the server explained. "The kooss has fed upon naturally-growing iisstth in the field, which imparts a delicate flavor to the milk. Then she adds a small bouquet of ssynkuuss to steep, as the milk is heating. This enhances the iisstth flavor; she removes the bouquet before finishing the custard."

"It's delicious," Omega averred, instinctively rubbing her full belly.

"Very much so," Eretigen and Entiyti agreed.

"Tell Chef the meal was wonderful," Ssiimiilav told the server, "and served its intended purpose excellently."

"Thank you, Captain; I shall certainly do that," the waiter said, removing the empty dishes to the cart before departing with the lot.

* * *

After the meal, they removed to Entiyti's sitting area for a brief time of chat over only mildly-alcoholic drinks—Eretigen would not let Entiyti have strong liquor yet, and Ssiimiilav may have been off duty, but was on call—before Ssiimiilav declared she needed to get back to her quarters.

"Because the start of shift comes early tomorrow," she noted. "And I need a bit of sleep so I will stay alert."

"And I need to try one more time to reach Franz before Werf shoos me off to bed," Entiyti averred.

"So I need to get gone for that," Omega observed.

"It would likely be best, if you do not wish him to know you are here," Entiyti agreed. "You know how astute Franz is."

"Good point. Okay."

"May I walk you back to your stateroom?" Eretigen asked the Agent.

"I would be delighted, sir," Omega said with a smile.

The pair headed out.

Chassav Ssiimiilav did not.

* * *

"Heh. And so we gave the lovebirds a few moments alone, before Chassav has to really leave," Omega noticed with a slight...if somewhat bitter and lonely...grin.

"You ARE as discerning as Pul has said," Eretigen decided. "And every whit as much as Lord Levy, from what I have seen. Yes, there is definite interest there, on both sides, and as he has never had a proper mate, I have hopes." He scrunched his scaly face. "Of course, I have also been disappointed before, too. We shall see, I suppose."

"You've known him a long time?"

"We were younglings together, so...yes. 'School chums,' as Franz used to put it. And this is the most serious I have seen him over a female in many a long annum. He was happily set to marry when he was a young male, but his lady was killed in an unfortunate accident, and he...never quite got over it, I think. And never found anyone who was her equal...at least, until now, perhaps. But Chassav piques his interest. Yes, I have definite hopes."

"She's new to the ship?"

"Yes. The previous captain had held the position since...I am unsure. A very long time. Perhaps dating back to Lord Levy's days on board," the physician explained. "But after the assassination attempt on the transfer station, several of the older members of Pul's team decided to retire, or move to less stressful positions. And he helped them find new positions, when needed."

"Who's heading up the bodyguard contingent aboard?" Omega wondered. "I know that Chief Dalgaard heads up estate security now, and Suud resumed the Chief Bodyguard position until Pulgey could arrange for something else, but I also know he couldn't leave Emdali, due to family obligations..."

"Suud's son Duuniiss is handling it, for now," the red Draconan noted, "but I think he has scarcely been out of the corps' barracks this trip. Pul is safe, and the corps is operating as it should, but there was some sort of mix-up regarding the on-board chain of command, and who reports to whom, and he has been attempting to work that out to everyone's satisfaction."

"Maybe I can pop by before I leave and say hi," Omega reflected, then reconsidered. "Or maybe it's best if he never knows I was here..."

"I think you should stop by and greet him," Eretigen advised. "You cannot isolate yourself, Omega, no matter what you think has happened to your life. Yes, I know what happened; Pul told me, only because he was worried about you and Echo, and wanted my medical opinion on what was occurring. He has told no one else, though I gave the captain a bit of a 'heads-up,' as you would say, about helping us ensure you ate decently tonight; that was one of our worries, because relative to your clothing, you are decidedly too thin. But none of us WILL tell anyone else, unless you wish it. However, realize this: we are trying to care for a friend, a member of Pul's extended, chosen family—you. And your behavior is not good, my dear. It is apt to get you killed, and sooner rather than later."

"It doesn't matter," she sighed. "Just let me nail the guy who hired Slug, and the rest is all gone, anyway."

"No! Now that is your depression and stress speaking," Eretigen reprimanded, stern, as they entered Omega's stateroom. He closed the door and stood before her, fisted hands on hips. "You think, because you have lost your heart's love, your life is over. What happened to the interest in working for Pul? To transfer to his bodyguard corps? You were an astronaut; you wanted to explore the universe. What better way to do it than with the galactic president, aboard his ship? There is a saying on Emdali, among Reptoid and Draconan alike—'Where one gate closes, another opens,' youngling. Remember that. Do not rashly throw away everything because you think one thing has gone wrong. Because sometimes that which we think is lost comes back to us again. And even when it does not, and sometimes it does not, there are always bends in the road. And something new to discover around each one."

He stared down the Agent, which was a rare thing; Omega was determined and strong-willed, and once her mind was made up, seldom swayed. But this time, recent months' events had beaten her down; she glanced away. Then, after several moments to consider, she met his eyes again, searching. He cocked his head and met that laser-like blue gaze, gentling his own; she bit her lip, thoughtful, then nodded.

"All right," she murmured. "You have a point. Several, actually. I'll do my best to do as you say. It wasn't so much that I wanted it as that, well, with nobody left to watch my back, I just figured it would happen eventually. And I'm tired enough of the pain, the constant embarrassment and hurt about what I am, not to care, if it did. But you're right. There are...options, even if they're not the thing I wanted most."

"Exactly. And sometimes, those options, if we persevere, we find BECOME the thing we want the most. Do not give up. I know it has been exceeding difficult for you these last few years, but keep fighting. You have friends on your side, family in your corner. We will help you fight. All you need do is ask."

Omega nodded, still thoughtful.

"Okay. I'm asking," she declared.

"And we are here," Eretigen said. "And already fighting on your behalf. Be patient. Relax, unwind a bit," here he walked over to the small wet bar in the corner and opened the tiny refrigerator, "perhaps have somewhat to HELP you relax...but not too much...and try to sleep tonight. Trust Pul, Chassav, and myself to handle the rest, at least for now."

"Got any whisky or Scotch in there?" Omega wondered.

"That, and a couple of other Earth liquors, several of what I think are called 'top-shelf' labels of each," Eretigen said, nosing about in the little fridge. "They are popular in the galactic community as a whole. Diplomats are particularly fond of them, so Pul tries to keep them in the staterooms. They are in the little single-serving bottles."

"Then I might knock back one or two of those, and go to bed," Omega decided.

"Excellent. I shall leave you to relax in your own way, then."

"Good night," Omega said with a slight smile.

"Good night, my dear," Eretigen said, returning the smile with a toothy one of his own.

And he was gone.

Omega drew a deep breath, let it out slowly, then began exploring the contents of the wet bar's refrigerator.

Chapter 12

By the time Eretigen returned to his own stateroom, Entiyti was alone next door.

"Werf?" he called. Eretigen came to the connecting door.

"Yes, Pul? Is all well? Have you reached Lord Levy?"

"Not yet," Entiyti replied. "Chassav only left a few minutes ago. How is she? Omega?"

"I gave her a stern talking-to," Eretigen said, "and a bit of a pep talk. I think it took. I left her exploring the wet bar, with instructions to relax—with mild assistance, if need be, hence the wet bar explorations—and trust us to help her." He drew a deep breath. "She actually asked us for help, Pul. Help, not merely in the task she has chosen. She needs us to help her fight her way through all this, and come out the other side. Alive. That is not in character, is it?"

"Ohhh," Entiyti murmured, mildly shocked. "No, it is not. She is quite independent, save for her relationship with Echo. Then she IS hurting, and at the end of her rope, as Franz would say."

"I think so, yes." Eretigen waved a clawed hand in the direction of the galactic president's desk. "This once, I am waiving my rules for you, Pul; I believe we have someone whose needs are greater than yours, and whom you can help. I think you need to contact Levy as soon as you can. Stay up late if you need to, as late AS you need to, but do it. I shall see that you are properly rested when it is done."

"Agreed," Entiyti said, turning toward the 'office' in the corner.

* * *

"...No, Pul, there's change all right, but not in the good way," Fox explained to the Draconan noble. "Echo's condition is deteriorating. If this keeps up, at the very least, he'll end up brain-dead, if not completely dead when the autonomic nervous system breaks down."

"Sssllltth ssshhiissh ttthhssiiss asssshh hiiisss hiigeessht,"

Entiyti cursed. "Is there any chance to stop it, let alone reverse it?"

"Yes, there is, but we HAVE to find Omega to do it," a patently worried Fox said with a sigh. "But no one knows where she is."

"Why do you need Omega, to save Echo?"

"Ambassador Zz'r'p reminded us that she has Echo's nd't'lq, his 'mind-clone,' and re-installing that in his brain should stop the deterioration, and pretty much reverse the whole mess, given a bit of time for everything to re-integrate. At least, that's what Zz'r'p says. And if anyone should know, he would."

"Wait—what?"

"If we can get Omega back here, so that Zz'r'p can facilitate reconnecting the copy of Echo's mind that she's carrying—but probably forgot she had—then we can FIX this. Echo will live, probably be back to normal, even. IF we can do it in time."

"Oh, giisshttt," Entiyti grumbled, smearing his palm across his face. "Forgive my betrayal, child. Franz, she is here."

"WHAT?!"

"I have her here, aboard my flagship," Entiyti reiterated. "She has sworn me to secrecy, but we ran across her this morning, while she was on this mission to close the Slug case..."

"Which was a mission of her own making; I didn't order it. Go on, Pul."

"Right. And I am not surprised, all things considered. Well, she was trying to pass as a Gurgev, but she did not count on my recognizing her voice, after spending so much time with her and Echo last lunation. So I had her and her vessel brought aboard my ship, and made her 'fess up, as you used to say..."

"She didn't want to come home?"

"She felt that she had no home left, Franz," Entiyti said quietly. "It seems she believes that the 'family' she has created is actually held together by...Echo. After all, we all knew Echo before we knew her...in many cases, by decades..."

"Oh, meshuge iung meyn tekhter," Fox murmured, biting his lip. "And so what did you think would become of you, my little girl...?"

"She hoped to capture the being who hired Slug to begin with," Entiyti noted, "most likely to help protect an amnesiac Echo from his own past, if I understood correctly...and apparently expected to be killed by perps at some point, because she was alone, with no one left to guard her back."

"Oy vey. Adonai have mercy." Deeply perturbed and not a little sad, Fox shook his head. "We need her back here, and fast, Pul. It's the only way Echo has a chance."

"Franz, I must first see if she WANTS to come back."

"I...understand." Fox bit his lip again, worried.

"Let me talk to her, and I will call you back shortly."

"I'll be standing by."

* * *

"WHAT?!" Omega screamed, as she stood in Entiyti's stateroom, whence Eretigen had fetched her immediately. "He's dying anyway?? They need ME to save him?! WHY?"

"Because you have Echo's...mind? in your head?" Entiyti tried. "I did not understand it, youngling, but Zz'r'p needs you to come back at once so that he may transfer Echo's mind back into his own head...?"

"The nd't'lq?"

"That was the word, yes!"

"Holy shit," Omega said blankly. "I figured, when that didn't download automatically, like it did in the Ennead mess, that it wasn't there any more. That, that when he...mostly died...it dissipated."

"The question now becomes, my dear girl...are you going back to do this?"

Omega paused, and eyed him.

"Are you sure this isn't just something they're coming up with to get me back? Some sort of scheme for convincing me?" she demanded. "You told him, didn't you? Told him I'm here?"

"I AM sure," Entiyti declared. "I have known Franz too long to be fooled. He is as close to frightened for Echo as that man can be. He fears he will lose his adoptive son. And daughter." He paused, then added, honest and open, "And yes, I told him you were here. ONLY after I was certain that the need was great, and urgent. This I swear to you, upon my honor."

Omega sat down hard—she didn't even look back to see if

a chair was there; Eretigen scrambled to grab a chair and shove it under her already-descending posterior—and studied Entiyti for long moments, looking for...and finding...the signs of his sincerity.

"Then yes. I'm going back." She stopped, considering, then added, "But you need to do something for me, in the meanwhile."

"Tell me, and I shall see it done if it is in my ability."

"Let me give you my evidence, and you take it forward, with my reasoning, to Chief Wuxullian," Omega said. "The two of you, chase my perp, while I go back to try to save Echo. But I want in on the end, if I can. Not for any credit; I don't CARE who gets the credit. I just want to see the bastard collared."

"Consider it done," Entiyti averred, placing his hand on his breastbone.

"All right. Let's call Fox," Omega said.

* * *

The viewscreen came up on a very pale and obviously agitated Fox; as Omega looked at him, she was suddenly and strongly reminded of the expression on his face when he had gotten news of the attempted assassination on Entiyti. And she knew, in that instant, things were serious...and completely unfeigned.

"Oh, meyn teyere tekhter," Fox said in deep and obvious relief, as soon as he saw her, "I am SO glad to see you! Are you all right?"

She flushed, pleased. "I'm...okay, Abba Fox," she tried, uncertain how he would react to the phrasing. Fox flushed slightly at the affectionate term, and a slight smile appeared on his tense face.

"That's good, tekhter, that's good. You're uninjured? Pul has been taking proper care of you?"

"Alla that," she averred, before breaking off and biting her lip. "Um. How is Echo?" she asked then.

"Eh. Not good," he sighed. "And very...remorseful...where you're concerned."

"Huh? What do you mean?"

"I decided to SHOW him how the two of you worked to-

277

gether," Fox explained. "I pulled out several hours of select video and gave him a running commentary while we watched it together. It didn't take long before he realized he skrud aroyf. And by the time I'd finished, he was all but cursing himself out. I think, if he could have remembered all the right words, he WOULD have cursed himself out."

"Wait—what do you mean, 'remember all the right words,' Fox?"

"I mean, as his mental condition deteriorates, he's starting to experience a certain degree of aphasia, something like a stroke patient. Once or twice, it has briefly deteriorated into what Zarnix says is colloquially termed 'word salad.' Kind of random insertion of words, with some made-up stuff thrown in for good measure."

"Oh, dear Lord!" Omega exclaimed, shocked. "What— I don't..."

"Hush, meyn tekhter," Fox soothed. "We think this can be fixed, but you must come HOME for that to occur. Did Pul explain about the nd't'lq?"

"Ye-yes..."

"All right. Then the next thing I want to tell you is, this IS your home, Omega," Fox said, earnest. "It is YOUR home. We are YOUR family. Yes, we have known Echo longer, but what I have been thinking of as Avendez'er Mishpacha—'Our Family'—and let me note that I lost my own birth family much longer ago than you lost yours, and I find I welcome Our Family—but Our Family did not come into existence...until YOU became part of the Agency. YOU are the glue that helps hold it together, tekhter...with your love, with your caring, with your truly gigantic heart and soul. We miss you—all of us, and would want you to come safely home even if Echo did not need you desperately."

The stateroom was silent for long moments, as Omega bit her lip, then bowed her head, casting her face into shadow. Moments later, something glittering fell from her face, and a single, tiny, wet spot formed on the deck. Finally she nodded once.

"All right," she said, voice husky, without looking up. "I'll come home, Fox. How are we gonna work this, and how fast do you need me...?"

* * *

Matters were arranged within moments after that. While Eretigen had gone to fetch Omega, Entiyti had pinged Captain Ssiimiilav. It had taken her a few moments to arrive from her quarters, but this had given Fox a chance to talk to Omega and convince her of her place.

And now all four beings stood in Entiyti's 'office' corner, talking to Fox while details were worked out.

"No, we need you five minutes ago, tekhter," Fox declared. "Every minute gone by means more deterioration for Echo. I don't think we have two more days, if that."

"How fast can the *Hsshthh* get to Earth from here?" Entiyti asked Ssiimiilav. She thought for a moment, then shook her head.

"We are TOO big, and we are already too far out," Ssiimiilav noted. "Our cruising speed is high, yes, but not high enough for this. We need a smaller vessel, one capable of hitting impressive velocity, but not so small that its range is restricted, as Omega's effectively is..."

"Yeah, it can go long-distance, or it can go fast," Omega agreed. "It can't really do both. And, while I could probably hot-rod it and increase its speed, we don't really have time for that..."

"I'll send the *Genesis*," Fox declared. "It can meet you partway, and transfer Omega between ships, then bring her back here at maximum emergency acceleration. The same numbers I hit to get from Earth to Emdali in considerably less than 'overnight' when you got nearly assassinated, Pul."

The three Draconans exchanged glances, considering, as a tense Omega watched.

"Yes, that should work," Ssiimiilav averred. "Let us work out a likely rendezvous point, and then I will call the bridge immediately and have our course diverted at maximum speed."

"Vunderlekh!" Fox exclaimed. "Omega, meyn teyere, I cannot leave to meet you, because Our Family is rather busy trying to help slow matters here, and Alpha Line is hustling to compensate for the lack of its leads—though Romeo is doing his best to split his time between Alpha Line and the medlab.

But will it do if I send Chi aboard the *Genesis* to meet you? That way, at least you will have a familiar, friendly face to keep you company on the trip back."

"That...sounds nice, Fox," Omega murmured, offering a hesitant smile.

"Now, as to the rendezvous..." he said, and Captain Ssiimi-ilav leaned forward.

* * *

As soon as the vidcomm ended, Ssiimiilav called the bridge and immediately diverted the *Hsshthh* as promised, aiming for the rendezvous point at maximum velocity, then headed for the bridge herself; half an hour later, Fox notified them in a ciphered blip that the *Genesis* had launched, with Agent Chi aboard.

"And now you two must get some sleep," Dr. Eretigen declared, waving his hands at Entiyti and Omega.

"Go ahead and put Uncle Pulgey to bed," Omega noted. "There's no way I'm gonna sleep at this point. I'll just head back to my quarters and...play video games on my phone, or something."

"Nonsense," Entiyti declared. "You can have my chaise longue; it is made for MY size, so you will certainly have plenty of room. And Werf can give you something to help you sleep."

"Well, I had rather not, Pul," Eretigen murmured. "I am not so experienced with humans, and you have different biochemistries, and she is considerably smaller, so will require a much smaller dose, and..."

"Oh," Entiyti said, deflating a bit.

"Besides, it's only gonna be a matter of hours, according to what Fox said," Omega pointed out, "because the *Genesis* is hauling ass. Like, max emergency acceleration, which got him from Earth to Emdali in about six hours, ish."

"And should not take much longer, possibly less, to reach the rendezvous point, which is slightly closer to us than to Earth, if memory of Franz's maps serves," Entiyti realized. "So...yes. We will be at the rendezvous point in about four hours, all told, and the *Genesis* will likely arrive very shortly thereafter. Werf," he said, turning to the physician, "she has a point. I know you want me to sleep, but..."

"All right, all right," Eretigen grumbled. "Provided you both at least REST, I will be satisfied. I have no doubt that Omega's colleagues will take good care of her once she is safely with them, and once she has departed us, then I will give you a soporific, Pul...and you WILL sleep."

"That will do," Entiyti agreed. "Oh, and Omega, I have already sent a ciphered message to Chief Wuxullian about your investigations, and he was MOST interested, and very glad to hear that you are safe with me, en route to Earth."

"But is he gonna follow up?" Omega wondered, nibbling her lip.

Before Entiyti could answer, Eretigen pointed Omega at the sofa, and grabbed Entiyti's arm, towing him to the chaise longue.

"LIE DOWN," he ordered, "BOTH of you. You may talk to your hearts' content, provided you both try to relax. Though I reserve the right to change the topic of conversation, should it become stressful or maudlin."

The pair obeyed the physician's orders, stretching out on the respective furniture. Omega grabbed a couple of throw pillows and tucked them behind her head. Eretigen took the overstuffed armchair close by. Once all were comfortably settled, Entiyti answered Omega's question.

"Oh, he will most definitely follow up, my dear. He was fairly delighted that you had what looked like such a very good lead on the cold case, and was surprised that those clues had been overlooked. He did not realize you were such a linguist. He thought Echo was the language student in your partnership."

"Well, I'm not, and he is," Omega explained. "I really...oh shit."

"Uh-oh," Entiyti said, sitting up in alarm, even as Eretigen sat forward, anxious. "What is 'oh shit'?"

"Aw, the whole figuring out the name clues? What they translated to an' all? It wasn't MY mental voice I heard, it was ECHO'S," she explained. "I'll bet it was the nd't'lq trying to reach out, find out what was going on, communicate with me. Only I don't have that telepathy chip any more, and I've been

SO upset..."

"That...sounds intriguing," Eretigen noted. "But not improbable, given what I understand of what is going on."

"Anyway," Omega sighed. "I missed a really HUGE clue that might have gotten me to turn around and go home a lot sooner. And prevented some of the deterioration, maybe. IF Echo had let me near him to actually, y'know, HELP."

"Hush that," Eretigen ordered. "You are en route now to do that very thing. And Echo, it sounds, has acknowledged to the others that he misjudged matters. Stop with the self-recriminations, youngling."

"Okay," Omega sighed again. "Go on, Uncle Pul. What else did the Chief say?"

"Ah. Well, let me see," Entiyti said, lying back down only when Eretigen glared at him. "He also grumbled something about, 'never quite trusted the bastard,' or the like. From what I gather, the rest of the family detection agency is above reproach, but the old reprobate who headed the clan, not so much. He seemed rather to be a bit of a throwback to olden days."

"That's what I kinda picked up on, too," Omega agreed. "So he's going after him?"

"It is all in work as we speak, my dear. Of course, he has a few more hoops to jump through than you did in your approach to the problem. So it will take a little longer. But in the end, it will be just as effective."

"Do you know how he's going to handle it? Is there any chance I can be present when it finally goes down, to at least, you know, close the loop?"

"He is looking into that. I believe he intends a sudden raid on Erushin and his resort, after checking a few things and verifying your notion that the resort is likely a money-laundering front. Which, given some of the things he has in place for such matters, should happen within the next day or two, possibly sooner; he said all he had needed was the knowledge of where to look." Entiyti watched as an expression of satisfaction spread across Omega's face. "As to your being present, he welcomes the notion, but we think the timing is going to be somewhat dependent upon how matters go with Echo."

"Mm. Right. Okay." Omega pressed her lips together,

considering. "Maybe...if I understood correctly, Echo's gonna need a couple days to let everything kinda reintegrate after we get the nd't'lq downloaded properly...assuming it works at all. I can probably pop over while he's still unconscious and 'processing,' as it were."

"Excellent. I will pass on that information, and have Wux contact Ambassador Zz'r'p and Director Fox for proper timing." He didn't tell her that he had surreptitiously notified Fox that Omega needed some medical care of her own, as much physical as mental—to include food, and rest—and that worthy had agreed.

"That sounds good," Omega averred, and the conversation meandered on to more innocuous topics and a physician-mandated heavy snack, as the two Draconans strove to take her mind off Echo's condition and the general situation.

* * *

Some four hours later, Captain Ssiimiilav's voice annunciated into Entiyti's stateroom.

"Pul, this is Chassav. Is Agent Omega there? She is not in her stateroom..."

"Yes, Chass," Entiyti spoke into the air, trusting the microphones to pick up his speech. "She is here. We have been keeping each other company, all three of us being a bit too anxious to sleep."

"Ah, good then. We have arrived at the rendezvous point, and the *Genesis* has already pinged us; she is on final approach. Do you have me on speaker?"

"I do, Chass."

"All right. Agent Omega, if you would be so good as to fetch your things and be ready, I will have someone come to get you and take you to the boarding hatch in about ten minutes. Normally we would use a shuttle for personnel exchange, but that takes longer, and time is of the essence, so we will use a spacebridge...rather like the skybridges to be found at your civilian airports, I suppose, but with an airtight seal on each side. But the spacebridge is, as you might think, a bit fragile when connecting two ships the size of the *Hsshthh* and the *Genesis*; a slight fluctuation in relative positions could shatter it. So we want to have you ready and waiting, and hustle you through, once it is established."

"All right. Yes ma'am, I can do that," Omega said, rising and heading for the door. "I just have to get my kit from my quarters, and I'll be ready. You want me to come back to Pulgey's stateroom?"

"Please. It has been a pleasure to meet you, my dear. I hope to see you again soon. And hopefully, you can then introduce me to your partner, Maker willing."

"Likewise, and I sure hope so, ma'am."

Omega slipped out, closing the door behind her. Entiyti and Eretigen exchanged glances; Entiyti nodded, and Eretigen addressed the captain.

"Chassav, has there been any more word on Agent Echo's condition?"

"No, Werf; I was about to ask you and Pul that very thing. I expect that Director Fox is more apt to contact the two of you than myself, especially here on the bridge."

"Well, no news is likely good news," Entiyti decided. "Or at least, status-quo news."

"True. Giisshttt hiigeessht!" Ssiimiilav suddenly exclaimed, and both males sat upright.

"What?! What is it, Chass? What has happened?" an alarmed Entiyti demanded.

"No, no, stand down, everything is fine," Ssiimiilav said, sounding vaguely sheepish. "The *Genesis* just came in and dropped her warp bubble, and she was hauling ass, as you are wont to say, Pul. She only slowed at the very last moment, and it caught me off guard."

"Ah. That would be one of Franz's old maneuvers, then," Entiyti decided, just as Omega re-entered his quarters. "And here comes Omega with her kit. We are ready to go, Chass."

"Sending an escort now, Pul," came the reply.

* * *

Entiyti, Eretigen, and no less than Duuniiss Guurn —who had been notified by Eretigen and Entiyti of Omega's presence earlier, and even invited to the dinner party, but had been unable to get away to greet her or attend—escorted Omega to the main boarding hatch. All three offered farewell hugs, as the two great ships' hatches connected in an airlock seal via spacebridge. Moments later the local pressures were equalized, and the airlock opened all the way through.

Agent Chi and Agent Zero, the *Genesis'* security chief, waited on the other side, already in the spacebridge.

"Keep us posted, young one," Entiyti declared, as Omega picked up her kit from the deck.

"I will, I swear," she said as she stepped through the hatch.

Within moments, the airlocks had sealed, the spacebridge retracted, the hatches closed, and the two huge starships parted company, as the *Genesis* whisked Omega back toward Earth.

* * *

Zero greeted the lone Agent, then excused himself and headed for the bridge, with instructions to Chi to bring Omega there...after providing for her comfort. Chi took her through several corridors and down one deck to the living quarters deck. There, he showed her to a small individual berth, where she deposited her kit for the time being.

"And if you get tired and need to rest, just come back here," Chi explained. "If you need company, grab me. I have the berth next door, so I can come 'round and talk if you need to. I was just off duty when the call came in from Fox through Crutch, so I napped a bit myself, on the way here."

"Got it," Omega agreed. "Now for the bridge?"

"Now we head to the bridge, yeah," Chi confirmed. "You ever been on the *Genesis* before?"

"Nope."

"It's big. REALLY big. And really cool! I spent a good part of the last four hours figuring it out, though—well, what time I wasn't asleep, so really about half of that, I guess it was—so I think I got it. It's this way." He turned and headed off, Omega beside him.

* * *

"Wow. Here we are, working together again," Omega noted, as Chi escorted her to the bridge of the *Genesis*. "It seems like forever and yesterday, all at once. And I'm NOT talking about the rescue mission!" She offered him an attempt at a grin, though it wobbled a bit. "And we are a LONG ways away from the solar system!"

"Yeah, I hear ya," Chi agreed, grinning back; he ignored

the wobbliness of her grin, in the circumstances. "That last bit? Like, out of the solar system? Damn, it feels SO good! I hadda tear myself away from the display on the bridge, just to get done what I needed to do! And we always did make a damn great team, Meg, the two of us. Maybe not as good as you and Echo, based on what I saw, 'cuz...wow, but still damn good, you an' me."

"Yeah."

"...I just wish you'd given me as many chances as you're giving him, that's all," Chi noted, seeming a bit discouraged.

"Aw. Look, Scotty," Omega tried to explain, "remember what I told you was done to me..."

"Yeah."

"And that I was programmed to kill him."

"Yeah. But you beat it."

"Yeah, I did. Barely. With a helluva lotta help. But as nearly as I can tell, when Slug programmed me? Insofar as I can figure out, he basically downloaded his dossier on Echo into me..."

"Hold it." He stopped dead in the passageway, and Omega stopped with him. "Is this the thing we're taking you back to download into him? The dossier on him?"

"No, no. The 'mental dossier' is one thing. That was just Slug downloading everything he knew about Echo into MY mind so that that part of my brain would recognize him when I eventually encountered him. The nd't'lq is another thing entirely. The nd't'lq is basically a kind of 'clone' of Echo's actual mind, stored in my head, BY Echo. The Deltiri ambassador showed me how to do it a couple months back, to combat a rogue telepath. Then, when Echo got set up during the whole Adita's Coup shit, in order to keep him from being brain-bleached—he was falsely accused and very nearly railroaded out of the organization on trumped-up charges, and if the coup had succeeded, we'd never have gotten him back; it's a long story—and to give us a chance to prove what happened, I showed HIM how to do it, and helped him clone his mind and install it in my head. It's supposed to stay in contact with the original mind, see, so when they brain-bleached him, since I can't be brain-bleached, his mind just downloaded back into his brain almost instantaneously...from where it was 'backed up' in MY brain. We called it a 'hot reboot,' him and me."

"But then why didn't...?"

"We talked about that a little, when Fox caught up to me," Omega said, hopscotching around the fact that she'd been hiding from Fox. "We don't know for sure, but we think it's something to do with Echo being almost-dead, combined with the fact that I had a special telepathy implant chip when we made the nd't'lq, but had to remove it a few days later, when my immune system pitched a fit."

"Oh, okay; I see, I think," Chi decided. "Different mental conditions, and a REALLY off-nominal situation."

"Right. So anyway, back to when I was a kid—Slug gathered all the information he had on Echo, and downloaded it into that part of my mind that he'd programmed..."

"Yeah. So?"

"So, by the time I ever MET Echo, for all intents and purposes, I already knew him—knew who he was, knew WHAT he was, what he was like, everything about him as a person... except outrightly meeting him." She shrugged. "Okay, I didn't know his background, because SLUG didn't know his background. But I knew what kind of person he was."

"Okay...I don't get it. What are you trying to say?"

"Scotty, I trusted him immediately. As soon as I met him. No matter what they put me through in training, in testing...I TRUSTED Echo. What does that tell you?"

"Oh. OH. That, that you already knew him, that you..." He broke off and stared. "Holy shit. Is THAT why you didn't wanna...? I mean, I know I kinda tried to press you into some stuff, 'cause several of the guys were givin' me grief about why we hadn't yet, and I jumped the gun on it, and I've always been really sorry for that...and we broke up soon after, so I always figured..."

"Aw. No, it's okay. It's always been okay, hon. When I said no, you accepted no for an answer."

"Well of course I did, and I'm glad you didn't get mad, but..."

"And it wasn't 'cause of anything to do with Echo; I'm just that old-fashioned. That wasn't why we broke up, either. I thought we were on the same page with it at the time, but maybe not. And if that's the case, I owe you an apology. It's only, well, I just felt like we made better friends than lovers, at that point. I guess THAT mighta been because of Echo in my subconscious, but still. Did you NOT want to just stay friends?"

"Waitaminit. Are you telling me...are you telling me you were already in love with him at that point? Before you'd ever even MET him?"

Omega sighed.

"I can't say for sure, but...I think so, yeah. It's the only thing that really makes sense of some stuff. Let alone how I was able to combat the programming long enough for Alpha Two to KILL the programming. I didn't realize it CONSCIOUSLY until a few months AFTER that, though."

"Well, then I never had a chance!"

"No, I don't think that's right," Omega said, thoughtful and considering the matter. "I know now that, well, that one reason why I didn't wanna sleep with you—aside from just bein' old-fashioned, an' the religious beliefs an' stuff—was what Slug did to me. It had...HAS...me scared of, of intimacy, Scotty. Like, even with Echo."

"Whoa. He didn't— I mean...oh shit. You're kidding."

"Nope; I wish I was."

"Did this Slug dude actually rape...?"

"Sexually, no. Every other way? Pretty much. And then some. A lotta 'then some.'"

"It was that bad?"

"Every bit, yeah. Think...think torture, here, hon. Think vivisection without anesthesia or sedation of any kind—fully conscious, fully feeling the least little thing—and it only STARTS there."

"...Oh damn." He grimaced.

"Yeah. My counselor and I are workin' on all that a whole lot, trying to get past my fear. But specifically, there were, um, well, there were what are called 'phantom sensations' that came from what Slug was doing, and...it HURT, Scotty. I...I don't know how else to explain." They were quiet for long moments, as he took that in, and she gathered herself to continue. "So that, buried in my subconscious, combined with my beliefs, are why I told you NO back then. It didn't have anything to do with you, personally. And it didn't really have anything to do with Echo as such, either."

"Okay, if you say so...but you were already in love with Echo!"

"It's...yeah, I was, but I wasn't," Omega tried to explain. "See, it's entirely possible that if something had happened, if another perp had already k-killed Echo, say, then I'd never have met him at all. If he'd gone offworld, you know, transferred, we'd never have met. If they'd sent another agent on the mission where he and I did finally meet, I'd probably never have met him. Well, maybe; they'd still have brought me into the Agency, I guess, and I might've met him that way. But there were all kinds of factors that stood in the way of me EVER meeting him; it was only Slug's determined and repeated manipulation that brought us together in the first place."

"So?"

"So, if he were already d-dead, or if he'd transferred off-planet, or any of a dozen other scenarios like that, my programming would have been rendered moot," Omega pointed out. "I'd never have met him, and any conscious thoughts of him that popped up, I'd have attributed to a book I read, or whatever—a dream interest, but not a real one. And I'd have been open to your...I hate to call 'em 'advances,' because except for the thing that one time, you were really gentle and thoughtful in your courting, Scotty. But you know what I mean. We maybe eventually could have made something of it. You'd have had to be damn patient, but it's a might have been." She hesitated. "I...haven't told Echo any of this. He was a little jealous of you at first, I think. Just that you and I even had a history at all." She shrugged. "To be honest, I hadn't thought about it in this kind of detail until right now, so I wouldn't have known to tell him, I guess."

"What about...about if...geez, never mind; that's just crass of me to even think it."

"What about if, if something bad happens here? If he... doesn't make it? I dunno, Scotty. In all honesty, he's the love of my life. If he...if we can't save him, I dunno how I'll react, what I'll do. I do have some options now that I didn't have a few days ago, so life will probably still go on, after a fashion. I dunno. Maybe, if you give me long enough...and just be a FRIEND who's there for me, in the meantime...maybe. I...dunno."

She swallowed hard, and struggled to keep her face normal. But Chi saw.

She's crazy in love with him, he thought. *That remark about 'options now' and 'life will go on'...she really DID figure on kamikazi'ing out, like Romeo thought. But now she probably won't, if she can halfway deal with the emotions. So...damn. Even for my own sake, I can't possibly wish that on 'em! I'd never be to her what HE is, anyway. Forget that shit, Scotty. There's somebody else out there for YOU. But not for HER. We gotta make THIS sitch work. For Echo's sake. For HER sake.*

"Okay, Pook," he said, voice gentle, as he apologized and tried to explain. "I'm sorry. I'm not really tryin' to steal Echo's girl, anyhow. Even though I suppose it sounds like it. I...I just mostly was trying to understand what happened, you know, 'back then.' And," he confessed, "maybe apply a little balm to a bruised ego, too. Look. Let's get you to Headquarters so we can render all the rest of this conversation moot, okay?"

"Sounds good," she said, heartening. "An' I get it, so don't worry about it."

"Okay. C'mon, let's go see what the status is." He got his legs in gear again, headed for the bridge once more.

"Right behind ya."

* * *

Fox rushed into Echo's room in the medlab, and Dihl, Zarnix, and Zebra looked up, even as Alpha Two and Zz'r'p ran to the door.

"We've got her, she's on board the *Genesis*, and they're en route for Earth as fast as they can go!" he declared. "It turns out that, as nearly as I've been able to tell from talking to Pulgey in several private little conversations, while there might have been a certain amount of...payback...involved in her quest to find whoever hired Slug—which, by the way, he's convinced she's done, she just didn't have a chance to confront the perp, so she turned the case over to the head of the PGLEIA to finish—one of her main reasons is right here." Fox met Echo's eyes. "She doesn't have enough of a handle on the rest of your past as an Agent to do anything about it, but evidently she decided that this was one perp that wasn't going to get a chance to blindside you, given your amnesia."

"She was protecting Echo," India murmured in sudden realization.

"Exactly," Fox confirmed. "And, I suppose, herself as well, to a certain extent. But given the number of times Echo's name came up in the conversation, as Pul coaxed her to explain, and the fact that she was willing to bite it if it meant taking the perp out, I think we can assume that was her principal rationale."

Echo bit his lip and closed his eyes.

"I'm such a b-bastard," he breathed, patently guilt-ridden.

"HUSH THAT," Zz'r'p reprimanded, sterner than they had ever seen him. "That will NOT do, Echo. You reacted based on your own logic, as determined by the information presented to you. You cannot help the fact that, unbeknownst to you, that logic was impaired."

"Listen to the male," Zarnix added his support to that of the ambassador. "He's right. Do not beat yourself up about it. Just realize what the situation really is, and how much she loves you, and accept it, if you can."

"I...can," Echo decided.

"Good," Zz'r'p decreed. "Now, I must prepare for the procedure. Dihl, will you stay here with Echo and see to his needs, while I take Zarnix and Zebra with me, and arrange for the medical side of the procedure?"

"Gladly, Your Excellency," Dihl noted.

"Just 'Zz'r'p,' if you please, my dear," the Deltiri said quietly. "You should not be using such honorifics with me, unless there is a formal requirement to do so. And there is not, here."

"All right...Zz'r'p," Dihl said with a slight, tired smile. "I will see to my son's needs for the time. You go see to his saving."

"Then let's go," Zebra said.

* * *

It took a couple of hours to get everything lined up, but with the entire medlab aware of what was transpiring, and the patient load relatively low for the time—they had gotten ahead

291

of, and managed to ward off the worst of, the usual Harrnakian flu season—it was all handled with skill and efficiency.

"And so you want Zebra and myself to handle this part of things?" Zarnix asked.

"Yes," Zz'r'p averred. "You may call in whoever else you need for the peripheral monitoring, and the post-procedure care, but I would like our two top physicians working this situation."

"I want Whiskey and Rglfrz to back us up, though, in case we have a crash-cart type emergency," Zebra ordered.

"Done," the human and the Kardorian said in unison. "And Yorker and Dihl and...who else, for the medtech team?" Whiskey added.

"Let's let Dihl simply observe the procedure," Zebra recommended. "I think she has enough on her mind without trying to provide actual support."

"But...why?" a puzzled Whiskey wondered, then suddenly hissed in recognition. "Their eyes! Oh shit, they're related! And she was the lady in the regen pod, back in the summer, so she looks a couple decades younger now than she was...is she his MOM?!"

"Shush!" Zebra and Zarnix chorused. "Remember how Omega was targeted," Zarnix added. "They do not need Dihl targeted as well. WE do not need it. This is classified information, gentlebeings."

"Ooo, right," Whiskey breathed. "Sorry, guys. I wasn't thinking." He and Rglfrz glanced at each other, then nodded. "Okay, so Dihl maybe does the post-op care, but she's with Fox and Alpha Two during the actual procedure. Family in waiting."

"Well considered," Zz'r'p declared.

"That's good," Zebra agreed. "You two throw together a team of about three or four of our OTHER best medtechs, and have 'em ready just outside the room, in case anything frazzes."

"On it," Rglfrz noted.

"Excellent," Zarnix ordered, "begin setup."

* * *

Once matters were well in hand, Zz'r'p called a family

medical conference in Echo's room.

"All right, I want you all to be aware that there IS danger in this procedure," Zz'r'p observed, as they all sat in Echo's hospital room. "I have already informed Omega—who is communicating with me again—but the rest of you should know as well: given the level of Echo's 'operating system' deterioration, should he experience a sudden...we will call it a 'core dump'... while Omega and I are in process of attempting to replace his mind via nd't'lq...well, that would generate a feedback which, when telepathically linked with Omega, could not only destroy the nd't'lq, but her mind, as well. I can and will try to protect her as much as I can, but that could simply create a domino effect, taking me with it."

Everyone in the room stirred in alarm at that information.

"Then we aren't doin' it," Echo decreed from his bed. "I'll die 'fore I take others with me."

"That is no longer your call," Zz'r'p noted. "Omega and I discussed it at some length—" he tapped his temple, "and decided that it was worth the risk, to recover my friend, her belovéd, the 'most badass Agent in the galaxy,' as she put it, the Assistant Director, the Director Successor..." Zz'r'p shook his head. "No, Echo. You are too important, to too many of us. The procedure is going ahead. She is desperate to get you back to normal, to keep you from dying in any sense of the word, and I not only respect that, I agree with it."

Echo gaped in shock, then dropped his gaze to the blanket, flushing.

"Can you accept that, my friend?" Zz'r'p pressed. "Please do not fight us when it comes to the last, because that is the certain way to disaster for all of us. Tell me now...can you accept this? That someone—that OMEGA—loves you enough to risk all? That your Agency family—because sometimes I think of myself as a kind of uncle, though given my age, perhaps great-uncle, in that family—loves you enough to risk our lives for you?"

Echo looked up, meeting the Deltiri's gaze, and opened his mouth to speak, but nothing would come out. Finally he simply nodded.

"Good. Because we are going ahead with it," Zz'r'p declared.

"Can any of the rest of us help?" Fox asked.

"Other than to petition the Maker for success, I think not, friend Fox," Zz'r'p considered. "Oh, but we WILL want Zarnix and Zebra monitoring their vitals, of course, and the medical team should be ready to establish intravenous lines for fluids and sustenance in the aftermath of this, because both of them will need to rest for an extended time, which I intend to ensure." He tapped his temple with a long blue finger. "And certainly other 'family members,' such as Dihl and India who have medical training, are welcome to help with the monitoring and such. I know I have frightened all of you, and I am sorry, but while I felt I needed to warn you of the potential, I do not think the probability is high of such a thing occurring. The more probable negative outcome is simply that the nd't'lq, mm, 'reload' will not succeed, and over time Echo will...die. At least mentally."

"I want all life sup-support off me, if that happens," Echo said quietly. "I know it'll hurt y'all, but I don' wanna..."

"We understand," Zebra observed, voice soft. "If it comes to that, and please God may it not, your family will see matters taken care of, Echo. I swear it."

"And she's not alone," Fox said, voice slightly hoarse. "I've had your...'terminal' paperwork for some few years now. It'll get done, zun. Omega has seen it, right?" Fox broke off, running his hand over his face. "Never mind. You don't remember. I'll...see that gets taken care of, too, just in case." He paused. "Well, how about this: there isn't really going to be a lot of time for her to go over such matters, so I won't worry her with it right now. I have the formal paperwork, and will see it gets executed if need be, and show it to her in the aftermath, explaining everything if I have to. And if all goes well, I'll also see that YOU show it to her, so she has the knowledge for any future events, though hopefully we'll never need it."

"Okay," Echo said, gruff. "That's all right, then, and that'll work, Fox. But Zz'r'p? You and, and O-o-um, Meg, y'all be CAREFUL."

"As much as is possible," Zz'r'p agreed. He paused, then observed, "Omega has made planetfall, and is entering the emergency maglev now. She will be at the emergency platform in a matter of minutes."

"Then Dihl, I want you and Zebra helping me get things ready," Zarnix issued orders. "Fox, who do you want meeting her?"

"Alpha Two," Fox decided, "come with me. I think she needs us there."

"Agreed, Fox," India declared.

"All over it, Boss-man," Romeo averred.

* * *

"How is he?" were Omega's first words when she stepped off the maglev at the emergency dock. Behind her, a worried Chi eased out and stood to one side, listening but silent, prepared to slip away once he found out how things had developed.

"What were you told?" India asked. "Fox talked to you before you rendezvoused with the *Genesis*, but you hadn't been updated since..."

"No, once y'all knew where I was, I dropped my telepathic block, and while the *Genesis* was en route, I reached out to Zz'r'p for a more detailed explanation of things," Omega clarified. "And he told me..." She broke off, voice cracking, and gathered herself. "...That he was dying, because the...'base operating system,' Zz'r'p called it...I guess y'all are usin' a computer analogy?...was deteriorating, on account of not being connected to a functional mind," Omega said. "He didn't seem to be sure if it would be full death, or just brain death, but either way. I know Echo left instructions not to be kept on life support in the event of brain death."

"Ah, so you already know about that paperwork," Fox noted. "I wondered, but had no way of finding out."

"Yes sir, I know all about it; when we decided to make each other our spokespersons in the event of incapacitation last winter, he showed me a buncha stuff like that. And helped me set up my own."

"Good. Well, NOT good, but...you know what I mean."

"Uh-huh. So how IS he? Zz'r'p's been too busy to fill me in much in the last couple of hours."

"Same sitch as Zz'r'p done told ya," Romeo offered. "I

ain't noticed a whole lotta deterioration in the last couple hours. He's kinda shaky, and his coordination ain't great, but he's still communicatin' at a pretty high level."

"Though I've noticed he's starting to struggle with word choices," India added. "And slurring a fair amount. And there have been a couple-three brief instances of word salad."

"Exactly, tekhter," Fox averred, turning for the space warp door. "So be prepared for that. And we need to get you to the medlab right away, so he DOESN'T deteriorate further."

"Oh, thank the good Lord," Omega breathed. "I was afraid I'd be too late."

"No, no, I don't think so," India said, putting a hand on her shoulder and gently urging her forward. Behind them, Chi slipped out, taking the side passage to the main concourse of Grand Central Station. "But Fox is right, we don't need to dawdle."

* * *

Once they arrived in the medlab proper, India took Omega into another room several doors away and around the corner from Echo's hospital room, leaving the men outside. There, she had Omega strip down, outfitted her with the newest wireless EKG and EEG leads, then gave her a medical jumpsuit.

"Here," she said. "Climb into this, while I tell Zebra you're here and almost ready. Once you're dressed, head down the hall to Lab D, room 12."

"Lab D, room 12," Omega reiterated, accepting the jumpsuit. "Got it."

* * *

Five minutes later, having struggled her way into the innumerable straps and hook-and-loop patches and strips that mostly seemed to comprise a medical jumpsuit—Omega sometimes wondered if there was any actual CLOTH to the garments—she headed for Lab D and located room 12. It was relatively easy to find, because Fox, Alpha Two, and Dihl awaited her there, in the corridor.

Dihl offered a brief hug, then simply gestured the younger woman through the door.

Hesitant, a shy, reserved Omega—now clad in the medical jumpsuit India had issued to her, which tended to be rather form-fitting by its very nature—entered the room where Zz'r'p and Echo waited.

* * *

Echo sat, more or less upright, on a partially-reclined medical bed, also clad in a medical jumpsuit; Zarnix sat beside him on his left, prepared to monitor his condition and subtly helping to stabilize his posture—no one wanted to alarm Omega any more than could be helped. Zz'r'p stood at the head of his bed, on his right; to the Deltiri's right was an empty bed, and on the far side of that bed Zebra sat, ready to monitor Omega's vitals while the alien telepath performed the transfer procedure.

Omega glanced at Echo for the barest fraction of a second, seeming wistful, then quickly turned her gaze to Zz'r'p.

"I, uh...I'm here," she murmured, voice barely audible. "Let's...let's get this taken care of, I guess."

"W-wait," Echo said, holding up a hand briefly. "O-omega? Um, Meg?"

Omega blinked, apparently startled not only at the familiar mode of address, but that he addressed her at all, and her wide-eyed gaze shot back to Echo.

"Shh, it's okay," he said, offering comfort. "Well, it's not okay, but, um, it's all my own fault it's not okay. Come over here, and um..." he broke off, then turned slightly. "Uh, all you guys, um, the Z's, could y'all give us a couple minutes? I...I need to t-talk to her..."

Omega blinked again, then glanced at Zz'r'p in concern.

"It won't take but a second," Echo said, seeing the look and the worry in it, "only I can't come over there, 'cause...well, I don't walk so good now..." He bit his lip and looked away. "I don't do anything so good now."

Omega's eyes grew even wider at that admission.

'The three Z's,' as Echo had been calling them—partly because it was easier for him to say—exchanged glances, then nodded. Zebra and Zarnix rose, and together with Zz'r'p, exited the room, easing the door closed behind themselves to allow the pair some privacy. Echo turned his attention back to his partner, and an apprehensive Omega cocked her head to one side in an inquiring fashion. Recognizing and correctly interpreting the gesture, Echo nodded.

"I s-swear, Meg, it's awright. Will...will you come over here a minute?"

Still hesitant, she moved to the bedside. Echo reached out and took her hand, his own hand shaking badly as his neural control deteriorated. He laced his fingers through hers as best he was able, turning the joined hands so that he could look at her hand. He grunted in frustration as he struggled to hold their hands still; Omega raised her other hand and wrapped it around his trembling hand, stilling it. He gave her a grateful glance. Echo studied her hands for a long moment, then looked up and met her eyes.

"I'm s-sorry," he said with a sigh. "I was so wr-wrong about you. Really, really wrong. I...when I read the files on ever'body, I picked up on some things an' not on others, Zz'r'p thinks on 'count of my de-um...of what's happenin' to me. And 'cause of that, I came to all sorts of...wrong notions. And I ran you off, 'cause of THAT. Which is why I'm in this shape now." He held up their joined hands, showing her the full measure of the tremor; within moments, the tremor had moved from his hand to his whole body, and his limbs spasmed slightly, beyond his full ability to control them. "If I'd been more ac-accepting, I wouldn't 'a run you off, an' we coulda had this fixed days ago, when there was a b-better shot of it workin'. So anyway, maybe this'll help, an' maybe it won't. Might be too late; I dunno. But I want ya to do somethin' for me."

"What?" Omega breathed, troubled.

"If...if this doesn't work," Echo said, earnest, "I want ya to...to 'member me the way I was, not the way I am now. Or... or however I end up. Okay?"

* * *

Abruptly Omega flashed back to the two of them, crashed on the protoplanet the previous spring, when Omega had suffered a severe concussion and skull fracture, causing her uniquely-wired brain to start shutting down. *"Look, it's like this, Ace,"* she had told him. *"I'll stay here and help you 'til I know Fox is close. Then I'll go away. I don't want Fox, and Romeo and India, to see me like this...Promise me you'll think about me once in a while?"*

Except he wouldn't let me leave, wouldn't let me die, she

298

remembered. *I can't let him, either. Not if there's ANYTHING I can do to stop it.*

* * *

"I...I..." Omega tried, then suddenly she flung her arms around him. "Oh, Echo!"

Echo's eyes widened, surprised; he had not expected her to react to him with such affection, after everything that had happened. Then he eased wobbly arms around her, holding her close as best he could.

"Hush," he murmured. "Hush, baby. Hush. It's okay. Whatever happens, it's okay. You an' me, we're...good."

"It's gotta work," she breathed in his ear. "It's just GOTTA. If I have to give you a piece of my own life energy to jumpstart things, it's gotta work!"

Echo pulled back only enough to look into her face, in utter shock.

"You...you'd do that?" he whispered, astounded. "After I...after I said what I did about you...?"

"In a heartbeat," she averred, meeting his eyes, her own gaze clear and sincere.

Echo bit his lip, studying her face for long moments before nodding.

"Okay," he murmured. "I...I guess this is the point at which th' ol' me woulda kissed ya, huh?"

"Uhm," was all she said, but it was Omega's turn to bite her lip. She dropped her gaze, flushing slightly.

"Okay, I c'n still read 'at message. Well, let's try this, then," he said, and he nudged her chin up with a fist before covering her lips with his own.

The kiss was gentle and chaste, but it still stirred something in the core of Echo's being. When he finally broke it, he found he was breathless.

"Wow," he muttered, staring into her face, wide-eyed. "And that wasn't even th' hot stuff."

"You want hot stuff?" Omega wondered, and he realized the offered kiss had revealed—to both of them—that, somewhere deep inside him, his love for her still lived, and that knowledge had given her back some of her confidence in their relationship—in his faith in her. "Here."

And suddenly he was being kissed just like the video he had seen from the secure confinement facility on Aleancë. Everything else seemed to vanish in the white heat of that kiss.

* * *

When Echo finally became aware once again of the world outside that kiss, he was lying back in the bed, and the room seemed a whole lot brighter. Omega had wrapped her arms around him, easing him down to the mattress, and now she slipped her arms from beneath his torso as she straightened into an upright position.

"Dayumn," he breathed, barely able to get the sound out of his mouth. "I hope I'm as good in bed as you seem t' be."

"Huh?"

"I jus' hope I been givin' back 's good as I got," he added, by way of explanation. "That 'bout curled my toes, honey, an' hot as it was, it 'uz still 'only' a kiss. I'm kinda hopin' my love-makin's been the ins-inspir-" he finally forced out the word, "inspiration f'r that kiss."

"Oh," Omega said, voice slightly flat, as her face flushed. "We, um, we aren't lovers yet. We're engaged, yeah, but...I, uh, I'm kinda old-fashioned; I wanted to wait until we got properly married. And you've been an old-fashioned gentleman, and gone along with it. I mean, we, uh, there was...we had to get to a certain level to complete the nd't'lq transfer, yeah, but...I mean, we...you know. There's an Agency charter amendment due out of the Ennead any day now...at least, we hope...that'll let us do it all legal and everything..." She bit her lip again and looked away. "That is, assuming...well, that you still want...if all this goes well today, and you, I mean..."

"Shush," he said, cupping his hand around her cheek and turning her back to face him. "My bad; I think Fox told me somethin' 'bout that a couple days ago, now you me-men-, um, say it. Then hopefully, if this shit that the three Z's 've cooked up really works, I've got somethin' really dynamite t' look forward to, I guess." He offered her a mischievous grin, then added, resolute, "As well as a damn good reason to keep on keepin' on."

Omega opened her mouth to answer, but there was a knock at the door. It cracked open, and a blue, fish-like face peered in.

"Omega, Echo, we need to get started," Zz'r'p said softly, "and see if we cannot get this whole thing taken care of, while we still can."

Omega nodded, then gently eased out of Echo's embrace. He released her, and watched as she moved to the nearby empty bed, climbing into it and lying down, as the telepath and the physicians came back into the room. Zebra promptly began ensuring the remote hookups to Omega's EKG and EEG leads were functional, as Omega scootched about in the bed, getting comfortable...or as comfortable as she could manage, under the circumstances.

Abruptly the Deltiri addressed the partly-open door.

"Yes," he noted, apropos of nothing that had been said, "you can, if you are all QUIET."

Just then, several dark-haired heads peeped around the doorframe, querying expressions on all.

"Yes, I know you are all there," Zz'r'p said without looking around. "And yes, I was talking to you. You can watch, but you must remain very, VERY quiet. None of the three of us can afford any distractions in this—neither Omega nor myself, especially. Even Echo becoming abstracted could be dangerous...to all three of us. We talked about this earlier, remember. Fetch chairs from the conference room, and position yourselves around the periphery near the door, now, before we get started."

All the heads disappeared; hurried, quiet footsteps pattered about, then four more beings entered the room: Fox, Dihl, India, and Romeo. All carried conference room chairs, which they positioned in an arc just in front of the door, careful not to block it, or the path into the room from it. All four sat quickly, settled in, and grew quiet. Outside the door, the on-duty medical staff—to include Whiskey, Rglfrz, and several medtechs—passed back and forth in the corridor, glancing through the door but saying nothing, and being as quiet as possible.

"Zebra?" Zz'r'p queried.

"All set," Zebra responded.

"Zarnix?"

"All is in readiness, my friend."

Zz'r'p bent over Omega, questioning, and she nodded.

"Do it," she said, determined.

"All right," he replied, and laid his right hand lightly on the top of her head, long blue fingers splayed across her skull. She shuddered once, then grew very still.

"C'n I ask a quick question b'fore ya put me under?" Echo wondered then.

"Of course," Zz'r'p said.

"What'd you just do to Ome-um, Meg?"

"I have placed her into what you might think of as a semi-comatose state," Zz'r'p explained. "This way, she is relaxed and resting—my various private inquiries of beings around her indicate she has slept but little since bringing you back from the space plane repair; aha, she admits it—and this way, she will therefore not tense up in worry and anxiety, and inadvertently fight the transfer."

"But...can she hear us?"

"She says yes."

"Can she move or anythin'?"

"No, she cannot."

"But...but," Echo said, growing upset, "won't that remind 'er of the whole...whadda she calls it...'tinkering' by that Slug dude? She couldn't move then either, right?"

"No, she could not, and she says that yes, it does," Zz'r'p noted, "but if it means you are returned to normal, she will endure it. And, she adds, she trusts me; I am a friend, a known quantity—Slug was not, nor did he take her personal feelings into account, in any fashion. Whereas I," the Deltiri admitted, "am doing my best to ensure her comfort, as much as in me lies the ability."

Echo caught his lower lip between his teeth, his face contorting in pain that was not physical. "What if..."

"If?"

"She's completely vul-vu-" Unable to form the word or even fully pull it to the front of his thoughts, Echo broke off with a huff of annoyance, then tried, "she's helpless like that, isn't she?"

"She is, but I have told her that her 'family' is all here," Zz'r'p said. "Or at least, those on Earth. She is depending on the rest of us to protect her...and you. 'It'll be okay,' she says."

"Aw," came the soft sigh from several voices, not just Echo's; three sets of shoulders squared, and every back in the room straightened with determination.

"All right, Echo, Omega, here is what is going to happen in general," Zz'r'p elaborated. "I am going to put both of you 'under,' in a specific semi-conscious mental state; Zarnix and Zebra are monitoring your vitals, to include EKG and EEG on both of you, and will let me know immediately if there is a problem. Then I am going to locate Echo's nd't'lq in Omega's mind. Once I have located it and ascertained it is in good condition—and no, I have no reason to doubt it, I am simply being cautious—I will communicate with it—after all, it is Echo's mind, or a clone of it—and explain what has happened. Then I will offer to be the conduit by which the nd't'lq can communicate with Echo's brain, allowing it access once more. It will almost certainly agree; it is the Deltiri experience of some long standing—think centuries, if not millennia—that the nd't'lq does not like to be sundered from the original mind. I fully expect the download to occur as soon as I open that conduit. Are you both accepting of this?"

"Yep," Echo agreed. "Can't wait."

"Good. Omega says an emphatic yes, also. Now, once the transfer occurs, Echo will then need time for re-integration to occur. This is to enable the memories he has of the time since the accident to be incorporated with his previous memories and being, as well as to resolve any conflicts that have occurred in personality development, and so on. So I plan to leave him in this same semi-conscious state for several days, as many as four or five Division days. This is why I have asked the Medical staff to be ready with intravenous and other such hookups, to provide Echo with nutrients, fluids, and the like, while this is taking place. Omega, you have worn yourself out, my young friend, so you get time off, as well, but not as long; I think a couple of Division days at most will suffice to return you to a properly rested state. And then you need to eat, and eat WELL. Though I shall want to see you for a counseling session soon after you awaken, also. Yes, I suppose we may do it while you are resting...toward the end of your rest, perhaps." He paused, seeming to listen. "Oh really, my dear? Well, you will still have several days to enact those plans, and I can always notify India and Dihl to begin some of your plans, if you will provide the details later." Dihl and India perked up, exchanging querying glances with each other before both shrugged in confusion. "And yes, Fox and I will discuss matters with the Chief, and try to work the timing for you. All right. Yes, that will work. Are you ready to go?" He paused, then added, "She says yes. Echo? What about you?"

"I BEEN ready, Zz'r'p," Echo declared. "This got old a long time ago."

"Say the word, my friend."

"All right. Well, let's get this done, then, one way or 'nother," Echo decided, and slid down in the bed, as Zarnix lowered it to fully horizontal. "Do it," he declared, not realizing he had just echoed his partner from moments before.

"All right," Zz'r'p repeated, and laid his left hand on Echo's head, fingers splayed. "Sleep, friend Echo."

Echo's entire body slumped, and he lay as still as death.

* * *

Please, Adonai, let this work, Fox prayed in silence, as he watched Zz'r'p enter the minds of Omega and Echo. *Don't let me lose my oldest living human friend, the closest thing I have to a true son. The son of my spirit. Not like this. If You need to take him, take him quick and kosher, in the course of duty, not a slow deterioration to nothing, like this.*

The Director stifled a worried sigh, and glanced at his mate. Zebra saw him watching, double-checked Omega's vitals, then gave Fox a thumbs-up. A quick, silent signal to Zarnix by Zebra resulted in the same behavior from the chief of staff. Fox drew a deep, soft breath, and relaxed...a little bit.

* * *

Damn, it's quiet in here, Romeo thought as he watched. *Nuthin' much is happenin' that I can see. Meg an' Echo 're just layin' there, an' Zz'r'p looks kinda like a blue fishy version of 'at Jesus statue over Rio, standin' there with one hand on Meg's head an' th' other on Echo's. I guess I shoulda known a telepathic mind transfer thingie wadn' gonna be much ta watch, though.*

304

He glanced at India, who was studying a data relay on her personal medical scanner. She looked up, saw the question in his eyes, and shrugged.

Oh man. I dunno if that means good shit, or bad, he worried. *An' we might not actually know, based on something Zz'r'p said earlier, until Echo wakes up. If he DOES wake up. It's gonna be one more long damn week. An' at the end of it, I might be th' Alpha Line assistant chief. Hell, if it don't go right an' Meg don't deal well with how it goes down, I might be the chief.* He paused, considering. *An' I don't think I WANNA be the chief. Not yet, nohow. Not like this. I got way too much t' learn. Unfortunately, those two are th' ones I wanted t' learn it from.*

* * *

India sat and studied the relayed vitals data coming in for both Echo and Omega, a relay she had set up with Zarnix earlier, at Zz'r'p's suggestion. *But I can't really tell anything about it,* she sighed to herself. *I see slight fluctuations in the vitals, but I don't know what they mean relative to this, or if they really mean ANYthing.*

She looked up and saw Romeo watching her, so she just shrugged, to let him know she didn't know what to make of it.

I got no clue on this, she thought, annoyed with herself. *And as a doctor, that's so frustrating. But humans just don't have much experience with telepathic...shit, as Romeo would put it...and Meg and Echo'd say that, too, for that matter. I only hope Zebra and Zarnix are making more sense out of it than I am.*

* * *

Oh, my son, my dear, beloved Alex, Dihl thought, on edge more than any of the others. *And Omega, the woman who was about to become my daughter in marriage. I cannot bear to lose them, not after losing James, after losing Shitaá, after so many years of thinking I had lost Alex. Then I got him back, and Omega—Megan, they told me her name was Megan when we had our first meal together as a family after their engagement, and the name is as lovely as she is—into the bargain. And now I could lose them both. No. Please, no. Dear Creator God, please let this work. PLEASE.*

305

She studied the medscanner Zebra had given her, which was tied into the vitals relays like India's.

I am uncertain what to make of all this, but...Omega's heart rate just jumped up a little. Perhaps that is an indication that she and Zz'r'p are in communication with Alex's mind-clone? I hope it is healthy. I hope it downloads properly, and stops this slow crash and burn Alex has been experiencing. And that Megan does not then pay for it, in some fashion.

She looked up from the medscanner and watched the silent, still tableau. *Not much to see there, either,* she decided. *I should not have thought it would take this long.* She glanced at her wrist chronometer, then did a double-take. *Oh damnation, as James would say—it has not yet been five minutes since they began! It has barely been three! Surely we are in a time warp! This will take an eternity!*

* * *

It's over here, I think, Zz'r'p, Omega told the Deltiri, as he searched for Echo's nd't'lq. *At least, that's where I had him put it, when we did it.*

I'm here, Meg! Echo's mental voice declared...from IN-SIDE Omega's mind. *It's been hard for me to talk to you like this, but I've been trying to help out, as best I can. And I dunno what happened to the rest of me; it stopped communicating a while back.*

Hey, honey! Omega immediately told the nd't'lq. *Oh, it's SO good to hear you again, Ace!*

Echo, do you recognize me? Zz'r'p asked the nd't'lq. *Omega's friend and telepathic counselor?*

Hey, Zz'r'p! Oh shit. If you're here, something bad is goin' down. What's happened?

What is the last thing you remember happening to you, to your body? the Deltiri asked.

Uhh, that'd be...lessee...the...oh damn.

I think he remembers, Omega decided, wry.

You mean the space plane, and the unholy mess of guts it had, and you nearly bitin' it, and...I bit it, didn't I? Am I gonna dissipate? Is Zz'r'p here to try to stop me dissipating?

Sort of, the telepath noted. *But you are not dead. You were what the medlab terms 'mostly dead,' and your body was re-*

vived, but your brain had already... Zz'r'p broke off. *Your brain was dying, and it had already dumped the memory, much like a computer that is without essential power to its core...*

Oh, I get it. So...am I still alive 'out there'? You said I wasn't dead...

You are. But you are dying again, as the incomplete mind in your body slowly 'crashes.' We need to get you back into your body, so you can re-establish the link and prevent that crash.

I've just been waiting and wondering what the hell happened, Echo's nd't'lq declared. *Let's do this thing. I wanna connect back up with the rest of me, not dissipate.*

All right. Since Omega does not have the telepathic chip implant that she used to place you, I am going to serve as the conduit. Is this acceptable to you, Echo?

Do it, came the by-now-familiar response from the nd't'lq.

Very well. Be ready...and...NOW.

And suddenly a brilliant flash of cognition seemed to light up in three minds simultaneously...

...Before everything went dark.

* * *

Both of the bodies in the beds arched, briefly 'bridging' head-to-heel, then seemed to collapse and lie still. Zz'r'p staggered back, into the wall, then slid down it into a slumped, seated position, head nodded forward, arms limp.

"Farkakte, verdammt, merde, glagaram, and argdun!" Fox exclaimed, as he leaped to his feet, and the others joined him.

"Dayum!" Romeo cried. "That looks BAD!"

A greatly alarmed Dihl clapped both hands to her mouth in an effort to stifle a despairing scream of grief. Confused, India glanced back and forth between the scenario before them, and her medscanner readouts.

"Hush, hush," Zarnix shushed them, studying Echo's vitals display intently. "I saw a vitals spike, but I've got solid, steady numbers here. Zebra?"

"Likewise," Zebra answered. "India, can you see to Zz'r'p? Make sure he's okay. Whatever just happened, it nailed him, but good."

India was already moving toward the downed ambassador before Zebra spoke; she reset her medscanner for Deltiri and ran it over the slumped form.

"He looks to be all right," she reported then. "Oh, the vitals are a little elevated relative to Deltiri norms, but..."

"Mmh," the telepath groaned, stirring. "Og'dm'n. That was far more than I expected."

"Are you okay?" India asked, concerned. "Stay put here, for a minute. You need to recover."

"Yes. Aside from a headache, and the sensation that my head has been carried off as what Fox would call a 'hood ornament,' I think I am all right," Zz'r'p said with a sigh, not protesting the medic's order to remain where he was. "That was rather different than what I had anticipated."

"It looked like lightning struck," Fox observed. "All three of you."

"It felt not unlike it, as well," Zz'r'p said with a rueful chuckle. "Zarnix? Zebra? How are they?"

"Solid vitals here," Zebra noted.

"Times two," Zarnix agreed. "Our patients have all survived the process...assuming the process is finished."

"The process is finished," Zz'r'p said, finally standing with India's help. "I must admit that it has been years since I have had to perform this procedure, and that was only once, between two Deltiri, one of whom had been injured. It seems the process between humans is rather more...energetic. Especially when both personalities are strong and forceful."

"Are they both all right?" The question fairly burst from Dihl.

Rather than answer immediately, Zz'r'p laid one hand on each head, brown and blonde. He closed his eyes briefly, then opened them and looked up.

"Echo says, 'Hi, Ma,' and Omega is crying and laughing inside," he reported.

Romeo and Fox scrambled to get a chair under Dihl as her knees buckled in relief.

Chapter 13

The medlab staff set up Echo and Omega for an 'extended stay,' as Zebra termed it; Omega would be there only a couple of Division days, but Echo would be there for the better part of a week.

"And we want them to be well cared for," Zz'r'p pointed out. "Never mind Echo's recent difficulties, Omega has hardly slept, and only ate when she realized it was essential to continued function, or when others—such as Lord Entiyti or Dr. Eretigen—insisted. I gather that this situation upset her so much that it not only took her appetite, but often threatened to cause regurgitation when she DID manage to choke something down."

"An' that sounds exactly like Meg," Romeo observed.

"Yeah, it sure does," India agreed. "It takes something really major to upset her, but once you get her to that point, barfing is a definite possibility."

"An' this 'uz, like, WAY major," Romeo added.

"No shit," Fox averred. "So we're talking IVs, with proper nutrients put in? Never mind other, um, tubes and whatnot?"

"Precisely," Zz'r'p confirmed.

"Which looks like exactly what the team is doing," Dihl noted, watching the medics and medtechs come and go around the prone pair.

"And we should get out of the way," India added. "They'll need privacy for some of those 'tubes and whatnot.'"

The 'family' slipped out.

* * *

A little more than an hour later, Zz'r'p, Dihl, and Alpha Two waited patiently in the Director's Conference Room. Within moments, Fox came in at speed.

"What's up?" he demanded. "What's wrong?"

"Nothing, nothing," Zz'r'p said, holding up his hands in a soothing fashion. "I am sorry, Fox; I did not consider that you might assume the worst, given recent events. No, this is rather

309

a nice little matter."

"Oh," Fox said, calming, as he took the seat Zz'r'p indicated. "That's good to hear. So what's this all about?"

"Well, Omega is, as you know, resting after her...ordeal... and getting proper nutrition and fluids administered," Zz'r'p explained. "But there were several things she had planned to do while Echo was unconscious and integrating..."

"Yes, I know about the case Chief Wux is working on," Fox said with a nod. "I'm trying to work out the timing on that for her, so she can be in on the take-down."

"Oh, has the Chief determined the resort was a money laundering front, then?" Zz'r'p asked.

"Indeed he has, and in short order, too," Fox noted. "And he's already contacted me about Omega's excellent detective work...as well as the assistance of other members of the perp's family."

"This sounds int'restin'," Romeo decided.

"It is, and we might wind up getting a few more members of Alpha Line involved, Romeo, so after Zz'r'p is done, let's talk," Fox agreed. "But somehow I don't think this is what he meant. Nor would Dihl be here, for that."

"You are right, Fox, and there is a specific reason why you four, and no others, are here," Zz'r'p informed them. "You see, there were TWO projects Omega wanted to see done. The case you mention is only one. The other, she needs the four of you to help with, where you can..."

* * *

When Omega woke up a little more than a Division day later, she had been moved to a different room; Echo was not there, but Fox and Zebra sat close by, waiting for her to wake, as Zz'r'p removed his delicate touch from her temple.

"There," the Deltiri noted. "How do you feel, my young friend?"

"Like I just woke up from a month-long sleep," she decided, slurring her words a bit, "after twelve ultra-marathons in a row." She stretched, sat up slowly, and smacked her mouth for several moments, still mildly groggy.

Fox and Zebra exchanged puzzled glances.

"Is that good or bad?" Fox wanted to know. Omega snorted.

"That depends, I guess," she said, fighting back a yawn as she tried to pull fully out of the deep sleep in which she had been. "How's Echo?"

"Coming along, coming along," Zz'r'p averred. "I am rather pleased, all things considered. There is some confusion, but that is to be expected, in the circumstances."

"Still 'asleep' though, right?"

"Yes, he is still in a deep unconscious state, though slowly moving up through various stages toward consciousness. His mind must reintegrate, and that cannot be rushed. And that is, I think, the source of the confusion."

"Okay, that's the way it is, then." Omega sighed.

"Tekhter, seriously, how do you feel?" Fox pressed. "We've been worried for you..."

"Decent, all things considered," Omega offered. "Nicely well rested, but a bit stiff, and a little on the hungry side. I know I had an IV in, so I'm probably not in need of it, but..." Her stomach let out a loud, prolonged growl...that ended on a wailing note. "Umm...then again..."

The other three laughed.

"Well, let's get you fed, cleaned up, and dressed," Zebra decided, "in that order, because then Fox needs you to go with him."

* * *

It turned out that PGLEIA Chief Wuxullian had only been waiting for Omega and the force Fox assigned to her to arrive at the designated rendezvous site. This force, under Omega's command, included Alpha Two; the Alpha Three Enigma Team, Gustav and Kilo; Alpha Eight—this was Kako's first mission since being released from the medlab, after he had been shot in the gut during Adita's Coup, and Monkey was a bit protective of his enthusiastic partner, so it all evened out—as well as standard field agents Orange, Berta, Como, Quintal, and Chi to serve as Omega's temporary partner; a dozen Division One agents in all.

"Excellent," Wuxullian declared, when they had arrived in one of the larger destroyer-class saucers, the *D1 Aeneid* by name. "A goodly squad, and the code-breaking and SIGINT team, as well; Fox promised he would send them, and I am

311

glad to see he remembered."

"We're glad to help out, sir," Gustav said, and Kilo nodded.

"Could you brief us, sir?" Omega requested.

"Most certainly," Wuxullian agreed. "Come with me, and I will brief you, along with my people, about the planet and our investigations which occurred subsequent to your own...which were excellent, let me add. You are responsible for breaking this case wide open."

"Thank you, sir, but it wasn't done in a vacuum," Omega murmured.

"Nevertheless, it was well done," Wuxullian averred. "Now, the lot of you, come with me."

* * *

Fox sat in his office, working out some very special plans, when a soft tone sounded. He glanced up, then hit a blinking orange 'button' on his virtual desktop; one of the dark wall screens came up with *Deltiri embassy—Ambassador Zz'r'p* on it. He hit the orange button again, and the screen lit with the alien ambassador's face.

"Hello, Zz'r'p. How are you feeling after the 'lightning strike' a couple of days ago?"

"Reasonably well, all things considered," the Arcturan replied. "Has Omega left with her team?"

"She has. I got word about half an hour back that their craft had dropped into warp."

"Good. Opaque your windows for a few moments, and let us talk."

"Ohhh, farkakte. THAT doesn't sound good," Fox decided, obeying the ambassador's recommendation.

* * *

"Well...SHIT," Fox said some twenty minutes later, with feeling. "And you really don't know how it's going to end up?"

"No, I am afraid not," Zz'r'p noted with a sigh. "I had thought matters would be fine once the nd't'lq transfer had completed. But...perhaps not."

"If...things don't go well...how will he feel about Omega?"

"I think he still cares for her, but..." Zz'r'p paused to consider. "It may throw them back to square one in their relationship. And she may have to take the lead in bringing it back to where it was."

"Meaning that, at least for now, the engagement is on hold at best, and off at worst."

"Exactly."

"That...may not go over well, given what else she has planned."

"I know. That is why I thought I should tell you at once."

"Damnation," Fox cursed bitterly.

* * *

It didn't take long to fill in the Division One agents on the situation; the planet was barely a planet at all. Doukeed, in the Mu Phoenicis system, was just above the official boundary designation between 'planet' and 'dwarf planet.' It was roughly the size of Pluto, being about 750 miles in radius, or some 1,500 miles in diameter. And this was how Erushin's holding company could afford to acquire the entire planet—it was tiny, had no intelligent life, originally had not had that much in the way of a surface inhabitable by anything except extremophiles, and even those had chosen to pass up the planetoid. It was basically a big, bare rock, saving that it did possess a rudimentary atmosphere, and it was in orbit about Mu Phoenicis.

But Tralosia, Limited had changed all that when it acquired the hunk of silica. The holding company had utilized a small fleet of huge spacecraft with powerful tractor beams to tow Doukeed into the Goldilocks zone, then ascertained that the dwarf planet's structure was sound and its crystalline lattices and rock strata strong. They then drilled down to the core at some considerable effort and expense, and added one of the largest artificial-gravity Higgs field generators that had ever been built, carefully tuned to provide standard gravity at the surface, without destabilizing the structure of the planet. After that, terraforming was relatively easy; artificial soil was mass-produced from local asteroidal material, enriched with imported compost and nutrients; atmosphere added via cometary ices, and the surface seeded with suitable generic flora from several different systems.

Once Tralosia had determined that it all 'took,' and that they now had a small, lush, habitable world, a site was selected, and expansive construction began, first on a spaceport

313

to ensure supplies shipping had a point of arrival, then on a sprawling, luxurious resort, complete with all the amenities—shops, a spa, no less than six individual five-star restaurants, high-end rooms and suites, the latest in security systems, indoor and outdoor pools, even a small 'sea' with beach adjacent, and salinity high enough to ensure safety from drowning accidents. Nighttime views of the Great Spiral were magnificent. The facility was dubbed the Eddelis Resort & Spa—'eddelis' being Veldorn for 'comfort.' It was the favored—and very exclusive—getaway spot for eight different galactic-media stars, half a dozen interstellar business moguls, the top three news reporting anchors, and innumerable Coalition representatives.

And approximately one galactic standard annum ago, Xoreplirg Erushin, the only legitimate stockholder in Tralosia, Limited out of a 'board of directors' of nonexistent beings, had come to live there permanently, in the largest suite in the resort—the isolated, and heavily secure penthouse suite, expressly designed for him.

* * *

"Hello, zun. Have we heard how matters are going with Chief Wux and Omega's team?" Fox asked several hours later, as Bravo entered his office to obtain his signature on some papers.

"No sir, not yet," Bravo noted, handing over the paperwork. Fox glanced over the pages, initialed a couple of places, then signed off on it and handed it back. "But it IS looking like we're going to need a change of venue for the other thing."

"How so, zun?"

"Do you have any idea how many people are showing up, Fox? As you'd say, 'Oy vey, that's meshuginah!' Look." Bravo pulled his personal tablet, brought up a display, and showed it to Fox. Fox took one glance and his jaw dropped.

"Oy!"

"Exactly," Bravo said with a wry chuckle. "Lima and I discussed it, and we strongly recommend the all-hands auditorium. It's not quite as...well, it doesn't have the same 'style,' I guess you could call it, but we think we can make it work. Move the decorations, add some steps or ramps up to the platform..."

"How many decorations for this little *farloy'fenish* are there?" Fox wondered, skeptical.

"Not many. You know them. They're not into all that, and wouldn't want a whole bunch."

"That looks like a plan, then. Get with the right people and make it happen." Fox resumed work on his virtual desktop computer.

"Um, one more thing..." Bravo was hesitant.

"What?" Fox looked back up.

"Well, we have some visitors coming in for this. IMPOR-TANT visitors." Bravo handed over his tablet. "Take a look at rows 12 through 16."

Fox stared, then smacked his hand to his forehead, smeared it down his face to his chin, then reversed the motion and slid it up into his hair, disarranging it.

"Farkakte, verdammt, merde, glagaram, and argdun!" he exclaimed. "Of COURSE they are. All right. Alpha Line is already up to their necks. Get with Uncle and Crutch and bring in plenty of security. Triple what we'd already planned on."

"Where do you want to put them?" Bravo asked, taking the tablet back and making several notations.

"Let me see that again, *zun*. Do you have the layout?"

"Yes sir. Hang on a sec." Bravo tapped several places on the screen and brought up a floor plan. "Here."

Fox studied it for a long moment.

"Ah. I see. Yes, put the top-level bunch here," he tapped the screen, highlighting the location, "and put the rest of 'em in the general section, directly behind."

"Right." Bravo accepted the tablet, then paused. "Fox? Change of subject?"

"Yes, *zun*?"

"Is...is Echo going to be all right? I mean, he's still in the telepathic induced coma-thing, with no time—or even date—being given for when he'll be awakened..."

Fox paused, considering the latest information that Zz'r'p had given him...AFTER Omega had left for her rendezvous with Wuxullian.

"I don't know, *zun*," he admitted. "Oh, he'll live. He's got a proper mind back in his brain again—full-up operating system and memory, if you will. So no brain death, and no full death. But the...the full mind, and the 'partial mind,' I guess we'll call it, have to integrate. And evidently that may not be going so well."

"What do you mean?"

"Evidently the 'partial mind' is being a bit...stubborn," Fox tried to explain. "I can't say I understand it all myself. But..." He sighed. "Close the door and sit down for a moment. I'll try to explain."

* * *

"So...Echo's fighting Echo?" Bravo wondered, puzzled.

"Sort of," Fox noted. "Technically, it IS a kind of dissociative identity disorder, but not in anything like the standard definition, given how he got that way, and it should be readily resolvable; Zz'r'p expected it to resolve more or less immediately, with a bit of a settling-in period, as I understand it... only it didn't quite work that way, due in part to the strength of personality and will that is the man we know as Echo. Anyway, it's making for a bit of confusion in his head, according to Zz'r'p. He's trying to help Echo sort things out, directing the various thought processes and memory integration. You'd think that would be relatively easy; I mean the nd't'lq was just stored in Omega's head. But it seems that it is also aware of Omega to some extent, and what she is thinking and doing. Which makes sense, when you realize that it's originally intended as a link between telepaths."

"Yeah..." Bravo shrugged. "Except Echo isn't a telepath, and Meg only sorta is."

"Exactly. So it seems that not only was Echo's nd't'lq aware of Omega's emotional upset, it was aware of her self-assigned 'mission,' and was trying to help her with it, as best it could," Fox continued. "So it DOES have memories of the time when it was separated from its body; it isn't like it was asleep or something. Never mind its ongoing memories of the things he's done in his life...many of which seemed impossible to the 'partial Echo' who woke up after the little on-orbit catastrophe."

"Urgh," Bravo murmured, pulling a face. "That doesn't sound good at all."

"No, it's potentially not," Fox agreed. "If the nd't'lq download doesn't end up in control, trying to figure out what to do with the leadership of Alpha Line, let alone my successor, will get complicated in a hurry. Never mind the relationship with Omega."

"Oh boy. And with what she's got planned..."

"Exactly. So...let me think..." Fox pondered for a few moments. "Notify our distinguished guests of the situation, but subtly. And um...ah. Put out a notification that Echo has been injured in Alpha One's most recent mission, and while there are plans, those plans may have to be put off indefinitely as we await his proper healing."

"Oh. Okay, yeah, I guess that'll work," Bravo sighed. "Poor Meg. I swear, it seems like she busts her ass to ensure everything goes great, and it heads south anyhow."

"You've noticed that, have you?" Fox said, wry. "Part of it is simply having enemies like Slug, who go out of their way to ensure things head south for 'em. But it does seem that our girl has some patches of bad luck, from time to time."

"Echo, too."

"Well, yes. Though he didn't, so much, before her advent. Still, I don't believe in such things, and certainly there's no evidence for it in her personal history before we ran across her. So it's likely just a run of probabilities coming up against her, coupled with some 'nastybad' enemies, as she likes to say, trying to ENSURE those probabilities. It has to turn, soon."

"As YOU like to say, 'From your lips to Adonai's ears,'" Bravo decided.

"Amein," Fox averred. "Anything else, zun?"

"No sir. I'll go fill in Lima, best I can, then get on alla this."

"Good man."

"Later, Fox."

"Later, zun."

* * *

Gentlebeings, this simply will not do, Zz'r'p told the two versions of Echo in the Agent's brain, as he stood next to Echo's hospital bed in the medlab. *You cannot share control, not like this. You must MERGE, become one.*

No way in hell, the fragment that had awakened in Echo's

317

body almost snarled. *I don't know any of you, and this...thing... you put in my head is either crazy, trying to drive me crazy by gaslighting the hell outta me, or trying hard to make me believe what y'all want me to believe. An' now I don't think I believe a thing Fox showed me, either! It had to be a kluged-up buncha videos! There's no bloody damn way I ever did all that shit! It's impossible!*

It's impossible according to what YOU know, the nd't'lq declared. *But not according to what I know. Because I lived it. I had the galactic tech, training, and science to make it work.*

I'm the one that woke up in this body!

No, you're the one that nearly DIED in this body. I'm the functioning, real-time backup to the mind that almost fully dumped when you—when WE—died.

Then why didn't you DO that? Provide backup? Why the hell did you leave me in the state I was in? Why did you let me nearly die again?

Because he could not download, Zz'r'p interrupted the argument. *When the body, the brain, began to die, the connection was apparently severed. There were difficulties in communication after the telepathy chip was removed from Omega's brain, to begin with. The organic body being 'mostly dead' when it was retrieved evidently cut what communication remained.*

Am I still dying?

No. You now have a fully-functioning mind working with the... 'operating system.' The deterioration has not only stopped, it has reversed. But YOU are not the fully-functioning mind. The nd't'lq is.

But why can't HE take the back seat and let ME drive, as it were?

Because he is the full mind. You are not.

What the hell does that mean?

It means that you do not have the resources to adequately 'drive,' as you put it. He does.

Well, let me ask you—

No. Let me ask you a question instead, Zz'r'p addressed the fragment.

Huh. Okay, that's different. Shoot.

Who are you?

Huh-wha? What do you mean?

Just what I said. Who are you? Zz'r'p shot a quick, private message at the nd't'lq. *Do not answer for him, or say anything, until I speak to you directly. I want him to grasp this.*

No, don't worry, I won't, the nd't'lq responded. *I see what you're doing.*

During this swift, fractions-of-a-second exchange, the fragment had pondered the question.

I'm Echo, he finally determined. *I'm an agent in this Division One Agency y'all keep talking about.*

What else?

The fragment 'shrugged.'

What else is there? it wondered. *I looked at the video, read the files you gave me. That's the answer you want, isn't it?*

And you? Zz'r'p now openly addressed the nd't'lq.

I'm Agent Echo, head of the Alpha Line department, Assistant Director of Division One, the intended successor of the current Director, he declared, starting where the fragmentary personality had...but not ending there. *I'm the senior member of the Alpha One team, fiancé of the junior member, Agent Omega, who is my partner and the assistant department chief. I'm one of the Originals, what Meg calls 'Agent Badass,' with a galactic reputation of some note, and I do this job in order to protect the innocent and get the guilty off the streets—whether those streets are on Earth, or anywhere else in the galaxy. I was once known as Alexander Ian Bryant, son of James Robert and Nalin Iyaaye Bryant. I'm half Apache and half Celtic Texican-American. I'm proud to be their son, proud to be Meg's intended husband, proud to be the father of her children one day, proud to be the man she loves, and proud to be the best damn Division One Agent I know how to be. THAT...ALL of that...is who I am.*

And so do you see the difference? Zz'r'p asked the fragment.

So he's got an ego the size of the galaxy, the fragment decided, sullen.

I wouldn't talk, the nd't'lq shot back. *Look who wants to run the show with about an eighth of a deck, if that.*

Stop it, Zz'r'p ordered, even sterner than either version of

Echo had yet seen him, almost fiercely angry. *You are part and parcel of one another. This constant sniping and outright arguing has to end. You must work TOGETHER if you want to return to consciousness and have a life. Else you will remain in the medlab, as a MENTAL PATIENT, for the rest of your life. You will NEVER marry Omega, NEVER become Director, never go on another mission, never leave the medlab again. And you will never wake up from this current state of consciousness... because you will never be ABLE to. Is THAT what you want?*

Oh shit, the horrified fragment said...

...Even as the equally-disturbed nd't'lq exclaimed, *Damn!*

* * *

"The first thing we need to do is to hack their security system," Wuxullian noted. "I thought that perhaps your Alpha Three team and my hacker team might handle that, Omega. Otherwise, we cannot possibly get in far enough to reach Erushin."

"That should work," Omega agreed. "I can probably throw in a bit of assistance there, too; Echo and I have had to hack a few things in the course of missions before, and I've caught onto a couple of little tricks that seem to work. Especially against—you did say that the security system was a Knorrised Security Systems setup, right?"

"Exactly. You have experience with their systems?"

"I sure do."

"Then by all means, do so! You and Alpha Three sit down with my people and see how deep you can get in," Wuxullian averred. "I already have all of the legalities lined up, so we have no worries there."

"Sounds like a plan," Omega agreed.

* * *

The half-dozen beings tasked with hacking the security of the Eddelis Resort & Spa took some time to manage it properly, but did magnificently. Within just four hours and with all the tools that the PGLEIA could put at their command, they took full control of the security system without the resort's security team being any wiser for it.

"EXCELLENT!" Wuxullian declared. "Now we need to see about some infiltration. Omega, your teams are best suited and trained for that kind of clandestine exploration...would you mind...?"

"Alpha Two, Alpha Eight, front and center, please," Omega ordered.

Romeo, India, Monkey, and Kako snapped to attention.

* * *

Three hours later, the two teams reported back.

"Yup, he's there, all right," Romeo noted. "Two guards at each entrance, front an' back, an' an emergency escape chute that takes him down and out to a waiting saucer."

"Except the escape hatch inside his suite is now jammed," India added with a smirk.

"What about the rest of it?" Wuxullian asked.

"Eqvipment is positioned, deployed and ready for actiwation, sir," Kako said in his soft Russian accent.

"Very, very good," Wuxullian averred. "And no one knew you were there?"

"No sir," Monkey confirmed. "While we watched from a clandestine location, the perp left his suite and went down to one of the ritzy restaurants for dinner. Then, with a bit of simple diversion, all four of us waltzed right past the guards with the personal sensor scramblers Omega ginned up."

"This will work, this will work," Wuxullian mused. "Phase One down, gentlebeings. We are about to commence Phase Two. Omega, are you willing to be our bait to draw in the wild beast?"

"You know it, sir," Omega answered, calm. "Just my showing up ought to unnerve him enough to convince him to act... one way or another. If he's the one who hired Slug, he knows who I am, I'm sure of it."

"An' I noticed that he ran from Veldorn 'long about th' time word woulda reached 'im that you an' Echo survived Slug's attack, back after ya came inta th' Agency," Romeo noted. "Which means he hadda have known about Slug's plans."

"Exactly," Omega agreed. "Given the extant contract, they probably were still in some level of communication. So when I show up, he's gonna realize I'm onto him..."

"And hopefully, panic and make a mistake," Wuxullian added. "So you are the obvious bait."

"Meg?" Chi, who had mostly sat by and watched to this point, murmured. Fox had given him a special job—to watch over Omega and see that nothing happened to her after what looked to be a reasonably successful 'resurrection' of Echo. "Are you sure about this? I mean, Echo an' all, hon..."

"I'm sure, Chi," Omega determined, firm. "This guy is smart, is sitting in an ivory tower, and if I'm reading the signs right, he could readily set up his own interstellar crime syndicate."

"Agreed," Wuxullian confirmed. "If he has not started already."

"And if he does that, and if he really is the guy who hired Slug, then Alpha One is a threat to him, and there's nowhere Echo and I can go that'll be safe," Omega pointed out. "Except maybe to go visit the Persan Premier, all the way in the Andromeda Galaxy. And even that's not a sure bet."

"Especially if Humn Aggum, the would-be usurper, left any sympathizers behind in his home galaxy," Wuxullian added.

"True," Omega agreed. She moved close to Chi, and took his hand. "It's okay, Scotty," she breathed, low enough that no one else could hear. "I'm calm, I'm rested, I'm well-fed, and I'm confident. I know what I'm doing on this. We got a plan, and it's nearly foolproof. Trust me."

Chi searched her sapphire eyes, seeing the assurance there. He decided to trust it, even as he trusted the woman possessing those eyes.

"All right," he capitulated. "But I don't wanna have to explain to Fox—never mind to Echo!—if something goes south."

"You won't," Omega said.

"No, I shall do that, if it comes to it," Wuxullian said. "However, I should say, in the circumstances and with the plan that Omega and I have devised, the probabilities are very low. Now, let us get this operation set up and going before the old reprobate gets back from his dinner. I already know I have him on money laundering. I just need to know if I want him on conspiracy, sedition, and attempted murder charges, as well."

"No sweat, Chief," Romeo noted. "Intel indicates th' guy loves 'is food. Bit of a gourmet, apparently. He got a multicourse dinner goin' on, an' gonna be in th' restaurant f'r at least three more hours."

"Ah, well then," Wuxullian said. "We have just enough time. Let us get started."

* * *

Xoreplirg Erushin returned to his plush penthouse suite several hours after he left it, well fed, sated, and content, scarcely bothering to acknowledge the armored and helmeted guards who stood at the front door. Nor did he notice that they were not the same guards who had been there when he left, nor would he have thought much about it if he had; he paid the guards well, and they had their own shifts, with which he did not bother, save to pay the head of hotel security to ensure they were trustworthy.

He provided no less than three biometrics to the door lock, and it opened within fractions of a second. One of the guards held the door for him, and he entered, listening with absent-minded satisfaction as the door locked firmly behind him.

He sighed with pleasure as he looked around the luxuriantly-furnished and -decorated great-room, into which the foyer entered, and moved to the wet bar in the corner, pouring himself a substantial drink—it was a lovely, and very old, Talisker single-malt Scotch, carefully imported from Earth via roundabout means, using his 'connections' and various holding companies, subsidiary to Tralosia. Then he dimmed the lights and carried his drink onto the force-field-encased balcony. There he stood, pensive, and studied the amazing view of the Great Spiral as he sipped, savoring the imported liquor.

This particular night, he was alone; there were several females who sometimes accompanied him, and provided him with 'evening diversions' from time to time. But he was careful to let none of them get too close. It did not do to allow affections to develop; he had realized that when he had had to ensure his nephew was duly taken care of by his 'undercover employees.' He hadn't cared for it, but Xerulass knew too much, and was starting to become too bold about it. Xerulass's daughter Xychaffa had been suspicious, but he had made certain that there was absolutely nothing for her to find outside of the desired cover story, lest he have to eliminate her as well, a thing he did NOT want to do; too many deaths in the family, too close together, tended to make the authorities suspicious.

In general, though, he decided, his plans had gone quite well over the years, and were now finally coming to fruition... though he had had to accelerate them the previous year, when certain news had come to him of an unwelcome nature. It seemed that the Division One agents were smarter and more skilled than his employee had given them credit for being, and said employee had not survived the attempt to tidy up some loose ends. Never mind the fact that the employee had made said tidying far more complicated than it had to be, in Xoreplirg's opinion.

Still and all, he considered, *these Division One Agents have no clue about ME. And I have hidden myself deeply. With more plans in the offing, if all goes well. I look forward to the visit from the head of Rrgllbrrgll in half a lunation; that is always a strategic maneuver, much like playing eschek, and I relish it. I suspect we will have much to collaborate upon, in future. And perhaps, when all is said and done, I can soon ensure the last loose ends of Azeln's xyeezic failed mission are done away with, the insane fool. Two beings...that is all I need to eliminate. And all he could not manage to do! Arguably, his schemes even made matters worse, by giving his real target a worthy ally, and thereby doubling the number of targets. Xyeez azh Bozhen e Riis!*

When his drink was finally finished, he came back inside, sat the empty glass on the bar for the carefully-vetted maid service to carry away on the morrow when they cleaned the suite, and headed for his private study.

* * *

But when he entered the study, the desk chair, facing the back corner, turned toward him. He stared in astonishment at the being sitting in it...one of the very beings he had been considering how to eliminate.

"Well, hello there, Nam Xoreplirg Erushin," the human with the platinum blonde braid and sapphire-blue eyes said with a harsh smile, offering the traditional honorific of his homeworld. "I don't believe we've ever actually met. My name is Agent Omega. I'm Agent Echo's partner. I think you've heard of us. I know we've heard of YOUR agent, Azeln AbdohNeléKein, the Bozhen of Wontwuun." She stood, revealing the black Suit of a Division One Agent.

"Khro di zhrat!" he spat viciously, and drew a concealed projectile weapon, aiming at Omega's chest and firing point-blank.

* * *

But Omega just stood there, smiling.

"A bit unnerving, those names, that history, eh?" she wondered.

Erushin emptied the remaining projectiles in his gun at her, to no effect. There was not even the flare of a force field intercepting them; instead, there were puffs of debris behind her, as if she were no more than a ghost.

"Security! SECURITY!" he bellowed then.

Within moments, four armored and armed guards burst in.

"KILL HER!" he ordered, pointing at the Division One Agent.

The guards drew down.

* * *

"NOW!" Chief Wuxullian ordered, yelling into the mic on his shoulder. "Take him now!"

Chi, Orange, Berta, Como, and Quintal, along with two dozen hand-picked agents from PGLEIA Galactic Headquarters, and some fifty Division Fourteen agents, moved out at speed.

* * *

Abruptly all of the security guards turned their weapons on Erushin.

"Surprise," Omega said in a cheerful voice. "Drop your weapon, Nam Xoreplirg. I think you're out of bullets anyway."

Erushin dropped the weapon, and one of the guards kicked it away. He started to bend, but Omega interrupted him.

"Anh, anh, anh! Oh no. You don't EVEN go there. Hands on your head."

Frustrated, Erushin complied, and one of the guards patted him down, confiscating another small energy-beam pistol that had been carefully tucked and secured just inside his trouser leg, in a cuff holster around his calf.

"Traitors! I will have your heads!" Erushin demanded, infuriated. "Who the riis are you?"

"Oh, you know exactly who I am," the Agent noted.

"I did not mean you!"

"Oh, you mean 'your' guards?"

"YES! Traitorous bastards!"

"Now, now, Nam Xoreplirg. Be polite. Boys and girls, your helmets, if you please," Omega ordered.

With their free hands, all four guards removed their helmets...

...To reveal Alpha Two and Eight.

Who were definitely not on the roster of security guards for the hotel.

"What the khreen?" Erushin muttered. "Who the riis are you?"

"Oh, surely you were notified when Echo and I survived Azeln's plan; it's why you moved here," Omega noted. "He and I run Alpha Line, the special forces department of Division One. These are some of MY people. Echo and I are VERY proud of them."

Just then, the doors of the suite burst open and agents from several Divisions poured into the apartment, weapons drawn.

"And these are my friends," Omega added, as Chief Wuxullian strode into the study. "I'm sure you know THAT guy. Hi, Chief Wux."

"Hello, Omega," Wuxullian said with a smirk. "Nicely done. Thank you."

"No problem, Chief."

"What the khro did that insane creature do to you?" Erushin demanded. "Why won't you die?"

Omega began to laugh, and Wuxullian chuckled, pulling a device and clicking a button. Suddenly Omega vanished.

"Because she was never here to begin with," Wuxullian averred. "Alpha Eight, will you please place this being in force cuffs? Wrist and leg, if you please. Oh, and his rights, of course; the standard things. Qof Twenty, if you would be so kind as to break down the solid hologram projector, and return it to our base of operations...?"

* * *

After Xoreplirg Erushin had been taken into custody and

led away—on charges of money laundering and attempted murder of a Galactic agent—Omega, accompanied by a much-relieved Chi, came into the suite.

"So! We have him, without doubt," Wuxullian said with deep satisfaction, "but now we need to prove your theory, Omega. Granted, he reacted as soon as he heard your name, Echo's name, and Slug's true name, and that is damning evidence right there, especially when coupled with the document file you found on Veldor."

"Yeah. But that damn contract would be proof positive," Omega noted. "Open and shut case, with a near-automatic conviction to boot. Let's see what we can find, shall we?"

They spread out to search.

* * *

In the end, an observant Chi found it, hidden in a secret compartment of Erushin's desk. There was both an electronic copy on a data chip and a printed copy, as well as two small containers, each with a carefully-preserved tissue sample in a special stasis tube. The tissue in one was an iridescent green; had the old Echo been there, he would have recognized it immediately.

"Whoa," Chi said, coming up with the entire packet. "THIS looks interesting. Meg, could this be it?"

"That sure looks like it," Omega noted, as soon as she saw the tissue samples. Wuxullian was already leafing through the printed copy of the contract.

"'This contract, made this 81st day of Orndras in the year 8941 after the Great Migration, by and between Uesleion Rushin and Azeln AbdohNeléKein, certifies that Rushin hires AbdohNeléKein for the following actions...'" he read. "Oh yes, this is damning, all right, Omega. Look." He handed her the document, and she scanned through it.

"...'To stop the completion of the negotiation at whatever cost,'" she read aloud, "'up to and including the abduction or elimination of the M'Queran Ambassador Quequar M'reth, as necessary and at the best convenience of the contracted Agent AbdohNeléKein...'" She broke off and shook her head. "Yeah, we got him. And if that right there," she nodded at the little green tissue sample, "doesn't match the DNA taken from

Slug's body, and the other match Xoreplirg Erushin, I'll be surprised."

"Shit," Chi remarked, "no wonder the guy hid it."

"Yeah, this is probably his death warrant, right here," Omega said, waving the printed copy of the contract. "Why the HELL he kept it around after Slug's death, I do NOT know."

"Well, even the smartest of beings pulls what I have heard Echo call 'a brain fart' now and again," Wuxullian noted. "Perhaps he did not know what to do with it, or the best way to destroy it. Or perhaps he thought that Slug had kin or descendants that he might be able to hold to the contract, in the stead of Slug...and take out Alpha One in the doing, once and for all."

"Yeah, any of those would make sense. Hey! Somebody grab that drink glass off the bar and put it in a forensics bag; that'll give us our DNA sample from Erushin, without havin' to fight him for it."

"Got it," came the call from Monkey, in the other room.

"Excellent. I brought my best forensics expert with me, and it brought a small but efficient laboratory with it, along with all of the genetic data from Slug, aka Azeln AbdohNeléKein," Wuxullian noted. "I can take all this to my flagship and have a response from it inside an hour, yea or nay."

"Good. Let's do it," Omega said. "I have a partner to get home to."

* * *

It proved even as Omega had said: There could be no doubt that the tissue sample 'signatures' for the contract were indeed those of the now-deceased Azeln AbdohNeléKein, and the very-much-alive Xoreplirg Erushin. More, a thorough search of Erushin's files—most notably, his email equivalent, though a bit of hacking had to be done to locate the hidden records—turned up the telling clue: it transpired that Azeln did indeed have kin, with whom Erushin had been in touch, attempting to coerce them into fulfilling the last of the contract by eliminating Alpha One for him.

"An' that's that," Romeo noted.

"It is indeed," Wuxullian agreed. "To the charges of money laundering and attempted murder of a Galactic agent, we will now add..." he ticked fingers, "sedition, conspiracy against the Pan-Galactic Coalition, conspiracy to commit kidnapping, three—possibly four—counts of conspiracy to commit murder, abetment in the murder of four Galactic agents, abetment in the brain-death murder of three Galactic agents, attempted kidnapping of a Galactic Ambassador, and attempted murder of a Galactic Ambassador. With plenty of evidence of each charge." He turned to Omega. "Are you satisfied, Agent Omega?"

"I am, sir," she said. "I'll be happier once he's convicted and serving sentence, though."

"Oh, he will not be getting away," Wuxullian vowed. "And at least two of those charges have a mandated death sentence for conviction. But even if he is not convicted of THOSE charges, he will certainly be imprisoned for the rest of his natural life. Given he is not a young Veldorn, well..."

"Then yes, I'm VERY satisfied," Omega decided, "and I think my job here is done."

"Then let's get home," India said, putting an arm around the other woman, "and see about getting some other things taken care of back there."

"Yeah, we need ta git back in time t' see Echo woke up," Romeo agreed.

"Then let's go," Chi declared.

"Go," Wuxullian gave permission.

* * *

Fox was waiting at the maglev platform in Grand Central Station when Omega and her team debarked after returning from the sting operation on Doukeed, in Division Fourteen.

"Well?" he asked, as soon as she stepped from the train car. Omega grinned widely.

"The idiot actually tried to shoot me as soon as I introduced myself," she noted.

"O' course, she WAS in his highly-secure apartment," Romeo pointed out. "In th' dude's office, no less."

"Not exactly," Chi snorted. "Her image was, though."

"Solid hologram," Omega succinctly answered Fox's mildly puzzled look. "We hacked the resort's security, located his suite, then programmed all of it so that the system recognized us. Alpha Two and Alpha Eight infiltrated and set everything up for the confrontation, including the hologram projector, came back and reported, then uh, 'relieved' the guards and took their places."

"Then," India tag-teamed, "when he came back from a really long dinner in the top gourmet restaurant in the whole damn place, Meg activated the projector from her remote location, scared the shit outta him, and he drew down and fired. While the rest of us used the hacked security cameras to watch. AND record."

"The idiot emptied his magazine," Monkey chortled. "And all he succeeded in doing was shredding a really nice desk chair."

"Zhen Chief Vuxullian called for action," Kako continued the story, "and ve all moved in."

"Oh, by the way, commendations for Agent Chi, here," Omega added. "He found the hidden safe with the contract AND both tissue samples, hidden in Erushin's desk."

"He did, did he?" Fox said, raising one eyebrow, impressed. "So soon after becoming an agent? I'll do that. And make sure Crutch knows all about it." He clapped the new agent on the shoulder; Chi flushed. "Very good, zun. You show considerable promise, even as your old friend here did, and does. I'll make your weapons assignments permanent. Oh, and I think it's about time we looked into finding you a partner, too. Crutch and I'll get right on that."

"That's a sign you're legal, both o' those," Omega said, elbowing Chi. "Congrats."

"Great!" Chi said, looking pleased. "Um...do I get a vote in who I get?"

"Of course," Fox noted. "We want the two of you to get along, after all. Many times our partnerships wind up being what I've heard some of the recruits—especially the younger ones—call BFFs." He put a fatherly arm across Chi's shoulders. "Come on; let's go find Crutch and see what she's got handy. Or rather, who."

As they headed off, and the rest of the team dispersed, Omega called out.

"Hey, Fox?"

He turned.

"Um, I woulda expected Echo to be here..." she tried.

"Oh," Fox said, and his face stiffened slightly. He turned to Chi. "Wait here, zun."

Omega felt the pit fall from her stomach. *And it feels like it went straight down the Mouth of Mitnal,* she thought, trying not to shiver. *This is bad, I can tell it.*

When she came out of her morbid thoughts, Fox was standing in front of her.

"Okay, what's happened?" she murmured in a low voice. "He...did it not work after all...?"

* * *

"He's not dead, tekhter, and he's not going to die," Fox said softly, resting a light hand on her shoulder. "But the last I heard, he wasn't fully 'integrated' yet, either. Evidently the 'piece of mind' that's been running the body is still being a bit stubborn...or confused...or something. Not being a telepath, and not part of the interaction, I'm afraid I don't quite understand. What I do know is, it's resisting, on the grounds of Echo's life being impossible according to ordinary reckoning. Or something like that," he added. "Zz'r'p says there's a lot of confusion there, and a lot of, of...jealousy, I guess, is one way of putting it. Envy. Anyway, the piece doesn't want to relinquish control, but the nd't'lq is smart enough to realize that IT has to be in control for Echo to get back to normal. Zz'r'p's been trying to mediate, or moderate, or however you want to put it."

Omega's face fell.

"So what's happening?"

"As best I could tell from what I got out of Zz'r'p," Fox explained, "there's a struggle for control, when they ought to be merging. Effectively it's created a kind of fragmented mind. In the unlikely event that Zz'r'p can't get this to resolve..." Fox broke off and sighed. "Well, an offworld mental institution might be able to produce positive results eventually."

Omega paled.

"Now, now," Fox murmured. "Zz'r'p doesn't think it'll come to that. Which leaves us with two options: the nd't'lq wins control, or the piece of Echo's mind that came back when we revived him takes control."

"So if the piece wins..." she almost whispered.

331

"Then you may have to start over with the relationship," Fox offered, hurting for her as he saw the pain in her eyes. "As in, from the day you met. But I can tell you this much, the...dammit, let's call him 'Fractional Echo.' It sounds better than 'piece of mind;' that just sounds like somebody is chewing someone else out."

That coaxed a grim chuckle from Omega.

"Okay," she agreed. "'Fractional Echo' it is, I guess."

"So. If Fractional Echo comes out on top, then as best I understood it, Echo will have the memories there, and the choice of acting on them, but will have an attitude more like the whole 'nobody can do that in real life' that he's had in recent days. Which will likely mean that his days as the head of Alpha Line—and as my successor—are over, but he can probably be retrained as a field agent or similar...if he's willing. Of course, all that puts you in the driver's seat for the department. And possibly as my successor. If YOU'RE willing."

Omega bit her lip; her bright blue eyes glimmered far more than they ought. *Oh, tekhter,* Fox thought, troubled. *I know, child, I know—all too well. I know the pain of loss. Of not having the life you dreamed. But this may not be that bad. I need to hurry and get to the heart of the matter, here. In more ways than one.* So he continued.

"That does not mean that Fractional Echo does not love you, meyn kind. I watched as he came to a full realization of what he had done, what and who he had rejected, while you were gone. I think that is why he wanted to speak to you before the nd't'lq procedure; he wanted to try to get across to you that he had realized that you WERE special, in many ways, but especially to him." He watched as Omega swallowed hard, then tucked her head. "So I think you could still have a relationship with him, and eventually get married...though probably NOT as soon as the amendment comes down from the Ennead. And...while I know this is not your wont...YOU will probably need to court HIM, this time."

Omega put her face in her hands.

* * *

Chi stood at a distance, watching. He could hear the murmur of low voices, but could not understand what was being

332

said.

However, he had known the woman once called Megan McAllister for too many years not to recognize when she was fighting back pain. And when her shoulders slumped and she put her face in her hands, he drew in a shocked breath, feeling as if someone had punched him in the gut, hard.

"Oh, no no no!" he exclaimed, and ran to the pair. "Meg! Pook, honey, it—he didn't?!" Chi grabbed her by the shoulder. "I thought everything was gonna be okay now! What's happened?"

Omega raised her head briefly; her face was tear-streaked. She buried her face back in her hands and croaked, "It—I..."

But nothing else would come out. She wrapped her left arm around her face, averting it slightly, and with her right hand, tapped Fox on the chest, then jabbed her finger at Chi. The communiqué was clear, despite the lack of words. Fox took Chi's shoulder, turning him back in the direction they had been going.

"Come with me, zun, and I'll explain for her," he murmured. "I think she needs some time to herself for a few moments. Omega, are you headed back to your quarters?"

She nodded, her back to them.

"Will you need assistance getting there?"

She shook her head.

"All right. Call me or Zebra if you need anything, tekhter; promise me."

She nodded.

The men left.

Omega found a bench in an out-of-the-way alcove and sat down hard.

* * *

Zz'r'p was in Echo's room in the medlab, still trying to help Echo sort out things...while simultaneously battling the headache of frustration that was threatening. After all, Echo had a strong personality, a strong will, and a strong sense of RIGHT, and always had. And that meant that BOTH of the versions of Echo currently residing in his brain thought that it should have control, because only in that way could each ensure that right was done.

And so Zz'r'p was once more trying to mediate, and get them to understand that NEITHER could DOMINATE or control, but that the nd't'lq needed to maintain the lead even as he led them into becoming a single being once again...

...When he became aware of someone he knew well, in deep pain, relatively nearby. He stopped dead, intensely worried.

Both of you, stop everything, right this moment, he told the two versions of Echo's mind as they wrangled for control. *I need to show you something, NOW. It is important, and it is urgent.*

What now? Fractional Echo wondered, mildly exasperated.

Yes, what is it, Zz'r'p? the nd't'lq download wondered.

Look.

And suddenly they 'felt' Omega, as she sat in the maglev station alcove, alone and crying.

Both versions of the man who loved her froze.

Wh-what's wrong? they asked in unison...for the first time.

Fox has just told her that, because the two of you are not cooperating, matters may not resolve as well as she had hoped. That the wedding the two of you had planned for as soon as the Ennead issued the charter amendment is likely off, and your betrothal may be, as well. She is devastated.

But...but it isn't that I don't love her, or that I couldn't love her, the damaged part of Echo's mind said. *I just...don't KNOW her yet.*

I do, the nd't'lq pointed out. *She's amazing, dude. We can't lose her, you and I. I don't know what I'd do without her beside me. Can't you trust me on even that much?*

I...I don't...know.

Can you trust HER? Zz'r'p asked then.

Both versions of Echo focused on Zz'r'p in surprise.

* * *

Omega, having gotten a gentle mental summons from a certain Deltiri, arrived in Echo's hospital room in the medlab a little later. Her cheeks had been thoroughly scrubbed, but her nose was still pink and her eyes red-rimmed and swollen. But Echo lay in the bed, eyes closed, and could not see what she looked like, she decided—and Zz'r'p already knew. It never occurred to her that Echo was using Zz'r'p's vision to see his partner, nor that both parts of his mind winced at her appearance.

"Omega, Echo—well, his minds, let us say—would like to ask you some questions," Zz'r'p said.

"Oh, Zz'r'p, do we have to do this?" she asked, her voice hoarse and low. "I just got back from helping to take down the dude that hired Slug, and I'm kinda tired."

* * *

"Do not lie to me, or to him," Zz'r'p reprimanded. "Yes, you did, and yes, you are, but that is an excuse."

"I don't feel like doing this," she admitted then. "I don't WANT to."

"Why not?"

"Because I don't know what to do any more!" she exclaimed in intense frustration and discouragement, raking a trembling hand over her braided hair, dislodging several silken silver strands. "I talked to Fox, so I sorta know what's going on. And I don't know what he wants, what he needs...I don't know how to deal with this!"

"Why not?" Zz'r'p tried again.

"Because I don't know what the...the part of him that was in his body through all this shit...I don't even know if he trusts me, let alone still wants anything to do with me."

Zz'r'p paused, seeming to listen to something Omega could not hear. Then he returned his attention to Omega.

"He indicates that he needs to get to know you, but you still hold his interest, my dear girl."

"All over again," she sighed, seeming to sag. "Two years' worth of working together closer than I've ever worked with anybody in my life. Trusting him, caring about him, picking him up, being picked up BY him. Saving his life, and having him save mine. And it's all out the window. From orbital altitudes."

"Patience," Zz'r'p counseled. "Could you not court him again?"

"I dunno that I ever really courted him," she pointed out. "We talked past each other for a long time. Then he evidently decided he needed to take action, when Mu got interested in me or something. Like, you know, 'Wups, I need to be more direct, or I might lose her to him,' kinda thing. And then HE did all the courting. I'm not even sure I know how," she admitted, earnest. "I...everything about how I was raised was kinda old-fashioned. What little I DID approach him, I was so embarrassed I thought I'd die. I just don't think I could handle starting over from square one, never mind ME courting HIM. I just know I'd mess up or something. I only..."

Abruptly she wobbled, and glanced around in almost-desperation, looking for a chair. Zz'r'p 'saw' her need and grabbed a visitor chair, shoving it in her direction just in time for her to all but collapse into it. She buried her face in her hands again and began to cry quietly once more, lightly rocking back and forth.

"I'm sorry, I'm so sorry," she whispered, almost keening the words. "I dunno what to do any more. I just don't know what to do."

* * *

Oh damn, Echo's nd't'lq download murmured in dismay.

What he said, the fragment agreed. *We're breaking her.*

And she's never been broken before, the download added. *Not like this. Not fully, anyway. Alla Slug's shitty machinations came close. Damn close. But this...it's ripping her heart out.*

Yes, it is, Zz'r'p interjected agreement. *You MUST integrate, and return to some semblance of your old self, or it is the ruination of your hopes and dreams...and her life. Oh, she may go on, even if you choose to deny your past. But she will never be the same. She will be but a shadow of her former self. And that, even if you manage to eke out a future together. Nor will that future be what it might have been. Because SHE will not be what she might have been.*

But...wouldn't she at least be willing to try? the fragment asked, somewhat plaintive.

She would, Zz'r'p averred. *And she is. But she is right; she does not know how. For all that she is a bold Agent, and presses forward on matters of capturing a criminal, or running the department—in her personal life, her relationships, she is deeply reserved and relatively undemonstrative, at least until she knows that demonstration is warranted, that it will be ac-*

cepted. Never mind how she was raised, which reinforced that innate reserve. You are asking her to go against everything that she is, every experience she has ever had. And she does not know how. More, the fact that you would consider forcing her to start over from the very beginning of your relationship speaks to her of a denial of trust. Deep in her heart, in her soul, in the core of her mind, she will no longer believe you trust her. She will believe that, deep down, you still feel about her as you expressed to her face—that she is an untrustworthy, alien thing, that you do not want around you.

Because... the fragment began, slow and thoughtful. *I'm making her prove herself to me, all over again. Her...and everybody, everything else.*

Right, Zz'r'p confirmed. *You say you trust her, trust the rest of us, but your actions in this say otherwise to her, to us, even if you mean what you say.*

* * *

They were silent for a long moment, while Omega sat in the chair and tried to regain control of her emotions. After several minutes, she scrubbed her hands over her face again, and squared her shoulders, sitting up.

"All right," she declared, determined. "I dunno if I can manage it, but if that's what he wants, dammit, I'll try to find a way."

* * *

And that should tell you all you need to know, Zz'r'p said. *She is, and has always been, willing to deny herself for your sake. That is how much she loves you. My question to you is: how much do you love HER? What are YOU willing to deny for HER sake?*

There was a long silence.

Then both Echos, the fragment and the download, responded in unintentional unison...for the second time.

Zz'r'p, could you give us some privacy to talk, please?

* * *

At Zz'r'p's gentle but firm instruction, Omega went home. But her quarters were cheerless and lonely without her partner next door. In the end, she wound up inviting herself over to Romeo and India's quarters, where they immediately guessed the situation and made her stay for dinner. Over dinner, Omega confessed the details of the matter, and the pair were concerned, but convinced her to be patient and give Echo time to "get it t'gether," as Romeo put it. Then the trio sat in the den with beers and chatted until it was bedtime.

"And now we're going to see you back to your quarters, Meg, with a little something in my pocket for you to take when you get in bed," India noted. "Don't worry; it'll just relax you, not make you go to sleep. You're understandably wound tight after everything and need something to help you loosen up a little."

"I really don't wanna have to take anything," Omega murmured.

"Well, I've already talked to Zz'r'p AND Zebra AND Zarnix," India declared. "They pinged me as soon as I got back into Headquarters. And the general consensus was that, one way or another, we were going to see to it you get a little medication for a while, to help you settle, and help Zz'r'p settle you for your counseling sessions."

"Oh," Omega said, and sighed. "What is it?"

"Nothing strong, and nothing that's gonna cause any problems," India said, rummaging through her medical supplies and coming up with a brand-new pill bottle. "That's the advantage to having access to galactic medications. They have a lot better understanding of the workings of the biochem, 'cause they've had a lot longer to study it, and so the dangers are a lot less. Here we go. This is the prescription we want you to have." She gave Omega the bottle. "It's just a little something for your anxiety. It'll help you relax and not get all wrapped around the axle about stuff."

"An' that, in turn, oughta help you fall asleep, girl," Romeo pointed out. "I got some 'a that shit—well, the Earth-based stuff—after my buddy got killed when I 'uz in the SEALs. Trust me, it helps."

"Okay, I guess. If it's safe," Omega decided. "I'm not, like, gonna get addicted, right?"

"No, not to this stuff," India said. "That's why we specifically decided on this. Just one dose a day, no addictive properties, and you don't even have to take it every day, so if you miss a dose, it won't hurt anything. I mean, you might feel a little more anxious if you do, but it's not gonna mess you up. And if something comes up to where you need to stop taking it cold turkey—like maybe you run out while you're off-world, or undercover or something—it won't hurt, either."

"Wow," Romeo said, surprised. "That IS better than the Earth-based shit."

"Yeah, it is," India agreed. "Now, let's you and me walk Meg around the corner and back to her place, where I'll see about helping her get ready for bed and put a dose of this in her, then we'll leave her to get some sleep and we'll come back home."

"All over it, girl," Romeo averred.

* * *

Omega did relax and was able to go to sleep, and sleep reasonably well, all things considered. The next morning she woke on time, then got up, plopped into her recliner in the den, and pondered what to do. It was Alpha One's normal day off, and she had had some very specific plans for the day...but those plans had predicated on the notion that Echo would be back to normal, and hopefully out of the medlab.

And neither looks like being the case, she thought, morose. *I dunno what I'm gonna do if he decides to just retire or something. Or even if they CAN retire him now, given the nd't'lq.*

Abruptly Zz'r'p contacted her mentally.

Omega! Are you awake, my dear?

Right here, Zz'r'p. What's up? Do you need me? Is everything okay?

Everything is fine, dear girl. I wanted to tell you that matters have resolved, and Echo is awake! We are proceeding with the plans as you have laid them out, so you need to follow through with your part, as well. India is coming over right now to help you.

WHAT?! Omega exclaimed, nearly shrieking the word mentally. *But...I mean, is he...?*

You will see soon. Go take care of things.

Omega wheeled for her bedroom to get ready for the day.

Chapter 14

"But I don't get it," Echo said, as Romeo and Yorker rushed him through showering, shaving, and dressing in a Suit. "Besides, I thought today was supposed to be our regular day off, anyway."

"Jus' hush, dude, an' do what we's tellin' ya," Romeo noted, handing Echo his tie and watching with hidden satisfaction as the Agent deftly tied the special knot—with rock-steady hands—without having to give much thought on the matter. "We got orders, here."

"Oh. Well, okay, then," Echo capitulated. "But I kinda expect that the medlab folks are gonna bitch if Fox wants to send me an' Meg out, with me just havin' woke up from the...shit...I been dealing with."

"The medlab thinks that what's planned will be very good for you," Yorker declared.

"Awright, dammit. Where's my holsters an' pieces?"

"Those, you ain't gonna need right now," Romeo averred. "Me an' India gonna have your backs on that. You c'n grab 'em later. Prob'ly stowed in your kit already; I think India said Meg told 'er somethin' 'bout that."

Echo eyed Romeo.

"This is a galactic commendation, or medal award, or some kinda shit like that, isn't it?" he wondered, annoyed at the thought.

"Some kinda," Romeo said with a grin. "Now let's get you into that Suit jacket and get going. Yorker got places t' be, an' so do we."

Grumbling under his breath, Echo shrugged into his jacket, as Romeo winked at Yorker, and Yorker grinned back.

* * *

The huge all-hands auditorium was full of agents, aliens, ambassadors, and administrators. A broad ramp had been installed that led onto the center of the low stage from the central aisle, and the podium had been set aside, replaced by a broad, short table decked with a white silk drape and a large, multi-colored floral centerpiece, and two big, imposing but stylistically simple, carved wooden chairs on either side. Matching floral baskets sat on either side of the ramp. Behind the table sat an inconspicuous row of stacking chairs. On either side of the platform, small holovid cameras recorded the scene, transmitting it in a ciphered feed to the other Offices, as well as to Aleancë and several other worlds.

In the audience sat significant numbers of agents from the Field department, Weapons Development and Testing, Sciences, and Medical, to include Madrid, Zarnix, and Zebra. Zarnix, unusually clad in a Suit instead of scrubs and a lab coat, and Zebra, also unusually adorned in a pale yellow cocktail dress which delightfully set off the golden tones of her brunette complexion, sat in the front row on the left of the aisle, beside Reptoid Lord Suud Guurn and his entire family—Suud and Duuniiss were both in Emdalian Bodyguard Corps livery—Deltiri Ambassador Zz'r'p in his finest dress robes, and Admiral Lyddhu Raiit in a special chair suited to her non-humanoid frame. Two empty seats were on Zebra's right, next to the center aisle.

Immediately behind this group sat all of Alpha Line, from all Offices across the planet, ranked in order of team number save for Alpha One and Two, who were absent. Even Alpha Seven was there, Fox having decided that Yankee's significant change of attitude prior to being brain-bleached a few months prior, and his impeccable behavior during his probation, warranted a shorter sequestration and another shot; given the situation with Alpha One had not looked promising, he and Tare had been brought back into the Agency and Yankee's memories returned while Omega was missing. He was delighted to be there...and just as delighted to be witness to what was about to take place. Meanwhile, the department members assisted Alpha Twenty-Four, as Torino hobbled in on crutches, and her partner Adam, the injured arm still weak and in a sling, cane in the other hand, followed behind.

Farther back, Agent Baker, the head of McMurdo Office, and Juliet, head of the Los Angeles Office, sat next to Agent Burbulon Vex, more commonly known as 'Klack' of the Atlantis Office, attired in an appropriately octopus-shaped pressure suit filled with seawater. Sugar and Gamma, chief and assistant chief of the Diplomacy department, sat nearby, accompanied by quite a few other department members, most of whom had seen action alongside Alpha Line during the original Cortian incident. Virtually the entire crew of the *D1 Genesis* sat in the audience, as well as Joe Beck and the staff of the Ranch, and several from the staff of the Farm, in addition. Mu and his partner Zeta sat side-by-side, holding hands. Agent Bi'hts'e Dh'u, a Glu'g'ik from Va'du'sha'ā, sat nearby, as did Agent Slekuwiss Jostek of Exinul, and almost all of the agents from Security...though most of them joined the several dozen field agents from Crutch's department, standing guard around the auditorium. Even newly-christened Agent Chi came in with his brand-new partner, Genova, an attractive brunette agent originally from the London Office and of some three years' experience, though she was slightly younger than Chi; Alpha Five waved them over, and the Alpha Line ranks made room for the agent who had helped out their assistant chief, and helped rescue their chief.

Dr. Psi unobtrusively eased an antigrav wheelchair into the auditorium; Kappa sat in it. Nun accompanied them, and Psi—who was now Kappa's full-time medical caregiver—parked the chair next to the last row of seats, then he and Nun sat down beside Kappa.

Moments later, a certain strawberry blond head floated through the crowd, as Dr. Travis S. Taylor, originally of Kirakalla—known to humans as Tau Ceti f—and late of Huntsville, Alabama, entered in an unaccustomed suit and tie, and found a seat in the auditorium. Seconds after that, a certain small red-skinned healer with large yellow eyes entered; Doron found a seat beside his equally-diminutive friend Indak. Seeming to appear from nowhere, a handsome gentleman looking suspiciously like the Harry Houdini of legend slipped into a seat near the back; moments later, the human was gone, and a Glu'g'ik of unknown antecedents sat there. A white-bearded and cheerful Nicholas Claus of Wintou, attired in a beautiful burgundy suit trimmed in gold embroidery, a rotund little white-haired Wintourn female in a matching burgundy tunic-dress—his wife—on his arm, entered and took seats near Klack, chatting familiarly with the octopus. Trifle, the segmented felinoid who ran Alpha One's favorite pizza parlor, hopped up on the back of Klack's chair and joined the conversation. Gianna Ricci, Italian restaurateur from Dekken, accompanied Sir Michael, the famous operatic lead from Yelfflan, sitting nearby.

Moments later, large wall panels around the room flickered and lit, as PGLEIA Chief Gwag Wuxullian, the Division Five PGLEIA chief Taassass Siisshiiss, and several other Division directors 'tuned in' to the proceedings about to take place. Several soft, friendly greetings were exchanged between those in the big auditorium and those on the other side of the vidcalls.

The soft buzz of conversation that filled the room abruptly ceased in a certain amount of awe and respect, as a new contingent entered the room—the entire Ennead, led by Pulgey Entiyti himself, clad in a pearly white Draconan 'suit' with a broad silver border on the long, draping vest. Captain Chassav Ssiimiilav, in full dress uniform, was on his arm. Behind them, Lady Teela Krimnet, acting chairbeing, was escorted by Lord Ari N'Do, with Lady Mrrp Prrow of Bast, and the other Ennead members attending; this included Zhaejoh kre Ranan of the Ke!endarian Coalition, who had recently been elected to the Ennead. Dr. Werfer Eretigen accompanied the group, subtly seeing to Entiyti's well-being.

Behind THEM—and rather to Klack's excitement—came a cheerful, animated Hsrs Syrsh, Premier of the Persis Federation of the Andromeda Galaxy, and his entourage.

The Entiyti Bodyguard Corps, joined by the Persis Imperial Guard, entered and spread out to join the security teams provided by the Division One agents.

"Holy shit," Zebra breathed to Zarnix, shocked. "No wonder we got security out the ass! I guess Fox musta known about all of 'em coming, but I sure didn't!"

The various dignitaries arranged themselves on the right side of the aisle, in the first few rows; Hsrs, in fine garb suited to a galactic premier, squelched into his seat beside Lady Teela opposite Lord N'Do, and the rest of the groups ranked themselves harmoniously. Entiyti seated Captain Ssiimiilav with them, then strode up the ramp to the stage and took the large, imposing seat on the right.

* * *

Romeo and Yorker escorted Echo to a small room across the hall from the auditorium, and Yorker left them there, slipping into the auditorium and taking a seat in the back with a female friend.

Inside, Echo's mother Dihl awaited him, attired not in her usual black scrubs, but in a soft blue evening gown, a single stargazer lily attached to her shoulder as a corsage.

"Here," she said, moving to a table. "Here are yours." She held up small lily buds—they were not-yet-unfurled stargazers—and attached them, first to Echo's lapel, then to Romeo's. "You have, ah, things in hand, Romeo?"

"Yes ma'am," the younger man said with a grin. "All over that one!"

"I don't get it," Echo complained. "What the hell is going on, here?"

"You will understand in a few moments, son," Dihl noted. "I know that you are likely still a little confused, having just been awakened only a couple of hours ago. But this has been carefully planned and worked out at the highest echelons. Consider it the honor it is."

"Damnation," Echo grumbled. "I don't want some sorta big award or whatever. And where is Meg? She oughta be here too. She's done as much of the big shit as I have."

"Th' pretty lady'll be along in a little bit," Romeo noted. "Calm down, big guy. It's all cool."

Echo paused and drew a deep breath, then slid a hand over his face.

"You're right, an' I'm sorry," he murmured. "I'm just...the last few days have been...hard. I was beginning to think it was all goin' to hell in a handbasket."

"We were worried about it, too," Dihl said, sobering. "Is everything okay now?"

"Near as I can tell," he decided. "I think we're—um, I'm—settled out. Finally."

"Got th' imperial 'we' thing goin', huh?" Romeo teased.

"Hell, junior! You try arguin' with yourself for a week and

see how you like it," Echo riposted, and they all snorted in wry amusement.

* * *

In the auditorium, from a side door, the chaplaincy filed in, most of them taking the seats behind the table; Father Papa, in his dressiest white clerical robes embroidered and fringed with gold, scurried about, adding a simple standing cross to the table in front of the flowers, and three candles—two small and one large—in front of that, along with a box of matches and a small cigarette lighter. Then he took the large chair opposite Lord Entiyti. He gave a slight nod, and the audio speakers in the auditorium came to life, as Pachelbel's *Canon in D* began to play.

* * *

Across the hall, the sound of music filtered into the room where Romeo, Echo, and Dihl waited.

"What the hell?" Echo wondered, puzzled. "I never knew an award or commendation ceremony to have music..."

"That's our cue," Romeo noted with a grin. "C'mon, dude. This is your big day."

He headed out the door and across the hall.

"Come, son," Dihl said, taking his arm and placing her hand in the crook of his elbow. "It is time."

"I just wish somebody would tell me time for what," he grumbled...

...But he bit his lip, thoughtful, trying to pull up a certain memory...

...And went with his mother into the auditorium.

* * *

There, he saw the huge crowd collected, with a suspiciously familiar altar table—from the Headquarters chapel—on the auditorium stage, as Father Papa rose to his feet and came to the top of the ramp to greet Romeo, who moved in a stately walk in time to the music, ahead of them.

"Oh man," Echo breathed. "She didn't."

"Of course she did," Dihl responded in kind. "She adores you, son. This has been in work for a long time. You are already life partners. But after nearly losing you twice in under a week, she decided she did not wish to wait any longer for the

Ennead's amendment, so this is the religious ceremony you both wanted, even if it is not yet 'official' in the Coalition. The specifics of timing were, however, determined on the day your nd't'lq was restored...and all these guests have been patiently waiting to be told when to arrive. We only hoped you would be..." She broke off, then tried, "...That you would still want it."

"What do you think, Ma?" he asked softly. She stepped forward.

"Then come," she murmured. "We have a ceremony to be officiated."

* * *

"Oooh," an anxious Omega murmured, hearing the music begin. She glanced down at the bouquet of stargazer lilies and red roses in her hands, as India adjusted her veil. "I think I'm glad I got that special medication after all, India. My butterflies have butterflies, and even THOSE have butterflies!"

"You look beautiful, Meg," India, attired in a soft rose gown, told her. "I'm so happy you got that wedding gown started as soon as you two got engaged."

"Me too," she admitted. "Though after recent events, the tailors had to take it up just a smidge."

"Then you EAT at the reception," Fox ordered, tweaking the position of the lily-bud boutonnière in his lapel. "India? See that she does."

"Roger that, Fox."

"Reception?" Omega said, looking up, startled. "I didn't plan a reception..."

"Did you really think that we would let the Alpha Line chief and assistant chief get married, and NOT have a proper wedding reception, tekhter?" Fox wondered with a soft smile. "Never mind two important members of our 'family.' Of course we have a reception planned. Given the number of guests—which is more than any of us had originally anticipated—it's heavy hors d'oeuvres rather than a sit-down dinner or luncheon, but it's quite a nice spread, if I do say so. Dihl, Zebra and I tried to pick out a menu we thought you would both enjoy. And that would have a few kosher items from which I could partake."

"And that would be safe for the guests," India added. "Not all of whom are from 'around here,' after all."

"All kinds of that," Fox agreed. "Oy. The menu planning was difficult in itself! No Brussels sprouts, no floral-derived foods OR garnish, no peanut anything..."

Just then, the song changed to a soft piano version of the traditional Wagnerian *Bridal Chorus,* more traditionally known as 'Here Comes The Bride,' and India grinned.

"That's my cue! Here we go, girl!" she said, and headed out the door, down the hall, and into the auditorium.

"Oh oh oh," Omega breathed. "Abba Fox, do you think he still..."

"I expect so, tekhter," Fox noted, "or the music wouldn't still be playing. We'll find out his reaction in a moment." He offered his unofficially-adoptive daughter his arm; she took it, and they headed out.

* * *

A nervous Echo stood on the auditorium stage beside Romeo and watched as India, attired in a lovely rose-tinted evening gown that matched the baby blue one his mother had worn, stepped slowly down the aisle toward the stage, carrying a small bouquet of stargazer lilies, with several more tucked into her hair.

Dihl had walked with him up to the minister and leaned up to kiss his cheek as he crouched a bit to enable her to reach. Then she had moved to the altar table and lit one of the two smaller candles, declaring that she did so on behalf of his parents—mother AND father—careful not to reveal that SHE was his mother. She then turned, walked down the ramp, and took one of the empty seats beside Zebra.

The music shifted, swelling to a full orchestral version of the *Bridal March* as Fox appeared in the auditorium entrance... with an angelic vision in white on his arm. Everyone in the audience stood and turned, as the rest of the world disappeared for Echo.

* * *

Omega dared a glance at Echo, seeing his tall, straight form standing at the top of the ramp, then dropped her gaze, shy.

"Oh my," she breathed. "He's gorgeous."

347

"Judging by the look in his eyes, I expect he'd say the same about you, tekhter," Fox replied in similar fashion.

The pair walked down the aisle in perfect time to the music, mounted the ramp, and came to a stop before Echo.

Before anyone could say or do anything, Echo caught Omega up in his arms, kissing her thoroughly.

Omega responded as one might expect, then broke off the kiss for a moment to meet the brown eyes gazing down at her.

"You still want this?" she whispered. "You want...I mean... after..."

"Damn straight," Echo declared to her, then bent back down to finish the kiss. They didn't look like coming up for air any time soon.

A soft, gentle laugh went through the onlookers, and after a moment, a smiling Father Papa cleared his throat rather loudly. The startled couple broke apart, then they flushed, grinning sheepishly, as Fox commented in a deliberately clear voice that carried to the back of the room, "I think you're supposed to wait for the end of the ceremony for that, kinder."

Another laugh followed this, then Fox moved to the altar table, lit the other small candle, and turned back to the couple.

"Thank you, Omega, for asking me to stand in for the parents who could not be here today," he noted. "I light this candle in your honor, for them." He took Omega's hand and placed it firmly in Echo's. "There," he said. "Just where it's supposed to be, now."

But before he could turn to go, Omega caught Fox with her free hand, pulling him in and planting a gentle kiss on his cheek.

"Thank you, Abba Fox," she whispered.

"Thank you, Tekhter Omega," he replied.

But his hazel eyes shone a wee bit more than usual, as he descended the ramp with straight, proud carriage and took his place beside Zebra.

* * *

The vows the pair had chosen, long before the events with the *Kitty Hawk* went down, were simple and short. It included a double ring exchange—for which Romeo and India were both prepared, Echo and Omega having acquired the rings while

348

on Emdali, in a local artisan's shop, and which matched the offworld alloy of Omega's engagement ring—the unity candle whose familial candles Dihl and Fox had already lit and which took but a moment for Echo and Omega to light with those smaller flames, and a simple but heartfelt blessing by Father Papa. Altogether, the wedding ceremony was succinct, short but beautiful, ardent and devout.

In a few minutes, matters came down to the final, momentous pronouncement.

"Echo and Omega," Father Papa intoned, as behind him, Lord Entiyti rose to his feet and came forward, "in so much as the two of you have agreed before a just and merciful God to live together in matrimony, have promised your love for each other by these vows, the giving of these rings and the joining of your hands..." Entiyti raised both of his hands and rested them gently on Father Papa's shoulders, even as he opened his wings to their full spread, "by the power vested in me by the Pan-Galactic Coalition and the Division One Agency..."

Papa allowed a pregnant pause, as the import of that statement, literally backed by the Coalition President and covered and shielded by his wings, hit home to all present. Over Papa's shoulder, Entiyti gave the couple a huge, guileless grin of sheer delight. Omega gasped; Echo stared. Then they both began to grin. A titter of excitement ran through the assembly before a now-smiling Papa continued.

"...I now declare you to be husband and wife. You may kiss your partner!"

The room erupted in applause and cheers as Echo once more swept Omega into his arms.

* * *

But before the pair could even turn, Ambassador Zz'r'p mounted the platform; Father Papa nodded knowingly and stepped aside, as Entiyti smoothly dropped his hands and stepped back, allowing his wings to fold.

"One more thing is left to do," the ambassador announced, "in the tradition of my people, and per the wishes of both members of Alpha One, especially in the wake of certain recent events."

Then he put a hand on dark head and blonde, and all three

beings became very still for long moments, as a hush fell on the auditorium.

"Is he doing what I think he's doing?" Zebra whispered to Fox.

"I don't know, but if you think he's formalizing a full-on nd't'lq exchange, I agree with you," Fox whispered back.

"N't'a ag'da at'l'o, ee'g'ay t'oy," the Deltiri intoned then, lifting his hands, but leaving them hovering over their heads. "An'd b'aa, Omega ag Echo."

"Thank you," Alpha One murmured...in perfect unison, as Zz'r'p lowered his hands.

"Yep," Zebra agreed. "Sure looked like it to me."

"Now," Papa decreed, "if Director Fox and Doctor Zebra will please come forward, I'll relinquish the pulpit...of sorts... to Rabbi Yod, then I'll come back to see to Alpha Two. Yod, do the others have the canopy?"

Fox and Zebra both started in surprise, as India and Romeo gaped at each other.

Omega clapped her hands in delight.

* * *

Forty-five minutes later, not only were Fox and Zebra properly married, but so were India and Romeo, with Alpha One and -Two standing for the Director and his mate, and said Director and mate, along with Alpha One, standing for Alpha Two.

"And now, Agency and honored guests, may the chaplaincy present to you the duly-legally-married couples, by the laws of God, Earth, the Division One Agency, and the Pan-Galactic Coalition," Papa said with a broad smile, as the three couples lined up across the front of the platform. "I believe there is a proper wedding reception, complete with THREE cakes, prepared and waiting in the Core, if you will all join us to celebrate. Surprise, Fox."

As Mendelssohn's traditional *Wedding March* from *A Midsummer Night's Dream* played in recessional, Alpha One, then Director Fox and Medical Assistant Chief Zebra, followed by Alpha Two, left the stage arm in arm, moved down the aisle between rows of standing, applauding celebrants, and out the big double door. Behind them, the huge, joyful, interstellar celebration spilled out of the auditorium, down the corridor, and into the Core.

* * *

"WOW! You sure surprised us!" a deliriously happy Omega told Pulgey Entiyti, hugging the big Draconan tight.

"Well now, after the delightful surprise of my new wing, could you expect me to do any differently?" Entiyti chuckled. "As soon as Zz'r'p contacted me about the successful completion of the nd't'lq download, I turned around and contacted Teela, asking about the status of the amendment. We had several days to push it through, and then the lot of us came here to share in your happy day, as you had invited us, some time back. And," he added, as Romeo, India, Fox, and Zebra came over, "arranged with your chaplain service to see the rest of you taken care of, as well. To hiigeessht with a 'vacation;' attending this has made me far happier!" He paused, then added, slightly concerned, "I hope the other brides were not disappointed by the lack of dresses and such little details."

"Not at all, Pul," Zebra averred, hugging Fox. "I'm glad I wore a nice dress, but that's basically all Fox and I wanted for a ceremony. Our tastes are simple, and we've been mated for months, now, anyway."

"Same here," India agreed. "I think my bridesmaid's dress made a lovely wedding dress! Unlike SOME bridesmaids' dresses I've worn! Thanks for THAT, Meg!"

They all laughed.

"So the newlyweds are all happy?" Lady Teela said, as she wandered over, a champagne flute in one hand. Nods and smiles met her question, and she raised her glass. Entiyti quickly grabbed the small hors d'oeuvre fork off his plate, and rapped it sharply against his own champagne glass; the high-pitched ringing drew the attention of the crowd throughout the giant room, and everyone silenced. Teela nodded her thanks at Entiyti, who sketched a slight bow. "Gentlebeings, let us raise a toast to the newlyweds! May they be, and remain, as happy and safe as their hard work allows the rest of us to be!"

Cheers went up, and the clinks of glasses sounded, as the crowd raised the first of many toasts to the happy couples.

* * *

351

Two hours later, Omega turned to Fox.

"Is it ready?" she asked then, gesturing at his watch.

"It's been ready for a couple of hours," he told her. "I have a complete off-duty wardrobe loaded, along with your travel kits, that you prepared for me this morning."

"What?" Echo wondered. "Are we going someplace, baby?"

"Of course," Dihl expostulated in gentle exasperation. "Where do old-fashioned newlyweds always go after the reception?"

"We've arranged a duly-secure honeymoon suite for you in the poshest resort in the capital city of Prini on Tiniken," Fox noted.

"Y'all're sending us to Eden on our honeymoon?!" Echo exclaimed, elated. "Whoa!"

"Ya better get goin', then," Romeo decided, glancing at his own wrist chronometer. "Your launch window's gonna be openin' soon. An' y'all still gotta change."

"And don't worry about your quarters," Fox added. "I already had the floor plan the two of you designed for the merger in hand before any of this went down, and I sent it to Facilities already. They've just been waiting for my go-forth on making the changes. It'll be ready by the time you get home, in two weeks."

"I think they're tellin' us to git, honey," Omega told Echo.

"I'm good with that," he agreed. "Let's go."

"Wait, wait, wait," Torino called. "What about tossing bouquets and such?"

"Oh, we do need to do that," Omega agreed. "And I got a garter on, too, so Echo, you gotta 'throw' that, though every time I've seen that done, it's more like a rubber-band shoot."

"I can do that," he decided.

"And now I know why Captain Ssiimiilav managed to smuggle in a bouquet for me," Zebra realized. "No garters though. Sorry, Fox."

"That's all right, bubeleh; I'll see to matters later," Fox replied with a smirk, and everyone laughed.

"No garter here either," India noted, "but the bouquet was awfully pretty."

"I didn't mean for y'all to have the same floral scheme for your weddings as mine, though," Omega apologized.

"I think these are pretty flowers," India averred. "I don't have a problem with it."

"Me neither," Zebra added.

"I just hope y'all didn't whack my poor planter of lilies down to the ground to get all those," Echo observed.

"Silly!" Omega said with a grin, pecking his cheek. "Florist!"

And suddenly she spun, pitching the bouquet backward, over her head and into the crowd of startled guests.

Mu's partner Zeta came up with it, much to her obvious surprise. Mu grinned from ear to ear as she flushed. Echo noted their reactions without comment or response, then knelt in front of his bride as she hitched up her floor-length wedding gown far enough for him to ease the baby-blue satin-and-elastic garter from its position just above her right knee. She eased her foot out of the white satin pump to aid him in removing the garter, then he turned, hooking his left index finger in the garter as he pulled it back with his right hand, rubber-band-style...

...And shot it directly into Mu's chest.

Mu was taken by surprise to judge by his expression, but he grabbed it, then shot Zeta a meaningful glance; she blushed, but grinned at him.

"And I think that takes care of that, if appearances are anything to go by," Echo murmured to Omega, who nodded, pleased. "We may be getting invitations of our own soon, though."

"Okay, so that was the blue," Fox observed then, missing the private communiqué. "What about the rest of it, tekhter? The dress is new..."

"Oh, you mean the old rhyme," Omega realized. "Well, the veil was my mom's. So it's the 'old.' The dress is new. I borrowed a turquoise-inlay hair clip from Dihl," she said, turning her head and pointing to the ornament in her hair, which was down and loose except for where the clip caught and held it out of her eyes. "The garter...and the turquoise in the clip, I guess.. are both blue. And I even have a lucky penny in my shoe," she noted, slipping her left foot out of her pump to expose the coin inside. "It's British, from, like, World War II; Daddy brought it home from a trip overseas when I was real little, and I've had it ever since."

"Cool, baby," Echo decided. "I don't remember anything about a coin, though."

"Well, it's not known as much," Omega said. "But the full thing goes, 'Something old, something new, something borrowed, something blue, and a lucky penny in your shoe.' Though I think the oldest version is something about a sixpence; I expect it changed in the US after the Revolution an' whatnot. Anyhow, I didn't have a sixpence, so I thought my British penny would do."

"I think that did nicely," Fox agreed.

"And now it's y'all's turn," Omega pointed out to her fellow brides.

"Huh?" India said, puzzled.

"It's time to toss those flowers!"

"Ah! So it is. Together?" Zebra asked India.

"Sure, why not?" India said with a grin of her own. The two women turned with their backs to the audience, and India called, "One...two...THREE!"

Both bouquets flew through the air. Genova, Chi's new partner, caught India's, much to the new team's discomfiture... though neither seemed particularly displeased. Slekuwiss Jostek, the Division One agent from Exinul, caught Zebra's; she was delighted.

"Because I have a...I think you call him a 'boyfriend'... at home," she told them. "We have been together long, and I will tell him of this, and perhaps we will become betrothed, as well."

"Then it's all good," Fox decided. "Now—Echo, Omega, off with you, kinder!"

* * *

An hour and a half later, Alpha One, attired in casual, off-duty clothes, sat at the control panel of a small interstellar skimmer, the *Republic*, as they headed out of the solar system, en route to the Zeta Aurigae system and their honeymoon destination.

"There," Echo said, setting the course into the autopilot.

"That's got it. Course, alerts and alarms, all of it."

"And I've got you!" Omega exclaimed, mischievously grabbing his waist with both arms.

"You do that, baby," he agreed with a grin, as he pulled her into a hug. "And you're stuck with me."

"Funny, I was gonna say the same about you bein' stuck with me."

"Then we're stuck with each other. And I, for one, like that."

"Me too."

They sat quietly together, arms about each other, watching the galaxy go by outside the main port. Finally Omega stirred.

"What?" Echo wondered.

"I...was just curious about something."

"What, then?"

"Well, yesterday, your head was still at war," Omega pointed out. "What...happened?"

"You," Echo said, succinct.

"What?! Me??"

"Yeah. Zz'r'p made sure we—the broken pieces of my head, I guess you'd say—got to 'see' what it was doing to you, the way we were fighting over control, when he had you come by the hospital room," he told her. "And it gave us common ground. We were both agreed that, after all you'd done to help us—to help ME—even going so far as to ensure I was protected from what could have been a vicious enemy that part of me didn't even remember, we couldn't risk breaking YOU just because I couldn't get my minds together. It was kinda like that NASA comm lingo. You know, 'break-break.' Break-break here, break-break there...I was broken, you were breaking...we couldn't let it happen. We had to fix our break before we broke you." He paused, then added, "And since I knew—and Zz'r'p confirmed—that you wouldn't be at all comfortable trying to court...mm, the other me...never mind that his reluctance was coming across as a lack of trust, even though it wasn't..."

"It wasn't?"

"No. He just wanted the chance to get to know you. He didn't, you know. It was like he was a version of me created after I 'mostly died'...I guess I really did die, when you get down to it, sorta...so he didn't have any knowledge of...much of any-thing, really. All he knew was what he saw, what he was told. When Zz'r'p and I finally got him to understand that, if he'd go ahead and merge with me like we wanted, then he'd have the benefit of MY knowing you, he started to get it, I think."

"So...you integrated."

"So we integrated. And now I'm me again. One Echo, one me, through an' through." *And me is really happy,* he told her through the joint nd't'lq.

Good. So am I, she told him.

Yeah. He paused, then added aloud, "I'm still working on a few things, I think. Zz'r'p told me to be careful, because my situational awareness and some junk like that was apt to be a little off for a bit. But he said if I stuck close to you for a week or so, everything should ease back to normal, even with that. Which, given that's about how long our honeymoon will last, works out about right."

Omega sighed then.

"Thank God," she murmured, fervent.

"Amen to that."

"How long will it take to get to Eden?"

"Mm? Couple hours at nominal cruising," Echo decided.

"Wanna smooch?"

"I could be talked into it."

And he bent his head to hers, as the *Republic* sailed on.

Author Notes

Many thanks to quite a few people, including beta reader Evelyn Zinn, who also helped me brainstorm a lot, editor Courtney Galloway, and Leo Champion and Richard Weyand, both of whom helped me brainstorm a bit, as well. Also thanks to new beta readers Randy Jones and Alisa Russell! Thanks as usual to my awesome graphics artist husband Darrell for the dynamite cover, and to my parents, Steve and Colene Gannaway, who brought me up to believe that I could do 'most anything I set my mind to do, at least within reason. (You be the judge of whether these books are 'within reason' or not.)

There are quite a few characters off my redshirt list in this story, too, notably among NASA personnel. They aren't technically redshirts, in that they don't die; I don't like the notion of killing off friends, even if it's only as characters in a story. Technically I guess that means I Tuckerized 'em rather than redshirting 'em. I hope they enjoy their portrayal.

(Yes, if you want to be redshirted or Tuckerized, ping me on social media or email, and ask. I'll probably add your name, along with any details about yourself that you provide, and use you at some point, though I can't promise any one title or series. That said, there have been some auction-for-charity redshirts placed on my list, so those will get the most glorious redshirtings.)

Also please note, for those who may think that space plane commander Dianus got short shrift, even mistreated, because Scotty Chadwick didn't really die, let me point out: Even when Alpha One were the only people on EVA, even when Chadwick went EVA to assist Echo, he never assigned — nor even asked for volunteers — for one or more crew to serve as backup/IVA. Nor did he function as such himself, at any time. (Let me also add that I have never met an astronaut who would have done such a thing in real life. Like any slice of the population, a select number do have, ahem, egos, but I have never encountered one who would have allowed a fellow crewperson to be in such harm's way without providing backup, never mind regs. I deliberately created a real jerkface person for this character.)

For those who may not understand the title of the book, given the wide- ranging locations and events contained therein: it is, plain and simple, a multi- layered pun. 'Break, break' is the standard nomenclature used by NASA flight controllers when an important bit of information must override the current communication. For example:

MS-2: Houston, *Kitty Hawk*. The experiment is progressing nominally. System readout is—

PLT: Break, break! Houston, this is Chadwick. We have an off- nominal situation. We believe the new propulsion system has catastrophically malfunctioned. We are calling a mayday.

FLIGHT: Prop, do you—

PROP: I see it, Flight. Prop confirms off- nominal condition, possibly catastrophic failure. Can we get other eyes on the bird to assess damage?

The initial pun is the fact that Dr. Megan McAllister, aka Omega, was to have flown aboard the *Kitty Hawk* on this flight. Her largely unexplained disappearance when she was drafted into the Division One Agency resulted in her break with the program.

The next pun is what happens to Echo, when his mind (and his nd't'lq) effectively 'break' from his body, resulting in what might be a 'breakdown' (yes, a double pun) of life systems.

And the final pun is when the sequence of events with Echo comes near to breaking Omega mentally and emotionally — breaking her spirit, if you will.

One more thing for the diehard fans of this series: when I envisioned these stories, this book was originally to be the culmination to, and end of, the series. However, as I wrote, several things happened. 1) I started getting to know the characters and the world, and I found I really loved writing these characters in this universe. 2) I started getting lots of ideas for other stories. 3) I started getting reader response that said, "Oh, please don't end it! I love this series!"

So I've decided to keep going. I may slow down the rate of production from 4 books a year in the series to only 3. But there are still quite a few more adventures/books left in this series and this universe, guys. Hang in there. The fun is still ongoing.

~Stephanie Osborn
January 2019
Huntsville, AL

About the Author

Stephanie Osborn is a former payload flight controller, a veteran of over twenty years of working in the civilian space program, as well as various military space defense programs. She has worked on numerous Space Shuttle flights and the International Space Station, and counts the training of astronauts on her resumé. Of those astronauts she trained, one was Kalpana Chawla, a member of the crew lost in the *Columbia* disaster.

She holds graduate and undergraduate degrees in four sciences: Astronomy, Physics, Chemistry, and Mathematics, and she is "fluent" in several more, including Geology and Anatomy. She obtained her various degrees from Austin Peay State University in Clarksville, TN and Vanderbilt University in Nashville, TN.

Stephanie is currently retired from space work. She now happily "passes it forward," teaching math and science via numerous media including radio, podcasting, and public speaking, as well as working with SIGMA, the science fiction think tank, while writing science fiction mysteries based on her knowledge, experience, and travels.

For more, go to http://www.stephanie-osborn.com/.

To subscribe to Stephanie's newsletter, visit here.

Don't miss any of these highly entertaining SF/F books by Stephanie Osborn!

The *Division One* series by Stephanie Osborn:
Alpha and Omega
A Small Medium At Large
A Very UnCONventional Christmas
Tour de Force
Trojan Horse
Texas Rangers
Definition and Alignment
Phantoms
Head Games
Break, Break, Houston

Coming soon:

Tourist Trap
Mega Moth
Everywhere Signs
Diplomatic Catfight
Shake, Rattle and Roll
Die Glocke
Forming Terra
With more on the way!

* * *

The *Burnout* series by Stephanie Osborn
The Fetish
Burnout: The mystery of Space Shuttle STS-281
Coming soon:
Escape Velocity
* * *

Sherlock Holmes: Gentleman Aegis series by Stephanie Osborn:
Sherlock Holmes and the Mummy's Curse
Coming soon:

Sherlock Holmes in the Wild Hunt
Sherlock Holmes and the Tournament of Shadows

* * *

The *Displaced Detective* series by Stephanie Osborn [being re-released by Enigma House Press, an imprint of Hydra Publications]:
The Case of the Displaced Detective: The Arrival
The Case of the Displaced Detective: At Speed
The Case of the Cosmological Killer: The Rendlesham Incident
The Case of the Cosmological Killer: Endings and Beginnings
A Case of Spontaneous Combustion
Fear in the French Quarter